A
NARROW
DOOR

D0879274

JOANNE HARRIS is an Anglo-French author, whose books include eighteen novels, three cookbooks and many short stories. Her work is extremely diverse, covering aspects of magic realism, suspense, historical fiction, mythology and fantasy.

In 2000, her 1999 novel *Chocolat* was adapted for the screen, starring Juliette Binoche and Johnny Depp. She is an Honorary Fellow of St Catharine's College, Cambridge, and in 2013 was awarded an MBE by the Queen.

Find out more by visiting her website: www.joanne-harris.co.uk or follow her on Twitter @Joannechocolat

JOANNE
HARRIS

A

NARROW

DOOR

ORION

First published in Great Britain in 2021 by Orion Fiction,
an imprint of The Orion Publishing Group Ltd.,
Carmelite House, 50 Victoria Embankment
London EC4Y 0DZ

An Hachette UK company

1 3 5 7 9 10 8 6 4 2

Copyright © Frogspawn Ltd 2021

The moral right of Joanne Harris to be identified as the author
of this work has been asserted in accordance with
the Copyright, Designs and Patents Act 1988.

All rights reserved. No part of this publication may be
reproduced, stored in a retrieval system, or transmitted,
in any form or by any means, electronic, mechanical,
photocopying, recording or otherwise, without the prior
permission of the copyright owner.

All the characters in this book are fictitious,
and any resemblance to actual persons, living
or dead, is purely coincidental.

A CIP catalogue record for this book
is available from the British Library.

ISBN (Hardback) 978 1 4091 7081 5
ISBN (Trade Paperback) 978 1 4091 7082 2
ISBN (eBook) 978 1 4091 7083 9

Typeset by Born Group
Printed and bound in Great Britain by Clays Ltd, Elcograf S.p.A.

FSC
www.fsc.org

MIX
Paper from
responsible sources
FSC® C104740

www.orionbooks.co.uk

To Dr Philip Oliver (1948–2020)

Preface
Thanatos

'Strait is the gate, and narrow is the way, which
leadeth unto life, and few there be that find it.'
(Matthew 7:14)

St Oswald's, September 2006

I often find that men like you underestimate women like me. You think we must be damaged, somehow. That we seek power to compensate for some real or imagined injustice. That we must hate men, for the way they have excluded women from their boys' clubs, holding them back, abusing them, exploiting them, for centuries. Well, yes, you may have a point. Some things make a woman fight back. And some things, though they challenge us, only make us stronger.

A woman Headmaster. To you it must seem a reversal of everything you believe. How did we come to this, you ask? How has the world been so overturned? Women like me, you tell yourself, should be this way for a *reason*. Our drive to succeed comes from weakness, you think. Rage, or hate, or fear, or insecurity. And that's why I'll win. Because you believe in the essential weakness of women in authority.

But that's where you're wrong, Mr Straitley. I have no insecurities. But for one early incident, my childhood was uneventful. My sexual partners have been dull to the point of uniformity. Except for Johnny Harrington, whom I fucked between the ages of sixteen and sixteen and a half, and who gave me a child, as well as the dubious novelty of having fucked, if not a murderer, then at least the next best thing. Otherwise, he too was bland, arrogant and predictable; riding on his privilege all the way to the Headship. In many ways, he was born to be Head. The model of a St Oswald's boy; so certain of his entitlement that he never questioned his fitness. And yes, I helped him along the way. Not out of any sentiment regarding his donated sperm – he never knew about Emily, or what it had cost me to raise her – but because it was expedient. I followed his career from afar, although he never followed mine. I saw an opportunity. By the time we reconnected, I had skills to offer him, and I became his Deputy; his trusted second-in-command. He accepted my services as he had always accepted them, never once considering that I might have ambitions of my own. And when he fell – as I knew he would – in the wake of last year's disastrous events, I was there to take his place, as St Oswald's struggled to survive yet another unfortunate scandal. After that, it was easy. Like you, they underestimated me. All it took for me to rise was flattery, a lot of hard work, some patience, time and, most of all, the strength to accept the snubs and humiliations that inevitably come the way of any woman with ambition.

But sitting in my office now – the office that once was *his* – drinking coffee from his machine, reading the names on the Honours Boards that decorate the panelled walls, I feel a sense of rightness. This is *my* office; this is *my* desk. My orchids on the window ledge. My parking space under the window. My coffee machine. My cup. My school. I earned this job, I belong here, and I have nothing more to prove. St Oswald's, with all its history, with all its relentless, patriarchal baggage, is mine. And today I sit in the Headmaster's chair, and will stand at the lectern this morning in Assembly as the new New Head – a title that in five hundred years has never gone to a woman before — and address a school filled with boys *and* girls, and lead them out of the wilderness.

An old St Oswald's proverb goes: *It is easier for a camel to pass through the eye of a needle than for a woman to enter these gates.* Well, not only have I entered, but now the gates are *my* gates, and the rules are my rules. The mistake you made was one of scale. Men always do, used as they are to taking the main entrance. Women must be more discreet. All we need is a narrow door. And when we have crept in unseen, like a spider through a keyhole, we spin ourselves an empire of silk, and fill you with astonishment.

I'm really very fond of you, Roy. Don't think that because I opposed you last year, I don't have a lot of respect for you. But you are part of the *old* school, and I belong to the future. I don't suppose you know what that's like. You've always been part of St Oswald's. Man and boy, you always belonged. You never needed the narrow door. And even after what happened last year, you still believe I have a heart.

How little you know me, Straitley. I have survived more setbacks than you could ever imagine. I had my daughter at seventeen without ever naming the father. I entered teaching at twenty-three, in a school very like St Oswald's. I fought for my place every step of the way, through prejudice, sexism and judgement. I have survived a double mastectomy without confiding in anyone. I have survived the death of a spouse and an elder sibling, a love affair. I have seen my parents die; my daughter move to America. I have committed two murders; one a crime of passion, the other, a crime of convenience. I am barely forty years old and, finally, I am starting to reap the harvest my ambitions have sown. This is my time, Mr Straitley. And no, I am not damaged.

I am whole.

PART I

Acheron
(River of Woe)

I

St Oswald's ~~Grammar School for Boys~~ Academy
Michaelmas Term, September 4th, 2006

I won't pretend it doesn't feel like some kind of an evil omen. A crossing-out on the very first page of a new St Oswald's diary. But, as of this year, we are no longer St Oswald's Grammar School for Boys, but St Oswald's *Academy* – a change that the new Head assures us will propel us into the stratosphere of fine independent schools in the north.

To an old lag like me, it seems like the end. The rebranding that began last year under Johnny Harrington's regime has spread like a pernicious weed to all parts of St Oswald's. From the removal of the Honours Boards on the Middle Corridor, to the workstations in the Common Room; whiteboards in every classroom and girls in every year, the new Head's influence has made itself known. We even have a new motto: *Progress Through Tradition*, as if Tradition were a tunnel through which the express train of Progress would someday emerge in triumph, having gleefully mown down everything we stand for.

But after the chaos of last year and the tragedy of the year before, some might say we've been lucky. The long-delayed merger with our sister school, Mulberry House, has taken some of the heat off St Oswald's, and the arrival of girls in the School has provoked a spate of approving articles in the local press, which, historically, has generally been rather negative towards us. The new Head is articulate, presentable and more than intelligent enough to understand how to manage the media. This week's issue of the *Malbry Examiner* has her on the front page, in one of her elegant trouser suits, surrounded by a selection of some of our more photogenic new girls, all in smart new uniforms (redesigned by the Head, of course) and smiling into the camera like a victorious general.

Yes, after almost a year of standing in for the absent Head, Ms Buckfast, who until recently constituted one third of Johnny Harrington's Crisis Team, has finally gained a permanent place in the Headmaster's office. Her counterpart at Mulberry House (Miss Lambert, aka Call-me-Jo) was offered the post of Deputy, but instead took early retirement, and has since been spotted at various prestigious venues, where she commands extortionate fees, I am told, as an after-dinner speaker. The other Crisis Deputy has moved to a Headship of his own, and Dr Markowicz, who joined the German Department last year, has taken his place as Second Master, much to the ire of Dr Devine, who, having championed the man last year, sees this as a betrayal, and of Bob Strange, the Third Master, a staunch supporter of La Buckfast, who assumed from the start that his own long-delayed promotion would henceforth be little more than a formality.

The Languages Department has not been untouched by the merger, with a number of older colleagues taking enhancement to accommodate their younger counterparts. Kitty Teague is still Head of French, and Dr Devine Head of German, while I, the only Classicist, remain to defend my department of one. Miss Malone (aka The Foghorn) remains, and we have two new members of staff, both appointees from Mulberry House: a young woman of the Low-Fat Yoghurt type, and a young man with a small moustache, too effete for a Young Gun, and yet too trendy for a Suit.

You'd think that all this change might have prompted me to walk the plank. I don't deny it crossed my mind; but what would I do with my freedom? Rarely does a Tweed Jacket ever thrive in retirement. Like the clothes of the dead, we wear thin: the air does not sustain us. Last year, we lost three: Harry Clarke; Pat Bishop, too young, of a heart attack – though his heart had been broken two years ago; and my old friend Eric Scoones, whose plan to retire in Paris was cut short by a stroke, followed by the savage onset of dementia. A shock will do that, my doctor says, and Scoones had suffered several that year, including the death of his mother. He ended up at Meadowbank – the hospice in which Harry had died – and died of a second stroke three months later. It was a mercy, I suppose: by then he had lost the power of speech, and his eyes were those of a lost dog. Of course, he was lost to me long before that – but we do not speak of that old affair, or of my suspicions regarding the boy, the erstwhile David Spikely. Besides, it's over now, isn't it? No need to go digging up the past. St Oswald's moves on, and I with it.

I have a new form this year. My old 4S have become 5M, with Miss Malone, aka The Foghorn, in charge. I dare not think what carnage my Brodie Boys – Tayler, Sutcliff, McNair and Allen-Jones – will manage to wreak under her reign. The Foghorn may sound imposing, but as soon as they realize that she is all sound and no substance, they will be in their element. And damn it all, I miss them. I've had them in my form for two years. They know my little foibles. Too much has already changed this year – new Head, new staff, new school. Is it really too much to hope that *something*, at least, would stay the same?

My own form is 2S this year, and I will be teaching both boys and girls. Thirty-two of them this year; but the merger with Mulberry House has increased our class sizes as well as proportionally raising standards and (according to the new Bursar) improving our finances immeasurably. Like a marriage of convenience between an impoverished nobleman and a merchant heiress, this merger will save our fortunes, while sadly curtailing our old way of life. Certainly, this year there has been no more mention of selling off the School playing fields. I have to admit that *is* a relief, but this is tempered somewhat by the fact that admitting girls to the School also means disruption: new scents; the sound of high-pitched laughter; the introduction of salads for lunch as well as the construction of various new amenitics. Hence the new netball courts, changing rooms, toilets, showers and even a new sports hall, complete with swimming pool, paid for by the parents of Rupert Gunderson, who have also lent their name to a prize: the Rupert Gunderson Medal for Academic Excellence. Not that Gunderson was ever outstanding in anything but his ability to exploit weakness in a younger boy, but most things can be forgotten, I find, with the help of a large enough donation.

However, the work on the Gunderson Building has, like the young Rupert Gunderson, been both slow and disruptive. Far from being a credit to the School, it has already defied deadlines, ignored planning permissions and finally come to a standstill, with the result that, instead of a brand-new pool block ready for the new term, we still have a muddy building site around an unsightly concrete shell, surrounded by a chain-link fence, awaiting a ruling from the Council

Planning Office next month. Thus I sensed that, during this term, Breaks would largely be spent patrolling the site, keeping it clear of intruders.

But I had other work today. The first day of term at St Oswald's is traditionally free of boys, while staff attend meetings, do paperwork and ease gently into the old routine without the hindrance of teaching. Which is why I was here at 7.30 a.m., drinking tea from a St Oswald's mug and surveying the view from my desk like Canute attempting to hold back the tide. A tide of Formica-topped tables, which, during the summer holidays, has taken all the old school desks, with their inkwells and lids scarred with over a hundred years of Latin graffiti, much of it woefully ungrammatical, but alive with a youthful exuberance that mere Formica cannot reflect. My Master's desk has remained untouched, in spite of an offer from the new Head to replace it with something more 'masterly'. I suppose she means something with gravitas, like Dr Devine's new cedar-wood affair, or her own mahogany writing desk with its ormolu inkstand.

But I have sat at this shabby old desk of mine for over a hundred terms. I know every mark, every cigarette burn, every piece of graffiti. The third drawer sticks, and there is a blackened residue of something at the back of the topmost drawer that might once have been liquorice. I shall keep my desk until the day I am carried feet first from St Oswald's. As for the new Formica desks, thanks to the Porter, Jimmy Watt, they will shortly be relocated to a different Department, and the old desks (currently in storage in the basement, pending disposal) returned to their original places. Rather a big job for Jimmy, who will have to carry them one by one up the stairs to the Bell Tower, but he has the advantage of being both good-natured and corruptible, and the promise of fifty quid, plus a round of drinks in the Thirsty Scholar, proved more than enough incentive to commandeer his services.

I lit a furtive, delicious Gauloise. The scent of smoke was moody and nostalgic. Autumn has come early this year; the trees in the Upper Quad look scorched, and at the top of the playing fields, the rosebay willowherb has turned from fiery pink to smoky white. It is my favourite time of year; melancholy, rosy and ripe, but this time, it is melancholy that dominates.

Ye gods, but I miss Eric. He was like the smell of chalk and mice and floor polish on the Middle Corridor; barely noticeable until it was gone. Now the Middle Corridor smells of floral disinfectant, and the chalk has been replaced by the reek of whiteboard marker. I know he's gone, but I still keep expecting to meet him on the stairway; to see him in the Common Room; to hear his greeting: 'Morning, Straits.'

It's the time of year. It will pass. But I do miss the old idiot, even after that sad business. Or maybe I miss who I *thought* he was. Who I wanted him to be. The thought makes me uncomfortable: that, during so many years, he could have kept his dark secret from me. Still, sixty years of shared history counts. I still remember the boy he was. I still remember him as a young man, before the Harry Clarke affair. And whatever he did, I know that, at heart, there was kindness in him, and love, along with the anger and darkness.

According to the Ancient Greeks, five rivers led to the Underworld: Acheron, the river of sorrow and woe; Cocytus, the river of lamentation, Phlegethon, the river of fire; Styx, the river of anger and hate; and, finally, Lethe, the waters of which conferred blessed oblivion. If this is so, then I am at least four-fifths of the way to Hades. The events of past years have taken me through fire and water, darkness and grief. All I can hope for now, I suppose, is the blessed gift of oblivion. Did Eric Scoones welcome Lethe? Or did he struggle against the flow? And in his place, what would I choose? Forgetfulness, or eternal remorse?

Tea, I think, to banish the ghosts. Barring Lethe, it is my preferred option. I have a kettle under my desk, along with some teabags and a small supply of single-portion containers of UHT milk. I draw the line at a teapot, but I do prefer my St Oswald's mug. Until recently, Eric's mug was still in the Common Room cupboard, but last term I saw that it had been removed. One less thing to remind me. Or maybe one of the new cleaners *really* likes Princess Diana.

I made the tea and sat down at my desk. Jimmy would be arriving soon. In fact, when I heard a knock at the door, I was fully expecting to see his round face peering through the marbled glass. Instead, I was surprised to see what seemed like a whole group of people, one of whom was wearing a neon-pink garment of a style that Jimmy would never contemplate.

'Come in,' I said, and the door opened to reveal a very familiar foursome. Sutcliff, Allen-Jones and McNair, along with Benedicta Wild – aka Ben – with whom they had made friends last year, in spite of the fact that she was now in the Upper Sixth and they were only fifth-formers. All out of uniform, of course, with Allen-Jones wearing a shocking-pink T-shirt emblazoned with the mysterious legend: *ON WEDNESDAYS WE SMASH THE PATRIARCHY.* Was it a joke, I wondered? I have to confess, schoolboy humour has evolved since those sunnier, simpler days in which *Caesar had some jam for tea, and Brutus had a rat.*

In fact, it took me a moment longer than I should to recognize them. A boy out of uniform is like a house cat at night; somehow more independent; skittish, more remote than by day. And, of course, they had *grown*: they always do over the long summer holidays. Except for Allen-Jones, who remains rather more boyish than the rest, and Ben – a Brodie Boy by association – who has acquired a new and very short haircut that would have driven Call-Me-Jo into spasms of disapproval.

At the sight of this delegation I put down my mug of tea and stood up. It was still only 7.45; too early for a social call. And the fact that they were all out of uniform ruled out the possibility that all four of them had somehow forgotten the fact that the first day of term is for staff only.

'Good morning,' I said.

'Good morning, Sir.' Allen-Jones had always been the spokesman of the little group, and he looked uncharacteristically serious. For a terrible moment I thought that something had happened to Tayler – the only one of my Brodie Boys not present. Then I remembered that Tayler's family had been on a kibbutz in Israel, and that young Tayler was not expected to be in School before the end of the week. I suppose my mind was still on old Scoones, but I already knew that something was amiss.

'What's happened?' I said. 'Is something wrong?' At any other time I might have followed with a cheery Latin quip, but there was something about their expressions that made me feel that in this case it would be inappropriate. Once more I thought of Tayler. So many things have already gone wrong that the thought of losing one of my boys made my heart lurch alarmingly. The ghostly digit that sometimes lurks at around the third button of my waistcoat – a reminder of the heart attack that laid me low two years ago – gave a twitch. 'What is it?' I said, rather more sharply than I'd meant.

Allen-Jones looked at the others. Ben gave a nod. Sutcliff looked pale – but then his redhead's colouring means that whatever the season, he always looks as if he has spent his life in a cave. The ghostly finger started to move gently up my ribcage. I wanted to ask after Tayler, but dared not say the words aloud. Give voice to your fear, and it will take shape. *Lupus in fabula.*

'What is it?' I repeated, in a voice that was gruff with anxiety.

'Sir,' said Allen-Jones at last, 'we think we've found a body.'

2

St Oswald's ~~Grammar School for Boys~~ Academy
Michaelmas Term, September 4th, 2006

It took them a while to tell their tale. Allen-Jones has – to my regret – never been especially concise or to the point. Besides, the others kept trying to add unnecessary details, so that the storyline soon disappeared in a burst of interjections.

The tale, in brief, was this. To celebrate the return to school, the little group had planned a practical joke. I had no doubt that this idea – had it come to fruition – would have been both elaborate and subversive. The site of the half-finished Gunderson Building – which lay beyond the playing fields close to the erstwhile Porter's Gate – a remnant from the old days when the Porter lived on site – had been left unattended inside its chain-link fence since the Planning Council's decision to suspend the works.

'We were trying to get through the fence,' began Allen-Jones. 'We were kind of thinking of starting the new term with a really classic prank. You know, like the time the Lower Sixth managed to get a Morris Minor onto the roof of the Physics block?' (In actual fact, it wasn't a Morris Minor, but a Mini Cooper, and the boys had transported it onto one of the tennis courts, not the roof of the Physics block, but I let that pass for the present. The point was that the prank had gone down as a legend in St Oswald's history, and my boys had predictably seen it as a challenge to their wits and ingenuity.)

'What kind of a prank?' I said, cautiously. 'Please don't tell me you've stolen a crane.'

Ben looked at the others. 'Not quite, Sir.'

'Ye gods!'

'It was my idea,' said Ben, now looking somewhat mutinous. I didn't doubt it; the girl was bright. 'I'd rather not go into details just now –'

'But, Sir, it would have been fabulous,' said Allen-Jones, his eyes shining. 'Honestly, if we could manage it, it would make the whole Morris Minor thing look puny.'

The others nodded, I thought with regret. By then I have to admit that I was starting to wonder whether the prank in question was this tale, designed to make me its victim, but their demeanour was still unusual enough for me to dismiss the suspicion.

'So, what exactly happened?' I said.

'Well, there's a part of the fence where the links have kind of pulled away,' said Allen-Jones. 'We thought that might be a good place to start, so we went off to investigate. There's a big heap of excavated rubble and stones beside it, waiting to be carted off, and on the other side there's the Glory Hole –'

'The Gunderson Building,' said McNair.

I know what he means. The section of the playing fields closest to the side gate is often waterlogged after rain, and the recent excavations have created a swimming-pool-sized hole, which promptly filled up with water. Since the commencement of the works, this pool has already yielded three shopping trolleys, a child's scooter, plus various aluminium cans, bottles and pieces of litter. This morning, there had been something else.

'A body,' I said gently.

They nodded, their humour forgotten. 'It looked like —'

The pile of rubble had recently slipped, probably because of the rains. A portion of the excavated soil had slid towards the side of the pit, revealing something that looked like —

'*Remains*,' said Ben.

I sighed. 'We'd better have a look.'

I had already dismissed the idea that *this* might be the practical joke. Their faces were too serious, the subject matter too grisly. I stood up, carefully placing my cup back onto the tabletop. My gown was hanging behind the door, and I slipped it on automatically, much as an elderly knight may don a familiar piece of armour. Thus prepared, with sinking heart, I strode out across the playing fields, a standard-bearer at the head of a decimated legion.

3

St Oswald's ~~Grammar School for Boys~~ *Academy*
Michaelmas Term, September 4th, 2006

Over the summer holidays, the site of the Gunderson Building
has gone from merely unsightly to something akin to a Circle
of Hell. Litter and other detritus form a kind of berg at the
flooded end, and the water is crazed and foxed with an oily
residue. I followed the boys through the broken fence – with
rather less ease of movement. With something of an effort, I
squatted by the side of the pit where the excavated earth had
slid. My knees protested violently.

'There, Sir!'

It could have been anything. And yet, it could have been
nothing else. A sense of inevitability, like something in a
troubling dream, started to take hold of me. I leant to inspect
a large wad of fabric, and what might have been a piece of
wood, there on the mound of broken earth at the edge of
the Gunderson Building.

But it was not a piece of wood. And there, against the
fabric, I saw the gleam of something familiar.

Once more, my knees protested. I have reached the age at
which a man thinks twice about bending down. One of my

shoelaces was untied. I took the opportunity to tie it with a double knot. Then I lurched to my feet with a grunt and turned once more to my Brodie Boys.

'Well, Sir?'

I felt an overwhelming urge to tell them that all was well, that they had made a mistake; that they should go back home and enjoy the final day of the holidays. I could see they wanted that. They might even have believed it. But they were my boys, and I could not lie. To others, perhaps, but not to them.

Instead, I said: 'You may be right. I'll have to inform the Head of this.'

'Will we have to make a statement?' said Ben.

I shook my head. 'I doubt it,' I said. 'But thank you for coming to me with this. I'll deal with it now. You leave this with me. But don't tell anyone else what you saw. You don't want to jeopardize a potential investigation.'

Allen-Jones looked hopeful. 'You really think it's a body, Sir?'

I suppose to a boy like Allen-Jones, such a discovery on School grounds was like a dog in the playground; a welcome distraction from dull routine; an exciting mystery. To a Master, it appears otherwise. The past two years have been hard for us all. Multiple scandals; a murdered boy; revenge, abuse and public disgrace have dragged the school's reputation down and brought us to near bankruptcy. The last thing we need this year, of all years, is any more excitement. I summoned my natural gravitas. 'I shall look into it, Allen-Jones. You need not pursue this further.' And with that, I squeezed back through the fence so forcefully that it gouged the tender roll of flesh around my stomach and my hip, leaving an angry spot of blood on my first-day-of-school shirt.

Another bad sign. That makes three today. But this one was by far the worst; a sign, not just of storm clouds, but of an impending hurricane. Because I'd recognized something in the knot of rags by the Gunderson Building; something my Brodie Boys would not have seen as significant. But *I* had seen, and I knew what it meant. Another postcard from the past. One that, if uncovered now, would jeopardize the School just as it was starting to recover – both financially and emotionally – from the disastrous events of last year, and those of the year before. One that might finally topple us, in spite of the efforts of our new Head and the rescue package from Mulberry House.

But nothing stays buried forever, I thought. The past is a gift that keeps giving, pulling names from a big black hat. David Spikely, Becky Price – now returned as Ms. Buckfast – Eric Scoones and Harry Clarke. One day, maybe my own name. I put my hand in my pocket. The object I'd found by the edge of the pool was cold between my fingers. It occurred to me that even now, I could just drop it somewhere on the fields, to be trodden into the mud. No one would know. No one would care about such ancient history. And the law must sleep in time of war. *Inter arma enim silent leges.*

Are we at war? Perhaps we are. Those desks are only the start of it. Whiteboards; gymslips; computers; e-mail; slogans. *Progress Through Tradition.* From my place by the chain-link fence, I watched my Brodie Boys cross the muddy field, Allen-Jones's pink T-shirt shining like a beacon. Sutcliff turned and waved at me.

I took my hand out of my pocket and waved back. I realized I had no choice. The School publicity brochure may read *Progress Through Tradition*, replacing the more traditional *Audere, agere, auferre*, but my personal motto remains; *Ad astra per aspera.* Even from the gutter, we are always striving for the stars.

I turned. The sound of youthful laughter rang exuberantly across the fields. Then, and with a heavy heart, I made my way across the fields towards the Headmaster's office.

4

St Oswald's, September 4th, 2006

Becky was an only child, and yet she had a brother. It sounds like a riddle, doesn't it? And yes, perhaps it was, in a way. Because my brother disappeared when he was just fourteen years old, leaving nothing in his wake but grief and a boy-shaped space I could never fill, that grew while I diminished.

It was not the first time that my parents had lost a child. A sister, who died before Conrad was born; of whom my parents seldom spoke. There were no photographs of her; no portrait in the living room. I understood that she had died shortly after she was born; that there had been something wrong with her. Whatever grief my parents had felt was tempered by that knowledge. Not so with Conrad. He had been altogether perfect.

I was just five when he disappeared. Too young to understand what it meant. Too young to know how my world had changed. Too young to know that whatever I did, however much I tried, I would never inhabit that space, never once stop feeling the cold draught of Conrad's absence, like an open door into the night. And it was there in my parents' eyes; the absence that endured throughout my childhood and adolescence; the absence of Conrad, more powerful than any mere presence could be, eclipsing me completely. Through marriage and widowhood it endured: through motherhood into menopause. Even now, as I take my place as Head of St Oswald's, I can still hear that familiar voice, saying: *Are you here? Are you really here?*

I pour another cup of coffee. Johnny left me his coffee machine – not that he really had much choice – and it is an expensive one; gleaming chrome that reflects my face, once more affirming my presence. At last, I am here. At last, I am real. Not just a reflection. Not just a name. Not just a ghost in the coffee machine.

I told you before that I was whole. That wholeness has been fought for. For all those years I was aware that part of me was missing. No one actually said as much. But children are aware of these things. I knew that there were days when I disappeared into a silent world of my own; days that seemed to vanish into a series of sink holes. And I could see it in their eyes; their longing; their disappointment. As if they wished that I, not he, had been the one to disappear. Perhaps that was why, as I reached my teens, I used sex as a means of control. I learnt I was desirable; I learnt how to make boys see me – at least, for as long as it suited them. I can't think of another reason for encouraging Johnny Harrington; I certainly never cared for him, although I enjoyed my new-found control. But still, to my parents, I was a ghost; a knocking in the water pipes; an everyday reminder of the day my brother disappeared.

Of course, my parents are both dead now. Everyone in this story is dead, or changed beyond recognition. No one compares me to Conrad now. No one blames me for his death. The house is no longer a shrine to him, but home to a nice little family with no idea of the drama that played out within their walls so many years ago. Two children and a Jack Russell dog. A little garden with roses. No one living there listens to the numbers stations anymore. The gurgling drains have been mended at last. I never fix down the toilet seat. I even get cards on my birthday.

But nothing ever lasts. The past is never completely over. And this is why I felt no surprise when you came to me with your story today. I think I was expecting it. I have waited these twenty years for someone to stumble over the truth. It seems almost poetic now that that someone should be Roy Straitley. Straitley, the shambling buffoon who somehow brought down Johnny Harrington. Straitley, the incorruptible; the heart and soul of St Oswald's. But it is *because* of St Oswald's that I will win. St Oswald's is his weakness, just as Conrad once was mine. But unlike me, Roy Straitley cannot exorcise his weakness. He wears it like a favourite coat, foolishly thinking it armour. And that's why I was not afraid when he came to me this morning. That is why I did not flinch when he took a small metallic object from his pocket and laid it in front of me on my desk.

Instead I felt a kind of relief, and thought: *At last. They've found him.*

5

St Oswald's ~~Grammar School for Boys~~ *Academy*
Michaelmas Term, September 4th, 2006

I'll say this for La Buckfast; she isn't easily shaken. She listened
to my story, then lifted the metallic object I had picked out of
the rubble by the side of the Gunderson Building between her
index finger and thumb, and gave her Mona Lisa smile.

'You recognize what it is, of course,' I said.

She nodded. 'Yes, of course.' She indicated the coffee
machine. 'The cappuccino's very good, though Johnny preferred
espresso. Can I tempt you?'

'No, thanks.' I was jumpy enough already. It isn't every
morning you find a body on the playing fields, but the Head
seemed to take it in her stride, as if the disaster about to hit St
Oswald's like a juggernaut were nothing but a minor annoyance.

'You realize what this means,' I said, watching her make
coffee. 'The police will have to be involved. There'll be an
investigation. The papers will be all over it. The building will
be suspended again, not just for months, but perhaps for *years*.
And the parents. What will the parents think? And once
the governors get involved – Headmaster, it could ruin us.'
I realized that, in my agitation, I had called her *Headmaster*.

La Buckfast showed no reaction. She picked up a small glass receptacle and sprinkled cocoa powder over her cappuccino. 'You're always so dramatic, Roy. The worst may never happen.' She sipped the coffee delicately, to avoid leaving lipstick on her cup. 'Let's start at the beginning, shall we? Tell me what you know about this.'

And she indicated the object that I'd fished out of the mud at the side of the Gunderson Building; no larger than my thumbnail, yet heavy with significance. Twenty years under the soil has scoured it of its colour: but I know it was once the rich, dark red of a fine old claret. The pin has been lost, and the metal has corroded to a dirty brown, but the shape is still recognizable; a shield, still bearing the ghosts of letters that were once emblazoned in gold; letters that would once have read:

KING HENRY'S GRAMMAR SCHOOL:
PREFECT

For a moment I looked at it. Such a small thing. Such a small thing, to bring down a school. In that moment I wished I had simply covered it again with earth, along with the bundle of rags and sticks that once had been a human being. But the rocky road that leads to the stars is filled with such temptations as this. A Master of St Oswald's must set the right example. He must be honest, brave and true, or else, what good is anything?

'You first,' I told La Buckfast.

'What makes you think *I* know?'

Oh, please. My stint at St Oswald's, man and boy, has taught me certain instincts. For a start, she's much too calm. And she never really looked at the badge; scarcely even glanced at it. La Buckfast has been *expecting* this. Maybe she knew about

28

it before. But if she already knew of a body in the School grounds, why would she not have reported it?

She smiled. 'It's quite a long story,' she said. 'Are you *sure* you want to know?'

'I'm here all week, Headmaster.'

'Of course you are.' She smiled again. It struck me how at ease she was; as if she was almost enjoying it all. Like a chess player who knows from the start the outcome of the tournament.

I said: 'I'll have that coffee now.'

'I thought perhaps you might,' she said. She poured me a cappuccino, with a sprinkle of chocolate over the foam. By accident or happenstance, it fell into the shape of a skull. Cicero, the cynic, refused to believe in omens and prodigies. I wonder if I should emulate him. After all, as Freud might have said, sometimes a Caunean fig is just another piece of fruit.

The cappuccino was good, although I still prefer the English kind. I remember when coffee came in just black or white. Things – and people – were simpler then. You always knew where to draw the line. But the Head must know the truth, regardless of where it may lead us. *Veritas numquam perit.* Truth never dies, unlike the poor chap by the Gunderson Building, reduced to a twist of sticks and rags. If my suspicions are correct, he wasn't one of ours. And yet his story should be told, whatever it may cost us. A school like St Oswald's is a stage for every shade of drama. This morning, Tragedy. Tomorrow, Farce. La Buckfast understands this perfectly. She was, after all, an actress, when she was still a Mulberry girl. She knows the value of suspense, and the pleasure of having an audience listening with bated breath. And yet she must be aware of how much damage such a revelation may do to the empire she is building. Does she mean to persuade me to ignore my find, for the good of all? Does she really believe I would, for the good of St Oswald's?

She finished her coffee and looked at me.

'Well, Mr Straitley,' she said with a smile. 'If you're ready, I'll begin.'

Her eyes are a curious shade of green; rather cold, but humorous. I thought: *Ye gods, she's enjoying this.*

I put down my cup. 'I'm listening.'

PART 2

Cocytus
(River of Lamentations)

I

St Oswald's, September 4th, 2006

I remember the day he disappeared, because it was my birthday. *Our* birthday, to be precise: we were born exactly nine years apart. At five, a birthday is magical: a long-anticipated day of presents, treats and indulgences. And it had started off so well, with pancakes for breakfast, and birthday cards, and even a present from Conrad. A little school satchel, much like his own, but smaller, and in lollipop red: exactly what I needed for my new term at primary school. But that was still six weeks away, after the summer holidays, and by then, Conrad would be gone, and everything would be different.

I remember that Friday morning with the clarity of certain dreams. The ninth of July 1971; with the radio playing 'Get It On', and butterflies in my stomach, and the long summer holidays so close you could almost smell the seaside. I've told the story so many times that the details have acquired a kind of unusual patina, like the prominent features on a bronze after repeated handling. I do not quite remember his face. All I remember is photographs. The one the newspapers published, of course, taken the day he disappeared: Conrad in his school uniform – charcoal trousers, red-striped tie; blazer

33

with the grosgrain trim. Then the one with my parents at Christmas; the one at the beach, with the sandcastle, and me aged three, with bucket and spade, laughing into the camera. And the one on the cover of that book that caused us so much heartache: *CONRAD: The Lost Boy of Malbry*, by a woman called Catherine Potts; with Conrad's face superimposed over a shot of a green door.

These photographs are my memories. The rest is a distant bank of fog. Even the dreams are forgotten now. Especially those dreams, and the voice of the person I called *Mr Smallface*.

I imagine you've heard the story. It made the papers, after all, though you and St Oswald's must have had rather more pressing concerns at the time. Nor would you have remembered the name of the lost boy's baby sister, even when she re-entered your life as a pupil at your sister school. But who could forget Conrad Price? He was a mystery indeed. A pupil at King Henry's vanished on his birthday, just before the end of the summer term, never to be seen again; no body ever found. And I was there when it happened, though my account of the day's events were useless to the investigation. They tried to make me remember, referred me to a psychologist, but the more they tried, the less they found, and finally they concluded that whatever I'd seen was gone for good into the sink hole of my trauma.

The basic facts were simple enough. My brother was supposed to have picked me up from my nursery school that day. I was excited. Conrad was in his School play, and Friday was the closing night. As a result, his birthday treat had been planned for the following day, which meant that, for the first time, I had a party of my own.

But when I came out of school that day, Conrad wasn't waiting for me. So I did what I usually did. I walked up to

34

King Henry's, which was only a few hundred yards away. Remember, it was the Seventies, and Malbry is a small town. In those days, children still walked home from school. The teacher was long since used to me joining my brother down the road. I'd made my way into the building via the Middle School entrance, and from there, to the Middle School cloakroom, where Conrad used to hang out with his friends: Milky, who looked like the Milky Bar Kid, Fatty – or sometimes Fattyman – and Mod, who wore a green parka, which explained his nickname. I was used to doing this. Conrad didn't like being seen at the gates of the nursery school. But, this time, something happened; something years of therapy failed to make me remember, and I had been found, hours later, crammed into one of the lockers like a small animal in hibernation. Of Conrad there had been no sign. When asked where my brother was, all I could do was shake my head – the red curls newly cropped – and say: '*Mr Smallface took him away. Took him through the green door.*'

The authorities had tried very hard to find out what I meant by *the green door*. The doors at King Henry's were mostly made of varnished natural wood, and the doors to the utility rooms – the caretaker's office, the boiler room – were uniformly painted black. The police investigated every green door in the area, without result. The *Malbry Examiner* pointed out that St Oswald's doors were painted green, which caused a brief excitement; but St Oswald's was five miles away, and there was no reason to believe that Conrad or I had been there at all. It was far more likely, they thought, that the boy had been abducted from school – perhaps by an intruder in a green car – and that the trauma of what I had seen had translated into a fantasy.

In any case, Conrad was gone, except in dreams and photographs. And for nearly twenty years after that, my birthdays passed without celebration: my sixteenth, my eighteenth, my twenty-first. That day was forever set aside; an offering to Conrad's ghost. And from that day, I too was a ghost; moving from room to room in a house in which Conrad's giant presence grew year by year, while I continued to shrink, until at last, in my parents' eyes, I had almost disappeared.

On good days, they still talked to me. They went through the motions of living. My father had taken redundancy the year of Conrad's abduction; he'd been a deputy at the pit, and he had a generous pension. There were the couple's savings, too; money they had put aside to pay for Conrad's school fees. They could have gone on holiday, or moved into a nicer house. But my father would never have touched the money put by for Conrad. On good days, he went to the football, or worked on his allotment. On good days, my mother went to church and helped out with coffee mornings. But on bad days, there was no reaching them. My mother went through phases of going to bed for weeks at a time and my father became increasingly obsessed with numbers stations, and the thought that Conrad's abduction was somehow connected with them. Throughout the early months and years following the abduction, he had played them incessantly, so that the soundtrack of my youth was not a series of pop hits, or television themes, but those haunted station idents – *Lincolnshire Poacher* or *Cherry Ripe*, the cheeriness of the little tune robbed of all life by the static – or worse, an unspeakable warbling that seemed to go on forever. And then came the lists of numbers: *Zero, two, five, eight, eight. Zero, two, five, eight, eight* – always with that little lift in the final delivery, as if the synthetic voice were discharging some jaunty message of hope. Perhaps that's what my father heard; a signal from beyond the grave. To me, they were the voices of the dead, and I would fall asleep to their relentless cadences, however much cotton wool I stuffed into my ears at bedtime.

I had just one friend at school: a girl called Emily Jackson. I remember her very well – those memories predate the thing my mind refuses to accept – a little blonde girl with a rosy face and a placid, maternal temperament. Her elder sister Teresa had cerebral palsy and Emily had taken on the role of elder sibling, putting Teresa's needs before hers without any sign of resentment. Her parents were plump and jovial; their house filled with cheery disorder. She and her family moved away in the winter of 1971, but I had never forgotten her, and my friendship with her remained the most loving part of my childhood. Aside from her, I had no one; lost in my imaginary world. Without the Jacksons, I would have been completely friendless and alone.

I'm not trying to gain your sympathy. I'm merely trying to set the scene. My parents' house, the numbers stations, the shrine to my vanished brother. Oh yes, they had a shrine: a photo of him in school uniform, his Prefect's badge in his lapel, his hair as blond and shiny-sleek as mine was red and untameable.

Red hair is a sign of bad temper, or so my mother used to say, but, by then, I had already learnt to keep my feelings safely under control. I was a model schoolgirl. I went to church every Sunday. At Mulberry House, I won prizes in Drama and Deportment. Yes, there was that little thing with Johnny Harrington when I was sixteen; but as soon as his name made the papers, I broke it off. I had more sense. The unplanned result – my daughter Emily – was born in summer the following year, and my parents, though shaken, greeted my decision to keep the child with the same helpless bewilderment with which they had faced *every* event in our lives since Conrad's disappearance.

But yes, I was a *good* girl. A quiet girl. An obedient girl. And if sometimes I had nightmares in which *something* pursued me relentlessly down the deserted corridors of King Henry's Grammar School, something I could never quite see, but which smelt of burning tinfoil and drains and the sourness of stagnant water – then that was surely not too high a price to pay for the privilege of having outgrown my big brother, who would never live to see fifteen, or kiss a girl, go to college, or give his parents a grandchild.

She should have been a boy, I suppose. *Then*, they might have loved her, loving me by association. But, cocooned in their grief like a pair of dead moths, my parents seemed hardly to notice their only grandchild, except when I suggested they allow me to convert Conrad's old room into a nursery, a suggestion they greeted with the same alarm as if I had suggested burning down the house. Perhaps, if she had been a boy, I might have considered giving her up. It had certainly not been my plan to get myself knocked up at sixteen and a half by a boy six months my junior. But the thought of leaving my daughter to the mercy of a patriarchal State – or worse, of flushing her away like a dying goldfish – filled me with a deep disgust. I would not abandon her as I had been abandoned. Nor would I turn to my parents for help, or contact Johnny's family. And so, as soon as I turned eighteen, I left for a council flat in Pog Hill, and a part-time job as a receptionist at the Meadowbank Care Home. The hours were good, the pay rather less; but between that and the Social Security, we managed to live, if not comfortably, then at least in a way that kept Emily fed, the bills paid, and the social workers off my back.

Every Sunday afternoon I would take the bus back to my parents' house on Jackson Street, and spend exactly fifty minutes drinking tea and trying to make conversation. Sometimes my father would offer me money, which I always declined. Sometimes, I would bring Emily. But no aspect of my life – neither my job, nor my daughter – seemed to hold their interest. Conrad's absence had swallowed them both, and they only ever came alive – briefly, and erratically, and then only on good days – at the mention of his name.

And so we spoke of Conrad: always in the present tense; as if at any time he might just walk into the living room. Above the relentless litany of the numbers station, they would go over school grades, his sporting successes, his qualities; while I sat watching the second hand of the living room clock go round and round.

'Conrad's so good with children,' my mother would say over her cooling tea. 'When he gets home, he'll be so surprised to find he has a little niece.'

'Have a Bourbon,' my father would say. 'Go on. They're your favourites.'

In fact they were *Conrad*'s favourites; I had never liked them. The same went for Coco Pops, Conrad's preferred cereal, which my parents had served me relentlessly for breakfast every morning, and Scotch eggs, which appeared in my school lunchbox every morning without fail, and which I would drop from the bridge into the canal on my way to school, where they floated like small orange buoys, and were eaten by the water rats who lined up solemnly on the bank like children in a dinner queue. It was almost as if, by feeding me Conrad's favourite foods, my parents could continue to pretend that he was still a part of our lives.

'I don't like Bourbons. Remember?'

'I suppose you're on a diet,' my mother would say. 'You shouldn't, you're thin enough as it is.'

'Honestly, it isn't that.'

'Conrad always eats like a horse. It's all that running about he does. You ought to get out in the open air. That'll give you an appetite.'

In the end I always gave in. It's only a biscuit, I'd tell myself. What harm does it do to indulge them? And so I'd eat one, very fast, to get it over with quickly, and she would look at me and say; 'See? You were hungry after all. I've got Scotch eggs in the pantry.'

Meanwhile, between caring for Emily and my job at the care home, I managed to finish my A-levels, then on to an Open University degree, then a teacher training course at the Tech and finally, aged twenty-three, ended up as a supply teacher at Sunnybank Park Comprehensive. It was not all I'd dreamt of, or what my parents had hoped for me. Nor was it the kind of life I wanted for my daughter. Over those six years, I barely slept; I bought my clothes from charity shops and lived on packet noodles. But over six years, I grew strong. I learnt to develop my talents. And that was how I met Dominic, and although that didn't work out as well as I'd hoped, you might say Dominic saved me.

I said *you* might say that, Roy. I'll even let you believe it. Men like you – like Dominic – love to think that of yourselves. You see us as fragile orchids, ready to wilt at the slightest change. But orchids are tougher than you think. We happen to flourish on neglect. Mine require nothing but a soaking every week or two: and when they flower, they do so for months, their blooms like moulded rubber. And yet they seem so delicate; so pretty and so vulnerable. They make you believe they are helpless things. Just like women. More fool you.

Dominic Buckfast was Head of Art, and some nine or ten years older than I. He was charming, funny and smart – much too smart for Sunnybank Park. He could have taught at the Grammar School, or even the University. But Dominic was a Labour man. He didn't believe in grammar schools. The son of a Trinidadian woman barely able to read and write, he was a born romantic, always looking for a cause to espouse: in this case, that of a single mother and her six-year-old daughter. To my surprise, he was aware of my family's history. He'd been the same age as Conrad the year my brother disappeared. He'd read about the case, and was shocked at what it had done to the family. He had a house on April Street – a three-bedroom house, with a garden. He took to Emily straightaway. Best of all, he was single.

And so I allowed him to save us. After six years of fierce independence, of working every hour I could; of buying clothes from charity shops; of always buying the cheapest food; of hoarding coins for the meter; after six years of refusing to be patronized, or pitied, or used, I let myself be saved by a man.

The things we do for our children, Roy. The complicated decisions we make. But Emily was six years old. Old enough to compare herself to the other girls at school. Old enough to understand that we were somehow different. Not because we were poor, but because there was something lacking. I'd taught her independence, determination and courage. But there was something missing, I knew; something I'd never had myself.

As a child, I'd always assumed that, one day, I would fall in love. It happened in stories and on TV. The newspapers were full of it. Even at six, Emily's life was dominated by fairy tales. But I had never been in love. Not with Johnny Harrington, or any of the boys I'd fucked. I'd never even had a crush on a pop star or an actor. I must have loved my parents once. I *knew* I must have loved Conrad – but all of that had disappeared into one of those sink holes that had swallowed so much of my past. And whatever I felt for Emily – that strange and fierce protectiveness – never came out in the normal way, as kisses and bedtime stories.

Remember, Straitley, I was young. I still thought a man could complete me. And he was a good man, in so many ways; and my child needed a father. It didn't quite work out as I'd planned. And yet, I would probably do it again, if I had the chance to go back. But this is where my story starts. I've always known I would tell it one day. It seems oddly fitting to tell it to you. And it starts, not the day Conrad disappeared, but eighteen years later, in Dominic's house, when Emily came home from primary school with a drawing, painstakingly labelled with the words:

Mr SmoLface.

2

St Oswald's ~~*Grammar School for Boys*~~ *Academy*
Michaelmas Term, September 4th, 2006

Yes, of course. I remember the case. A tragedy for all involved.
Conrad Price, a Third-Form boy at King Henry's Grammar
School, who disappeared on the last day of term, never to be
seen again. If he had been one of ours, I probably would have
made the connection sooner, but King Henry's is six miles
away, as well as being a rival school, and I suppose it had slipped
my mind.

'I'm so sorry, Headmaster,' I said. 'It must have been a
terrible loss.'

'Are you going to keep calling me that?' Her eyes still shone
with amusement. I realized that my sympathy was neither
welcome nor warranted.

'*Headmaster* is traditional,' I said.

She laughed. 'Then by all means use it. But my brother's
death was a long time ago. Don't feel the need to sympathize: that isn't why I'm telling you this. But I owe you a
full explanation before we decide where to go from here.'

For a moment I was puzzled. Where else to go with a
body but to the police? And yet, if these were her brother's

remains, then maybe she deserved the right to decide when to make the announcement. Then a terrible thought crossed my mind, and I forbore from comment. Why would a boy from King Henry's be buried in St Oswald's grounds? Could there be another link than accidental geography?

La Buckfast gave me a pitying smile. 'Your friend Eric Scoones used to teach at King Henry's, didn't he?'

'Ten years after Conrad's death,' I said, a little too quickly. 'Between 1982 and 1990.' I heard the defensiveness in my tone, and winced. Of course La Buckfast did not mean to imply anything inappropriate. But on the subject of Eric I am more than a little sensitive. The man is dead. Now let him lie. And yet, her words had troubled me. What was she implying? That Scoones, with his predilections, might have been a suspect in a boy's disappearance? No. That isn't possible. Eric may have been deeply flawed, but he was never a murderer. I would have known it if he were. I would surely have seen it.

La Buckfast gave that smile again. 'I was once a supply teacher at King Henry's myself, for a while. Just for a term, in 1989. One of their French Masters fell ill and they needed someone at short notice.'

'Really?' I was a little surprised. King Henry's — even more than St Oswald's — has always prided itself on its enduring trad-itions. What survives at St Oswald's as a slightly grubby kind of academic folklore has evolved at King Henry's as a Gothic edifice of pretension, including doctoral robes in Assemblies, straw boaters for the rowing team and a multitude of arcane traditions designed to make outsiders feel uncomfortable. Our boys call theirs 'Henriettas', and even though the school has since evolved to include some of the more prestigious and lucrative policies of the twentieth century (mixed-sex classes, Academy status, Drama, Social Sciences), it still retains a (somewhat undeserved) reputation for exclusivity. As a result, predictably, Ozzies and Henriettas have always been bitter enemies, which made old Eric's abrupt defection even more bitter to swallow.

La Buckfast smiled. 'It was an experience.'

'I'll bet it was.'

'In fact, I worked with Mr Scoones. I'll tell you about that, too,' she said. 'But for now, I have a meeting with Dr Markowicz and the Chairman of Governors. Would you allow me a day's grace? All this has rather shaken me.'

Has it? I thought. She looked calm enough. And yet, now I came to think of it, wasn't her smile a little forced, her face rather paler than usual? I felt a stab of sympathy. It couldn't be easy, thinking back to those old, traumatic events. The death of a brother is hard enough. But a disappearance is far worse. It tears at the soul. It never rests. And Hope is the ghoul that will not die, and will not lay the dead to rest.

Of course, I was an only child. I lost my parents years ago, and mourned them out of duty. But losing Eric has taught me about grief. We were only two years apart; brothers in everything but name. I know how sometimes an absence can feel more substantial than flesh itself, like an amputated limb that still demands attention. I'll admit it. I wanted more. I wanted to hear what Eric had been like during his time at King Henry's. Perhaps, most of all, I needed to hear that his abuse of one of our boys had been but a single incident. One long-ago aberration, revealed at the end of his career. I said: 'Of course. I understand.'

'Tomorrow, after school? Shall we say, five-thirty?'

I nodded. 'It's a date.'

3

St Oswald's, September 5th, 2006

The things we say from embarrassment. *A date?* I must have really shaken him. Good. I need him shaken. The mention of Scoones will have done that. Most importantly, I need him to believe that I am vulnerable.

And so I am, but maybe not for the reason Straitley thinks. Scheherazade may have lived a thousand nights under sentence of death, but she was always the one in control. And I do not need a thousand nights: a week or two should cover it. Straitley is a romantic at heart. Like the White Knight in *Alice*, he sees himself in the chivalrous role; allowing me to tell my tale as he leads me to security. Of course, this is very far from the truth. *I* direct the narrative: I tell him only what he needs to know. A tale of misdirection, to keep him on my side until the danger is averted. The rest – the deeper history, the messy, tangled guts of the tale – will stay securely packed away, like handkerchiefs in lavender. And yet, I can feel the echoes of the woman I was all those years ago; that young and brittle woman, still under the shadow of Conrad, and under her show of confidence, still awaiting the inevitable.

Mr Smallface. Oh, that name. That name, in my daughter's handwriting. How naïve I was to believe that scars such as mine could just disappear. Two words on a piece of paper. That's all it took to bring them back. Two words and a shapeless picture: a figure with a tiny head. Two words, and a sudden memory, as sharp as the scent of burning: myself, aged five, in a plastic chair, and two adults in uniform, one at each side; shiny, hopeful faces flushed with mounting fatigue and frustration:

'Did you see where Conrad went? Did he go off with anyone?'

And my answer, again and again, in that tiny, whispery voice: *Mr Smallface took him away. Took him through the green door.*

'Where does he live, Becky? Where's the green door?'

Down the sink hole.

'Underground?'

It wasn't much, I know, but it was the only possible lead they had. They followed it as far as they could: asked me to draw Mr Smallface; asked me where he lived, who he was, and why he would want to take Conrad. They tried again and again to find out what I meant by *the green door.* They searched the basement of the school, as well as the basements of various abandoned buildings in Malbry, Pog Hill and the neighbouring villages. They searched in culverts and clay pits and the sites of disused collieries. The literal-minded idiots even went as far as to bring into the station a local man afflicted with microcephaly, in the hope that I might give them a lead on a potential suspect.

But although the man did indeed have a small face (and a hopeful, nervous smile revealing a set of short, stumpy teeth, and a habit of pulling out hairs one by one from the crown of his head as the officers kept repeating: *Look at him, Becky, is that the man? Is that the man who took Conrad?*), I would only shake my head. Even so, the local papers got hold of the name of the small-headed man, whose house unfortunately happened to have a greenish door. He finally left the village, was tracked down again by the *News of the World*, and ended up taking his own life in a caravan park near Blackpool. And as the trail grew colder, Conrad was – if not quite *forgotten*, simply pushed to the bottom of the pile, as other cases took precedence.

Except in my own home, where instead of fading, his image had grown, eclipsing everything else in our lives. His room was kept just as he'd left it, except that his bed was made afresh every day. A place was set for him at meals. My parents spoke of him all the time, as if he had simply stepped out for an hour instead of having disappeared a week (ten days, six months) ago. Time passed everywhere else, but in my parents' house it did not. It simply crystallized, like a roll of black velvet gathering salt in the Dead Sea. Even all those years later, as my daughter came to me with her primary-school drawing, the house on Jackson Street had remained just as it had been in 1971, with Conrad's photos on the walls; his place set at table; the poster of The Doors by his bed. Our parents hated that band so much. But Conrad loved them, so it stayed. Sometimes my mother even played his records when she cleaned his room, as if he were still there at his desk, listening to the music. It was better than the numbers stations, but I didn't like it. I much preferred classical music, the hymns we used to sing in church. I later discovered I had a voice, and I enjoyed deploying it. But however hard I sang, my parents did not hear my voice above the tinnitus of grief. And so I left, and found my voice again – this time, as a teacher.

The day that Emily came home with her picture of Mr Smallface, we'd been living with Dominic for six months. Six months of not worrying about food, or money for the meter. Emily had her own room; new clothes, new toys, new shoes, new books. What was more, I had just received good news. After twelve unsuccessful months of seeking a permanent teaching post, I'd had a call from King Henry's. One of their French Department staff had died, suddenly, of a heart attack, at the start of the summer term, and they needed someone to stand in until they could find a permanent replacement. Although I mostly taught English, I had a dual-honours degree, which qualified me for the job, and I had been waiting for such a long time to go back to King Henry's.

From the School's perspective, the timing could not have been any worse. So near the end of the school year, all the likely candidates for a September post are already taken. Even newly qualified staff are often unavailable, leaving King Henry's with no choice but to consider a supply teacher.

I was invited to take up the post for the remainder of the term, with the possibility of extending my contract in September, assuming I settled in adequately. The verdict, which was delivered that afternoon via the Headmaster's Secretary, was both condescending and vaguely suspicious, like a colonial missionary addressing the representative of a hitherto uncontacted tribe. And Dominic didn't like it, of course; Dominic, who had saved us, and who hated King Henry's with all the evangelism of the newly converted zealot.

'You deserve better than that,' he said. 'That shower of snobs in their Oxbridge scarves and House ties and doctoral robes. Imagine having to work with them!'

I shook my head. 'The money's good.'

'You don't need the money anymore.' That was true; since we'd moved in with Dominic the previous year, I was actually starting to feel less anxious about money. 'And anyway, how do you think you'll feel, being back where your brother disappeared?'

49

'It's only temporary,' I said. 'Don't worry, I can handle it.'

'You ought to have got that Sunnybank job.' There'd been a vacancy that year, in the English department at Sunnybank Park. I'd applied, at Dom's request, but the post had gone to someone else. Even now, he resented the fact. Maybe even blamed me.

'There'll be other jobs,' I said.

'Not as good as the Sunnybank job.'

He turned away, and started to make tea. Dominic always made tea when he was upset or angry. I suppose he'd imagined both of us teaching side by side, every day, just as we had when I first arrived at Sunnybank to teach supply. But I'd set my sights higher, and now his disapproval was palpable. His dark face was as hard as a piece of oak. His eyes were fixed on the tea things.

'You know I tried. They turned me down.'

Dominic shrugged. 'If you say so.'

'Do you think I didn't try hard enough? That I failed the interview on purpose?'

My voice was rising. I was aware of Emily in the corner with her colouring book. Emily was always very aware of any tension between us. Dominic rinsed two cups in the sink, using more water than required. The water pipe protested, making a moaning, rattling sound. I have always hated that sound. It always reminds me of Conrad, somehow; of stagnant air; of darkness.

That's where he lives. In the sink hole. That's where he takes the children.

I lowered my voice again, and put my hand on Dominic's shoulder.

'It's only a temporary post,' I said. 'I promise, I can handle it. As long as you're still on my side.'

I saw his posture relax. 'I am. I overreacted.' He looked at me again, and smiled. 'I'm sorry, Becks. I'm only looking out for you and Milly. You know that, right?'

'Of course I do.'

Crisis averted, I told myself. Dominic was always so keen in his defence of me. He was like a good dog; trusting and dependable. He was kind and funny, too: attractive; clever; good in bed. Not for the first time, I wondered why it was I didn't love him. There was nothing *not* to love; and yet where my love for him should have been, there was a kind of whistling gap, like a broken window. Or maybe the broken part was where my love for *anyone* should have been. My parents. Dominic. Emily —

From her corner, Emily said: 'I drew a picture in class. Want to see?'

'Of course we do,' said Dominic. He beckoned her towards him. I still remember her rosy face, the piece of art paper in one hand, scrawled with that name from the shadows. I opened my arms to welcome her, but still she went to Dominic first. She always did. Maybe she sensed that broken window inside me.

'Mummy got a job,' I said.

'She's going to be an artist someday,' said Dominic, taking the picture. 'Here, sweetheart, let Mummy see.' He held it up. From a distance, all I could see of Emily's art was a blur of colours, but the *shape* of the image chilled me. As I drew closer, I recognized the formless body. The tiny head. The words, in yellow crayon —

'Who's this?' My lips were cold and numb.

'Oh, Mummy. Look. It *says*.' She traced the words with a finger. 'Mister Smallface.'

I felt my throat contract. My voice was down to a tiny whisper. 'Tell me, sweetheart. Who is he?'

'He lives down in the sink hole. He comes up through the drains. He looks up through the plughole and he sometimes makes a sound like *this –*' She made a terrible, slurping sound, and I felt the hairs on my arms prickle. Suddenly I was four again, hands pressed against the bathroom door, with the ominous sound from the drain unfurling like a long black flag.

'*He's coming,*' whispered a quiet voice from the other side of the door.

'No!'

'*He knows. He can always tell. He's coming to get you, Becks.*'

'No!' My own voice was disappearing now, collapsing and spiralling into itself like water down a plughole. All that was left was a whisper, an airless sucking in my throat, all my senses lost beneath a weighted blanket of terror. Behind me the ratcheting, slurping sound had become a kind of guttural squealing.

'*Close your eyes,*' whispered the voice. '*Close your eyes, curl up very small and maybe he won't notice you.*'

And so I made myself very small, very small against the door, and closed my eyes and waited, as little by little, the sounds from the drain receded to a series of hiccuping burps. And I remember sitting there, eyes closed, hugging my knees to my chest, just as I would sit inside the locker at King Henry's.

The plumbing had always been bad at the house in Jackson Street; the drains were always protesting. My parents had said there was nothing to fear, but at four years old, the world is filled with superstitious terrors. And Conrad had told me it was true; Conrad, who could do no wrong; Conrad, who was my brother.

Mr Smallface lives in the drains. He knows if you don't brush your teeth.

Mr Smallface can squeeze through the pipes. That's why they make those noises.

Once there was a little girl who wouldn't say her prayers at night. Mr Smallface came up through the plughole in her bedroom sink and pulled her into the drains by the hair. Some people say she's still down there. People sometimes hear her, crying to be let out.

Yes, I suppose you could say it was cruel. But children are sometimes cruel, and my brother was just a child. He had no idea how much Mr Smallface terrified me. He didn't know how every night I would secure the bedroom sink, and weigh down the lid of the toilet seat with books before I went to bed. He didn't know how often I dreamt of Mr Smallface, with his eyes like holes in his blank, dark face and his body all coated with dark slime. Or how sometimes I held my breath and looked into the dark of the drain – and how, sometimes, the drain looked back.

Of course I said none of this to Emily; nor will I say it to Straitley. Those things I shall keep to myself. No need to resurrect them. But *someone* had told Emily. Someone had passed on the story. Maybe, after all those years, Mr Smallface, like so many monsters, had found his way into urban myth, passing from small mouth to small ear over playgrounds far and wee.

I handed back the picture and forced myself to smile at her. 'You know he isn't real, right? You know he's just a story?'

'Of course I know he's a story,' said Emily, from the height of her six years. 'I'm not a baby anymore.'

'So where did you hear this story?' I said, keeping my voice very gentle.

Emily shook her head. 'It's a secret,' she said.

'From me?' I said.

She looked at me. *Oh, please. You think you know me?* Children are like cats, I thought. They have evolved behaviours that make them appealing to humans. Feral cats are silent, you know. They do not mew among their own. But to humans they mew, they purr; they rub against our legs and beg. Childish behaviour, designed to cajole and conceal the fact that they are killers.

'Who told you about Mr Smallface?' I said. 'Was it someone at school?'

She smiled and shook her head.

'Then who?' I tried to hide my impatience. Emily had never been a talkative or outgoing child. She'd always been quiet, secretive; happy playing alone with her dolls or reading one of her picture books. Given the choice, I would have preferred my child to be a happy little confiding girl, like her namesake, Emily Jackson. A smiling girl with rosy cheeks and not much imagination. But Emily was too much like the little girl I'd been at her age. A little girl with a quiet voice and big eyes full of secrets.

'Who told you about Mr Smallface?' I said.

For a moment she looked at me. Whoever had told her the story, I thought, it must have been someone at school. These legends spread like nursery rhymes, invading every playground. *Awd Goggie* and the Trapper-Lad; Tom Poker and the bogeyman; all those childhood monsters that we fondly think we have outgrown. Mr Smallface has joined them now. Perhaps that means he's forgotten me. This was what I was thinking as I looked at my daughter's picture, brought to me as a kitten brings its owner the gift of a headless mouse.

And then she gave me a brilliant smile and said; 'Conrad told me.'

4

St Oswald's ~~Grammar School for Boys~~ *Academy*
Michaelmas Term, September 5th, 2006

May, 1989. Yes, Eric would have been there at the time; though he returned to St Oswald's in the autumn. A woman at King Henry's must have been unusual enough, but such a young and attractive one had surely raised a few eyebrows. I wondered that Eric had not recognized her when she came to St Oswald's at Harrington's side as part of the ill-fated Crisis Team, designed to save our failing school. Nearly twenty years later, of course, and even her name was different then. But surely, he would have known her. And yet if he did, he never said.

I remember 1989. A relatively quiet year, mercifully uneventful, except for the hasty departure of a new appointee named Fentiman, who took one look at my current 3S and fled before the end of the first day of term, never to be heard of again. Well, yes. It happens sometimes. And that year's 3S were a boisterous lot, even more so than my current Brodie Boys. But Fentiman was an Oxford man, who came highly recommended, and at over thirty years old, was surely no stranger to expressions of juvenile high spirits. Still, you never know just what a new man will amount to until his courage

55

is tested: in this case, by a practical joke engineered by a boy called Darren Milk – another version of Allen-Jones, unruly but basically harmless. The joke was rather a classic of sorts: the old mouse-in-the-teacher's-desk jape, but substituting Milk's pet tarantula for the rodent in question. And to be fair to young Milk, the boys could have had no previous knowledge, either of Fentiman's arachnophobia, nor of the opened packet of Digestives he'd left in his desk for Break time, in which the arachnid sought refuge.

The result, once the Break time tea arrived, was enough to satisfy even the most hardened prankster, and Fentiman, having fled the scene, decided to keep on running. Some days later, his letter of resignation arrived, and the rest of us in the Languages Department spent the rest of the term filling in for the absentee. What happened to the tarantula is not known: rumour has it that it saw its chance for freedom and escaped, becoming the founder of a race of giant spiders that still dwell in the ceilings and skirting-boards of the Bell Tower.

As for Eric, I saw him from time to time, though not as often as I had when we were colleagues at St Oswald's. I think he missed the old place. He always pretended not to, but he wanted to know what was going on. We'd meet in the Thirsty Scholar on a Saturday night at six, and we'd have a couple of pints and a smoke (no restrictions in those days), and I'd bring him up to date with the perpetual soap opera of St Oswald's. The Scholar was rather out of his way – his local was called the Shanker's Arms – but that was a Sunnybanker pub, and Eric would not frequent it.

'Too many rowdies, Straits,' he would say. 'Too much salt of the earth in there.'

Yes, my old friend was rather a snob. I can't claim the moral high ground, of course: I too favour the Scholar, with its battered old oak bookcases. Some of them are allegedly even from the old St Oswald's library, which was rebuilt and refurbished in 1834, and refurbished by Jeremiah Smarthwaite, a local mining millionaire with delusions of immortality. St Oswald's library is still officially called The Smarthwaite Library, and a portrait of our benefactor – a rather forbidding-looking man with a bad beard and a judgemental expression – hangs above the fireplace, along with the plaque that commemorates him.

Perhaps that's why Eric preferred it; it linked him with St Oswald's. And it was there that we used to discuss the ongoing drama of the place; the petty triumphs; the conflicts; the dirt; the day-to-day tragedy and farce. In return, he would tell me about his mother; his prospects; his health. He seldom spoke of King Henry's outright, or his relationship with the staff. His defection lay between us like a silent bank of cloud. But he came back to us in the end, in the wake of the hapless Fentiman, whose flight from the French Department provided a suitable opening, plus a chance for Eric to save the day.

'Milk,' he said. 'That rings a bell. I used to teach a boy called Milk. Any relation?'

'Probably. These boys get everywhere.'

'Got a B in French, I think.' Eric remembered boys by their grades, rather than their personalities. I have no idea what Milk got in his O-level Latin, but I do recall a quiet boy, with dark-blond hair in a shiny fringe. Predictably, the other boys called him Milky, or the Milky Bar Kid, like the advert. If Darren Milk was perturbed by this, he did not let it show. Instead, he specialized in the kind of quiet revenge and stealthy jackanapery that doubtless precipitated the departure of the hapless Mr Fentiman.

'A bit of a joker,' I went on. 'But any St Oswald's Master who can't cope with a spider or two in his desk isn't worthy of the name.' Alas, poor Fentiman. I can't say I really knew him at all, except for the brief conversation we had outside the staff room the day he arrived.

'That's what comes of hiring an Oxford man,' Eric said. 'Always expecting an easy ride. No experience of real life.'

This was a regular complaint from old Scoones, who tended to blame his lack of promotion on the fact that he had studied at Leeds, rather than at some place with bowler-hatted Proctors. Still, he'd nailed it with Fentiman, who had chosen to arrive on his first day wearing a College boating blazer and tie, which had earned him some ribald commentary among the inmates of 3S.

'You look like a Henrietta, Sir. Did you come to the wrong school?'

'Are you a student teacher, Sir? Is this some kind of school exchange?'

Boys can be merciless at times, especially when they scent weakness. The new Master's resemblance to one of their arch rivals must have acted as a challenge to my boys, who otherwise would probably have given him a week's grace to settle in.

'What about King Henry's?' I said, trying to lighten Eric's mood. 'Any interesting newbies this year?'

Eric huffed. 'A few,' he said. 'One of them's a woman.'

'Oh.'

That was Rebecca Buckfast, of course. Miss Price, she would have been then. Twenty-three, with jade-green eyes and hair the colour of embers. I wish I'd taken more interest in that snatch of conversation, but I couldn't have known. I simply shrugged.

'That Supply from last term,' Eric went on, lighting a Gauloise. He never smoked at work. He thought it made him look unprofessional.

'I thought you said she wasn't staying on. She must have more to her than you thought.'

He sniffed. 'Can't say I really noticed.'

I suppose I should have known. Eric was hiding something from me. I try to imagine the impact Miss Price must have made at King Henry's, standing out like a cockatoo in a flock of sparrows. Of *course* he must have noticed her. So why pretend he hadn't? Under his gruff exterior, Eric was a gossip. And he'd already had the previous term to gather more than his fair share of scandal, speculation and dirt. Why then this reluctance to speak? At the time I simply put it down to his general sullenness, but knowing now what I do, it seems there may have been more to it.

I wonder what La Buckfast knows. I wonder if she suspected at all. I wonder if her reluctance to call the police immediately has anything to do with —

No. Her brother vanished years ago. Thirty-five years. A hundred and five terms. Which also happens to be precisely the time that I have spent at St Oswald's, following a five-year stint at a lesser school in Leeds. It's hard to remember being so young; entering my first term. Everything was at the same time both familiar and strange. The Staff Room; the Quiet Room; my form room in the Bell Tower. The rules, which I had never kept when I was there as a schoolboy, but which I was now expected to enforce on a daily basis. The older Masters, some of which — like the Chaplain — had even known me as a boy.

But Eric was there to show me the ropes; Eric, my old friend from childhood. Eric, whose ugly secret life it has taken me thirty-four years to discover. Nothing was ever made public, and Spikely — that troubled, sullen boy — was not a reliable witness. Even now I find myself thinking of ways to absolve him. There was never any proof. Surely a man remains innocent until he is proven guilty. And yet, I know in my heart that Eric abused David Spikely, and fled the school when Harry Clarke fell victim to the same kind of scandal.

And here we are again, he and I, with another dead boy to account for. Not one of ours, not this time, of course. But can I *really* be certain that Conrad Price wasn't one of *his*?

No, it is unthinkable. And yet I think about it a lot. Eric used to drive a green Austin Morris he referred to affectionately as *Bessie*, and which he replaced without explanation over the summer of 1971. Could my friend have driven to King Henry's on July 9th? Did Rebecca Price suspect that *he* was the man behind the green door? And what had happened between them both in the summer of 1989?

5

King Henry's Grammar School for Boys, April 10th, 1989

Well, yes. I knew Eric Scoones, at least inasmuch as I really *knew* anyone at King Henry's. But when I arrived at St Oswald's last year he totally failed to connect me with the brittle young woman I had been almost twenty years before. To be fair, I have reinvented myself more than most women: as a mother, as a wife, as a widow. I'm aware that I have changed since then. My body has thickened. My hair has been tamed. And at twenty-three I was quite unaware of how often men turned to look at me. I was the mother of a six-year-old child. I felt mature beyond my years. Truth is, I was a child myself. Alice, down the rabbit hole.

I arrived in my new post at eight o'clock on Monday, 10th April. I parked my ancient blue Mini in the Staff car park, among the Audis and Jaguars. I'd taken pains with my outfit. Dark-blue trouser suit; white silk shirt; my hair pulled back into a bun. At Sunnybank, the teachers wore whatever they liked: which mostly meant jeans and open-necked shirts. I knew that at King Henry's, I would be judged on every little thing they could find to use against me. My red attaché case was new, an early birthday present from Dominic, who had greeted the revelation that I didn't celebrate birthdays with a mixture of pity and disbelief. Of course, he'd not met my parents yet. Nor had they shown any interest in him on the few occasions I'd mentioned him. But his gift was the first I'd had since the day Conrad disappeared, and although I couldn't help but see the similarity between my new attaché case and that little red satchel from long ago, I took it as a gesture of reconciliation; a sign that in spite of his principles, he wanted me to succeed at King Henry's.

The School is a handsome building, built on rather grandiose lines. An avenue of cherry trees, now just coming into bloom, leads visitors from the wrought-iron gate up to the main building. A broad and sweeping flight of steps leads to the main entrance, which is reserved for visitors and staff. Two side entrances for the boys; one on the left for the Lower and Middle School, one on the right for the Seniors. A short flight of steps leads down into the cloakroom. That's where I sometimes used to wait for Conrad when I came out of school. My school – its name was Chapel Lane – was just down the road, behind some trees. My day ended ten minutes before Conrad's, so at the end of the school day, I would walk the few hundred yards along the road to King Henry's to meet him. I would go in through the Pupils' entrance, make my way down to the cloakroom, and wait for him by his locker, after which he would take me home, before going off again with his friends.

I remembered Conrad's friends; Fatty, Mod and Milky. They were always together at school, or at the children's playground, or hanging around the railway lines, or on the stretch of waste ground that people called the Clay Pits. Our parents didn't like them much – Milky's parents were divorced, Fatty was less than athletic (my father, especially, disapproved), and Mod was, worst of all, *coloured* – but no one had ever been good enough in their eyes for Conrad. To them, he was always an innocent, led astray by others. Too good for this world. Too good for *anyone.*

I don't know what impelled me to go into the cloakroom on that first day. Perhaps I wanted to see what had changed. Perhaps I still thought, after all this time, that I might remember something new. Memory is a place of shifting sands, overgrown with creepers. But sometimes, you can still find a way to an almost forgotten place. Scents can sometimes help; and sounds. With me, it's especially scents and sounds.

I bypassed the main entrance and went in by the side door. A sharp gust of April wind slammed the door behind me. The corridor was mostly clear; I recognized a familiar scent of old wood and furniture polish. The Middle School cloakroom was on the left, down a little flight of steps. I started down the steps, and a blast of sound emerged from below. The cloakroom had a high ceiling, which made the noise reverberate. And there were boys everywhere, pushing up and down the steps. A Master in a black gown was trying to keep order.

'Keep to the left! Keep to the *left*!'

Of course, I didn't know Scoones at the time. And of course, he was younger then. But you would have recognized him, Roy. The heightened complexion, stentorian voice. The eyes like chips of mica. The boys never had much respect for him, not even in the classroom, and here, on the steps to the cloakroom, he didn't really stand a chance.

'You, boy in the Murray House tie! *I* saw that! Who's your Form Master?'

Of course I didn't know it then, but Scoones never bothered to learn the boys' names. Instead, he dwelt on details shared by dozens – if not hundreds – of boys. House ties; spectacles; colours blazers; Prefects' gowns. As such, it was hardly surprising that his brief and violent outbursts were largely disregarded.

'You, boy with the ginger hair! Why aren't you wearing your School tie?'

I stared. The Master was glaring angrily at me from the locker room floor. Behind him, the cool morning sunlight angled through a strip of glass bricks near the ceiling. I remembered that undersea light filtering from the top of the room, and the feet of the passers-by, ghostly through the pebbled glass.

'Well?' said Scoones. 'Where's your tie?'

It took me a moment to realize, first, that he was talking to me, and second, that in the dim light of the staircase, my trouser suit and shirt combination might have looked something like the boys' uniform.

'I'm talking to *you*, boy!' trumpeted Scoones. By now, several of the boys on the staircase around me had understood the Master's mistake. Laughter buffeted the air.

'Sir, that isn't a boy, Sir!'

'Don't you know the difference?'

More of that mocking laughter. It was not, by and large, directed at me, but I was swept into it nevertheless. It broke against me like ocean waves. It mocked me in my brother's voice. Scoones took a handful of furious steps and faced me on the stairway. Far from being apologetic, his face was congested with fury.

'What the hell are you doing here?' he shouted into my look of dismay. 'This is not a gangway! Visitors take the *Main Entrance!*'

I managed to stammer something about having wanted to look around. This seemed to infuriate him even more, and his voice, already thunderous, seemed to fill the whole building.

For a moment I was five again, in the belly of the whale, with the voice of Mr Smallface booming through the pipework.

'This is a school, Madam, not a zoo! Go to the Main Entrance, and ask for the School Secretary!'

Yes, it must seem impossible to imagine me being afraid of Scoones. But Straitley, I was very young. I was unprepared for this. And the smell – the smell of the cloakroom – bleach and football boots and boys, as well as the darker underscent of something much more sinister – was just the same as it had been that afternoon, on my birthday, the day that Conrad disappeared; the day I could never remember.

I turned and fled on another wave of boisterous, juvenile laughter, and I wondered – not for the last time – whether accepting the job hadn't been a dreadful mistake.

6

St Oswald's ~~Grammar School for Boys~~ *Academy*
Michaelmas Term, September 5th, 2006

The first thing I did on this first day of the Michaelmas term
was to check the site of the Gunderson Building. Nothing there
has been disturbed; except that the gap in the chain-link fence
has been mended with thick wire. Looking through the mesh,
I think I can just see the bundle that, to the overly imaginative,
might possibly look like a body. Since yesterday, the resemblance seems to have become less marked. Perhaps this is
because yesterday was a day of mists and today is one of bright
sunshine. In sunlight, everything looks better. The ominous
shadow against the wall that looked so like a monster now
looks a lot more innocuous. In fact, it seems more likely today
that the bundle of rags and sticks by the pool is indeed nothing
but rags and sticks, and that the old King Henry's badge was
simply there by coincidence. There is no sign the police have
been here. Then again, why should they? La Buckfast has a tale
to tell, and I have pledged to hear it. Perhaps she will call the
police tonight. Perhaps she will call them tomorrow. In any
case, the evidence has been there for a long time. Whatever
remains must surely survive for a day or two longer.

What should I tell my Brodie Boys? Of course, they are in school today. But I doubt there will be any time for lengthy conversation. The first day of a new term is always a time of disruption, and now that our gates have been opened to girls, the possibility of a quiet Gauloise before class, or a leisurely cup of tea during Registration, has been drastically curtailed.

Fortunately, the new forms are segregated. Kitty Teague, the Head of French, is in charge of a form comprised entirely of girls, while I have the masculine counterpart. According to the new Head, sound academic studies suggest that girls perform better in segregated classes, while on a more social level, boys can benefit from the civilizing effect of girls. Our system is designed to take advantage of both, as well as giving the School a much-needed influx of new blood – and of course, the added fees will serve to pull the old ship off the rocks on which she currently finds herself.

Still, that doesn't change how I feel. We love what we love, regardless. Harry Clarke taught me that, and although St Oswald's chances of survival may be vastly improved by this injection of fresh talent, I cannot find it in me to embrace the change wholeheartedly. *Ad astra per aspera.* The rocky road leads to the stars. And if those rocks should prove too great, the Captain should go down with his ship.

Not that I *am* the Captain, of course. I am still the cabin boy, now grown whiskered, grey and old, like a sailor under a curse, doomed to sail forever beneath the same old and tattered flag. At lunchtime, sitting with my form, marking a set of grammar tests and eating a ham and cheese sandwich, I saw Allen-Jones looking in at the door. I could tell that he wanted to talk to me, but School protocol dictates that I should invite him to enter. Instead, I gave a dismissive smile, and turned back to my marking, hoping that he would be satisfied.

But Allen-Jones was never the type to take the hint. He stood there a moment longer, then knocked and came in, looking both anxious and determined.

I looked up from my marking once more.

'Sir, do you have any news?' he said.

I gave him a quizzical look. 'News?'

'News,' he repeated. 'Of the – you know. The B-O-D –' He indicated my current 2S, sitting around the form room in groups. Some were eating their packed lunches. Others played chess, or cards, or read. I noticed with a slight pang that Allen-Jones's erstwhile desk was taken by a nondescript boy called Tebbitt or Tibbett (my recall of boys' names on the first day of term isn't as good as it used to be), who was thoughtfully eating Hula Hoops while reading a battered copy of *Viz*.

'Ah. That,' I said to Allen-Jones, assuming my most senatorial smile. 'That's currently being dealt with by the – er – relevant authorities, thank you.'

He looked at me. 'You reported it, Sir? What did they say? Was it –? You know.' He lowered his voice. 'Was it what we thought it was?'

'That I can't tell you at present,' I said, choosing my words very carefully. 'Time will tell. Tests, and so forth. But thank you for coming to me, and now I think it's best if you and the others refrain from discussing the matter, even with each other.' I allowed my gaze to return to the group of second-formers clustered about the room. 'Don't want trouble in the ranks.'

He nodded, looking dissatisfied, and I went back to my marking. I hated to be so dismissive, but I didn't want to engage in conversation. Allen-Jones may be lax when it comes to Latin grammar, but he is unusually bright when it comes to judging people. I'm not sure he would understand why

I am so reluctant to act; or why the situation needs to be handled with such delicacy.

'Sir, there's one more thing,' he said, lowering his voice a little more.

I sighed and looked up from my marking.

'It's about Ben,' said Allen-Jones.

'What about her?'

'That's the thing.' Allen-Jones was watching me. 'Remember when I first came to you and told you I was gay, Sir? You never asked me how I knew. You just asked me if I thought it was going to interfere with my Latin.'

I nodded. I remembered it well. The truth is, I've never been entirely comfortable around issues of sexuality. As far as I'm concerned, the less said about it the better.

'Are you telling me *she's* gay?'

Allen-Jones shook his head. He looked as if he were struggling with a difficult Latin phrase.

'Then what?' I was genuinely confused. It wouldn't have surprised me. The short hair, the blunt manner, the outright refusal to wear a skirt. Today's young people are so much more complicated than they seemed to be in the old days. Dick and Jane. Janet and John. Pigtails and puppy dogs. You never needed to ask yourself which was which, or why that was. When I was a boy, girls might well have been visitors from a different world.

'What does Ben want to tell me?' I said. 'And why isn't she telling me herself?' Allen-Jones looked up at me. His blue eyes were very earnest. 'He is, Sir. He's been telling you ever since he came here. Telling us all who he *really* is. And when people tell us who they are, we really ought to listen.'

★

After Allen-Jones had left, I thought about what he had told me. It wasn't the first time I'd heard of a pupil claiming the opposite gender, but this was the first time with one of my own. I'm sure that, twenty years ago, I would have dismissed the claim out of hand. Even now, I am aware that I am one of the Old Guard: laden with the prejudices of my generation. And yet, a teacher of Classics *should* be aware of the concept of metamorphosis. Perhaps this will pass. I hope it will – surely any child must want to be like other children. But Ben never was; and, like Allen-Jones, seems more self-aware than most. *When people tell you who they are, we really ought to listen.* It might have been Harry Clarke speaking: the thought filled me with a poignant and unexpected melancholy. Harry tried so hard to be himself. But when our friends tell us who they are, do we ever *really* hear them? I sighed and reached in my desk drawer for a Liquorice Allsort. I wish I could believe that this essentially pastoral matter, like the remains by the Gunderson Pool, could be dealt with swiftly and according to the proper procedure. But already this term seems to be fraught with peculiar challenges.I put my hand in my pocket, and found the old King Henry's Prefect's badge, washed clean of dirt now, and starting to shine once more from repeated handling. A kind of punctuation mark on the reverse of the painted shield marked where the pin had broken off. I stropped my thumb reflectively against the ragged metal, wondering if it would turn out to be a full stop, or a colon, or maybe an ellipsis. Something must be done, I thought. A boy is dead. Not one of ours, and so long ago – but that should not affect the way in which we deal with his murder.

Tonight I will speak with La Buckfast. Explain to her that, whatever comes next, we must alert the authorities. And yet, I want to know her tale. I want to know what happened that year, at King Henry's, with my friend Eric Scoones. Of course, there is as yet no hint that Scoones was even aware of the boy. Maybe I am flinching at shadows. And maybe La Buckfast's undoubted charm is taking me down a dangerous route. *Will you walk into my parlour?*

No: whatever she tells me, I must talk to her tonight. Tonight –

Maybe tomorrow.

7

St Oswald's, September 6th, 2006

My audience of one is restless today. I saw him at Break on the playing fields, ostensibly keeping pupils from the new site, his black gown flapping in the wind. He looked like a mournful graveyard crow. He tried to make another appointment with me through my Secretary, after school, but I already had two hours of meetings with the Bursar and the new Heads of Year, and therefore could say with no certainty when I would be available. He waited out in the corridor for an hour or so, nevertheless, then eventually gave up. The sound of his footsteps down the hall echoed like a ball and chain.

Straitley is looking unwell, these days. The new regime does not suit him. In his old black gown and his chalk-smudged suit, he looks like the last piece of dead skin left on a quickly healing wound. The new staff do not wear gowns, of course. The old guard – what remains of them – have made an effort to change with the times. Only Straitley stubbornly clings to the trappings and methods of the past. I wonder how long he thinks he can last on his hopeless quest to hold back the tide. But he was there at our meeting at five-thirty last night, on the dot: I poured him a cup of coffee and resumed my story.

'I hadn't made a good start,' I said. 'I'd embarrassed myself, and humiliated a member of King Henry's staff. Mr Scoones wasn't the type to laugh at his mistake and move on, so the atmosphere was already strained before I'd even started the job. If we had been at St Oswald's, I might have contrived to avoid him, but King Henry's is not like St Oswald's, where teaching rooms are like islands, standing in a sea of boys. King Henry's was run on formal, almost military lines, with a Headmaster's briefing every morning in the Common Room, and a formal mentoring programme for the induction of new members.

According to this inaptly named 'buddy' system, members of the Department who did not have a form would be the first point of contact for any new members of staff. You can guess what happened next. I was a new member of staff. Mr Scoones did not have a form. Thus I arrived to find myself paired with Eric Scoones as my mentor. If I had a problem, I was to take it to Scoones. If I needed advice, Scoones. If anyone made a complaint, Scoones.'

'I see. That can't have been easy.'

You should know that: you were his friend. But I was everything you were not. Young; inexperienced; female. That, more than anything else, I think, infuriated him. The phrase 'confirmed bachelor' was created for Eric Scoones. Of course in those days it would never have occurred to me to ask, or even to think about a colleague's sex life. And to my eyes, Scoones already seemed old. His hair was already greying. His manner was patriarchal, veering between condescension and the outright judgemental. His stiffness, his formality seemed to belong to another age. And like the other King Henry's staff, he wore his academic robe over his charcoal suit and University tie. Later, it would occur to me that all this posturing

73

was simply a means of concealing his very real insecurity (the university was Leeds, after all), but at the time I found him not only terrifying, but monstrous.

I had no academic robes. At King Henry's, however, they were more or less mandatory. Even Prefects wore them in Assembly, and for carrying out duties. Without them, I was likely to be mistaken for a pupil – or, worse, as one of the School Secretaries. Scoones explained all this to me in glacial tones at our first 'buddy meeting' that morning, in the Common Room, while the boys were in Assembly.

He made no further mention of his outburst in the cloakroom. In a way, that made it worse; he seemed to assume I'd ignore it. He simply introduced himself, in that stiff, fussy manner he always had; he shook my hand (just one dry pump), and then went on to fire at me the series of toneless bullet points that counted as my induction.

'School begins at eight o'clock, with the Headmaster's Briefing. Registration, eight-thirty for members of staff in charge of a form. Eight-forty till nine, Assembly. During this time, I shall be free to address any queries or concerns. The Head of Department is Dr Sinclair, but he has a form to administer, therefore you will address your concerns to me inasmuch as possible. Every Friday we shall review your progress. This' – he handed me a sheet printed in purple ink – 'is your timetable. Where possible, I shall observe lessons, inasmuch as my own timetable permits.'

'Oh,' I said, rather weakly.

He fixed me with his watery gaze. Scoones always looked as if he was peeling onions. I suspect he should have worn glasses, but didn't want to be judged, somehow. The result was a narrow, peculiar gaze born mostly of short-sightedness.

'I'm assuming you do *have* your lesson plans?'

I opened my red attaché case. I could tell it looked childish to him, in his world of masculine monochrome. My class notes were written out neatly in a new spiral-bound notebook.

'Oh dear, oh dear,' said Eric Scoones. (It was something he said rather often.) 'Have you not received your copy of the Book?'

The Book, it transpired, was a series of Departmental lesson plans, designed to ensure the seamless transition from one Master to another, without enabling such dangerous things as personal style to surface. Written over ten years ago by the current Head of Department, it concentrated on grammar, spelling and precis, and had been built to dovetail with a curriculum set by the Oxford and Cambridge Board when I was still in utero.

'If you'd arrived at the *start* of the year, you would have had your own copy.' His tone implied that this, too, was my fault. 'Still, you'll have plenty of time during the summer holidays to get to know it properly.'

Thus were my careful lesson plans, with their role-playing games and activities, rapidly dealt with by Eric Scoones, who gave them a summary glance, then sighed and took out a ring-bound file from his black leather briefcase. The file (which was also black) was marked DEPARTMENTAL LESSON PLANS.

'This is my personal copy,' said Scoones. 'You can use it for the time being.'

I opened the file, which was filled with mimeographed pages. I recognized the same purple ink as the class timetable sheet. I noticed that the course book my brother had used was still in circulation. Whitmarsh's *Simpler French Course* – with its distinctive orange-and-black cover. I remembered it very well. Conrad had spent many evenings sighing over its contents.

'Oh,' I repeated, not knowing quite what else to say. 'Thank you.'

At the back of the book was a messy folder of worksheets, purple-inked on duplicating paper. 'These are your masters,' said Eric Scoones. 'No photocopying without permission. The Banda machine is in the Departmental Common Room. You'll need to get there early.'

I'd heard of these duplicating machines before, but I had never actually used one. Most schools had moved on by then to less unwieldy methods. Even Sunnybank Park had a staff room photocopier. 'I'm not sure I know how to use one,' I said.

Scoones made a kind of huffing sound. 'Better learn, then, hadn't you? Go on,' he said. 'It's a quarter to. Lessons start on time here.'

8

King Henry's Grammar School for Boys, April 10th, 1989

The Departmental Common Room was on the Middle Corridor, where the Languages Department had its rooms. It was a smallish office room, with four desks, two armchairs, a phone on the wall, and in the corner, an item that I took to be the Banda machine. It was a primitive thing, comprised of a kind of metal barrel, turned by a metal handle, with a tray holding blank paper. A kind of grille served to protect the paper from the mechanism. In the sunlight, it seemed to snarl like the grille of an approaching car.

These are your masters, Scoones had said. I understood that the inky sheets were supposed to be fixed onto the barrel somehow, where the print from the master would be transferred onto the blank sheets of paper. I selected a worksheet marked *Four Lower*, and fixed the master sheet into place. I turned the handle experimentally. The printed sheet shot out from beneath the barrel and landed face up on the floor. The print – which was smudgy and rather faint – came out in the same bilious purple. I tried another sheet, which crumpled and jammed under the rim of the barrel. I smoothed out the master and tried again, smelling that characteristic scent of ink, and metal and solvent.

The handle turned. The barrel clanked. It sounded like a clockwork toy. Printed pages shot out one by one, landing pell-mell on the floor. I bent down to gather them and found my hands stained purple with ink.

'*Fuck*!' I said, at the moment at which the door opened, revealing a grey-haired man in a doctoral robe and wearing an expression of distinct disapproval. He made no comment at my outburst, but my face lit up like a flare.

'You must be Miss Price,' he said.

I made a meaningless little sound and gathered the rest of my papers.

'I'm Dr Sinclair. Head of French. Scoones should have brought you up to date. Copy of the Book, and so forth.' He looked down at my inky hands. 'I see you've worked out the Banda machine.'

I nodded again. 'Yes, thanks.'

'Good.' He eyed me coolly. 'I'm afraid there are no bathroom facilities for ladies at King Henry's. You'll need to ask the School Secretary for the key to the disabled toilet.'

'I'm sure that will be fine,' I said.

'One more thing.' He looked me up and down. 'Ladies at King Henry's do not, as a rule, wear trousers. We have a formal dress code here: business suits for the gentlemen; a skirt suit or frock for the ladies.'

'Oh,' I said, rather taken aback. The trouser suit had cost rather more than I usually spent on work clothes: I'd assumed it would count as business wear. I wanted to protest, but there was something about Sinclair that was intimidating, in spite of his quiet demeanour. Perhaps it was the gown he wore, or his effortless air of authority. He had been a teacher at King Henry's for over thirty years: he was practically part of the building. I tried to imagine how it would feel to have that kind of confidence. Instead, I could feel a lump in my throat; an alarming stinging in my eyes.

Sinclair went on without seeming to notice my expression. 'Any trouble with the boys, just tell Scoones. He'll sort it out. Good chap, Scoones. Knows what he's doing. He'll talk you through the Detention procedure, and so forth.'

'I won't have any trouble,' I said.

His look was politely incredulous. I suppose, in his world, a woman teacher – especially such a young one – was inevitably going to have trouble with boys.

'Well, if you do, talk to Scoones,' he said, and left in a swirl of scarlet-tipped robes.

I rearranged the crumpled sheets with hands that trembled a little.

I don't belong here, I told myself. What on earth possessed me to think that I could ever teach here?

I thought of the School curriculum, nestled in the black file. Sinclair and his doctoral robe. The Banda machine, with its snarling grille. Scoones saying: *These are your masters.* And, on that memory, there came another, more distant memory: Conrad's voice across the years; black smoke carried on the wind.

'*My French master's name is Dr Sinclair.*' Conrad's voice was very close. '*He's super-strict, but he's OK. My Classics teacher's the Chaplain. Mr Farrelly, Rugby. Then there's Miss Macleod, Drama. Looks a bit like Diana Rigg.*'

At four years old, I had no idea of what Diana Rigg had looked like. But I did remember my brother's voice; its not-quite-pleasant undertone. So, Conrad must have known Sinclair? How strange. I thought I'd forgotten. What other things might I recall over the course of the next two weeks? What buried thoughts, what memories?

It's only for three months, I thought. Three months, and you can breathe again. Three months, and you'll have the whole of the summer holidays to –

To do what? Prepare?

Escape?

My thoughts were interrupted by the sound of the school bell, announcing the start of lessons, bringing with it memories of myself at five years old, waiting in the strip of light at the foot of Conrad's locker. I picked up my briefcase and work-sheets, and headed into the corridor, where the bell was louder still. A simple clapper-and-bell design, triggered electronically. The noise of it was relentless. Boys were already lining up outside their respective classrooms. Some of them had their hands on their ears. Finally, it stopped, and I made my way to my first lesson; a Four Upper French class in L14, on the Middle Corridor.

I missed it the first time, because the boys lined up outside the door seemed too young. I checked my black file again and discovered that, at King Henry's, 'Four Upper' is what they call the Third Form. Another eccentricity, like the wearing of academic robes, designed to make outsiders feel conspicuous.

The boys were lined up quietly on the left-hand side of the door. A little too quietly, I thought: the quietness of teenagers is usually linked with uncertainty. As soon as they felt secure again, the disruption would begin. The trick has always been to identify the troublemakers and defuse any misbehaviour before it becomes disruptive.

I followed the boys into the class. I counted thirty-one of them; the black folder gave me their names. The class was a smallish, L-shaped room, with a bank of windows facing east. Golden sunlight filtered through, picking motes out of the air. The teacher's desk was on a kind of stage overlooking the classroom. Over the door hung the classroom bell, and an old-fashioned box calendar. The desks were in rows of six, except for the back row, which extended further into the corner. I noticed a blond boy wearing a Prefect's badge choose a desk on the far end of the back row, and marked him for attention. The back row is traditionally the troublemaker's domain, and this boy had an impudent look – a slightly clownish walk, a grin that suggested some inner hilarity – that told me he might be the one to lead the class into mayhem.

The boys stayed standing as I came in. Another King Henry's tradition. I said: 'Please, sit down. My name is Miss Price. I'll be taking over your class.'

The blond boy in the back row said: 'Asda Price.'

A murmur spread among the boys. I knew it. That blond boy was trouble. His hair, in the morning sunlight, was almost dazzlingly bright. I tried to see his face, but the sun had bleached his features of detail; he looked like the shadow of a boy reflected in a sheet of foil.

'Are you new, Miss?' one boy said. 'Or are you just another Supply?'

Another said: 'What car do you drive?'

'A Mini,' said a third, and grinned.

I said: 'I'll need to learn your names. Please write yours on a sheet, and put it on the front of your desk.' I handed out sheets of paper. The boys took the opportunity to start talking among themselves. I felt my cheeks begin to burn: even at such an early time, the classroom was already warm.

'No talking, please,' I said. The noise subsided a little. Only the blond boy at the back seemed not to have heard me. Instead, he grinned and started to fold his sheet of paper into the shape of an aeroplane.

'We'll have none of that,' I said.

The boy's grin widened still further. Around him, the other boys had begun to talk among themselves again. Several were drawing on their name sheets. In a moment, they would be riotous.

'You at the back. What's your name?' I said in a crisp tone, addressing the blond boy.

The boy in front of him looked up. 'Persimmon, Miss.'

'Not you,' I said.

Persimmon feigned confusion. He had a broad, comic face and a habit of sprawling across his desk, like a lazy seal on a flat rock. Behind him, the blond boy met my gaze, unabashed; grinning triumphantly.

'All right. We'll try this again,' I said, trying to sound confident. 'Everyone stand. In silence.' The boys stood up, rather noisily, grinning at one another.

'We'll wait until you're quiet,' I said. This was a technique that had worked pretty well at Sunnybank Park — but then again, at Sunnybank Park I'd always felt like a teacher. Here, I was something different. Someone who drove a Mini instead of an Audi or a Jag. Someone who didn't even know that academic gowns must be worn in Assemblies, and that ladies wore a skirt suit, or a frock.

'Asda Price,' repeated Persimmon, tapping his trouser pocket like the woman in the advert.

'What did you say?'

'Yes, Miss Price,' said Persimmon innocently, tapping his back pocket again. The boys on either side of him grinned. The boy on the back row capered and danced like the conductor of a mad orchestra.

'Yes, Miss Price,' said the rest of the class, all tapping their pockets in unison. A ripple of laughter went through the group, a ripple that soon became a wave.

At the back, the blond-haired boy was in paroxysms of laughter, lolling half in, half out of his chair. There was something strangely familiar in the way he moved, I thought. The sun was too bright for me to see his features properly, and yet, there was something in his smile that I found deeply unsettling.

'You at the back – stop that – sit *down*!' My voice was sharper than I'd thought; I sounded almost close to tears.

The class fell suddenly silent, but not at my words. The glazed classroom door had opened and I saw Eric Scoones in the doorway.

'What in hell's name is going on?' trumpeted Scoones in his locker room voice.

The boys had stood up at his entrance, and now remained in silence, wooden as toy soldiers.

Scoones went on: 'I could hear you all the way to my office!'

The boys stood there in silence, heads bent as if it made them invisible. I said to Scoones; 'I'll handle this, thanks.'

Scoones ignored me completely. 'Any more noise from this classroom,' he said, 'and you'll *all* be staying in after Break. Is that understood?'

'Yes, Sir.'

'I didn't hear you!' said Scoones.

'Yes, Sir!'

'You'd better,' said Scoones, and left once more, without having a said a word to me, or even having acknowledged my presence. For a moment I stood there in silence, feeling my embarrassment turn to inarticulate rage. *How dare the man! How dare he!* The boys were still standing, awaiting my reaction in silence.

'Oh sit down, for pity's sake,' I said. Then shifting my gaze to the sunlit back row, I looked for the troublemaker –

And in that moment, I realized two things. One, the reason the boy in the back row had looked so very familiar was that he was the very image of my brother at fourteen, two, in the moment between my outburst and Eric's intervention, the blond-haired boy in the back row had somehow completely disappeared.

9

St Oswald's ~~Grammar School for Boys~~ Academy
Michaelmas Term, September 7th, 2006

Three days into the new term, and still no word of the body. It is starting to weigh on my mind. The thought of that bundle lying there is like an itch in an unreachable place; it makes me distracted, irritable; it colours every moment. I find myself looking for reasons to walk past the flooded building site. I tell myself that the Porter's Gate is closer to the Bell Tower than the Main Gate, and use this as my daily excuse to check out the Gunderson Building.

This morning, I noticed that the remains had been covered with orange tarpaulin. Does this mean that the police have been told, and have secured the crime scene? It would make sense if that were so, but so far there has been no sign of police anywhere on the School grounds. Perhaps La Buckfast has asked for their discretion at this difficult time.

I managed to catch her this morning, though not for as long as I would have liked. The first week of term is a busy one for any new Head, and especially given all the changes that she has implemented over the holidays. I managed five minutes with her alone, in her office, after Assembly, but when

I asked her the question outright, she remained evasive.

'Mr Straitley,' she said. 'Do you know what happens if a builder discovers human remains during the course of an excavation?'

'I imagine he informs the police, and they secure the site,' I said.

She smiled and poured herself a cup of coffee from the machine. 'Would you like one?'

I shook my head. 'What I'd like, Headmaster, is answers.'

'Nine times out of ten,' she said, 'the builder pretends he didn't see anything, and just bulldozes whatever it was back into the ground. Why? Because to do otherwise would involve stopping work for months, maybe even longer. It means letting the client down. It often means laying off the crew, unpaid, returning hired machinery. It means being out of pocket at best, maybe even losing the contract. And there are so many human remains buried under this piece of ground. Some are very, very old. Some date back from coal-mining days. Did you know that there was once a coal seam running under our land?'

'Of course. When we were boys, we used to go looking for pit tags on the fields.'

She smiled. 'You and Eric.'

'Yes,' I said.

'So a lengthy, damaging investigation might ultimately reveal your find to be ancient remains, unconnected to Conrad's disappearance.'

'You don't really believe that,' I said.

She shrugged. 'No, I don't. But it's possible. And if the police *were* informed, they would have to follow every lead, including those that might further damage the School's reputation.'

'We've weathered storms before,' I said. 'The past two years are proof of that.'

'But all that came at a high cost,' she said. 'That business last year – and especially the loss of the new Head in a time of crisis – was the final straw. The parents need assurances that the old ways are gone for good. They needed a change. Girls in the School. New buildings. A cull of the old staff.'

'*You* certainly thought so,' I said pointedly.

She smiled again. 'Oh, Roy,' she said. 'You know that was nothing personal. And you know as well as I do that parents don't send their children here to learn Latin. They send them here for peace of mind. For shiny new facilities. For sporting fixtures, foreign trips, Drama clubs –'

'*Progress Through Tradition*,' I said, quoting the School's new motto.

'Some traditions are best left behind,' she said. 'And if ever word gets out that someone found a body, everything I've done to try to distance us from the past will be swallowed up in a tidal wave of scandal and speculation.'

'If you're asking me to lie to my boys –'

'Oh, get off your high horse, Roy. Did you ever tell your boys that Eric Scoones was a paedophile?'

And there she is, I told myself. Do not be fooled by the quiet voice, or the hint of vulnerability. La Buckfast is made of tempered steel, snugly wrapped in lambs' wool.

'I can't be certain he was,' I said. 'It was only last year that –'

'And yet you were friends since childhood. If that story got out, Roy, would anyone believe you *didn't* know?'

I felt an unpleasant tightening around the waistcoat region. The past is a dark magician, pulling bouquet after bouquet of poisoned flowers from his hat. What was La Buckfast telling me? That she believes that Eric Scoones was involved in the death of Conrad Price? That, by association, I too might be a suspect?

'Be patient, Roy,' La Buckfast went on, 'and let me finish my story. If, after that, you still believe that we should inform the authorities'– she shrugged – 'I'll respect your opinion. But wait until you have the facts. And, of course,' she gave me a tight-lipped smile, 'if you were to decide to take the decision unilaterally, then I don't think I could continue to keep you in my confidence.'

How does she do it, I wonder? It is a kind of hypnosis. She does not raise her voice, and yet, she has such an air of authority. Accustomed as I am to the traditional kind of Headmaster – bullishly, reassuringly rude, arrogant in his doctoral robes – it comes as a surprise that *she* should be the one to inflict on me this singular paralysis.

Of course I know it cannot last. The body – if that's what it is – must be turned over to the authorities. But, in some ways, she is right. An investigation will reopen wounds that have only just started healing. The Harry Clarke affair will be back in the news and, with it, a new set of rumours. How does she know what Eric was? Was it Johnny Harrington, the boy who nearly brought down the School, only to return as its Head? Or did she witness an incident during her time at King Henry's?

I told La Buckfast I did not know about my old friend's proclivities. Only last year did I suspect, following my discovery of that letter from David Spikely. But now, I wonder whether perhaps I knew all along and ignored it, as a man might ignore a suspicious mole or lump that presents no symptoms. But *were* there symptoms? His secretiveness. His stubborn refusal to be a Form Master. His swift departure from St Oswald's in the wake of the Harry Clarke affair. His equally swift departure from King Henry's in 1989. Did I never question these things?

Or did I simply let them pass, in fear of a diagnosis? I do not *think* I suspected him. And yet, when I read that letter to him, I do not remember feeling surprise; simply a terrible sense of loss and loneliness and betrayal. Have I been fooling myself all this time? Worse still, if Eric's story came out, would anyone think that I *didn't* know?

IO

King Henry's Grammar School for Boys, April 10th, 1989

I struggled to keep it together until the end of the school day. One more lesson; Break: Lunch; two more, plus one free, in the afternoon. During my free period I sat in the empty classroom vacated by Four Upper S, and tried to make sense of what I'd seen.

Could I have imagined the boy? Could a combination of nerves and stress and the desire to finally exorcize Conrad have culminated in a full-blown hallucination? Or could it have been a practical joke, and somehow the boy had managed to hide, or maybe even leave the room during Scoones's intervention?

I tried to familiarize myself with some of the contents of the black file, but the words were meaningless to me. I couldn't concentrate for long enough to understand even a sentence. *Shirt sleeve order must be declared by the Head in Morning Assembly. Jewish boys should assemble in 3L every second Tuesday with Rabbi Goldman. To save space, Lower School Boys will sit on the floor during Assemblies. Chapel is on Fridays, and is mandatory for all staff.*

Whoever – *whatever* – the blond boy had been, his face kept resurfacing in my mind, and now it was beyond doubt

Conrad's face; Conrad as I remembered him; Conrad saying in my ear: *He knows. He's coming for you.*

I closed the file. My throat was dry. I longed for a drink of water, but didn't want to risk going into the Departmental Office. Scoones might be there, or Dr Sinclair. Nor did I feel like going downstairs to ask the School Secretary for the key to the disabled toilet. Instead, I went into the boys' toilets on the Upper Corridor, feeling absurdly furtive. I told myself I was being ridiculous. It was hardly my fault that they had no women's facilities. Besides, the boys were all in class. No one would see me going in. And still it felt wrong to be there – a woman in a man's space – a social taboo instilled into girls from the very earliest age.

The place was austere; institutional. White tiling on the walls; steel mirrors; urinals; cubicles with black-painted doors. I noticed that the gap between the cubicle doors and the floor was unusually wide; I could see right underneath without even having to bend. The room was windowless, and the light was both dingy and strangely powerful, like the sky on a muggy day. A running tap poured a steady stream of cold water into a chipped stoneware basin.

I walked to the basin and turned off the tap. The silence yawned around me. From the plughole there came a sound; a kind of ominous gurgle. Conrad used to tell me that Mr Smallface lived in the drains. Now I knew better. I no longer heard the voices from the plughole: I no longer needed the toilet seat to be closed and held down during the night. And yet the sound unsettled me a little. It seemed to say: *You're not meant to be here. Little girl, sneaking around in the places she shouldn't go. No one would know if you disappeared. No one would even really care.*

It was a voice I knew very well, although I hadn't heard it in years. I'd called it *Mr Smallface*, but I'd long since understood that it was the voice of my childhood; the voice of the Conrad-shaped hole in my world; the voice of my absent parents. My childhood loneliness and fear had taken the shape of that bugbear, the creature of nightmare teased into life by what had happened to Conrad. But I was no longer that child, that girl. I had survived. I had moved on. I was no longer broken.

I looked the plughole in the eye. It looked back at me steadily. The bar of metal halfway down looked like the eye of a grinning goat. *Think you got away, Becks?* the drain seemed to say in its whispering voice. *Think you escaped Mr Smallface?*

'I did escape him,' I said aloud. 'He's dead. He died a long time ago.'

The plughole made a gurgling sound, like a hungry child's stomach.

'I'm not afraid of you anymore,' I whispered softly into the drain. 'I'm all grown up now. I have a home. I have a daughter of my own, who knows that she is safe, and loved –'

The drain gave a dark and fruity belch, spitting foul water into my face and onto my white silk shirt.

I recoiled.

The drain gave its lopsided smile. I looked down at my wet shirt: but instead of dirty water, I saw a shocking slaughter-house spray of red –

I took an instinctive step backward, my high heels skidding on the tiles. In the steel mirror I saw myself, open-mouthed; a bloodstained ghost. The pipe had stopped gurgling and the room was filled with my ragged breathing. The air was alive with broken shards of that sick, peculiar light. For a moment I was stunned – my eyes stung as if I'd been slapped. And then, from the drain, came a final sound; a tiny, low and hiccuping sound that could almost have been a word –

Becks.

I managed to keep it together, though. I was proud of *that*, at least. The last thing I wanted was for Scoones – or worse, one of the boys – to see me hysterical, covered in blood. I closed my eyes and counted to ten; forced myself to breathe again. *Slowly, slowly, slowly.* Then I opened my eyes again.

The blood was already almost dry; a rusty red against the silk. I stripped off my shirt, dropped it onto the tiles and slipped on my jacket over my bra. If I buttoned it all the way, I could do without the shirt. Then I went back to the sink, squirted thick green soap from a dispenser and washed the blood from my hands and face, rinsing with warm water from the tap. The drain stayed docile and quiet throughout. No blood; no sound; no whispers. I rinsed the soap ring from the basin and stepped away from the row of sinks. In the mirror I looked very pale; without my make-up I looked very young.

'There is no Mr Smallface,' I said.

Silence.

'I dare you to come back,' I said. 'I fucking *dare* you to come back.'

Nothing. No buzzing, slurping sound from the drain.

'I thought not,' I said softly.

I bent down, picked up my shirt and bundled it into my jacket pocket. I turned towards the door – and then, behind me, from one of the stalls, I heard the sound of a toilet flush.

The gap beneath those doors was wide; far too wide for a boy to conceal his presence in the cubicle without actually standing on the toilet seat. *Could* a boy have been hiding in there? A mental image appeared in my mind: a blond boy wearing a Prefect's badge, perching on the toilet seat like a crow on the side of a dustbin.

It was ridiculous. There was no boy. That was just what I'd *expected* to see; a kind of flashback, brought on by the stress of being here again, after all those years. The drains at King Henry's were noisy because they were the drains of a three-hundred-year-old building: God knew what was in those pipes, or what kind of build-up had accumulated down there. The red stain on my shirt was rust. The rest was imagination.

From the empty toilet stall came a tiny knocking sound. It could have been the sound of a boy's shoe against the toilet seat, or that of someone leaning against the locked door. Or it could have been nothing at all.

I opened the door to the corridor just as the school bell rang for lunch. I had just enough time to run back to the classroom, and to hide my discarded shirt inside the red attaché case. Then I picked up the case and made my way towards the Common Room. The Master on duty at the top of the stairs eyed me appreciatively as I passed and, glancing up, I saw him looking down at me over the railings. Presumably to check out my cleavage – of course, I wasn't wearing my shirt.

'Enjoy the view, creep?' I snapped at him, and the man – tall, around thirty-five, with furtive eyes and a *Magnum* moustache – retreated hastily behind the balustrade. The boys on the staircase gave me a look of mingled surprise and grudging respect. I recognized two of the boys from Four Upper S that morning; Persimmon and another boy, a rather mousy boy with a fringe and with glasses taped at one corner.

Seeing them gave me an idea. I stopped and addressed the two boys.

'Persimmon,' I said.

'Yes, Miss?'

'What's the name of your class Prefect?'

'We don't have one, Miss,' he said. 'Prefects are all Sixth Form and Upper School.'

'So – you didn't see a boy wearing a Prefect's badge in the lesson today?'

His eyes widened. 'No, Miss. Don't think so.'

I nodded; in a way, relieved. 'All right. Thank you, Persimmon. I'll see you tomorrow.'

'See you, Miss.'

When I got home, I found Dominic on the phone in the living room. He rang off as soon as I came in, but it gave me the excuse I needed. I ran upstairs and quickly changed my work clothes for jeans and a pullover – I didn't want to have to explain to Dom why I'd taken off my shirt at school. I took it from my attaché case, hoping to put it in the wash before Dominic saw those rust-red stains, and bumped into him coming up the stairs.

'Hey,' he said. 'How was your first day?'

'Fine.' I smiled and kissed him, keeping the shirt from his line of sight. 'Who was on the phone just now?'

'Only my sister Victoria. She sends her love.' He looked down. 'What's that?'

'Just laundry.'

He frowned. 'That's dry-clean only, isn't it? Here, let me look.' He took the shirt, and turned it to look at the label. Numbly, I thought of the terrible scarlet spray from the plug-hole. I struggled to find a convenient lie – an accident, a fight between boys, a fall, a bloody nose. Anything but the voice from the drain, and the boy who looked like my brother.

'We should invite her over some time,' I said, with forced enthusiasm. In fact, I was rather nervous of meeting Dominic's sisters – we'd been briefly introduced at a New Year's party in Malbry, where I'd been shy and uncomfortable, and had not made a good impression.

Dominic ignored me. 'What's this?'

I felt my mouth go dry.

Dominic looked more closely at the label on the shirt. 'No, it says here that you can hand wash it in cold water.' He passed it back to me. 'It should be fine, as long as you don't use the biological powder. Use the hand-wash stuff under the sink.'

I took the shirt, still feeling numb, and took it into the laundry room. There, I inspected it, front and back, inside and out. I stood there with the shirt in my hands for a full five minutes, unable to understand what I saw. There was no sign of a stain on the silk. No blood, no rust, no residue – not even a watermark. Apart from a little creasing, the shirt I'd been wearing was spotless.

I I

King Henry's Grammar School for Boys, April 19th, 1989

Over the following week I came to know everyone in the Department. There was Sinclair, polite and remote; Scoones, of course, and two younger men called Higgs and Lenormand. Higgs was the man with the *Magnum* moustache who had peered down my cleavage from the Upper Corridor stairwell; Lenormand was French, with an accent, which caused great hilarity among the boys. None of them were particularly friendly – I sensed that Higgs might have said something about my outburst on the stairs – and so I avoided the Languages room, preferring the Masters' Common Room, where all Masters assembled in the mornings to read the newspapers and drink coffee before Headmaster's Briefing.

It was there that I made my first friend – my *only* friend – at King Henry's. That was Carolyn Macleod, who had been Conrad's Drama teacher; a redhead with a smoker's laugh and a strong scent of patchouli. Twenty years on, she no longer looked quite as much like Diana Rigg, but she still had the kind of defiant look that spoke of karate and combat boots. She introduced herself to me as I grabbed a coffee before class. 'I heard you had a run-in with Scoones,' she said. 'I hope you gave him what for.'

I looked around uncertainly. The Masters' Common Room was an imposing space, dark wood and ceiling mouldings stained with a hundred years of smoke. Masters lounged on worn velvet chairs, reading, drinking, talking. An ornate clock hung over the door like the Sword of Damocles. I felt as alien here as I had sneaking into the boys' toilets.

Miss Macleod saw my face. 'You didn't?' she said. 'Well, that's a shame. You have to stand up for yourself here. When I got here in '62, they'd never had a woman teacher before. They kept thinking I was the School Secretary. I had to fight tooth and nail every day, just to keep from going down. You'll have to do it too, love. Nothing much has changed since then.'

'I can imagine,' I said, looking round. I could see two other women there; both grey-haired, in their fifties or sixties. Otherwise it could have been a nineteenth-century gentlemen's club; smelling of leather and coffee and smoke. 'I mean, how did *you* manage?'

She grinned. 'Oh, I was a piece of work then. Fresh out of Girton, and stagy as hell. Incense, patchouli and long, loose hair. There was no Drama Department at the time, just a Head of English with the *Complete Works of Shakespeare*. I took the job from necessity, expecting my big break at any time, and here I am, thirty years on. Ten shows a week. No curtain call.'

I gave a reluctant grin. 'Yes, there *is* an element of performance, isn't there?'

Miss Macleod gave her raucous laugh. She sounded like a parakeet among a flock of pigeons. 'Oh sweetheart. It's *all* performance, both in and out of the classroom. You're *always* on show – to the boys, to the staff, and most of all, to the parents. The parents were my angels. They wanted a Drama Department. That's why I'm still here, raising hell at every opportunity.'

I grinned again. 'Thank God,' I said. 'The French Department hasn't exactly made me feel welcome so far.'

She shrugged. 'Oh, Scoones is all hot air,' she said. 'And Sinclair may look stiff as a board, but he's not as bad as he looks. Lenormand's a softie. Higgs is a snitch. Watch what you say when he's around. But most of all, stand up for yourself. Don't let Eric Scoones bully you. And if you need a listening ear, come to me. I'm always around.' She held out a hand. I'm Miss Macleod. You can call me Carrie.'

'Thanks.' Suddenly I found myself almost tearful with gratitude. I took her hand, which was dry and thin and covered in chunky silver rings. 'I'm Becky. Pleased to meet you.'

'My pleasure, sweetheart,' she said. 'Don't let the bastards grind you down.'

I spent the rest of the school day feeling rather more hopeful. In spite of our unfortunate start, the boys of Four Upper S proved surprisingly co-operative, and I even got to know some of their names. There was Persimmon, the class clown, and Spode, his sidekick; then there was Orange, who stuttered, and Fenelly, whose mother was French, and who spoke it like a native, though his spelling was atrocious. There was Akindele, who was Nigerian, and Sato, who was Japanese, and Birdman, who had asthma, and Andrews, whose father had hired a French au pair, who seemed to take pleasure in teaching his son as many unsuitable terms as possible. The unfortunate nickname that Persimmon had given me was hard to suppress: it appeared on the cover of several exercise books as well as on the classroom door, and I had to threaten reprisals, but the organized misbehaviour of that first lesson was not repeated. A small step towards acceptance, I know – and yet it was a start.

By the end of that week I had met all of the next term's classes, but, to my surprise, it was Four Upper S that I warmed to most. Third-year pupils are often disorderly, especially at the end of a term, but they also have a kind of charm that comes from enthusiasm and energy. Well, you'd know that, Roy, with your Brodie Boys. I found, to my surprise, that Four Upper S improved with acquaintance; in spite of — or maybe *because* of — that intervention by Eric Scoones.

Scoones was not popular in the School. He had a reputation of being both unfair and volatile. The boys called him *The Eggman*, and made jokes about his temper, but he was not respected, like Dr Sinclair. Instead, he provoked a kind of secretive laughter coupled with unease, as well as a large amount of graffiti on desks and on the covers of French books.

Mr Scoones est un doofus.

Mr Scoones is the Eggman.

And, once, on the back of the teacher's chair, scratched deeply into the dark wood with what must have been the point of a compass: *Mr Scoones is a nonce.*

Well, yes. Our boys always know when one of their teachers isn't quite right. If you hadn't been his friend, I think you would have seen it earlier. You would have seen the graffiti; the way the boys avoided his company. You would have seen why he preferred to be without a form of his own. You would have seen what the pupils saw, instead of your easy illusions. Of course, he was more careful with you. He wanted to impress you. You had known him as a boy; you remained the custodian of all his justifications.

Yes, Roy: he looked up to you. Envied you your calling. Envied you the ease with which you laughed and joked with your class, while he could only watch from afar, tormented by his appetites. Of course, you would never have seen that. It would never even have occurred to you that your old friend might have had secrets. But we all have secrets, Roy. I should know; I have more than most. The question is, what should I tell? And will you want me to hide them?

PART 3

Lethe
(River of Forgetfulness)

I

St Oswald's ~~Grammar School for Boys~~ *Academy*
Michaelmas Term, September 8th, 2006

Friday of the first week of term usually heralds a shift in pace. Names learnt; tests run; seating plans in action. Authority established in class; troublemakers identified. Next week, we begin in earnest. Next week will be back to business. Except, of course, for the bundle of sticks by the side of the Gunderson Pool: the bundle of sticks that might once have been a boy in a King Henry's blazer.

As junior Ozzies, Eric and I had shared a healthy contempt for King Henry's. Their boys were richer, softer than ours, in line with the somewhat higher fees. Their school had better facilities, with its gymnasium and its swimming hall, than St Oswald's, with its patchy fields and its ridges of mining subsidence. Their Classics students learnt Arabic, as well as Latin and Ancient Greek. And their Honours Boards were filled with the names of Oxbridge scholars and rugby Blues, while ours favoured more local universities; Sheffield, Manchester and Leeds.

That said, Eric had always had a tendency to aim higher. He had had aspirations beyond a job at St Oswald's, and the great disappointment of his life was that he had never achieved them. Working at King Henry's must have been a dream come true – and yet, he came back to St Oswald's at last, with scarcely a word of the past seven years, except that it hadn't suited him. Had he eventually realized that his face would never fit? Had he missed St Oswald's? Or had there been some other, more troubling reason to make him return? If so, he had never revealed it, but simply grumbled a few times about colleagues who didn't respect him, and boys whose parents took them to watch the tennis on the centre court at Wimbledon during the busy summer term, expecting their teachers to somehow suspend the exam process until their sons were ready.

I, of course, was too grateful to see him again to ask too many questions. Scoones could often be secretive, and I knew he would only tell me what he chose, and in his own time. Besides, St Oswald's is a world set apart from the rest of civilization, and we were already too preoccupied with timetables, school trips, lesson plans, newbies, the Porter, incidents both major and minor, and all the tragedy and farce that accompanies any grammar school on its journey across the turbulent seas of masculine adolescence. And so I never really did get to the bottom of why he had left King Henry's, or why he had chosen to return, or whether he was glad to be back. We simply went on as we always had, drinking tea, dissecting Common Room scandals, eating ham and cheese sandwiches and, in my case, snatching a furtive Gauloise in the stockroom at Break times. We continued our weekly pub visits – ploughman's and beer at the Thirsty Scholar.

We discussed Eric's elderly mother, and his growing concern for her mental capacity. We discussed the Sunnybankers who pushed their litter into my hedge. Year by year we discussed the Departmental newbies; saw them come and go while we stayed at our posts like sentinels, growing greyer year by year. I had my bit of heart trouble; and Eric was even quaintly alarmed; as if it were the first time that he had even considered the possibility that someday, I might not be there.

'You never think it will happen,' he said, standing at my bedside the day after my first coronary. 'One tends to think some people are beyond the reach of mortality.'

Rather poetic for Eric, that. It showed how troubled he must have been. It's also very much what I thought after the Harry Clarke affair: surprise at the persistence of the illusion of a man's permanence. It is a dangerous illusion, shared by us all. *Folie à tous*, as Eric would say. That feeling that our little world is impregnable; unbreakable. That we, too, by association, must remain forever.

I'm feeling rather maudlin today. Maybe this is why I'm thinking so much about Eric. And there is a tightness in my chest, which feels like something more than the effects of all the coffee I've been drinking. I do not generally drink coffee. My doctor advises against it, along with stress – which is inescapable – and cheese, fruit cake, Liquorice Allsorts, Digestive biscuits, ploughman's lunches, beer, port, sugar, Gauloises and, in short, most of the small, delicious things that make a life worth living. I ignore him most of the time, as befits a Latin Master saddled with a middle-aged version of one of his pupils as his heart specialist.

And yet, this time, he may have a point. Perhaps I should drink less coffee. It makes me feel breathless, and jumpy, and fat, and more than usually old. Most days, I feel like a boy of fourteen with inexplicably white hair: today I am a scarecrow Methuselah, shedding pieces of myself all the way down from the Common Room. And yes, I miss my Brodie Boys. My current 2S is likely to be rather a pedestrian form, I fear. There are no comedians, no rogues, no flamboyant eccentrics like Allen-Jones, no wise little elves like Tayler. No troublemakers either, of course; which I suppose should be a comfort, and yet it is not. A little disruption is good for morale. It gets the pulses racing. Instead, all I can think of is *that* boy; that boy who wasn't one of ours. Nor am I alone in this. Benedicta Wild has been trying to catch my attention since the start of the week. Today, at Break, she managed it as I stood with my morning cup of tea, watching the Middle Corridor.

As always, she was in trousers. In theory, there is a choice for Mulberry girls to wear trousers, encouraged by La Buckfast, who nearly always wears them herself, but Benedicta Wild is the only one of our girls to have taken this option so far. Then again, Benedicta Wild is not at all like her classmates. Her new haircut is significantly shorter than that adopted by Allen-Jones, and, unlike her classmates (and, again, Allen-Jones), she never wears nail polish or make-up. She sidled up to me and said in a low and meaningful voice:

'Well, Sir?'

I had been dreading this. And yet, as I try to tell myself, sometimes a lie is better. Benedicta Wild was not the type to let an exciting discovery pass. Nor was she likely to under-stand the repercussions of such a discovery, and its impact on a failing school.

I smiled and said: 'Good morning, Miss Wild. I trust the first week of the new term is proving both joyous and invigorating.'

She gave me a look. 'I'd rather you didn't call me that, Sir.'

'Miss Wild?' To be honest, I'd almost forgotten my conver-sation with Allen-Jones.

She nodded. 'I'd rather you called me Ben.'

'Ah, yes. I heard about that.'

Ben nodded encouragingly.

'I'm not sure how this concerns me,' I said, with an attempt at levity. 'As I once told Allen-Jones, unless it affects your Latin –'

'He said you might say that,' said Ben, with alarming forthrightness. 'It won't affect my Latin, but it's important to get it right. You do understand that it isn't the same as me coming out as gay, Sir?'

'Well, as I said to Allen-Jones –'

'It's easy. Just start with the pronouns.'

'Pronouns,' I said, feeling flustered. This is what happens, I told myself, when you allow issues of gender to escape the Latin grammar book. Well, at least, perhaps this would help provide a much-needed diversion from the remains at the Gunderson Pool.

No such luck. Ben lowered her voice. 'Sir – *what about the body?*'

'The body?' I said.

That look again.

'Oh, *that*. It's all being dealt with.'

'Is it?' said Ben, with, I thought, some disbelief.

'Oh absolutely,' I went on with an affectation of nonchalance. 'In fact, the police have already called. You'll have noticed the excavation site has been covered, in order, no doubt, to preserve any possible forensic evidence.'

'Oh,' said Ben.

There was a pause, during which I finished my tea and longed for a Digestive biscuit.

'*And*?' said Ben. 'Do you have any news?'

'I have no news, or conclusions,' I said. 'I am making no judgement here. It could be that there is no case, and that what you saw was nothing more than a bundle of oddments.

But I, like you, shall leave it to the authorities to determine. And, like you, I hope, I shall henceforth try to put it out of my mind and enjoy the last of the summer.'

'It's been raining all morning, Sir,' said Ben, who seemed about to say more, but was interrupted by the bell, signalling the end of Break.

'Off to your lessons now,' I said, trying not to sound as if the invisible finger that so often lurks beneath the third button of my waistcoat wasn't playing my chest like a drum. I could feel it – *boom-boom* – counting out the measures of my life.

'But Sir, what about –'

I finished my tea, feeling another, less playful stab from the invisible finger. 'I think we can safely leave it to – *damn it!*'

'Sir? Is anything wrong?'

I tried to tell her there was not. But the words wouldn't come; they seemed to have lodged somewhere at the back of my throat. I saw the polished parquet floor of the Upper Corridor tilt, and I noticed a scrap of foil on the ground, like a patch of mica. For a second the silver foil was all I could see, or understand. The pain in my chest – no playfulness now – swelled like an accordion. And then I hit the ground, and heard my teacup skate across the floor, and voices calling, and Ben's sharp voice above the rest, saying: '*Get help. Straitley's collapsed.*'

I'd always rather hoped that my last words would be something profound. Maybe some Classical reference. *Morior invictus*, perhaps. Or should it be; *Melita, domi adsum*? But that eventuality had always seemed comfortably remote, and I had assumed that I would have time to plan my exit accordingly. But now here I was on the parquet floor, which smelt of polish, and chalk dust, and feet, and all I could feel was annoyance that my final utterance was likely to be no more than a mild profanity.

From somewhere behind me I heard the voice of the Head of the French Department, Miss Teague, raised in sudden, sharp alarm. I've always been fond of Kitty Teague. A sensible, practical woman, who has had a few trials of her own. There came the sound of running heels, and a surge of renewed activity.

I became aware of a presence, and a hand on my forehead.

'Hang on, Roy,' said Kitty Teague. 'You've just had a little fall. You'll be fine.'

'*Eric*,' I mumbled. '*Find Eric.*'

Then there was nothing but darkness.

2

September 11th, 2006

At last. I'd been wondering how long it would take for the stress of it all to get to him. Not that he's in much danger – a simple panic attack, that's all – and he was already recovering by the time the ambulance arrived.

The doctor has ordered some hospital tests, plus a week's rest, no fuss, no espressos, and a change in his medication. I arranged for a Sixth-Form girl – *not* Benedicta Wild – to check on the patient once a day, to bring him his groceries, make his tea, and otherwise ensure that he does not even think of going out until the enforced rest period is over. The girl, whose name is Emma Wicks, is under instructions to report anything of concern, and has embraced the task with enthusiasm – not least because she believes that it will count towards her Duke of Edinburgh Gold Award.

I called round before school to see how he was, and found Straitley already up, though still in his pyjamas, listening to the radio and reading a copy of *The Malbry Examiner*.

'Tell me, Mr Straitley,' I said. 'Do you *ever* do as you're told?'

'Very seldom, Headmaster.'

I smiled and made a cup of tea. It was decaffeinated, I noticed. Probably for the best; I thought the old man looked strained and colourless. He took it with little enthusiasm, his hand on the saucer not steady.

'How are you feeling?'

'*Cedere nescio*,' he said. 'To yield is not in my nature. Unless you happen to have with you a packet of Digestive biscuits, in which case I'm all yours.'

I assumed a stern expression. 'No biscuits for you, Mr Straitley. You know what the doctor said. In fact, you're going straight back to bed, after you've drunk this cup of tea. I shall remain to make sure you do.'

Straitley gave me a narrow look. 'I will if you finish your story,' he said. 'Did you speak to your daughter? Did you ever find out the truth about your brother's disappearance? And what was the link with St Oswald's?'

That look. It cheers me to the soul. It's the look of a man who needs something. I'm rather good at meeting men's needs: I've had to, over my career. Women who say what they *really* want tend to succeed less often. In my experience, female success comes with a degree of guile. The ability to fool men into thinking that your ideas were theirs all along, and that you don't need validation.

Men are surprisingly fragile. You could see that in our boys, who, as soon as they got a low mark in French, would immediately stop working, and pretend they didn't care, preferring to be thought lazy rather than mediocre. Men are often no different. They need to hear their praises sung. Johnny Harrington was a case in point. You might have thought that, as Head of St Oswald's, he would have been able to manage without. But half of my job then was telling him how well he was managing, even when I was managing most of it.

King Henry's was an excellent training ground. Carrie Macleod taught me that: behind her brash exterior there was a quick and subtle mind. She had joined the English Department at a time when Drama was seen as an indulgence; a trivial addition to a serious academic subject. Thus, as a Junior Mistress, Carrie ended up with the lower sets, and the tasks her Head of Department had seen as unimportant. But in time, her influence grew. She organized the School play. She led trips to the theatre, and encouraged her boys to dream of careers in acting and directing. Finally, came recognition – one of her pupils, Sam Noble, achieved success via a popular TV show; another moved to America and directed a series of movies. Suddenly, King Henry's had a reputation for nurturing the creative arts. It was largely undeserved; but Carrie was happy to let the rest of the Department – and, by association, the rest of the School – reap the benefits. In 1968, the Head of English, Dr Foulstone, was awarded an MBE *and* an honorary degree in Performing Arts from the University of Sheffield, and the following year, Carrie Macleod finally got a designated teaching space.

King Henry's Little Theatre was the result of this development. Replacing the Old Refectory, left redundant after the construction of the New Cafeteria, it now houses a good-sized stage, some three hundred velvet-upholstered seats, four dressing rooms, two bathrooms, a rehearsal space, a stunning stained-glass ceiling dome and a sizeable wardrobe facility for the storing of costumes and props. Paid for by the Sam Noble Foundation, it was officially opened by Margaret Thatcher in the winter of 1970, among protests from the State sector over the impending withdrawal of free milk. For Carrie, it was the start of a golden age at King Henry's. The Little Theatre was her new domain, and she had extended her empire, slowly but surely, ever since.

'It was a small enough victory,' she told me in the Common Room. 'But for a woman, a room of one's own is essential in a place designed to serve men. I even had my very own glass ceiling to look up at.' She shrugged. 'Still no ladies' toilets, though. The Head has a private bathroom, but women have to ask the School Secretary for the key to the disabled loo. They literally think being female is a disability.'

I thought of the Upper Corridor, and the sink, and the boy with the Prefect's badge. Over a fortnight had passed since then and nothing unusual had happened. The outfit I'd worn on that first day – the trouser suit and the silk shirt – had been put to the back of my wardrobe, to be replaced by a series of twin-sets and skirts in line with King Henry's dress code.

I did not tell Dominic about my clash with Philip Sinclair. His disapproval of King Henry's was already a source of tension between us, and I didn't want to give him any further cause for comment. I hadn't told him about the boy in the Prefect's badge, either, or the boys' toilets. Instead, I racked my brains to find funny, light-hearted anecdotes to tell him and Emily – how Scoones had mistaken me for a boy; the stories Carrie told me at Break. I thought that if I could make Dom see that I was settling in, then he would relax his attitude.

He didn't. 'It isn't healthy,' he said. 'Being in Conrad's old school. It's bound to be full of sad memories.'

'It's not.' That was a lie, of course, but I knew that if I told him, he'd worry. Dominic was protective. I was so much younger that he sometimes thought of me as a child. No matter that I had a child of my own, no matter what I'd already survived, he thought of me as delicate. I wasn't – or not in the way he thought. And the memories weren't exactly *sad*. There was something I needed there, something that would put Conrad to rest, if only I could find it.

Dom, however, remained unconvinced. He'd made no secret of the fact that he thought I'd made a bad choice, and by the time I'd reached the end of my second week, his disapproval was almost oppressive. However much I tried to be amusing and light-hearted, he always seemed to go out of his way to seek out a negative angle. On several occasions I walked in to find him on the phone, speaking in a low voice that altered as soon as I came in. Of course, he was close to his family, and often spoke to his sisters by phone. But I wondered just what he was telling them about our domestic problems. And, of course, none of this was helped by the fact that Emily had acquired a new, imaginary friend she persisted in calling *Conrad*.

Conrad wants pancakes for breakfast. Conrad doesn't like broccoli. Don't disturb me, I'm in my room playing dolls with Conrad. It was a phase, I told myself. Children have imaginary friends for all kinds of harmless reasons. But, needless to say, Dominic blamed my new job for that, too. Emily's behaviour, he said, was a classic cry for help, from a child in need of attention.

'At her age, she needs stability,' he said one day when I came home late. 'I don't like her spending so much time alone. Look at that picture she brought home from school. And now all this business with Conrad –'

'It was only a picture, Dom.'

'I saw how much it frightened you.'

'It didn't. I was surprised, that's all. All it means is that we need to be more careful what we say around her. That's why I stopped taking her to visit my parents. That's where she must have picked up his name. And lots of children have imaginary friends. There's nothing unusual about that.'

Dominic looked unconvinced. 'You've been different since you started working there. Distant. Hardly sleeping. Obsessed. Staying up till three every night.'

'You're exaggerating, Dom. I have to prepare my lesson plans.'

'I thought you said the lesson plans were in a departmental file.'

'They are, but −' I paused, feeling suddenly annoyed. 'Dominic, you don't understand. French isn't my main subject. I have to read the set texts. I have to know what I'm doing. I can't just turn up and teach, like you.'

'I'm just a Sunnybanker. Right? Just a grunt with a palette knife.'

'That's *not* what I meant.'

He turned away. 'And this is how it begins,' he said. His Trinidadian accent − which was dormant most of the time, but which sometimes emerged when he was upset or excited − was suddenly, startlingly prominent. 'Being around them bastards with their Masters' gowns and their Oxbridge degrees. Before long you'll be right at home.'

'That's ridiculous,' I said. 'Nothing's going to change.'

'Really?' He turned back to me with anger in his dark eyes. 'Because you haven't worn your trouser suit since that first day. Did anyone tell you it wasn't appropriate? One of those snobby old men, maybe?'

I felt a flush rise to my cheeks. 'I'm trying to settle in, Dom.'

He laughed, not quite unpleasantly. 'That's what you tell yourself,' he said. 'You try very hard to be invisible. You think that if you follow the rules, and do everything you're supposed to do, then someday you'll be accepted. Well, take it from me, Becks. Some of us have already learnt that lesson the hard way. A square peg won't fit a round hole. And it never will.'

That night, as he slept beside me, I went over and over what he'd said. He was right about one thing, I thought: a square peg won't fit into a round hole. Carrie was living proof of that, although she'd paid her dues, and more, in over twenty years at the school. Young as I was, how could I expect to change the shape of King Henry's? And as for my brother, what did I hope to discover after all these years?

Unable to sleep, I finally got up at two in the morning. I went down into the kitchen and made a cup of herbal tea. The house was very still; not a sound came from the water pipes or the drains. I sat on the sofa to drink my tea in the light of the street lamp opposite. I remember the silver light through the blinds; the dancing silhouettes of the trees; the warmth of the mug between my hands. I must have slept a little, because the next thing I remember was feeling cold, and looking down, and seeing grass under my feet. Had I gone outside in my sleep? The grass was damp and very cold; looking over my shoulder I saw the open kitchen door and golden light pouring out onto the ground. But the door to Dominic's house was white. This one was a poisonous green; and I realized that it *wasn't* Dom's house at all, but some kind of painted scenery, behind which lay some terrible knowledge that, once seen, could not be forgotten.

There came a sound from under my feet; the ominous sound of something big approaching through a tunnel. There was a ventilation grate in the grass right at my feet; the rising air lifted my nightdress. In a moment I would rise just like a Chinese sky lantern. Behind the ominous green door, the golden light had faded. A shadow, like that of a tall, tall man, crawled out onto the bright green grass. And I heard a voice: *I know where you are. You can't hide from me, Becks.*

And the worst of it was that the terrible voice was *not* the voice of the monster, but the voice of my brother Conrad, and when I awoke, it was daylight, and the kitchen door was open wide, and there was grass between my toes, and the dry salt of tears on my face.

3

King Henry's Grammar School for Boys, April 25th, 1989

It never ceases to amuse me how, in films, a character always wakes from a nightmare suddenly, with an audible gasp, sitting bolt upright, as if someone had slipped an ice cube into their pyjamas. My nightmares have always been silent; suffocating; heavy as sand; and I awake in darkness to a dreadful paralysis. Eyes unable to open; limbs weighed down, unable to move; and the knowledge – the *certainty* – that, this time, there will be no end to this, no awakening to the world; that I will stay here in the dark for all eternity, with *him*, relentless; inescapable –

My therapist tells me this phenomenon is called *sleep paralysis*, and that it lasts only seconds. Sadly, this waking knowledge does nothing to change the experience. It had been a long time since I had had an episode, and it was the first time that I had ever knowingly *walked* in my sleep, although from the open kitchen door and the muddy state of my feet I understood that this must have been the case. I had no memory of getting up, or going into the garden, or of going back into the house. The dream of the green door and of Conrad's voice from out of the ground was already losing coherence.

The rest had already vanished into one of those memory sink holes that I knew so well from childhood.

I checked the time: it was five-fifteen. I showered quickly and, silently, went back into the room I shared with Dom. Dominic was still asleep – I slipped in naked between the sheets. Dominic said something in his sleep – he was a frequent sleep-talker – and threw an arm over my shoulder. I pressed my body closer to his, smelling his musky night-time scent. I was not expecting to sleep, but I must have dropped off after all, because I awoke at seven o'clock to the alarm at my bedside, feeling surprisingly rested. The sun was shining through the blinds, and I felt suddenly, unexpectedly good. I kissed Dominic on the mouth – he was still mostly asleep – and went to the wardrobe, where my school clothes were hanging. I looked at my unworn trouser suit, hesitated over a powder-blue twin-set and matching skirt, then decided against it. Instead, I pulled out something from the back of the rack, pulled it on quickly, and said to Dom: 'I have to go. Make sure Emily has breakfast, OK?'

Dom opened one eye, then both. 'You're going in like *that*?' he said.

I grinned. 'You were right, Dom. There's no point in trying to fit a square peg into a round hole. I've done my best to follow the rules, and I'm tired of trying to hide.'

At that, I grabbed my attaché case, quickly brushed my teeth and hair, and set off to King Henry's in my little blue Mini. I knew that Scoones and Dr Sinclair always came in early; Scoones to use the Banda machine before the other members of the Department came in, Sinclair to drink coffee and read the papers before Assembly. Most of the rest came in later, and boys very rarely arrived before eight. Thus it was that I was able to enter the Departmental Office at 7.40, carrying a dry-cleaning bag, and watch both Scoones and Sinclair's mouths drop open at the sight of me, in a scarlet miniskirt, black sweater and high-heeled knee-length boots.

'Dr Sinclair,' I said, and smiled. 'I've given a lot of thought to what you said to me on my first day regarding the dress code at King Henry's.'

Sinclair's face was marble. Scoones's appeared to be made of ham. I smiled again, and held up the dry-cleaning bag: 'As you see, I'm wearing a skirt. But if you feel that you would prefer to update the King Henry's dress code, I've also brought my trouser suit.'

There was a pause, as Scoones and Sinclair stared at me, bereft of speech; Scoones with a look of horror, and Sinclair with a quiet kind of surprise. I held his gaze in silence: I was always good at poker.

For a moment I thought he would call my bluff. His eyes were − I would have sworn it − amused.

Then he gave a tiny nod.

'Wear the trousers, Miss Price,' he said. 'You can change in my office.'

4

King Henry's Grammar School for Boys, April 25th, 1989

It was the smallest of victories. And yet it was significant. I had found an opening in the patriarchal façade: not quite a door, but a *weakness*.

I've never understood why men think of us as the weaker sex. Women are built for endurance. If men had to bear even half of what women typically endure – menstruation, childbirth, hormone surges, menopause; not to mention the daily attrition of catcalling, mockery, silencing – they would be reduced to tears. Men are surprisingly easy to break. Maybe it's because they have fewer trials to overcome. The men and boys of King Henry's were served their privilege every day with a generous side of tradition. None of them ever questioned their right to enter through the hallowed gates. I have had to hack my way through the stone and sinew. I have had to fight a war for every step of progress. But that was the first of my victories – a small one, but it mattered. I had faced Dr Sinclair and found that, far from being a giant, he'd been a windmill all along.

I spent the rest of that morning in a warm haze of triumph. It was as if the terrible nightmare had released some power in me. 4H were inclined to misbehave; I squashed them without flinching. At Break, Higgs made some lewd comment; I swatted him away like a fly. I met Scoones on the narrow stairs leading up to the office, and *he* was the one who flattened himself against the wall to let me pass; another little victory that filled me with hope and confidence.

'You're looking a lot more cheerful today,' Carrie said, when I joined her for lunch in the Common Room.

'I'm feeling all right,' I said with a smile, and told her about my encounter with Scoones and Sinclair that morning.

Carrie gave her smoker's laugh. 'I told you Sinclair was a pussycat. And Scoones just wants to be Sinclair, like a vampire's assistant who thinks that one day, if he toadies enough, he'll get to be immortal. Good for you. You stood your ground. I think you'll find things a whole lot easier from now on.'

I smiled again. 'Now the only person I need to convince is Dominic.'

'Is that your guy?'

I nodded. 'He doesn't believe in private schools. Thinks I'm going to end up like Scoones, an old bat in a dusty gown.' I told her about Dominic, his disapproval of my job; his continued hope that I would leave at the end of the summer term. 'I know he's just being protective,' I said. 'It's partly because he's so much older than I am. But I can fight my own battles. I think today proved that.'

'Sounds like you're fighting on two fronts,' she said. 'Still, if he's a good guy –'

'He is,' I said. 'He really is.'

But even as I said so, I felt strangely uncertain. And for the first time that day I remembered my dream of the green door, and the voice from the grille, and that peculiar certainty that Dominic's house was nothing but a piece of painted scenery.

And I thought, what if he likes me weak? What if he likes me dependent? What if the only reason he wanted me in the first place was because he wanted someone to save? Books are filled with tales of knights in search of maidens to rescue. But none of those tales ever questioned the maiden's need or desire to be saved. Stories show the maiden grateful and obedient. The knight's job is to fight and be brave; hers is simply to be his reward. But what if the maiden chooses to fight the dragons on her own behalf? What happens to the brave knight then? And if he slays no dragons, then how do we know he's a knight at all?

5

St Oswald's ~~Grammar School for Boys~~ Academy
Michaelmas Term, September 12th, 2006

Excellent question, Ms Buckfast. And one that applies equally
well to St Oswald's Masters. Our identities are constructed from
the small but significant ways in which we present ourselves to
the world. Our suits; our academic robes. Our honours. Our
pronouns, as Ben might say. Without them, who are we really?
If I am not teaching a Latin class, can I be said to be a teacher
at all? And how long will it take before my place at St Oswald's
vanishes altogether?

I begin to see that even at such a young age, La Buckfast
was a live wire. I would have given a lot to have seen her
standing in front of Scoones and Sinclair, wearing that red
miniskirt. This begins to explain why Eric assumed that mute
and gammon-faced aspect every time the subject of his new
colleague arose in our conversations. Unpredictable, volatile,
clever, and – worst of all – female, she must have represented
everything he found intolerable.

In his place, I suspect that I would have enjoyed her disruptive
influence, but Eric and I never saw eye to eye on the subject
of subversion. The Tweed Jacket, though loyal, typically lacks

ambition, and Eric was always a would-be Suit, although, like the vampire's apprentice, he never managed to gain acceptance into the members -only crypt. St Oswald's was more accepting, because – I say this with the greatest loyalty and affection – St Oswald's was never a *really* first-rate grammar school. *I* can say this with impunity, although I would never allow an outsider to say so. The fact that La Buckfast ended up as Head here, rather than at King Henry's, is a case in point. Not that I have any doubts as to the genius, vision and efficiency of La Buckfast; it is simply that, at King Henry's, between its layers of old money, tradition and academic excellence, she would have found the way to the top all the more difficult to find. And yet, I begin to think that she is capable of anything. And as I await my doctor's all-clear with growing impatience and boredom, her visits are all that sustain me. Her visits, and the window to the past with which her stories provide me – a window that I find myself increasingly eager to open.

'Don't flatter yourself,' she tells me when I express anxiety for my lessons, my form, my Brodie Boys – and most of all, the situation evolving in and around the projected Gunderson Building. 'No one is irreplaceable. Concentrate on your recovery, Roy, and let St Oswald's take care of itself.'

That's all very well, I tell her. But I have had half a dozen days off in over thirty-five years at the School, and most of those have been this week. During that time, who knows what mischief has been wrought in the Bell Tower? Plastic-topped desks reintroduced; dead plants replaced by living ones; The Foghorn covering my classes – or even worse, Dr Devine.

He called by yesterday, you know. Although he and I have been on less chilly terms in recent months, I was nevertheless surprised. I had not considered Sourgrape Devine the type to check on an absent colleague. He was more likely to use the opportunity afforded by my indisposition to annexe my Departmental Office. Dr Devine has long since been a campaigner for the removal of Latin from the curriculum, and only the strength of our shared dislike of last year's new New Head united us for a brief time. Now he was back to his usual self; brittle; officious; a Suit through and through. Ah, well. Times change. *Tempora mutantur*, and so on.

He called by on his way home from work, still carrying his briefcase. He greeted me in typically curt style, saying; 'Straitley. Still alive?'

I raised an eyebrow. 'Apparently.'

He gave the sharp, percussive sniff, which, in his nasal repertoire, often denotes disapproval. 'Overdoing it a bit, eh? I thought you were looking peaky. Well, if you will persist in trying to run a department single-handedly while simultaneously trying to hold back the tide of progress –'

'Simply a precaution,' I said. 'I'll be back at my desk in a day or two.'

That sniff again. 'Well, don't rush back. You're not as young as you were, you know.'

'I know you're no mathematician, Devine, but that applies to all of us.' Damn the man. He's a shade younger than I am, that's all. But the fact that he sometimes plays badminton at weekends (as well as having a younger wife) seems to have given him the idea that he is a comparative stripling. 'Who's covering my classes?' I said. 'Don't tell me *you*'re having to do some teaching, for a change.'

Devine made with the nose again. 'Don't flatter yourself, Straitley,' he said, unconsciously echoing the Head. 'Nothing's going to grind to a halt just because a few classes miss Latin. In fact, they'll probably appreciate the extra time spent on something else.'

'Something *else*?'

'Well, if there's no other Classicist –'

'I sent in a whole week's lesson plans. I expect my cover to follow them. No sneaking in an extra French or German class under the door, do you understand me, Devine?'

He made a face. 'Always so dramatic,' he said. 'I suppose it never occurred to you that your colleagues might be concerned for you?'

'What colleagues?'

'Anyone,' said Devine, his nose turning a little pink. 'I mean, you're a long-standing member of the Department. Obviously, colleagues will feel some concern for your well-being.'

I smiled. 'I didn't know you cared. Why don't you come in for a cup of tea?'

He sniffed. 'I won't, thank you for asking. But I thought maybe you might enjoy these.' He opened his briefcase and handed me a small box of Black Magic chocolates, cellophane-wrapped, with a red bow, and labelled in his fussy script:

To Roy,
Get better soon.

'Why, thank you, Dr Devine,' I said, touched.

He gave a final, percussive sniff. 'I think that after all these years, we could probably consider being on first-name terms.'

I was almost too surprised to speak. First-name terms? I mumbled some kind of agreement, but, to be honest, I couldn't recall whether I had ever *known* his full name – to me, he'd always been Sourgrape.

Chocolates, forsooth. And now, this. How ill did the idiot think I was? Did he not know I'm unbreakable?

'Right. That's that,' said Dr Devine. 'Must be on my way, I suppose.' He turned on his heel and made for the gate. Then, turning back for a moment, he said – with the tiniest of smiles: 'It's Malcolm, in case you were wondering.'

And then he was gone, except for the receding outline of his charcoal suit through the dusty privet hedge.

6

King Henry's Grammar School for Boys, April 28th, 1989

These little victories. They make us feel as if we are invincible. For the next two days, I walked King Henry's corridors like a conqueror. Scoones watched me with the air of a man who expects a violent outburst at any moment; Sinclair with new and grudging respect. The lecherous Higgs; the cold Lenormand; even the boys themselves – all seemed to have realigned and moved towards acceptance. No one disrupted my lessons, or called me 'Asda Price' in class. There was no sign of the blond-haired boy – if indeed he had been there at all. There were no rattling, sucking sounds from the pipes in the boys' toilets. Even the Banda machine behaved. For two days, I believed I had won.

But life has a way of pulling down the victories of women. It was a lesson I learnt that Friday, at my very first Chapel Assembly.

Sinclair's Book had made it clear: *Chapel is on Fridays, and is mandatory for all staff.* It was mandatory for all boys too, irrespective of religion. I'd managed to miss it until then, but Sinclair's eye was on me now, and I was keen to maintain my advantage. There was a reason I'd been avoiding going into the chapel; there was a memorial to Conrad there, and I had never seen it.

I suppose I was too young when he died to follow all that happened. I do remember certain things; the searches all over Malbry; hundreds of people with flashlights and dogs, combing the waste ground, calling his name; the journalists who came to my school; the tabloid reporters at our house. None of it interested me very much, and so mostly I ignored it, lost in a little world of my own. But now, I began to understand what the scandal had done to King Henry's; the uproar his disappearance had caused; the inevitable loss of revenue. My brother had disappeared *from school*. Most likely, he'd been abducted. That kind of thing leaves a shadow on any school, but for a fee-paying school like King Henry's, which prided itself on its superiority, it must have been a terrible blow.

I wondered how many parents of third-year boys had decided to withdraw their sons after the Conrad Price affair – after all, there were other grammar schools, all eager to pick up the pieces. I wondered how long that shadow had lingered over the school's reputation. Maybe this was why they had chosen to create a memorial; as an act of contrition, a gesture of faith, or perhaps in the hope of moving on.

You'll probably have seen it, Roy. It's actually quite famous now. Based on artwork by Frazer Pines, it features in several of the school's brochures. Time has elevated my brother's disappearance. Once a grubby scandal, filled with gossip and speculation, now his death has become a part of an artistic legacy. That day as I came in, and took my place at the end of a row of boys, I found myself staring directly at a stained-glass window opposite, and realized almost at once what it was.

The design is simple; a plain white dove above the King Henry's emblem (a fleur-de-lys, a Tudor rose) and the words, inscribed in copperplate:

CONRAD PRICE
(1957–1971)
OUT OF THE STRONG CAME FORTH SWEETNESS.

I felt a sudden, stinging shock of memory at reading the words. I knew the Biblical reference, of course, although it had been a long, long time since I'd thought of it. But I associated it most with the Golden Syrup that I took with my porridge on winter mornings: a green tin, with a picture of a lion, and that inscription.

Now at last, I remembered how Conrad had told me the story. It had been late, one winter's night, and I had had nightmares afterwards. It was the story of Samson and the riddle of the bees who had made their nest in the dead lion's body. *Out of the eater came forth meat: and out of the strong came forth sweetness.*

Who had chosen that epitaph? Surely not my parents. What was it supposed to mean, and why did it make me feel so strange? And it came with a burst of memories; seemingly unconnected, but buzzing like a swarm of bees. Out of the sink hole they came, and I remembered my childhood bedroom, and my shelf of toys, and my high-sided cot, and my favourite nightdress; it was pink, with a pattern of little blue birds. Conrad's pyjamas were black, with a yellow piping. Conrad often told me stories at bedtime; but the stories were often scary ones. I remembered the way he used to hold his pocket torch under his face, making his round, rather chubby face look unexpectedly ghoulish.

Voices from a haunted room: *Conrad can put you to bed tonight. Won't that be nice? He's so good with her.*

And then came the stories, all of them filled with monsters and ogres and demons and ghosts. *Be a good girl or Awd Goggie will come. That sound you heard was the Trapper-Lad, walking the buried coal seam.* And of course, Mr Smallface himself, squeezing through the smallest of pipes; peering out from the toilet bowl; always on the lookout for meat. And yet those nights must have been precious to me. I remember how excited I was when it came to bedtime, and the way my heart used to flutter and pound when he said: *How much do you love me, Becks?* And I would shout: *This much! This much!* – and fling my arms wide.

Eric Scoones was glaring at me. He'd never liked me, of course, but on that day his hatred was tangible. I wondered why. As far as I knew, he was not devout. I looked away from the window and tried to concentrate on the service.

The Chaplain announced the first hymn: 'When a Knight Won His Spurs'. I turned my attention to my hymn book, but the words on the page were dancing. Not far from me, Persimmon and Spode were mouthing along to the words of the hymn. From their furtive expressions, I guessed that they were singing some unauthorized, probably obscene lyric. I tried to concentrate, but I felt as if the ceiling were about to crash down. The words from the Golden Syrup can had started to release the swarm.

Try to be strong, I told myself. *Only thirty minutes to go.* I could survive thirty minutes, I thought, as long as I kept my eyes on the page, and not on the stained-glass window. I tried to breathe; my chest was tight. I wanted to sit down, but the hymn – the hymn seemed to be interminable. How many verses could there be? In spite of myself, I glanced up again at the window. And there I saw him, at the far end of the row, right under the stained-glass window. His hair was illuminated by the sun, the lenses of his glasses reflecting the scarlet of a Tudor rose –

It was the boy of my first day, the blond boy with the Prefect's badge. He looked at me, crazed in the coloured light of my brother's memorial window, and grinned at me, as if to say: *How much do you love me, Becks?*

And at that, clapping a hand to my mouth, I ran from King Henry's Chapel, just as the final line of the hymn rang out into the gilded air.

7

King Henry's Grammar School for Boys, April 28th, 1989

Eric Scoones had been watching me. He must have seen how upset I was. He caught up with me in the passageway that led to the main school building – a passageway lined with memorials to boys and Masters dead in the War. The passageway was filled with light; it was like being in a fish tank. I put my hand against the wall to steady myself. My head was buzzing with nausea.

There was no boy. There was no boy. And yet I had seen him clearly; under my brother's memorial –

'Miss Price. Are you feeling unwell?'

Scoones was looking rigid and pinched. He looked like a man who is forced to touch a wasp's nest, or a dying dog. I wondered how much it had cost him to come after me in the first place, to try for that semblance of sympathy. All in the name of duty, of course; Scoones was a stickler for that.

I said, 'It must have been the heat. I'll be all right in a minute.'

He made a kind of huffing sound. I realized his anxiety was less to do with concern for me, and was entirely due to the fear that he might find himself having to deal with an unconscious woman in a narrow corridor just as a thousand boys emerged from chapel on a Friday.

Nervously, he cleared his throat. 'Maybe you should see the School Nurse.'

I shook my head. 'I'll be all right. All I need is a minute.' I closed my eyes again, although I no longer felt dizzy. Instead, I felt a kind of glee. The bully was afraid. What of? My femininity; my essential alienness in this masculine place. From the chapel I heard the sound of a thousand schoolboys standing up. It must be almost time, I thought. I could feel their eagerness, their restlessness to be up and away.

I opened my eyes and said to Scoones, with a touch of malice: 'I must be starting my period. Sometimes I have fainting spells – and I have a heavy flow.'

Scoones's face had changed colour. His usually pink complexion had veercd to Banda-ink purple. 'Let's get you to the nurse,' he huffed, and taking me by the elbow, began almost to drag me down the passageway. His alarm was tangible; his hand clenched the fabric of my sleeve. I really think he might have swooned if he'd accidentally touched my skin. I followed, smiling a little, hearing the muffled sound of the Head giving his valediction.

And then the boys came rushing out, just as Scoones and I turned the corner into the Middle Corridor, which led to the Little Theatre.

'You can sit in there,' said Scoones, manoeuvring me through the double doors, away from the stream of school-boys. 'Just sit in one of the seats and breathe. I'll go and fetch the School Nurse.'

'No, please, don't,' I said. 'I'm sure I'll be fine in a minute.'

Scoones seemed rather put out at this; clearly, his intention had been to leave me in the care of a woman as quickly as he could. The malice that had led me to simulate a fainting fit returned, along with the germ of an idea. I thought of those bits of graffiti I'd seen on desks up and down the school. *Mr Scoones is the Eggman. Mr Scoones is a nonce.* School graffiti is mystic, I thought. It dares to dance and caper around a truth that cannot be spoken.

I sat down heavily on one of the upholstered theatre seats and put my hand to my temple. Scoones lingered at the door, eyes fixed on the passageway.

The scent of the Little Theatre, a compound of sawdust and velvet and paint, settled all around me. The light from the stained-glass ceiling dome fell like autumn leaves upon the rows of red-velvet theatre seats and the stage, with its painted safety curtain. It all felt very familiar. Had I been here once before? Perhaps on the day Conrad disappeared? I could feel the buried memory waiting to reveal itself. But try as I might, I could not bring it out of the sink hole.

'I really think the *nurse* —' said Scoones.

'Really, no.' I looked up at him. 'I'll be all right in a minute, but seeing that stained-glass window —'

'Window?' said Scoones, with another of those desperate glances down the passageway.

'The memorial window to Conrad Price.'

I thought I saw him flinch. '*Price?*'

'The boy who disappeared,' I said. 'The boy who was murdered. My brother.'

8

King Henry's Grammar School for Boys, April 28th, 1989

In spite of all my caution, Roy, I am a creature of impulse. It's one of the reasons, after all, that I chose to tell you this story. It's also why I decided then to push a little further. It wasn't that I really suspected him of anything. But Scoones had been so hostile to me when I arrived at King Henry's that the thought of making him feel a little discomfort of his own was almost irresistible. And whether it was Conrad's name, or the unwanted intimacy, or the thought of menstruation, but for a moment I thought the man was going to have a heart attack. His face had turned the delicate shade of a Banda sheet nearing the end of its life, and his stiffness was almost painful.

'You couldn't have known Conrad,' I said. 'You weren't even a teacher here then. Were you, Mr Scoones?'

'I was at St Oswald's,' he said. 'It was only my second year as a Junior Master.'

I tried to imagine Eric Scoones as a Junior Master, and found that I could not. That reddish face, the greying hair must have been with him since childhood. And that stiffness that seemed part of him, like the spine of a particularly dull book, must have been with him then, too. I couldn't imagine him differently. I suspect he never was.

'I was only five years old,' I said. 'But losing him changed everything. Nothing has been normal since then. Whoever took my brother that day took my parents, my childhood. My life.' I kept my eyes on his face, and went on in a tone-less, quiet voice; 'I still sometimes dream of meeting them. Whoever it was who took Conrad away – I'd like to look into their eyes and tell them what they did to me, to my parents, to everyone. Taking a child out of the world is like taking a supporting block out of a game of Jenga. Everything destabilizes. Everything comes falling down. *That's what you did*, I'd tell them. *That's what you did to all of us.*'

Scoones was very pale by now. The purplish cast to his features had faded to a washed-out mauve. His eyes, which always seemed to weep, now seemed more watery than ever. He opened his mouth, but nothing came out but a kind of stifled moan.

'Are you all right, Mr Scoones?' I said. 'You're looking awfully pale.'

Scoones gave a furtive glance sideways into the corridor. I hid a smile, like a gleeful child who has outwitted a bully. And then his expression changed to one of sudden and desperate relief. 'Miss Macleod,' he said in a voice that wavered like a schoolboy's. 'I'm afraid Miss Price is feeling unwell.'

I heard the sound of heels on parquet, and Eric Scoones looked back at me. 'I'll leave you with Miss Macleod,' he said, and was that a note of triumph in his voice? 'I'll keep an eye on your class, Miss Price, until you're feeling better.'

And then he was gone, and Carrie was there, Carrie with her cynical smile, and Scoones was off like a schoolboy on the last day of term, and I found that, instead of triumph,

I felt a great rush of anguish and grief, and I sobbed like a heartbroken child for the first time since I could remember.

Of course, his reaction wasn't necessarily proof of guilt. You'd be the first to tell me, Roy, that Scoones was profoundly uncomfortable with any display of emotion. The prospect of having to cope with a female colleague's fainting fit, and then her apparent breakdown, might well have been enough to plunge him into anxiety. But my initial mistrust of Scoones, on top of his unflattering reputation among the boys, had made me newly suspicious. Was it possible that Scoones could have known something about Conrad's disappearance? St Oswald's and King Henry's were traditional rivals. They often played rugby and cricket together; their chess teams often competed in the same tournaments. It was perfectly possible that Scoones *had* been at King Henry's that day. Of course I knew that declaring myself so early had its drawbacks. But the man had been shaken. Surely that had to mean something. Now all I had to do was wait and see if anything came of it.

Carrie had been speaking to me, but only now did it register. 'I'm sorry. What did you say?' I said.

'I said I've never seen old Scoones so very glad to see me before. You must have given him quite a scare.' She passed me a lace-trimmed handkerchief, and I caught her strong patchouli scent. 'Here, use this. You're leaking.'

I smiled at her and wiped my eyes. I was no longer feeling faint. Instead, I felt as if a light had come on in some part of my body. I remembered Christmas lights as a child, draped over a balding silver tinsel Christmas tree. I remembered how, every year, my father always had to tinker interminably with the fairy lights, and how it always seemed to take him hours to make them work. Later, I learnt that the fairy lights were wired in series; if a single bulb was out, then none of the other lights came on. Every bulb had to be tested. It was a source of particular stress for both of my parents, and yet they never replaced those lights, because my brother had chosen them.

'Feeling better?' Carrie said.

I said: 'It was nothing, really. Probably just my period.'

'I hope you told that to Scoones,' she said.

I grinned. 'As a matter of fact, I did.'

Carrie gave her rich, strong laugh. 'No wonder he ran, the idiot. He's terrified of women. I remember him when he arrived. Stiff as a board, and about as friendly. He disapproved of me so much that he used to turn the other way if he saw me coming down the corridor.'

I thought back to my first day. 'It doesn't seem like he's changed much,' I said.

Carrie smiled. 'Oh, people don't *change*,' she said. 'They just become more themselves with age. Scoones and the other old boys here are in their natural habitat. Their entitlement knows no bounds. Anyone who challenges their view of the world is a danger. They live in a kind of boys' clubhouse, where the only women allowed are there to bring them coffee and biscuits at Break, and to clean their classrooms after hours. You and I exist as an awkward reminder that the world outside has different rules and that women are not a minority, or a resource, or someone for them to protect from the world.'

'Now I can see why you're single,' I said, thinking of Dominic. Then I said; 'I'm so sorry. That wasn't meant to be a —'

'No, you're right,' she said and grinned. 'I wasn't meant for marriage. And frankly, there are easier ways of making a body feel good than signing up for a lifetime of bed farts, dirty laundry and arguments over money. Not to mention the mortgage, the kids and having to pretend to yourself *he knows best –*' She broke off and grinned again. 'Do you know? When I was a lot younger, I nearly married Philip Sinclair.'

'*Sinclair*?' I said in astonishment.

Carrie lit a cigarette in contravention of School rules. The smoke was sharp and nostalgic, and although I hadn't smoked in years, I suddenly longed for a cigarette myself.

'You and *Sinclair*?' I repeated.

'That's right.' She laughed. 'Oh, it would never have worked. We were both too different. I thought he was Mr Darcy. Turns out he was just a controlling guy who didn't like being challenged.'

I thought of Dominic, and his anger over my acceptance of the King Henry's post. I thought of his generosity, and of how much I owed him. I thought of how my life had become a part of his reality. And then I thought back to that moment of clarity I'd had on the day of my victory over Sinclair. What if Dominic hadn't known about my troubled past when we'd met? What if the damage I'd suffered was the reason he'd been drawn to me?

Carrie seemed to read my mind. 'You're thinking of your guy,' she said. 'What was his name? Dominic? He sounds to me like someone who needs to be challenged once in a while.'

'Oh, he's not like that,' I said. 'Dominic's the real thing.'

'Good for you, sweetheart,' said Carrie.

But later, and throughout that day, I found myself going back to my words, not only with wonder, but with doubt.

9

St Oswald's ~~Grammar School for Boys~~ *Academy*
Michaelmas Term, September 14th, 2006

The joys of being a Centurion are vastly overrated. A little
limited wisdom, perhaps; but impaired digestion, thinning hair,
an overactive bladder and a great deal of unnecessary lower
back pain. And, as of my most recent episode, a worrying little
tremor, somewhere in between my ribs, less radical than the
moving finger, but troublingly persistent.

My doctor tells me I need to relax. Stress and hypertension,
he says, are at the root of my problem. He has changed my
medication again, and speaks to me once again of retirement.

'This could be the wake-up call you need,' he said, on his
visit this afternoon. 'You're still in reasonably good shape. A
change of pace could be all you need.'

I suppressed the urge to tell him that a change of pace
could well be the death of me. We Old Centurions thrive on
stress. Take it away, and we fall apart. Look what happened
to Eric Scoones.

La Buckfast, too, has been most attentive. That too is
vaguely troubling, for reasons I cannot quite put into words.
She comes to see me every day, and tells me a little more

of her tale. She also tells me that she means to contact the police this week regarding the gruesome discovery by the side of the Gunderson Building. This comes to me, I'll admit, as something of a relief. I should have insisted upon it from the start, but somehow, she managed to hypnotize me. Perhaps it is simply the force of her personality, or the fact that Eric seems to be such a persistent part of her tale. In any case, I'll be free of it soon, once she has finished her story.

And I do *want* her to finish. I want to know more of what Eric was like when he was at King Henry's. Not at all like the Eric I knew — if indeed I knew him at all — but I do not believe he could ever actually have been violent. And yet that tremor in my heart tells me that there is more to come. My old friend, now disgraced in my eyes, and yet no less my friend than he was. The heart is a stubborn pacemaker, which persists in unruly emotions, regardless of the schoolmaster brain. Eric was an abuser. I know this, and it has destroyed me. What will happen if I find out that my friend was also a murderer? Will I have the courage to take what I know to the outside world, or will I allow it to fester? And fester it will, I'm aware of that — in my soul, and in that of the School. What began as a story is now something else; a test of faith; a fight to the death; a fight for the soul of St Oswald's.

The girl assigned by La Buckfast came by to check on me this morning. Emma Wicks, her name is — a pleasant enough girl, but here out of duty rather than affection. She brought some more of La Buckfast's tea, which would be greatly improved by a shot of brandy, but which La Buckfast clearly believes to be a universal panacea. It contains St John's Wort — whatever that is — as well as hawthorn and liquorice, and is meant to clarify, purify and somehow rejuvenate my decrepit old self. I sincerely doubt it will. But the Wicks girl also brought a get-well card from my Brodie Boys, along with a large box of Liquorice Allsorts, and a card from Ben which read: *Please get better soon!* The little gesture touched me more than I might have expected, and yet, as with Devine's chocolates, it also made me uneasy.

'I'm ready to go back, now,' I told La Buckfast as she called in that night at her usual time of 6.30. I welcomed her into the kitchen, and put the kettle on to boil. Yes, she and I have found a routine – and I, alarmingly, welcome it. Of course we of the Old School are all the playthings of routine. The timetable dictates where we go, whom we see, what we wear, even when we have tea. Even those times at which we are allowed to sneak a Gauloise or a bite to eat are subject to the vagaries of Bob Strange's labyrinthine supervision timetable, which is why most St Oswald's Masters suffer from a digestion impaired by over-hasty consumption and an over-reliance on baked goods. Perhaps this is why I currently still feel rather below par, in spite of a week's enforced repose – although I was careful not to reveal this to La Buckfast, who seems to believe that I am about to succumb to the Reaper at any moment.

'I'm ready to go back tomorrow,' I repeated. 'This has been a thoroughly pleasant sinecure, but I don't believe I need to impose on my colleagues any further.'

This was certainly true: it has always been St Oswald's custom that members of the Languages Department should not seek external cover until a member of staff has been ill for a week or more; which meant my lessons (and the administrative duties connected with my new form) must have fallen to one of my colleagues to cover.

'Which brings me to the question; which of my unfortunate friends has been covering my form in my absence? Dr Devine? Kitty Teague? A newbie? Gods help us – The *Foghorn*?'

La Buckfast smiled. 'You still don't look at all well, Roy. Are you sure you're getting enough sleep?'

I sleep as much as I normally do, which is generally as long as my overactive bladder allows. After that, I lie in bed with the wireless on until daybreak, when I get washed and shaved, make a pot of tea, mark some books and set off to work by eight o'clock.

'I don't feel tired, if that's what you mean,' I said. 'I'm fully recovered.'

This was not entirely true, but I'd hoped that my appearance would deceive her. I had taken pains to dress and shave properly before she arrived. To be sure, my suit was crumpled, but I don't seem to own one that isn't. But it seemed disrespectful somehow, to receive the Head in slippers and robe, quite apart from the fact that it made me look as if I were at Death's door. Even so, I was aware that I did not cut what you'd call a dashing figure; but I'd rather hoped that, suited and tied, I would pass the inspection.

La Buckfast looked at me critically. 'I think you need more time,' she said. 'Besides, I've already got a Supply.'

'What, really?' I was surprised. This suggested that she believes I will not be fit for another week. 'What do you mean, you've got a Supply? I've never needed Supply in my life. Where did you even get him from? Don't say it was Sunnybank Park.'

'It's a *her*,' said La Buckfast. 'And no, it wasn't Sunnybank Park.'

I hid my annoyance. La Buckfast was perverse enough to take pleasure from my discomfiture. Instead, I made a pot of tea — making sure to reach for the tasteless herbal infusion that she had provided instead of the usual Darjeeling — and poured us each a cup of the brew. It isn't often I use my mother's set, left to me with the rest of her things after her death in the Meadowbank Home. The cups are too small, too fiddly, the saucers decimated by time, but there's something about La Buckfast that seems to demand something more refined. Besides, I thought, the less I drank of her tea, the better.

The cup on the saucer tinkled and I realized with annoyance that my hand was shaking. I reached across to put them down on the kitchen table, but the table was overloaded with papers, books and crockery, and the little saucer slipped and fell, to smash onto the linoleum.

'*Damn it!*' I'd managed to keep hold of the cup, which now dangled from my finger like one of Liberace's oversized rings.

La Buckfast knelt down to pick up the broken pieces. 'Let me do that, Roy,' she said. 'I hope it wasn't valuable?'

I shrugged. 'I seldom use them,' I said. There was a sliver of china just beside my left foot; the gilding on the edge made it shine like a tiny crescent moon. It was my mother's tea set, a wedding present from some aunt or other. A cheap thing, as most of them were in those days, but hoarded and stored for many years, and kept in her china cabinet. La Buckfast gathered the pieces and dropped them into the pedal bin.

'You don't want to rush things, Roy,' she said. 'Another week will do you good.'

I sighed. I was feeling quite ill by then. I sat in my kitchen armchair, and wished for a comforting Gauloise. 'Then indulge my one remaining vice,' I said, as she sat beside me. 'Open my window into the past. Did Eric speak to you again? And what do you think he had to do with Conrad's disappearance?'

IO

King Henry's Grammar School for Boys, May 24th, 2006

I have been playing for time, of course. Like Scheherazade, I
have managed to make a temporary respite last for almost long
enough for me to outlast my adversary. Not that he thinks
of me that way. In his own eyes, he is still the White Knight
leading Alice to safety. Unimaginable, that he might have been
outmanoeuvred by a woman, especially one who seems to him
so fundamentally damaged. But I have achieved my objective.
Straitley wants to hear my tale now – no, he *needs* to hear it.
The stress of all this uncertainty is doing his sleep patterns no
good at all, and on top of everything else, I'm sure his health
must be suffering.

Still, it will soon be over. On Monday, I have a meeting
with the Council planners, the architect, and the head of the
Residents' Committee, during which I hope to break the log-jam
that has so long impeded the completion of the Gunderson
Building.

It would be good to see it complete before I move on
from this Headship. I never meant to stay here long. Just
long enough to wind up my affairs. After that, the School can
move on, safe in the wake of my legacy. Not that I mean a

swimming-pool block to be my legacy at the School, although it will look very nice on next year's publicity brochures. No, my enduring legacy is bringing girls into the School; not as a merely financial exercise, as Johnny Harrington meant it, but as a genuine move to improve the way in which girls are formed and taught to see the world around them. Not as outsiders, facilitators, mothers, sisters, daughters, supporters, comforters, cheerleaders, but as experts and pioneers. To replace the narrow door by something that opens for everyone.

I said as much in Assembly today, but I'll admit my thoughts were largely elsewhere. I suppose it's natural enough. Telling my story to Straitley has opened a gateway into the past. I'm hoping it will be cathartic; that it will close that gateway for good. But until then, I am aware of a certain constraint in my movements; a certain uneasy feeling. Not that I feel at all threatened, but I will rest easier once this is done. Maybe he, too, will rest easier – not that he deserves to.

The following weeks at King Henry's passed with little incident. There was no further sighting of the blond boy with the Prefect's badge. I went back into the chapel twice, in the hope that my brother's memorial might have more to offer me, but the memories released that day remained unfinished, incomplete; pieces from a puzzle from which the original picture has been lost.

The rest of the Department remained on largely cordial terms. Higgs kept his distance; Sinclair was polite; Lenormand was almost friendly. Scoones did his best to avoid me, except for my weekly progress report, which he delivered on Fridays on a single sheet of paper. He did not mention Conrad, or allude to our conversation, and I was inclined to believe that he had kept the details to himself. Occasionally, he would come into my class, always sitting at the back, to check that I was following the lesson plans set out in the Book. But after that day in the theatre, his visits became less frequent, and he never stayed more than five minutes or so, which meant that I was able to introduce more lively activities to the boys, reserving the Banda worksheets for Scoones's occasional visits. My pupils' behaviour improved. Even Persimmon and Spode directed their exuberance to the study of Whitmarsh.

At home, my daughter's invisible friend continued to make his presence felt. I was not especially surprised by this. Emily was at an age where everything she overheard was stored and processed and integrated into her expanding world picture. And only children often find the presence of an invisible friend convenient in all kinds of ways. *Conrad wants more ice cream. Conrad said a bad word. I didn't break it, Conrad did.* Why did she choose my brother's name? Conrad's story was like lint; it somehow stuck to everything. Dom, however, still believed that the reappearance of Mr Smallface was a cry for help; a sign of something more sinister.

'She's just being imaginative,' I said, when he voiced his concern. 'Did you not have invisible friends when you were her age?'

'I had *real* friends,' Dominic said. 'Emily should have them, too.'

Dominic was always talking about the friends he'd had at school. To him, I sensed that school had been a mostly happy, carefree time: he was still in touch with friends that he had made in primary school, and his memories of those years were filled with pranks and adventures and problems shared, and the warmth of easy companionship. My own experience had been very different. Apart from Emily Jackson, I'd had no friends − not at school, or anywhere. And after Conrad disappeared, even Emily drifted away, as if I, and not he, had gone from the world. No one was unkind to me, no one bullied me, and yet there was a kind of mark on me that warned the other children away.

As I'd entered secondary school, I had tried my best to fit in. I had joined clubs and societies. I had taken up Drama and Music. I had played hockey and gone on school trips. I had been pretty, and sporty, and good. I had not been exactly *unpopular*; but still I'd had no close friends. It was as if the hole that was left behind when my brother had disappeared had made a space around me; a space that no one could occupy.

I shrugged. 'You were different. Emily has always been a lot more quiet and self-sufficient.'

'Like you,' said Dominic. It didn't sound like a compliment.

'Yes, like me,' I told him.

'Well, maybe that's the problem,' he said. 'You know, Becks, it's sometimes possible to be *too* self-sufficient. It's OK to ask for help, you know. You don't *have* to deal with everything alone.'

'I know, Dominic.'

He shrugged. 'Doesn't seem that way, sometimes. And you're still talking in your sleep. Something's wrong, and you know it.'

I waved aside his objections. It was true that my sleep had been troubled, but there had been no repetition of the sleep-walking incident, or of the sleep paralysis, or of the disturbing dream of Conrad's voice and the green door. To be sure, I found it difficult to get off to sleep in the evenings, and I often awoke in the early hours and found myself unable to sleep again, but it was summer, and even as a child I had always been sensitive to light.

And I *felt* fine; more energized, more confident than I'd felt in years. I had conquered King Henry's. I had faced the dragon and won. I had acquired immunity to the disease of my childhood. The obstacles in my way were gone, and all that was left was sunshine.

II

May 29th, 1989

Of course, that feeling didn't last. And, of course, I was very naïve to think I could make a difference. But I was like a child in a boat on the surface of a lake: under the water, there could be any number of dangers – sink holes; currents; clutching weed; blind creatures with gaping jaws – but all the child can see is the sun shining on the water; the golden midges in the air; the ripples on the surface.

The weekend of May 29th was a Spring Bank Holiday. Dominic had booked us all a weekend away at the seaside. A guest house in Scarborough, that was all; but it would take my mind off work, he said, and give us the chance to spend some time together, before the rush of activity that heralded the School exams.

'Emily'll love it,' he said. 'It's where we always used to go when we were kids.'

I remember that weekend; sunny, and filled with families making the most of the sunshine. I remember being unsurprised that Dominic had loved it here; the games arcades; the ice-cream stands; he and his sisters on the beach, building sandcastles and playing games. Emily loved it, too: she and I had never been on holiday together. But then, I'd only ever been on holiday once, with my parents; a time I remembered only through my parents, and a single photograph. Myself, aged three, and Conrad; on a nameless beach in France, laughing into the camera. It was one of the photographs my parents kept on the mantelpiece. They often spoke of that holiday. But I had no memories of my own. Any that I might have had were overwritten by stories of Conrad; stories I'd heard so often that they had become my reality. The time that Conrad had given me his ice cream when I'd dropped my own. The time that Conrad had saved me when a big wave had knocked me down. And the sandcastle in the picture, which he had spent all day building for me. It was my first and last holiday. After Conrad disappeared, we had always stayed at home, even during the long summer holidays. Without the Jacksons and Emily, I would have been completely alone: alone with the ghost of Conrad.

Perhaps all this was why I did not warm to the idea of a seaside holiday as much as I had expected. The beach was too crowded, the water too cold; in May, the sun is deceptively warm, but the sea still remembers winter. But yes, I was convincing. Dominic's photographs proved it – hundreds of them, taken on the promenade, the beach, the tiny garden that ran alongside the stucco-fronted boarding house. Photos of me with Emily, flying a kite by the seashore; or building a castle, or on the street, or paddling in the cold sea. They look so real, those memories; and yet they were a performance. Emily, too, knew how to perform; posing for the camera; indulging in the kind of kittenish, pre-sexual behaviour a young girl may sometimes adopt when a man she loves is watching. I was not fooled. It was pretence, just as her antics with 'Conrad' had been a kind of performance, designed to divert attention away from the fear of the monster.

Over that weekend, there was no mention of Emily's invisible friend. Apparently, 'Conrad' had stayed at home, and not followed us to Scarborough. Dominic felt vindicated: over a candlelit bottle of wine, when Emily had gone to bed, he expounded his theory.

'It proves she needed attention, that's all. It's done us a world of good to be here, together, as a family.' *A family.*

I did not reply. Is that how he thought of us? It occurred to me that he, too, had been playing a part. The generous father; the bringer of mirth. He liked himself in the role, I thought. He liked the feeling of being in charge, of fixing what was damaged.

Damaged. That feeling of doubt returned. The feeling that Dom had known who I was *before* he got involved with me. It would not have been difficult to find out a little about my history. My name had not changed, and at fourteen, he would have been quite old enough to follow the details of Conrad's case. What *had* Dominic seen in me? Could it have been my damage, and not my resilience, that had first attracted him?

'Hey.' His voice was caressing. 'You're not zoning out on me, are you?'

I looked up. His familiar face was so kind; so sincere; so warm in the candlelight. And yet a part of me struggled to escape, just as I longed for acceptance.

'Dominic. Did you know who I was before we started dating?'

He frowned. 'Why do you ask?'

'I wonder what you see in me.'

He laughed at that, a good rich laugh that should have chased my doubts away. 'What *I* see in *you*? Are you joking? You're gorgeous, Becks. Way out of my league. I still can't believe I'm with you.'

'Not – damaged? Something to be fixed?'

He pulled a comic face. 'Oh, Becks. If only you could see yourself. You're by far the most wonderful thing that has ever happened to me. You're tough, and strong, and clever, and all I ever dreamt of –' He took my hands in his, and pulled me gently towards him. He smelt of wine, and of the sea, and of something else, like ozone and sweat. And I accepted his embrace and pushed away that feeling of doubt, born from a lifetime of feeling that I didn't deserve to be happy.

We made love that night to the sound of the sea, and afterwards, I should have slept, except that everything was wrong; the shadows on the painted wall; the sound of the ancient plumbing. *Victorian boarding houses have Victorian plumbing*, I thought, but that sound was too familiar; too sinister to be ignored. I got up at one in the morning and went to check on Emily; she had a little room of her own, with an en-suite bathroom. I opened the bedroom door, and listened for her breathing. It was light and regular; I could just see the top of her head from underneath the duvet. Just as I started to close the door, I heard a sound from the bathroom.

Rrrrrrrk –

Those Victorian pipes, of course. But it sounded so familiar. I stopped. The bathroom door was shut. Quietly, I came into the room, and turned on the bathroom light. Behind me, Emily slept on; the light from the passageway caught her cheek and torched her hair into autumn fire. I opened the bathroom door and looked in. I saw Emily's toiletries on a shelf; her bathrobe, with the kitten print, was neatly hung up behind the door. And I saw that the toilet seat was shut, held in place by a number of items piled with a haphazard urgency: a Bible from the bedside drawer; a bundle of holiday brochures.

Who had taught her to do that? I thought. Who had brought Mr Smallface into my daughter's little life?

From the pipes, that sound again, like a dog with a bone in its throat. *Rrrrrk. Rrk-Rebecc-aaaa —*

I shut the bathroom door and fled.

12

King Henry's Grammar School for Boys, June 14th, 1989

Returning to my life after that, I found myself experiencing a strange kind of paralysis. Things were good again at home; Dominic was happy, and there were no more of those furtive phone calls to his sisters. Work, too, was good. That summer term at King Henry's was like the summer Conrad died; all sunshine on the surface, and the giant presence of what was to come no more than a shadow at my feet. Emily seemed happy at school, although she still spoke of 'Conrad', and weighed down the toilet seat with books before she went to bed. I wanted to find out the reasons behind her behaviour, but Dominic's opinion was that we should simply ignore it, and try to encourage her to be more outgoing, and to try some new activities.

I allowed him to persuade me, not quite believing his tactic would work. Like the child I had once been, Emily had always been quiet and introspective. The idea that she would respond to a programme of outdoor activities, cooking, TV and board games seemed almost unbelievable. And yet, to my surprise, she did. The gift of a shiny new bicycle, presented to her strategically at the start of the half-term holiday, served to tempt her out of doors, after which Dom announced his long-delayed plan to redecorate her bedroom. This meant that, while he was working there, repainting the walls in her favourite colour (pink) and converting her bed into a fantasy tent, draped with gauzy fabric, she would have no choice but to vacate her room and spend more time playing out in the garden.

Thus, under Dominic's influence, Emily spent less time alone, and more time in the kitchen with him, or riding her new bicycle, or watching TV in the living room. She even invited a couple of friends to come and sleep over one weekend, which entailed a great deal of giggling and pillow fights and sugary snacks.

I knew I should be pleased for her. My daughter was adjusting. And yet I could not shake off the idea that, somehow, I was missing something. Was it simply jealousy of her affection for Dominic? Or was it that persistent fear that he was controlling both of us?

Back at King Henry's, the Middle School exams took up most of my time. Written exams took place in the Gym, and oral exams in the theatre. Scoones was in charge of the latter, and he took immense pleasure in the role, allocating each member of staff a dressing room in which to conduct the face-to-face language interviews, while the rest of the boys worked in silence in the main part of the theatre. The interviews were all recorded onto a stack of cassette tapes, then taken home and marked according to the new GCSE guidelines. This was far more unwieldy and time-consuming than marking scripts and took up most of my evenings, much to Dominic's disgust.

'I thought we were trying to make more time together with Emily,' he said.

'I know. It won't be for long,' I said. 'I just need to mark these oral exams.'

'Twenty minutes per candidate – with how many candidates? Sixty? That's twenty hours' solid marking, even before you get on to the written papers.'

He was right, of course, which made it all the more annoying. Under the pretext of being in charge of exam administration, Scoones had offloaded most of his marking onto a junior member of staff. This was Departmental policy, I discovered, and I was torn between the desire to complain, and the knowledge that if I did, I would be viewed as a malcontent, or weak, or not a team player. And so I accepted the extra work, and ploughed through the stack of cassette tapes, noting with sly satisfaction that Scoones's French was considerably less fluent than mine. As a result, Scoones was complacent – even almost avuncular. Sinclair, too, was approving, and Lenormand quite sympathetic. Only Higgs still kept aloof. But finally, I was starting to feel as if I could be accepted.

I made the mistake of saying so to Dominic one Sunday night. I'd finally finished the marking; Emily had gone to bed and we were watching late-night TV and sharing a bottle of red wine. 'What does it matter what they think?' he said. 'It's not like you're staying on.'

'I haven't made that decision yet.'

He looked at me sharply. 'Becks,' he said, 'you've spent the whole weekend shut away, listening to those fucking tapes. You barely talk to Emily. And you're run ragged. I know you are. What time did you go to bed last night? One? Two?'

'The hard bit's done. Now I can afford to relax.'

He pulled a face. 'That's what I'm afraid of. Don't get too comfortable there, Becks. Next thing you know, we're all playing bridge with someone who went to Eton.'

I had to smile. 'It's nothing like that. There are some people you'd really like. Good people, like Carrie Macleod –'

'The hippie Drama teacher you keep going on about?' He laughed. It was not an entirely pleasant laugh, and I felt a touch of annoyance. I'd only mentioned Carrie to him a couple of times, at the start of term, and certainly not often enough to qualify as 'going on'.

'I don't think I called her a hippie,' I said. 'She's great, and not at all snobbish. Maybe we could invite her over for dinner or drinks one weekend. You'll love her, she's hilarious –'

'*No.*' His tone was suddenly harsh.

'What?'

'You're not inviting her here,' he said in the same cold and angry voice. 'I think I've made it clear I'm not interested in socializing with anyone from that place. *Ever.*'

'Oh.' I suddenly felt like a child, helpless in the face of some incomprehensible adult rage. It was the same kind of feeling I'd had when Scoones had lashed out at me on my first day. I felt my features taking on that look of frozen politeness; that strangely *apologetic* look that women assume when they have been hurt. Men are allowed their reactions, but good girls never make a fuss, even when they have every right to do so.

Dom saw my face, and softened. 'Look, I didn't mean to upset you,' he said. 'It's just that we've been going to invite my family over since Easter, but you always say you're exhausted, and I'm running out of excuses –'

'A couple of drinks with a friend from work is hardly a dinner party for twelve,' I said. 'And you're right. I *am* exhausted. I'm going to get some sleep.'

He did not stop me from leaving. But when I crept down, some time later, still upset and unable to sleep, I heard him speaking on the phone; too low for me to make out the words.

PART 4

Phlegethon
(River of Burning)

I

King Henry's Grammar School for Boys, July 7th, 1989

The last days of the summer term are never easy on supply staff. No comforting routine, no plans; no punishments; no homework. Boys can already see the summer holidays unfolding before them like a stretch of unbroken beach, all sunshine to the horizon. Upper School boys are long gone, having finished their exams, and the Middle and Lower Schools are kept as calm as possible by a series of trips, sports, and other diversions.

Not having a form of my own, I was exempt from writing reports, and end-of-term administration. As a result I was given the task of helping with the school Sports Day, to be held on the penultimate Friday of term. I'd always rather enjoyed sports. I felt that my contribution might help me in my improved relationship with the boys. Thus I was looking forward to Sports Day, and to the rare informality of a day spent outside.

But on Thursday night, it rained. Six inches of rain fell on Malbry, and the school fields were waterlogged. Instead of spending the day outdoors, I was obliged to supervise a group of assorted misfits and malcontents while the PE staff organized indoor games with the sporting elite of the School. The result was not what I'd hoped for. Forty frustrated Grammar School boys – including most of 4 Upper S – crammed into one classroom for the whole of an afternoon was already bad enough. But add to that the end of term, the cancelled treat; the pouring rain; the smell of wet socks and the way the condensation ran down the walls and fogged the small, high windows, and my charges were getting restless. I had no work to give them – except for Scoones's lesson plans – and my attempts to get them to read in French were doomed before I started. I had to do something quickly, or risk an intervention by Scoones – who was always on the alert for an excuse to wield his authority.

And then I had an idea. 'All right. That's quite enough of that,' I said. 'Follow me to the theatre, boys. I think we could all use a change of scene.'

I hadn't looked in the theatre since the day of that first Assembly. King Henry's was a traditional school and mingling between Departments was definitely frowned upon. But Scoones was with Sinclair that day, unlikely to notice my absence, and Carrie was the only person in the School I could count upon to co-operate.

She was there with a trio of fifth-formers, sorting out props by the side of the stage. I filled her in on my Sports Day predicament, and found her sympathetic.

'I thought we might be able to use the theatre this afternoon, instead of being stuck in a classroom,' I said. 'I thought perhaps some foreign-language role-plays might be more fun than Sinclair's lesson plans.'

She raised a cynical eyebrow. 'Role-plays? Sweetheart, we can do better than that.'

And with Carrie's help, we did. First, I sorted the boys into groups, and asked them to each write a short piece in French.

'It can be a poem, a role-play, a song, a sketch. Anything you like,' I said. 'In forty-five minutes, we'll see you perform. The audience will judge the work and the winners will get a prize.'

'You mean, like a *performance*?' said Persimmon.

'More like a concert party,' said Spode, his eyes shining behind his taped glasses.

I smiled. 'As long as it's in French.'

'Excellent!'

'All right. Off you go.'

The others, a little doubtful at first, soon flung themselves into the work. Carrie and I oversaw the groups; and Carrie opened the prop store for the boys to take props where required. Orange – a shy boy, whose stammer made it difficult for him to speak any lines – was designated *le costumier*, bringing out clothes from the back room. Birdman was *le directeur*, and Akindele *l'ingénieur*. Fenelly checked the French for mistakes, and Andrews added invective where necessary.

Persimmon and Spode already formed their own comedy double act, and with the help of the rest of the team, managed to create a kind of satirical playlet, featuring Persimmon as *Monsieur Oeufmann* and Spode as *Madame Asda-Prix*. (These characters were clearly versions of myself and Scoones.) There was also *L'Ours*, played by Sato in a bear costume left over from a production of *The Tempest*; *Le Mouton Anglo-Français* and (perhaps inevitably) *Le Pétomane*. There was even *l'Orchestre*, consisting of two boys called Winstone and Potts, perched up in the band loft, playing the drums and the keyboards. The result was absurd, profane, surreal, but nevertheless, oddly endearing, and I found myself once again feeling touched by the energy and humour of these boys, and the underlying *seriousness* which they brought to the whole ridiculous affair. I suppose, Straitley, that you must feel much the same for your Brodie Boys.

Finally, the curtain rose on the finished performance, which was as absurd as you might expect. The audience response was lively, but manageable: the boys stayed mostly in their seats and clapped every sketch with enthusiasm. It was clearly the first time that any of them had been allowed to exercise any kind of creativity in the subject, and they welcomed it with obvious glee, stepping very close to the line between slapstick and outright disrespect (especially with the portrayal of Scoones), but never quite crossing it. The sound of juvenile laughter rang across the theatre, and I felt a strange sensation, almost of *belonging* –

And then it happened. A figure emerged from a trapdoor on the left of the stage: a tall figure draped in a long, dusty robe. A murmur swept across the auditorium, followed by an expectant silence. The figure moved slowly, and I saw that its face was grotesquely small in proportion to the bulk of its body. The face was that of a mime in reverse – a black circle on a white ground – and it seemed to float in silence, like a balloon, in the darkly gleaming air, in which motes of coloured light danced like shoals of tropical fish . . .

Suddenly, all the strength and laughter went out of my body. I was back in the boys' toilets; I was back in the cloakroom. I felt my facial expression become a kind of terrified rictus. His long black robe, his small, round face, blank as a disc on a turntable –

How had they known? How could they have known?

There are two kinds of people, I realize. Those who freeze under pressure, and those who go on the attack. I had never been quite sure which kind of woman I was until then. But to see the monster in the flesh – the monster that had haunted my dreams – given new life so close to the place the event had happened, was enough to force a reaction. I vaulted out of

my seat in the stalls and raced towards the front of the stage.
I don't know what I would have done if I had reached the
monster in time, but I was wearing high heels, and one of
them snagged the carpet, so that during the fifteen seconds or
so that it took me to reach the front of the stage, the sinister
figure had disappeared, down into the trapdoor.

I turned to Carrie. 'Where does it lead?'

'To the trap room,' Carrie said. 'It's a kind of storage area
where I keep old costumes and props —'

I ran up the steps and into the wings, then round the back
of the little stage. Here there were dressing rooms, prop stores,
and finally, down a small flight of stairs, the trap room: a
cramped area below the stage, filled with boxes and suitcases.
A set of wooden steps led up to the open trapdoor. This was
how the cloaked figure had made both his entrance and his
escape; at the bottom of the steps lay a cloak and a kind of
black mask. Otherwise, there was no sign of life.

Above me, the boys were applauding, as if this had all been
part of the show. I turned and ran to the side door and looked
out into the corridor. No one was there but the caretaker, Chris,
who carried out odd jobs and routine maintenance around the
School, and who was currently standing on a ladder, adjusting
a light in the ceiling.

'Did someone come out just a moment ago?'

He looked at me rather curiously. A lightly built man in
overalls, with lank blond hair that fell over his eyes, and little
John Lennon glasses. Mid-thirties — which made him too young
to have been working at King Henry's when my brother was
at school — and though I'd seen him around once or twice,
I had paid little attention to him until now.

Chris shrugged. 'I had my back to the door. A boy went
past just a moment ago. Was that him?'

'What boy? What did he look like? Was he blond? Glasses?'

'Who knows? They all look the same to me.'

I felt the hairs on my neck rise.

'Little bastards, all of them. What did he do?'

With an effort, I smiled at him. 'Nothing. It's fine. Are you sure there was no one else? No one in the corridor?'

'Only Mr Scoones just now.'

'Mr Scoones?'

'I saw him, yes.'

'Coming out of the theatre?' I said. My hands were beginning to tremble.

'Told you. I had my back to the door. Are you all right? You look a bit pale.'

'No, I'm fine, thank you.'

Chris shrugged again and returned to his work. I went back into the theatre. The house lights had come on by then; the boys had all regained their seats. Persimmon and Spode were still in their costumes, grinning; visibly pleased with themselves. I scanned the rows of seats, wondering who could be missing. No one was. I checked again. All my boys were accounted for. Whoever had been in that costume must have come from elsewhere.

'What was all that about?' Carrie said.

'Nothing,' I said. 'Some kind of prank.' I gave a meaningless little smile. It might even have been true. So close to the end of term, with so many unplanned activities going on, it was all too easy for boys to go wandering outside their class. But under my skin, a million volts were pulling at my muscles and nerves: behind the blank-faced canvas, the machineries of panic.

'So, Miss, who's the winner?' said Spode.

'Excuse me?'

'Who's the winner, Miss? You said the winner got a prize.'

I forced myself to look away from the stage. 'Everyone was terrific,' I said. I glanced at my watch. Twenty minutes remained until the end of School. 'All right,' I said. 'The prize is . . . The prize is . . .' I faltered.

Carrie spoke up briskly. 'The prize is you all go home early,' she said, to an eruption of glee from the stalls. Looking at me, she said softly; 'Are you all right, Becky?'

I raised my voice a little and said: 'Quietly, gentlemen, as you go. Leave your costumes on the stage. I don't want a riot as you leave.'

Rather to my surprise, they obeyed, voices down to a low hum. There was no running in the aisles, or any misbehaviour. As he left, Orange turned and faced me with a beaming smile. 'Best French lesson ever, Miss,' he said, without a trace of a stutter.

Carrie smiled. 'You've got a new fan. Maybe more than one, in fact,' she said as Persimmon and Spode filed past, their faces flushed with success.

'You were all very good,' I said. 'I especially appreciated the personal homage to Mr Scoones.'

Persimmon grinned. 'Thanks, Miss.'

'Oh, by the way –' I went on. 'Who was that supposed to be, coming out of the trapdoor?'

The two boys looked at each other and shrugged. 'Wasn't one of ours,' said Spode. 'Must have been one of the other class.'

Once more I felt the mounting fear buzzing at my insides. *My skin is filled with bees*, I thought, *soon my head will split open like the lion in Samson's riddle*. I went back onto the empty stage; looked through the open trapdoor. Many theatre trap-doors have lifts and mechanical sliding doors: presumably the School budget had not allowed for such things. A simple set of hinges; a door that could swing both out or in; a simple set of wooden steps leading underneath the stage.

Carefully, I climbed down the steps and back into the trap room. I picked up the black cloak and mask from the ground. The mask, especially, was odd; a perfectly round, velvet affair, as featureless as a record.

'A void-face mask, a *moretta*,' Carrie said, coming in from the side entrance. 'It's a kind of Venetian mask they wore in the seventeenth century. I used them once in a production of *Othello* we did years ago.'

I lifted the mask. It was perfectly round, with no space for a mouth, and no strings attached to hold it in place. Instead, there was a kind of flat button on the inside.

'You were supposed to keep it in place by biting down on the button,' she said. 'That meant the woman wearing it was mute, as well as faceless. I thought it was an interesting visual for the women characters: I had them wear one every time they didn't have to deliver a line.'

'When was this? What year?' I said. All my strength was keeping me from flying apart.

''Seventy-one,' she said. 'The year the theatre opened. We did it all in period dress. I played Desdemona, in fact. I could still get away with it in those days.'

But I was no longer listening. I had found something else on the ground under the abandoned cloak. Something the size of a large purse; shiny and patent red. I would have known it anywhere. It was the little red satchel that Conrad had bought for my birthday; the one that I had mysteriously lost the day my brother disappeared.

2

King Henry's Grammar School for Boys, July 7th, 1989

I stayed alone in the theatre long after Carrie and the boys had gone. Without them, the space was less comforting; the shadows at the edges of the room seemed filled with silent menace. I looked at my watch: it was four o'clock. Dominic would be wondering where I was: school finished at three-thirty.

Once more I looked at the little red satchel in my hand. Time had not faded the colour, but the patent surface had crackled and crazed to the shiny, sticky consistency of a scarlet candy-apple. How I'd loved it! I thought to myself. How frantically I'd searched for it as soon as I'd realized it was gone!

I stuffed it into my briefcase. Short of simply leaving it there in the Little Theatre, there wasn't much else I could do with it. How had it arrived there? Combined with the sudden appearance of a figure in a mask − a mask that happened to have been part of my brother's School play − it could not be accidental. It was real, just as the figure was real. Someone with knowledge had planned this. Could it be Scoones? He knew who I was. He knew his way around the theatre. And Chris had told me he'd seen him nearby. But why would he do it? And how had he found the satchel I had lost as a child?

I reached for my jacket, which I'd left on one of the velvet-covered seats, and heard a sound from the back of the room – the sound of a toilet flushing.

Such an everyday sound, you'd think. Nothing to be alarmed by. But the toilets were only accessible from the theatre. To get in, someone would have had to have done so by the main entrance. I would have seen and heard them come in. And yet, the only alternative was that *they had been in there all the time* –

I picked up my jacket and briefcase and walked slowly towards the back of the auditorium. My heart was thudding sickly, and there was a taste at the back of my throat like biting onto tinfoil.

Scoones?

There stood two identical doors, one marked with a little stick-man, one with a stick-man in a wheelchair. Carrie was right; in this school, to be female or disabled amounted to more or less the same thing. I opened the door with the stick-man. There was nobody inside. A row of sinks; two urinals; two cubicles with half-open doors. It was cleaner than the boys' toilets on the Upper Corridor: the mirrors were glass, and not polished steel, and there was a faint, medicinal scent of pine. None of the taps were running. There was no buzzing sound from the pipes. I turned and went to the other door. I tried it. It was locked.

I put my ear to the door and heard the sound of running water. The metallic taste in my mouth had become almost overwhelming. I tried to say: *Is anyone there?* and found that my throat was too dry to speak. I rattled the door handle.

'Is anyone there?' My throat was still dry, and the sound of my voice was very small. I might have been a child again, huddled on that bathroom floor. Something in my memory seemed to suddenly *loosen*, like a long-blocked water pipe that finally gives up its sediment. I remembered the green door of my dream, and with it, a scent of sawdust and paint, and a light that came through from above in coloured puzzle pieces. I remembered looking down a hole, and seeing the shadows stirring there, and hearing a voice behind me, saying: *This is where Mr Smallface lives. This is where he takes his prey. Do you want him to take you, too?*

The green door. The mysterious hole. The images were clear, though the time and context were not. *Had* I been in the theatre that day? The presence of my satchel certainly seemed to suggest it. And that memory of coloured light falling onto bare boards – could that have been from the ceiling dome, with its abstract pattern of coloured glass?

Once more I rattled the toilet door. 'Hey!' This time my voice was louder. 'Hey, is anyone in there? Mr Scoones?'

The sound of running water stopped. There came a sound from behind the door. The sound of bees in my head increased. I clenched my fists around my briefcase – I don't know quite what I was expecting, but that combative streak in me was still there, and had not been subdued by my unease. Thus it was that when the door opened, and a stranger emerged from the stall, he was rightly alarmed to find himself faced by a young woman holding a red briefcase above her head like a mallet, her face rigid with tension, her eyes crazed with dancing lights.

He was a pleasant-looking man in his early thirties; tall, athletic, with mousy hair, and wearing a King Henry's Prefect's badge on the lapel of his blazer. He looked surprised to see me – as well he might – then gave me a rather cautious smile.

'Was it something I said?'

I took a deep and calming breath. 'Dammit, sorry – you scared me,' I said, putting down the briefcase. 'I thought you were an intruder.'

'No shit,' said the stranger. 'I thought you were going to brain me.' He gave a warm and winning smile. 'I'm Jerome. And you are –?'

His smile was infectious. 'Rebecca Price. Modern Languages.'

'Then maybe we'll be colleagues next term. I've just been speaking with Dr Sinclair about the new French Master's job.'

It took me a moment to process this. 'But – there *isn't* a French Master's job.'

'Apparently there is,' said Jerome. 'You lost a staff member earlier this term, and managed to find a last-minute Supply, from Sunnybank Park, of all places. There *was* some talk of keeping them on, but I got the feeling from Dr Sinclair –' He broke off abruptly and looked at me. 'Oh, shit. *You're* the Supply.'

'How did you hear about the job?'

'I'm sorry.' He looked uncomfortable. 'I honestly wouldn't have said anything if –'

'How did you hear about the job?'

'I was at Oxford with Daniel Higgs. I met him for a drink in the pub, and he said there might be a job here for me.' He reached out to put a hand on my arm. 'I swear I didn't know,' he said. 'Danny led me to believe that you were not likely to stay.'

'Did he?' I thought about Daniel Higgs, and the way he'd stared down my cleavage on that first day on the stairs. Since then he had mostly avoided me – alarmed, perhaps, at my tirade. It occurred to me then that he had probably been spreading rumours about me ever since among his friends and colleagues.

'What did Sinclair say about me?'

'Really, nothing much,' said Jerome. 'Just that you were very young, and not quite up to –'

'Standards?' I said. My former unease had rapidly been replaced by a kind of swooning rage that I was struggling to control.

'I was going to say, not entirely used to the way things are done at King Henry's.'

I forced myself to stay calm. I've become very good at hiding things. Conrad's death and what followed it has taught me that, if nothing else.

'Well, I'm sorry you wasted your time,' I said. 'There isn't a vacancy at all. I'll be staying on until the end of my contract. After that, I mean to apply for a permanent post here.'

I found myself almost surprised at the fierceness of my reaction. I realized how badly I *wanted* to stay, in spite of all I'd encountered. Even in spite of Dominic's increasingly sullen objections. I wanted to prove myself to those men who had already written me off, who had ogled me, and bullied me, and made me feel unworthy. I wanted to prove to them what I could do, *that I could kill the monster –*

The memory caught me unawares. It came, as before, in fragments of light; flashes from a corrupted archive. I remembered the green door, and the dappled, forest light from above, and the sound of something hitting the ground, and the taste of tinfoil and chocolate –

Jerome was looking uncomfortable. 'I completely understand,' he said. 'I shouldn't have approached Sinclair. But I happened to be between jobs, and this one seemed like such a good fit. I was a pupil here once, you know. Happiest days of my life.'

'Really?' I said. How different we are. How different our experiences.

'I know. Right?' He smiled at me. 'I *liked* school. I really did. I know I'm a walking cliché, but I like to think it makes me a better schoolmaster.' He tapped the Prefect's badge in his lapel. 'That's why I wear this badge, I suppose. To remember the friends. The Masters. The games. The feeling of belonging to a long and proud tradition.'

I looked at him again. Mid-thirties, maybe. *Old enough to have known him*, I thought. 'You're lucky. Some kids have a rough time at school.' I paused. 'Remember that boy who disappeared?'

He looked at me rather blankly. 'You know about that story?' he said. 'You must have been *very* young when it happened.'

I shrugged. 'It's kind of famous.'

'Yes, I suppose it must be,' he said. 'That all seems very long ago.'

'Did you know him at all?' I said. The metallic taste was back in my mouth, and I wondered if he could see from my face how much I needed to know the truth. Then he slowly shook his head.

'I may have seen him once or twice,' he said. 'I didn't know him.' He looked at me rather closely, and said: 'Price, his name was. Colin Price.'

I forced myself not to correct him.

'Price,' he repeated slowly. 'That's *your* name, isn't it?'

I shrugged. 'It's a common name around here.'

'Well, I didn't know him. I think he might have been in a different year. Or maybe a different House. In any case, I don't remember much about it.'

Well, Roy, I knew that was a lie. Conrad's disappearance was the single biggest event in King Henry's history. Books have been written about the case. There was even a TV documentary. Of course he would have remembered, I thought. Add to that the look on his face when I asked him if he'd known Conrad –

What did he know? Why would he lie? Could it be something important?

Once more I schooled my expression. I glanced at my watch. 'Well, look at the time. I have to get home. But maybe we could meet somewhere?' I smiled at him. 'I have to admit, I could use a chat with someone who knows King Henry's. People like your college friend Higgs haven't been making it easy for me.'

I know. Having a pretty face can also have advantages. It means I'm taken less seriously. But when it comes to directing men towards what I want, it seldom fails. I reached up to unpin my hair from its bun, and shook it loose over my shoulders. 'That feels *so* much better,' I said. A cheap shot, but it drew him in. I could feel his eyes like hot fingers on my cheekbones.

'We could meet tomorrow,' he said. 'There's a pub in Malbry that I like. It's called The Thirsty Scholar.'

I nodded. I knew where it was. Down the road from St Oswald's.

'Meet me there at four o'clock. We'll have a chat.'

I smiled. 'It's a date.'

3

July 7th, 1989

It was late when I got back to April Street. Emily, in pyjamas, with her slippers shaped like tiger feet, was watching cartoons on the sofa. There was a rich scent of cooking – garlic, chillies, tomato, rice – I supposed that Dominic must have already made dinner.

I came in and put down my briefcase. The clock in the kitchen said 6.45. For a moment, I felt a stab of unease. Had I really been with Jerome for over two hours? And if not, where had the time gone?

Dominic was washing up, his back to me as I came in. He did not turn round, but spoke to me in a deceptively neutral voice.

'Saved you some jambalaya,' he said. 'I didn't know when you were coming home.'

'I'm sorry. Something came up,' I said. 'Thanks for feeding Emily.'

'Kid has to eat,' said Dominic.

'I'm sorry,' I repeated, putting my arms around him. He felt as stiff as a block of wood. 'I'll make it up to you later.'

Dominic shrugged. 'Whatever. Sure.'

I said nothing more, but went to investigate the covered dishes on the hob. He would come around, I thought. He would learn to be proud of me.

I spooned jambalaya into a bowl. It looked good, though it was no longer hot. I sat down to eat it in silence. There was chicken, and sausage, and rice, cooked with chillies and garlic. Dominic was an excellent cook. Far, far better than I was.

I poured myself a glass of wine, realizing how hungry I'd been. Sinclair and Scoones and the others always went to the school refectory at lunchtime, but in between marking, and setting up my lessons, and moving from one room to another, and supervising the boys, I hadn't joined them even once.

'Don't bother,' Carrie had said. 'You're not missing anything. I don't think I've used the refectory more than twice in thirty years. Besides which, the place is full of men, ready to comment on what you're eating. *Chips, Carrie? You'll get fat!* And all the time they're stuffing their faces with steak and kidney pie, the pigs, and jam roly-poly, and custard.'

I had to laugh. I knew what she meant. To be a woman, I have learnt, is to be the constant recipient of unwanted pieces of male advice. *Cheer up, love, it might never happen! You shouldn't eat that! You need to eat more! Ladies don't wear trousers!* Once more I thought back to that trouser suit. I thought I'd *earned* the right to wear it. But all the time, Sinclair had been on the lookout for my replacement. *I'll show that bastard*, I told myself. *I'll show him who's up to his standards.*

I finished the jambalaya and rinsed the dishes in the kitchen sink. By then it was Emily's bedtime, and though I was happy to put her to bed, Emily asked for Dominic. That was just like Emily; she gave her affection freely to men, while I tried in vain to earn it. Dominic had been in our lives for less than a year, and already my daughter loved him. I wondered if *I* loved him. I wondered if I was even capable.

He came downstairs some time later. By that time, I'd drunk two more glasses of wine, and I was feeling light-headed and a little reckless. Dom looked at me for a moment or two, then seemed to relax.

'You're looking tired.'

'Well, it's been a tiring week.'

'One more to go, and then you'll be free.' He poured himself a glass of wine. 'I thought we could go away for a while, afterwards, once my term's over. Robin Hood's Bay, or somewhere like that. I bet Milly would enjoy that. It hasn't been easy for her this term, with you so busy all the time.'

I drank my wine in silence. I knew that my decision to stay might be a challenge for him to accept. But Dominic had never believed that I would succeed at King Henry's. He'd never *wanted* me to succeed. Not for the first time, it struck me how Dom's disapproval always resurfaced when I was making progress. And hadn't his reaction to Emily's 'imaginary friend' been to limit the time she spent alone, to make her more dependent on *him*? Perhaps that's what he fears, I thought. A woman's independence.

'You're very quiet,' said Dominic.

'I told you, I'm just tired,' I said. 'But if I can keep on top of it now, next term will be so much easier.'

'What do you mean, next term?' he said. 'I thought you'd decided not to stay on.'

I shook my head. 'I never said that. And why would I leave at this stage? I've done most of the hard part already.'

I could tell he didn't approve. But maybe it was the wine I'd drunk, or the scene in the theatre, or the rediscovery of my little red satchel, but I was feeling a strange and unusual sense of exhilaration. For the first time since my arrival at King Henry's, I felt I was close to something. And after everything I'd seen, I couldn't possibly give up now.

'I'm worried about Emily.'

'Don't be. Emily's perfectly fine.'

'You know she's been showing signs of stress,' said Dom. 'The invisible friend with your brother's name. That creepy picture she drew at school –'

'That was ages ago,' I said.

'It isn't the only one, Becks.' He was still concerned, but I sensed a low kind of triumph in his voice. 'I warned you. She's very sensitive. She can tell when things aren't right.'

'Then why didn't you tell me?' I said. 'Why wouldn't *she* tell me?'

'I didn't want to worry you. And maybe she confides in me more.' He opened a cabinet drawer and pulled out a dark-green folder. 'Go on. Have a look,' he said. 'These are the ones I've found so far.'

'Found?'

There were maybe twenty of them. Some in crayon, some in paint, some doodled manically across long strips of what looked like discarded bus-ticket roll. All of them so familiar, in their garish red-and-black, and marked with that name, which haunted me still –

'She was hiding them under her bed. I put them away,' said Dominic.

I stared at the paper in my hand. A piece of butcher's paper of the kind they hand out in primary schools, with the words printed painstakingly underneath. 'But how does she *know* Mr Smallface?' I said. 'I've never even mentioned him.'

Dominic shrugged. 'Kids talk,' he said. 'Maybe it was someone at school. Or maybe your parents said something.'

My wine suddenly tasted vile; sour and metallic. I put down my glass. 'They didn't,' I said. 'She hasn't been to my parents' since –' I cut off the phrase abruptly. She hadn't been to my parents' house since we'd moved in with Dominic. Not because I was afraid of what she might hear, but rather from what she might say to them about our new circumstances. My parents were not the kind of folk who would welcome a man like Dominic. I knew they would think him too old for me; too left-wing; too different from Conrad. Most of all, his racial background would have caused them to comment, I knew. I remembered the day when Conrad came home with an Afro-Caribbean friend. The questions. The comments. The silences.

'My parents are – complicated,' I said.

Dom raised an eyebrow. 'You can say that again, babe.'

I'd only met Dominic's parents once. His mother was an exuberant Trinidadian woman; his father a soft-spoken Yorkshireman. He spoke of his three sisters fondly, but they always seemed to be arguing; plus there were several aunties on his mother's side; a generous handful of cousins, and a grandmother in her nineties, who lived in nearby in Pog Hill. Dominic's siblings fascinated me. Their closeness; their constant squabbling; the way in which their features reflected every generation of their large and chaotic family. All the family I'd ever known was still in that house on Jackson Street; my parents, and the ghost of that boy who has been at my side for so much of my life.

'But Emily isn't the only one who's been acting strangely. *You*'ve been different ever since you started at King Henry's. The nightmares, the insomnia, the fact that you're never quite present. I've been worried about you, Becks.' He took my hand gently between his own, making me want to slap it away. The urge only lasted a moment; then I felt guilty I'd felt it at all. Dom was trying his best, I knew, which made me perversely resentful.

'Please. Listen,' he went on. 'I know why you took the King Henry's job. You wanted to learn about Conrad. You thought that maybe you could find out where he went, all those years ago. That maybe, if you could find out the truth, your parents –'

I stood up abruptly, knocking my glass so that red wine spilt over the tablecloth. 'Lay off the amateur counselling, Dom. I'm not one of your students.'

He looked hurt at that, and I felt a hateful stab of shame.

'I'm sorry. I care about you,' he said.

'Then try believing in me, for a change, instead of assuming I can't cope.' I was close to tears now, and I hated it, and him, too, for seeing them. 'I'll admit it was tough at first. But things are so much better now.' I looked at him. 'I'd hoped that you, of all people, would be happy for me.'

He stood up and put his arms around me. 'I'm sorry,' he said. 'I believe in you. And if you're happy, *I'm* happy.'

I forced myself to try and relax. I could feel his breath against my hair. I knew he was trying to be warm and sincere, but I'd never felt so distant. I've always had that problem, Roy, ever since my childhood. I don't seem to feel things in the way that others do. Things that women are meant to enjoy – candlelit dinners, Valentine's Day, lavish displays of affection – fill me with embarrassment. It all seems so fake. So empty, somehow. So wholly, depressingly meaningless.

'I promise I'll do better,' he said. 'Let's sit down and start again. Tell me all about your day. I promise I'll be supportive.'

It was all I'd wanted to hear, and yet when it came to confiding in him, when it came to *trusting* him, I couldn't tell him about Jerome, or what had happened in the theatre. In the same way I couldn't tell him about what had happened in the boys' toilets, and what had happened to my silk shirt. Most of all I couldn't tell him about the little red satchel, and how it had come back into my life, and how I had brought it home with me in my new attaché case.

Instead, I took his hand and led him upstairs to the bedroom. I've found men never turn down sex – and sex, unlike its sibling, romance, is never mawkish or insincere. Perhaps that's why I prefer it to romantic declarations. Its decent sweat; its rhythm and slap; its ugly, panting honesty. I came twice, and so did he: and I slept like a child until morning.

4

King Henry's Grammar School for Boys, July 8th, 1989

The next day was Saturday, the day of my meeting with Jerome. It was easy to get away; on Saturdays I usually went to see my parents in Malbry. Never for more than an hour at a time, and most of it in a silence that was broken intermittently by the sound of the gurgling pipes and my father's radio, on very low, but perpetually tuned to one of his numbers stations. A ticking clock on the mantelpiece; a smell of unaired laundry; the kettle screaming on the hob. The tea, which was always too milky. Those Bourbon biscuits I hated. The pictures of Conrad everywhere; on the walls, over the mantelpiece. My mother in her dressing gown, my father in his slippers. And the script, repeated so many times that I knew it word-for-word:

You should eat more. You're too thin. You're not on a diet, are you, Becky?

Conrad always eats like a horse. Must be all that running around.

Go on, have a Bourbon. You know they're your favourites.

I could leave early, I told myself, go to meet Jerome at the Thirsty Scholar, then tell Dominic I'd had to deal with some minor household emergency at my parents' – a blocked sink, a broken lock, a pigeon in the water tank – to account for the extra time. Dominic would not question the lie. He was always absurdly trusting. But this time, as soon as I arrived, letting myself in with my key, I sensed an unusual atmosphere. Something had changed since the previous week, something that charged the air like quartz. I could smell it; a lemony scent like sheets that had dried outside in the sun. I could hear it like tinnitus. And most of all, my parents were strangely, eerily energized: my mother in a blue dress, my father in a summer suit I hadn't seen him wear for years. Both were in the kitchen; the table was strewn with utensils. A jar of flour stood open; a bowl of chocolate cake mixture stood ready to be spooned into a pair of lined tins. A window was open above the sink, and the sun was shining onto the tiles, bringing with it a harmless memory of being very small, and of playing under the table in the hazy golden light.

My mother turned as I came in. 'Becky!' she said. Her eyes were bright. She might have been ten years younger than the last time I'd seen her. 'Becky, I'm so glad you're here. I'm making Conrad's birthday cake. Should I ice it in yellow or blue? Blue's his football team, of course, but yellow's his favourite colour.'

I gave an inward sigh. I'd seen my mother like this maybe three or four times over twenty years. Each time, in the few days before Conrad's birthday, and each time, the short but frenzied period of activity had been followed by a sharp decline in cognition. I'm not sure which one hurt the most: the brief illusion of life, or the subsequent silent weeks in bed, the changes of medication, before the drab return to routine. My father, too, was affected, of course, and the hope in his eyes hurt even more than her inevitable relapse. But today, he too was energized: alert; heartbreakingly normal.

'She looks so well today,' he said, drawing me aside under the pretext of making tea. 'She even talked about going to church. Thank God it's happened, Becky. Thank God. I've been waiting so long for this.'

I tried to smile. 'Relax, Dad.'

'Bourbon? I got some in special. The biscuit, not the whisky.' He laughed. It was an old, old childhood joke that hurt my heart like a physical blow.

'No thanks.'

'You're looking well, Rebecca. Teaching suits you. How's it going? And how's little Emily? It's been a while since you brought her to see us.'

That was new, I thought: I couldn't remember either of my parents expressing an interest in my job, and as for my daughter, I was surprised that either of them remembered her name. They certainly never used it – she had always been '*the child*'. I took the cup he offered me. As always, the tea was too milky. And yet that look of awareness in his eyes made my pulse race. Could it be – *could* this time be different?

'You don't mind yellow, do you, love?' That was my mother, with a cup filled with icing sugar. She spooned a little water into the cup, then a drop of food colouring. 'I could make you a pink one too, but yellow works for boys *and* girls.'

'Yellow's fine, thanks, Mum,' I said. 'But I might not be there tomorrow.'

Of course, I'd forgotten our birthday. I usually tried to avoid it. And since the celebrations were always for Conrad anyway, I never found myself sharing the day with them unless it happened to coincide with my weekly visit.

'Oh, but you'll *have* to be there,' she said. 'Now that Conrad's coming home.'

It's never the fall that kills you, I once told my therapist. *It's always the fucking landing.* My parents had been in freefall for years: for years, I had dreaded the moment at which they finally realized Conrad was dead. And yet, without that, I was condemned to an eternal waiting – 'Oh, Mum.' The taste in my mouth was like pennies steeped in brandy. 'We've been through this so many times. Conrad's never coming home. Whatever happened, it's over now. You need to try and –'

'Oh, but he is!' She was laughing now, her face illuminated with joy. 'He's *written* to us, Rebecca. We got the letter yesterday. He's been away for so long, but now, *finally* –'

'No,' I said. 'Please, Mum. Not this again.'

Well, of course, this had happened before. Several times during my adolescence, we'd had letters from people claiming to know – or sometimes, even to *be* – Conrad. Maybe two dozen of them in all, each one a heartbreaking journey of hope and disappointment. Hope is the thing that kills you, Mum. Hope is what breaks when you hit the ground.

My father looked concerned. 'Oh no. This is different. Not like those other chancers. This is our boy, no doubt about that.' He put a warm hand on my arm. 'He even asked after you, love. Asked how little Becks was. Look, I'll show you.'

'Please, Dad, no.'

But my father was already halfway to the living room mantelpiece. There was an envelope there by the clock, under the portrait of Conrad. In seconds, my father was holding it out; a stiff manila envelope, labelled in a strong, round hand.

'Go on. Take it. Read it, love.'

For a moment I wanted to run. To run away and never go back. But that was never my style, Roy. If there was an enemy, I needed to confront him. Of course, it never crossed my mind that the letter could be genuine. I'd been through every scenario, and only one fitted the facts. My brother was dead: most probably abducted by the person my traumatized memory still refused to identify, except as a kind of monster. Children see the world differently. They filter their realities through fairy tales and metaphors. The person I called *Mr Smallface* had been the embodiment of my fear, but *someone* human had triggered that fear: someone real and living.

I took the envelope and turned it over. The postmark was blurry, unreadable. No return address: just ours, correct down to the postcode.

That was interesting, I thought. Most of the letters we'd received had been unconvincing from the start – the postcode absent, the names misspelt. Some had clearly been sent from some kind of institution. I'd come to recognize the style; the thin, cheap paper, the words written in pencil, underscored. Some had asked for money at once. Some had sent messages 'from beyond', claiming Conrad's spirit had contacted them from the afterlife. One had latched on to my father's obsession with numbers stations; claiming they were signals from extra-terrestrials who abducted boys for use in secret experiments. And my parents had received all of these with the same kind of febrile, fluttering hope, even the ones that even I could already tell were fakes.

This one was rather different. Written on a single sheet of creamy letter paper, inside a matching envelope; the hand-writing neat, in fountain pen; the tone both calm and intimate. I read the words:

Dear Mum and Dad,

I've been waiting so long for the right time to send you this letter. There are all kinds of reasons I didn't before. Some are my fault, and I'm sorry. I know how much my going away must have hurt you, and little Becks. I suppose she must be grown up now. I bet she's a proper beauty. I've missed you all so much, you know. I really need you to know that. But life is often very strange, and takes us to strange places. I don't want to tell you too much about that before I meet you face-to-face, but know that I never stopped loving you, or thinking about you. Not ever.

You won't believe all the things I've done since I left home. I've travelled the world. I always said I would, though maybe not in that way. And I've found myself at last – it's a cliché, I know, but I never really knew who I was until I had to learn for myself, the hard way. Dad, I think you'd have been proud to see me pulling myself up by my bootstraps. And you were right: I never did find a career in football. I played a lot – I still do, actually – but it's not what you'd call a stable job. You'll laugh when I tell you what I do, but I promise it's decent, and legal.

I know all this must come as a shock to you all, and I'm not expecting the fatted calf. But I'd love the chance to explain myself, and to see you all again. I've already missed out on so much. Little Becky's graduation. Mum and Dad, your silver anniversary. Now that I'm able to see you again, I'll try to make it up to you. And I hope, that when we meet at last, you'll understand that sometimes things really do work out for the best, and that out of the strong, comes forth sweetness.

All my love till then,
Conrad

I looked at the sheet for a long time, reading and rereading the words. It could have been Conrad at thirty-five, his phrasing more adult; his handwriting more assured. And of course it was not. It couldn't be – but the fact that it was so plausible filled me with grief for my parents. The reference to one of my father's favourite sayings. That was clever, even though it was a very common one. The silver anniversary, too, was a clever, plausible touch. Worst of all was the use of that phrase – the one from the Golden Syrup tin. *Out of the strong came forth sweetness.* Of course it was a coincidence. People buy Golden Syrup every day. And anyone could have been aware of my brother's memorial window. But the fact that Conrad had told me the story of Samson and the lion gave me a kind of chill inside, like looking down a long, dark pipe and seeing a face looking back at me –

I realized I'd dropped the letter. My father bent to pick it up. 'Now you understand,' he said. 'Conrad's back. He's really back. We're going to see him again at last.'

I shook my head, feeling suddenly sick. 'I can't do this again. Please.' I turned to go, not wanting them to see how close I was to tears. 'I can't. I'm really sorry, Dad.'

'But Becky, you haven't finished your tea.'

I shook my head, but did not turn. I heard my mother's voice say: 'Leave her, Stan, she's still upset. Give her some time to get used to it.' My father said something I did not hear, but I heard his footsteps behind me. I moved quickly towards the front door, hoping to avoid him, but I felt a hand on my shoulder, and turned instinctively to face him.

'Becky, please,' he told me. 'Give this one a chance, right? I know it hasn't been easy for you, what with your mother and everything, but this is different. I feel it.'

I wanted to remind him how he'd 'felt' the others, too; including the one later revealed to be from a woman in her fifties claiming to be a medium, to whom he had given eight hundred pounds in exchange for a 'message' from Conrad.

Instead, I took a deep breath. 'Dad, I have to go. I promised Dominic I wouldn't be long.'

'That coloured boy she took up with,' said my mother, from behind me. I could not see her face, but I knew her eyes were hard as agates. 'She hasn't been the same, Stan, not since that job at Sunnybank.'

'That's not where I am anymore,' I said.

'Right, love, you're at Conrad's school. He'll want to hear all about it.'

'Oh, Dad.' I looked at him. 'Please don't get your hopes up again.'

'This time's different,' he said. 'You read the letter. That's Conrad's voice. All these years we've kept the faith. Finally, God sent us a sign.'

I shook my head. 'I can't do this. I can't do this again, Dad.'

'You will,' he said. 'You always come back.' His voice was warm and confident. 'I know you, Becky. You're stubborn,' he said. 'But you'll be back tomorrow. You wouldn't let your mum and me down. You wouldn't miss your birthday.' He put his hand on my arm and gave a sunny, heartbreaking smile. 'Try not to worry, Becky, love. Everything's going to be fine,' he said. 'Everything's going to be fine again. Now that Conrad's coming home.'

5

St Oswald's ~~Grammar School for Boys~~ *Academy*
Michaelmas Term, September 18th, 2006

It's funny, how quickly a person can become institutionalized. Of course, St Oswald's itself is a bubble, in which a perfectly ordinary man can become a Senator merely by dint of surviving a few years longer than his friends. But I feel slightly alarmed at the rate at which, in just a few days, my world has shrunk from the size of an empire to the corner of some foreign field that is forever St Oswald's.

I am still feeling slightly unwell. The palpitations have increased, and my breathing is troublingly laboured. The doctor puts it down to the recent change in my medication, and expects to see an improvement soon. In the meantime, my days have fallen into a comforting routine. I wake at around 5.30, and turn on Radio 4 just in time to hear the daily broadcasts begin. I lie in bed for an hour or two before I get up to make breakfast. A cup of tea and two slices of toast. *Woman's Hour*; *Desert Island Discs*. At lunchtime, Emma comes to bring me my bit of shopping. Half a dozen eggs; a loaf of bread; some currant teacakes; sausages. No Gauloises, though I asked for them; the girl is under orders.

Kitty Teague called once, to bring a bunch of chrysan-themums and a card from the rest of the Department. Dr Devine called round again, ostensibly to bring me some books, but in reality, I suspect, to check for further signs of decay. My day is punctuated by my visits and the wireless. These are my lessons; my free periods; my Breaks. They help me keep track of the passing time. I suppose that, when I finally retire, this is how I shall proceed; gliding listlessly from one radio show to another, stopping for tea at ten-thirty sharp, maybe taking a walk in the park if the weather seems up to it. And then, as regular as the news, La Buckfast's visit at six-thirty.

I like that she is punctual. A Headmaster needs to be punctual. Her dedication to duty, too, is pleasing – though I cannot imagine that she comes to visit me out of anything but a sense of responsibility to an old man long past his prime. And I'll admit that her unfolding narrative has become the highlight of my day.

I have never followed soap operas. Perhaps this is because St Oswald's itself is a kind of long-running drama. Our small but intense community; our comings and goings; our conflicts; our deaths. I have known Masters refuse to speak to each other – sometimes for years – for something as relatively small as taking a colleague's board rubber out of his room without permission. From La Buckfast's story, I guessed how many enemies she must have made during those few weeks in the summer term of 1989 at King Henry's. She was clearly unaware of the extent of the effect she must have had, both on boys and on staff. Young as she was, and with more on her mind than the volatile chemistry of the Languages Department, she would have been as unconscious of the effect she'd caused as a child stepping on an anthill. And yet, I could tell from her story that she must have made quite an impact – on Mcleod, on Sinclair, on Higgs, even on my friend Eric Scoones, although he had tried hard to hide it from me.

But with time on my hands to recall just what he had said to me, I realize now that Eric *did* mention her to me several times, each time with a kind of chilly indignation. I even actually *saw* her once, when I was with Eric in the pub. I'd almost forgotten it until now, but memories gather together like lint, and now I remember it clearly.

The Thirsty Scholar was always a traditional Northern pub. You didn't see many young people there – except, on week-days, our sixth-formers, and some of the Junior Masters. There was always an unwritten rule that Masters and boys should never acknowledge each other, the boys removing their blazers and ties in a pretence of anonymity. At weekends the tap was mostly filled with middle-aged and older men, and to see a young woman – especially one as attractive as Becky Price – was already unusual. In spite of my long and comfortable bachelorhood, I'm not unaffected by female beauty, and even if I had been, Eric's reaction to seeing her would surely have alerted me.

We'd been sitting at a corner table some distance away from the bar. We'd already had a couple of pints, and I was about to suggest we order a ploughman's or something. Then the door opened and Eric stiffened like a dog. 'Dammit, Straits! What's *she* doing here?'

'Who?' I whispered.

'Asda Price.'

I looked at the woman who had come in. Young, in jeans and a sleeveless top, red hair torched by the sunlight. I'll admit I was a little surprised. From Eric's use of that nickname, I'd expected someone older – perhaps a little frumpy. Instead, I saw a woman of the kind I'd only ever seen before in certain Victorian paintings, though without the quiet serenity that seems to come with the territory. Instead, she looked edgy and ill at ease, scanning the bar for someone. I remember the way her hair caught the light through the open door; the graceful curve of her collarbone revealed by the simple neckline.

Eric hid his face with his hand. 'Is nowhere sacred anymore?'

'Oh fine. Drink up and we'll go somewhere else,' I said with some annoyance. Eric could be remarkably over-dramatic at times, and I doubted whether even he believed some of the things he claimed to think. One of these persistent claims was that women worked to undermine our traditional spaces, making it impossible for men to enjoy each other's company. The fact that Miss Price was young, too, must have served to annoy him, because I remember him saying then:

'She's barely older than one of our boys.'

'Give her a chance, Eric,' I said. 'Even you were young once.'

He shrugged. From the height of his forty-eight years, she must have seemed ridiculously young. Now, it is we who seem ridiculous in retrospect. At forty-eight, the world is still new, and rich, and full of promise. At forty-eight, the prospect of old age – sickness, dementia, death – is nothing but the shadow of a summer cloud against the sun.

I don't remember much more of that day. Eric finished his drink and we left, by which time Miss Price had settled down at a table by the door. There was a man sitting with her, but I couldn't tell you anything about him, except that for a moment I felt a fleeting stab of envy. Sometimes a woman will do that to you, a woman you'll never see again.

Except, I *did* see her again, some fifteen or so years later. She has changed of course, and yet I can see the girl she was. Maybe it's hearing her story that makes her come alive again. Or maybe *I'm* the one coming alive, after a long and dismal dream.

I only wish I felt better. I have made an effort to rest; I have taken my medicine; I have avoided fatty foods; I have even forced myself to drink La Buckfast's herbal tea (three times a day, after mealtimes). In spite of all this, the promised recovery does not seem to be forthcoming. She commented on it earlier, when she made her usual call.

'I hope you're taking it easy,' she said. 'I don't like to see you looking so pale. Shall I make some herbal tea?'

'I'd rather have a brandy,' I said.

'Tea,' said La Buckfast firmly. 'And maybe something light to eat?'

I let her make me scrambled eggs. She makes them better than I do, with herbs and a little grain mustard. I wondered briefly how it would feel to have her cook for me every day, to sit with her in the mornings and talk, and listen to the wireless. It was an odd and troubling thought, and very unlike me. I have very few regrets in life, and having avoided marriage has certainly never been one of them. And yet, as I sat in my armchair, watching the lamplight against her hair and the sure, quiet way she handled the utensils – the wooden spoon I'd made as a boy in woodwork class at St Oswald's; the little aluminium pan that once belonged to my mother – I felt a little pang in my heart for a life that might have been. A life of companionship; of shared moments in the kitchen. It lasted a minute or two, no more, and when she turned back with the food on a plate, flanked by two generous slices of toast, I was fully recovered again.

'Thank you, Headmaster. You're very kind.'

'And you're a very stubborn man.' She smiled. 'Mr Straitley, how many times must I ask you to call me Rebecca?'

I took a bite from a piece of toast. She even makes *that* better than I do. 'At least once more, Headmaster,' I said. 'Today – as always – at least once more.'

6

King Henry's Grammar School for Boys, July 8th, 1989

Once more, it is, Mr Straitley. I have to admit I enjoy our routine. The delightful uncertainty that characterized our first interactions has settled into something quieter and more affectionate. He will not betray my confidence now. He wants the rest of the story. And so I can allow myself to confide in him a little more – not *everything*, but nevertheless, more than I'd intended. Nor had I intended to cook – I've never liked domesticity – but there's something about him now that brings out something unexpected in me. Could this be what Dominic felt? The urge to care for someone who is suffering?

After the scene at my parents' house, I wished I hadn't arranged to meet Jerome at the Thirsty Scholar. My immediate impulse was to run back to April Street and tell Dominic all about it; to feel his arms around me again and have him tell me I was safe.

But that would have been too dangerous. Dominic would have welcomed that as a sign that I needed protection. He would have been only too happy, too, to protect me from my parents, my past, my teaching job, even myself – but that would have meant telling him about Jerome, and Scoones, and Sinclair, and the blond boy with the Prefect's badge, and although he *would* have protected me, he would also have placed unbearable pressure on me to leave King Henry's, seek counselling, to go back to my medication –

And so, instead, I went to meet Jerome at the Thirsty Scholar. How strange to find out that you were there too – though of course I didn't know you then. I suppose you were in your element, though; the Scholar is filled with bookshelves. It even *smells* like St Oswald's, somehow: a smell I associate with old books, chalk and centuries of dust. An *old* smell. Even older than the smell of King Henry's. I noticed Scoones, sitting in a corner with another man – *you*, Roy – looking irked and uncomfortable. There was as yet no sign of Jerome.

I found a place to sit by the bar, as far as I could away from Scoones, and waited, trying not to look as if I wanted company. Three men – all of a certain age – asked me if I wanted a drink, in spite of the fact that I already had a full glass of Coke in front of me; but five minutes later Jerome came in, and my would-be admirers melted away.

He saw me sitting at the bar and greeted me with a cheery smile. He was wearing the same blazer as the previous day, this time over stone-washed jeans and a plain white T-shirt.

'Can I get you a drink?' he said.

'Thanks, I'm fine.' I shook my head.

'Because you look like maybe you need a bit of something stronger than Coke.'

I looked at him. I knew his type; I'd met a lot of them before. Good-looking; athletic; outspoken; with that awkward, bluff good cheer that so often comes with having been largely unused to female company during the formative years. It is a form of behavioural over-compensation that reflects a boyhood spent in studying women from afar, as if they were a kind of rare bird, to be collected and noted down, rather than interacted with. The staff of King Henry's was filled with men of this type; men like Higgs, who eyed me lecherously from a distance, and men like Scoones, who glared at me openly as if they couldn't believe my impertinence at daring to enter their space at all. Jerome was playing it cool, but I could see how hard he was trying to look as if he wasn't watching those *other* men, watching him with the pretty girl. But I knew that look on his face, and I knew that in a minute he would order a vodka for my Coke, as if I were a child whose desires could be overridden.

I'm not at all vain. Really, I'm not. Even then, when I turned heads, I found my beauty an impediment that by far outweighed the small advantage it gave me. I never wore makeup. I tried not to wear clothes that emphasized my figure. None of it made any difference to the catcalls, the propositions, the compliments. None of it made me feel safe, or gave me the comfort I needed. And yet men – and even some women, too – seemed to think I ought to feel grateful. After all, isn't beauty what every woman really wants? The chance to be seen, to be wanted by men, regardless of whether *she* wants *them*? Since entering my forties, I find I have become less visible. After the mastectomy, I refused to get implants, which means that men now look me in the face instead of a few inches lower. I do not miss my breasts at all. I like the sensation of freedom. I like the fact that I can wear suits. I have become the kind of woman who used to be referred to as 'handsome'. Thinking back to who I was, I wish I could have told her then: *This will pass. The smirking looks. The men who think they know better. In less than ten years, you'll be free. Of him. Of them. Of everyone.*

'Pop a vodka in there, love?' That was Jerome, as predicted, handing my glass to the girl at the bar.

She took it without comment and poured in a measure of Smirnoff. A girl a little younger than me, with a barmaid's smile, all teeth and no eyes. I wondered if she disliked him as much as I was starting to; or whether *I* was the one she disliked. Maybe she hated both of us.

I took the vodka and Coke. 'Thanks.' I needed to keep him on my side, at least until he had told me what I needed to know. He might have known Conrad or his friends; might even have seen something without realizing its importance. 'I really appreciate this chat,' I said. 'I haven't found it easy to settle down at King Henry's.'

He gave me a smile that doubtless was meant to be sympathetic. 'Oh, I can imagine,' he said. 'It's not at all the kind of place I would have expected to find someone like you.'

Hardly a flattering thing to say, although, to be fair, the man was right. I smiled and drank some more of my vodka and Coke. It tasted vaguely metallic, as if the barmaid had added a handful of change.

'Why *did* you come to King Henry's?' he said. 'What were you hoping to find there?' His voice was friendly enough, but I thought he was laughing at me. 'I heard you made quite an entrance,' he said. 'Managed to upset both Sinclair *and* Scoones before you'd even been there a day.'

This meeting had been a mistake, I thought. I could already tell that Jerome wasn't going to tell me anything about Conrad. Instead, he was trying to make me feel ill at ease and insecure. It might even be his way of trying to be charming, I thought. Some men like to put women down: they think that kind of bullying makes them more attractive.

Jerome put a hand on my bare arm and leant in closer to talk to me. 'I did a little research,' he said. His voice was low and confiding. 'I thought there was something odd in the way you talked about that murdered boy. Conrad Price. You're Becky.'

I felt something tighten around my heart, which I recognized as anger. 'Did Scoones tell you that?'

Jerome looked surprised. 'Scoones? No. I looked you up at the library,' he said. 'That book, *The Lost Boy of Malbry*. There's a whole chapter in there, just on you.'

'Oh,' I said in a small voice. 'Of course. I'd almost forgotten.'

Jerome looked sympathetic. 'I imagine you'd want to,' he said. 'But you were so young. It must have been hell. Is that why you came to King Henry's? Because that's where he disappeared?'

I shook my head. 'I don't know. I wanted to remember.'

'And did you?' I thought his voice trembled a little.

I might have misjudged him, I thought. That self-assurance was a façade. What I had said had touched him. He was trying to be kind.

'Little things,' I told him. 'Little things that don't make much sense. Of course I was hoping for more. But I'm broken. I'll always be broken.'

It was an extraordinary thing for me to say to a stranger. On the other hand, maybe it was *because* he was a stranger that I'd dared to say it so plainly. I would never have said such a thing to Dominic. Dominic would have cared too much. Dominic would have used it in his ever-growing armoury.

'I'm sorry,' I said. 'I shouldn't be unloading my private life on you. But I've had a horrible day so far, and I can't tell my partner about it, and everything feels like it's falling down, and now today, my parents –'

And I told him about my visit to my parents, and the letter from 'Conrad' they'd received; the final blow to my self-esteem in a series of attacks.

'I thought all that would be over by now,' I said, and sipped at my second drink (he'd placed it quietly by my side, and it was far stronger than the first). 'I thought that, after all these years, at least people might leave us alone.'

Jerome took my hand. There was a crease between his eyes that made him look almost close to tears. 'You shouldn't say that, Rebecca,' he said. 'I can tell you're incredibly strong. Danny Higgs said –' He broke it off, looking suddenly mortified. 'Well, never mind. Danny Higgs is an idiot, and he doesn't know what he's talking about.'

I looked at him. 'You can tell me,' I said. 'Go on. What did Higgs call me?'

Jerome cleared his throat and lowered his voice even further. 'He said you were *a stone-cold bitch*. I'm sorry. But you wanted to know.'

I had to laugh. It was the first time I'd *really* laughed in days. I laughed until my eyes watered, then finished my vodka and Coke in a shot. 'Praise, from the cut-price *Magnum* man,' I said, with another peal of slightly hysterical laughter.

Jerome looked around in a hunted way. Several people were staring at us. The Thirsty Scholar was not the kind of place where women laughed aloud. I noticed that Eric Scoones and his friend had gone at some point during our conversation, and felt a little better.

I said: 'I'm sorry. Really. I shouldn't laugh. But I've tried so hard to fit in at King Henry's, and this is *by far* the best compliment I've heard from anyone at the place –' I broke off, laughing helplessly.

Jerome sighed. 'It must be tough. King Henry's isn't what you'd call an inclusive environment. But they're not really such a bad crowd. Sinclair's a stiff old bugger, but I remember him being a decent sort when I was a boy. And Higgs – that's just banter. Locker room talk. Maybe –' He paused. 'Now *here*'s a thought. Maybe I can help you. It must be so hard to concentrate on trying to remember the past, as well as doing a new job, and dealing with the less civilized elements of the Department.'

I laughed again. 'You could say that.'

'So maybe – if we went there alone, some time after the end of term – we could visit the school together. Just walk down the corridors and into the hall, and the chapel and the refectory; see if anything you see or hear sparks off a buried memory?'

I was starting to like the man. And yes, it was a good idea. 'You'd do that?' I said.

'Of course. If it helps.'

I nodded. 'Yes, I think it might.'

'Good,' he said. 'Then we have a date. I'll have a word with the Porter. Shall we say – next Saturday? At ten?'

For a moment I held his gaze. 'You did know Conrad, didn't you?'

He looked at me and nodded.

'Why didn't you tell me you were friends?'

He looked away. 'I'm sorry. I know. I should have told you sooner. But Conrad –' He paused, and I thought I saw a shadow flicker over his face. 'Conrad wasn't exactly a *friend*. I'm not sure Conrad *had* friends.'

'What do you mean?' I said.

He shrugged. 'Conrad was – difficult. Vengeful. You never knew what he was thinking. He had a way of hiding a grudge and taking it out on you later.'

'Oh. Really?' I was surprised. A lifetime of stories about Conrad – his goodness, his popularity – meant that I'd never considered that he might have been anything different. And the thought that my brother could have been – what was it? *Difficult. Vengeful* – filled me with a kind of guilt. How could I believe such a thing? Conrad was my brother. After all, he'd been looking after me the day he'd disappeared – you might even say that if it wasn't for me, he might not have disappeared at all.

How much do you love me, Becks? How much?

This much!

'I'm sorry,' said Jerome again. 'I shouldn't have said that. Don't be upset.'

'I'm not upset.' I was aware that my face was flushed, and that my heart was racing. 'I don't remember much about my brother, really. Thank you for your help. In fact, I'd like to hear more about him. It might help recover my memories.'

He nodded. 'All right. See you Saturday?'

I smiled. 'Saturday it is.'

7

July 9th, 1989

I awoke the next morning from a dream of falling to the sounds
of activity downstairs. Dominic was already up – unusual for
a Sunday – and the scent of roasted coffee filtered through the
half-open door. I sat up in bed and checked the time. It was
only 9.30.

I was about to get up to see what was happening in the
kitchen, when Emily came dancing in, closely followed by
Dominic, carrying a breakfast tray. 'Happy birthday, Mummy!'
she said. 'Dom and I made French toast!'

'French toast, orange juice, freshly ground coffee,' said
Dom. 'And after that, a birthday surprise, because we have
some catching up to do.'

He placed the tray by the bedside and kissed me on the
top of the head. 'Happy birthday, Becks.'

I was too surprised to react. He knew I didn't celebrate
birthdays. It had been hard for him to grasp – his sister Victoria
had turned forty in January, and the celebrations had spanned a
whole week, including a weekend in Paris, and a family party
that I'd had to miss due to a bout of stomach flu. Dominic
had always believed my illness was psychological. He himself

loved parties, and felt that if only I could bring myself to put aside my anxiety, then I would be halfway to being cured of all my childhood trauma.

'Thank you, Dom,' I said at last. 'I didn't expect any of this.'

'There's more,' he said, grinning. 'I've booked the gang in at the Shanker's Arms for lunch. We're throwing you a party!'

The Shanker's Arms was the Sunnybank pub, which Dominic liked because it was where his chapter of the Labour Party had their meetings. I'd been there a few times, though politics wasn't really my scene. Dark wood; a pool table; dart boards; a lot of old miners' lamps hanging from the ceiling; some portraits of local celebrities by an artist called Frazer Pines who specialized in regional history. And a little suite of party rooms at the top of the building, which Dominic had hired for what he, no doubt, would have thought of as a 'little gathering'.

'A party?' I repeated.

'Just a small one. The family. And a few friends and colleagues from Sunnybank Park. Open bar, disco, balloons – trust me, you're going to love it.'

I tried to summon a smile. That was Dominic in a nutshell. So kind, yet so lacking in empathy. His celebration sounded to me like a list of everything I feared. Noise; a crowd; the smell of beer; music blaring through speakers. Balloons, streamers, inedible cake, a drunken round of 'Happy Birthday to You'.

I wondered if I was being snobbish. My parents would find all this vulgar. But Dominic embraced it all with a childlike enthusiasm. He was so excited, so pleased with himself and his birthday surprise for me. I couldn't disappoint him, I thought. I had to go along with it. I thought of the way he had worked on Emily over the past few weeks. The board games, the cooking, the weekend away. The expensive new bicycle. *This is how he does it*, I thought. *This is how he gets us to change.*

'What about Emily?' I said.

'She'll be fine. It's a private do. She's just not allowed in the tap room.' He put his hands on my shoulders and smiled. 'You'll see. It's going to be great, Becks. The gang are all dying to meet you. Now eat up your breakfast, and get frocked up. We're going to show you a fabulous time.'

8

King Henry's Grammar School for Boys, July 9th, 1989

The day my brother disappeared, I was meant to be having a party. A party all of my own, the first I would not share with Conrad. Of course, the party was cancelled when Conrad failed to come home with me. Emily came with a present, but my parents sent her away. The cake, with its pink-and-white icing, stood in the pantry for over a month until my father threw it away. All our presents and birthday cards – including the one from Emily – were left on top of the wardrobe, forever unopened, gathering dust. And it was another three months before I was able to see Emily again; I had been ill, and my parents thought it best for her to stay away.

Looking back, I realize that my parents had never approved of Emily: she came from a working-class family, and her accent was common. And her sister made them uncomfortable. To them, to have an imperfect child was the worst thing a parent could endure. And yet Teresa's parents seemed to love her all the same – a child who would never make them proud by bringing home a trophy, or write them a letter from summer camp, or wave to them from the football field. I sometimes think perhaps that was why I was such a disappointment to them. Because now I was imperfect, too. Because I had been damaged.

It took me a long time to understand what form that damage had taken. I looked the same; I *felt* the same; and yet something had been taken away. It wasn't simply the stolen pieces of my memory; whatever it was went deeper. As I grew I began to feel it like an absence in my heart: a numb place where there should have been the ability to love.

How much do you love me, Becks?

This much!

And yet I don't remember how it felt to love him. I remember saying the words – my parents made sure of *that* – but where the feeling should have been, there's only that sink hole in my heart, a sink hole that has swallowed up not only my memories but the part of me that was able to love. There's no point pretending otherwise: I don't feel much for people. Not for my parents, or Emily, or Dominic, or anyone. Mr Smallface took that away the day he took my brother. I used to think it might come back; but it never did, although I learnt to fake it well enough to persuade the men in my life.

Emily sensed something, though. She knew something was missing. Perhaps that's why she loved Dominic. Perhaps that's why she had chosen my brother as her invisible friend.

How much do you love me, Becks?

He had a way of hiding a grudge and taking it out on you later.

I remembered Jerome's words with a kind of furtive guilt. The thought that Conrad might have been something other than lovable seemed almost sacrilegious. More disturbing still was that momentary sense of *recognition* I'd felt at his words; that feeling of overhearing something that I wasn't allowed to hear.

Shhhh. We don't want to get caught.

Are you sure it's safe?

Shh.

Voices from a haunted room. Voices from –

The sink hole.

I pushed away the breakfast tray. My cup of coffee had gone cold. Although it was July, my skin had come up in hectic goosebumps. The metallic taste was back in my mouth, and there was a ringing in my ears, as if from a bump on the head. The memory was small, but clear, like something glimpsed through a long, dark pipe. And the voices were clearer, too; as if a blockage had shifted.

Come on, man. She's just a kid.

It's only a joke. Lighten up, man.

I got up and grabbed the first dress I could find in the wardrobe I shared with Dom. It was green, with thin straps, one of Dominic's favourites. I paired it with Dr Martens boots; a choice that Dom's mother would no doubt deplore, but which made me feel more at ease. I brushed my hair and tied it back, leaving my face without make-up, and felt a little better, though my mouth still tasted like pennies.

Some memories will do that, Roy. They lie in wait under the surface. I hadn't thought of Conrad's friends since I was a little girl. Maybe it was the prospect of having a birthday party, but suddenly the memory was almost close enough to touch. A memory, but of what?

I sat on the side of the unmade bed and looked at the tray Dom had brought me. Coffee; orange juice; French toast. A pink rose in a jam jar. The toast had gone cold. I tried a piece. It was too sweet, too greasy. Dominic always made French toast with far too much Golden Syrup.

From downstairs I heard the sound of Dominic washing the dishes. The pipes gave a sudden, clunking groan, then a croak that was almost a word.

Water pressure, that's all it is, I told myself automatically. *There are no monsters in the drain, or lurking in the toilet bowl. No Mr Smallface, watching me.*

I went to the sink to wash my hands. I looked into the plughole. There was a clump of long hair snarled into the chrome grid: Emily's, probably, or Dom's. Gingerly, with my fingernails, I tried to pull out the clump of hair before it clogged the drain: it came, but it was far longer than I'd thought, longer and matted with debris and scum, and under the black slime that coated it, I realized the hair was my own.

And then, as if the memory had been attached to the plug of hair, came the sound of my brother's voice, close enough to be shocking: *That's where he lives. In the sink hole. That's where he takes the children.*

And the old and long-buried memory came gushing out like a blockage from a pipe, and I found myself falling into the dark, like Alice down the rabbit hole.

9

King Henry's Grammar School for Boys, July 9th, 1989

Like so many Northern coal-mining towns, Malbry has had its tragedies. Ours was the 1924 Smarthwaite Colliery Disaster, which claimed the lives of thirty-two men and boys, after an inrush of water from some older, unmapped workings flooded the tunnels and collapsed the main shaft, trapping the miners underground.

My father said he remembered it, though he must have been very young at the time; the thunderous rumbling under the earth, the keening of women in the streets. And later, over the next few days, hearing voices from under the ground, voices that already sounded like ghosts. Not all the men died at once, he said: a handful of them survived for some days in a dwindling pocket of air, but all attempts to reach them failed, and later, the mine was abandoned.

Nowadays there's nothing much left, except for some local ghost stories, blocked tunnels and the raised bed of the railway line that once led to the colliery, joining the edge of St Oswald's fields to the woods behind King Henry's. It runs through a deep cutting, through which runs a tunnel just over a mile in length, now long since filled in, its entrance overgrown with drifts of bramble and rosebay willowherb.

For Conrad and his friends, the site was a playground all the more attractive for being strictly forbidden. The tunnel was still accessible then, as was the air vent above it, which looked like a tiny castle on top of the ridge. And if you were lucky and dug around, you could sometimes turn up a souvenir – a discarded pit tag, a nail from a boot, a broken lamp, a snap tin. When the weather in summer was dry, the grass that covered the discarded site would go brown and shrivel in patches, revealing the shape of the earthworks and the path of the tunnels that had collapsed. Even as far as St Oswald's fields, there were signs of subsidence, especially in the corner down the far side of the rugby pitch, where there was a stubborn little lake, which shrank during the summer months, and spread over the winter.

There was a persistent smell too; sour and vaguely ominous. By dint of yearly deliveries of topsoil and grit, the place was made sound, and the sour smell finally disappeared – at least until Johnny Harrington declared the site a perfect location for the Gunderson Building – which shows how much he *really* knew about St Oswald's history.

Of course, my brother would have known all about the dead miners. When my father was a boy it was common to hear of ghostly voices from underground, or to see the local ha'nts, including the infamous Trapper-Lad, reputedly a ten-year-old boy who perished in the tunnel collapse. And of course, the village was filled with reminders of the disaster. They lived on as street names, monuments and the names of pubs. Even St Oswald's library bears the name of the owner of Smarthwaite Pit, and now, as the memory returned, I remembered his face, and the way he looked down at me like something from a nightmare.

I must have been four, maybe four and a half, the first time I went to St Oswald's. My mother was excited. Conrad was in his school chess team, and had been selected to play against the St Oswald's Middle School champion in the regional quarter finals. My mother drove us both to the school, and brought me to the library, where the chess matches were held, with instructions to be quiet, and wait on a little chair by the door, under a big old portrait of a bearded man in black.

I remember the smell of the library. The smell of old books, and polished wood, and dust, and damp, and mildew. I remember the boys in uniform, sitting face-to-face at their desks, with Conrad sitting to one side, in a patch of sunlight. Several St Oswald's Masters in gowns oversaw the proceedings, and there was a section at the back with refreshments for the parents. A kind-looking Master with a red face brought me a chess set to play with. I remember the little horses and the little pointy hats. I remember taking them onto the floor and making them gallop on the wood. I was so absorbed in play that I failed to see Conrad's look of annoyance, or hear him say *Shhh!* at the tiny sound of the pieces on the polished floor. Mother was having a cup of tea in the parents' area, and when I looked up, Conrad was there. He had already finished his game, and his face was hard and set.

'Get up. We're going,' he said.

I hurried to pick up the little chess pieces from the floor. Conrad kicked at them savagely, making them skitter over the boards. 'Hurry *up!*' He kept his voice low, but I could tell he was furious. 'You always ruin everything,' he said. '*I* should have won that game.' And then he looked up at the portrait above me, and said: '*He*'s watching you. He knows when you've done something bad. And he knows where to find you.'

I looked up at the portrait of that bearded man in black. I'd been so absorbed in my game that I had barely noticed him before. But now I could see him looking at me; his eyes like holes in the canvas –

'Who is he?' I said.

And Conrad grinned, and whispered:

'Mr Smallface.'

IO

King Henry's Grammar School for Boys, July 9th, 1989

Of course, that's not what he *really* said. But memory is a dangerous thing, promising much, but delivering nothing more than fragments and dreams. The name he whispered meant nothing to me, and so in my mind *Mr Smarthwaite* became *Mr Smallface*, which in turn became the monster that was to haunt my dreams for so long, and still periodically winks at me from the occasional plughole or drain.

And Conrad was relentless. He stoked my fear incessantly. His anger at losing that chess match had turned into something vengeful. Everything that frightened me was ascribed to Mr Smallface. Shadows; the dark; the wind in the trees; but most of all, the sucking sounds of water pipes and gurgling drains. Whenever a toilet flushed, or a pipe rattled, or a plughole sucked noisy water into a drain, I knew that Mr Smallface was there: always aware, always hungry.

I started to wet the bed again, after almost a year of being dry. I had nightmares, in which Mr Smallface pursued me through a series of ever-decreasing pipes. I piled books onto the toilet seat in case he came up through the drains. I had been a combative child: but now, the threat of the monster ensured my co-operation.

Do as you're told, Becks, or Mr Smallface will know.

Brush your teeth like a good girl. Mr Smallface is watching you.

I know. If it sounds cruel, it was. But at that age, such casual cruelties are part of our everyday business. And children are like house cats: they lead astonishing double lives. Inside the home, they are docile; sometimes even affectionate. Outside, they are alien things, predatory and merciless.

He's so good with his sister, my parents would say adoringly. *You wouldn't have thought a teenage boy would cope so well with a four-year-old.*

And Conrad, smirking, would look at me and cover the bottom half of his face with his hands; a code sign that only I understood.

If you tell anyone, he'll know. I won't be able to save you. He'll come up out of the drains and drag you underground by your hair.

And then, one day, Conrad and his friends had taken me to the railway bank, where the land had slumped and shrugged and dropped and fallen into the cutting. From the top, you could still see the half-closed mouth of the tunnel; and above it, along the ridge, the vent they called the Pepper Pot. I remember them climbing the brick-built sides, and looking down into the dark, where the earth seemed to be draining away like water down a plughole. And I remembered Conrad's voice, saying:

That's where he lives. In the sink hole. That's where he takes the children.

And for eighteen years that memory, and what came next, had stayed in hiding in my mind. For eighteen years the door to the past had stayed shut, keeping the truth inside. And then, on my birthday, eighteen years to the day after Conrad disappeared, that narrow door had opened up like a sink hole in the ground: releasing the past like a swarm of bees. All from a piece of French toast, drenched in Golden Syrup: *Out of the eater came forth meat: and out of the strong came forth sweetness.*

Why that moment, I wonder? I've never really understood. Perhaps it was my talk with Jerome, or the troubling scene at my parents', or the stress of having to hide it all from Dominic; but, in any case, here came a memory, bringing with it the dusty smell of St Oswald's library, and the sour dark scent of the sink hole, and the sound of the pipes in my parents' house, and the picture of Mr Smarthwaite. Memory and, with it, a surprising realization. I'd always believed that my five-year-old self worshipped my big brother. My parents had always told me so, and I had always believed them. His image on the mantelpiece looked down at me like the face of God, dominating my childhood. He was in our prayers every night; my parents spoke of nothing but him. And over the years my brother had come to embody every quality I lacked. He was grown up; clever; good at sports; outgoing; popular; good-looking. Most of all, he was a boy. Boys achieved things. Girls did not. If they were pretty (and good, of course), they married well. But I was not good. I had shamed the family, first by getting pregnant, and then for *taking up with that coloured boy.*

But here it was at last, the truth; perhaps too late to serve me now, but strong and undeniable. A truth even my therapist had never managed to extract; a truth that had been left for years untouched, like a flooded mine shaft, until one day the wall was breached, and the knowledge came rushing through; deadly; dark; unstoppable. Conrad, my brother, my hero; my friend; the angel at our table; the martyr; the one too good for this world –

I'd hated him.

PART 5

Styx
(River of Hate)

I

July 9th, 1989

Memory is like a young child: it is immensely suggestible. It is coloured by feelings; dreams; other people's convictions. And, like its friend, the subconscious, it loves to deal in metaphor, so that Memory often leaves home dressed in a sensible outfit, and returns in a tutu and fairy wings, with its face painted like a tiger.

Throughout my childhood and adolescence, I'd believed that my memories of Conrad were real: but now, I began to realize that the truth had been overwritten by years and years of guilt, suggestion, mythology. The brother I knew was not the boy whose face hung over the mantelpiece, flanked with a pair of candles and a little vial of water from Lourdes. He was not the boy the press had described – handsome, popular, loved by all. Throughout my childhood, he had stood, monolithic, over me. Now I saw him for what he was: cruel; petty; bullying.

Now that the dam was broken at last, I remembered all kinds of incidents, tricks and childish cruelties. The times he'd locked me in the bathroom and threatened me with Mr Smallface; the times he'd lied to my parents, and taken me with him to hang out with his friends by St Oswald's playing fields, or along the old railway, or smoking down by the Clay Pits, while he claimed to be taking me to the playground, or the park, or the children's library.

It occurred to me that the boy I'd seen on my first day – the blond boy with the Prefect's badge – might have been my subconscious mind, trying to make me see the truth. The fact that I hadn't recognized Conrad was wholly understandable: through the lens of my memory he had been unrecognizable. But as a teacher, I'd seen him at last without the rose-coloured spectacles – as a grinning little shit, no different from any other disruptive pupil.

If only you'd been on the scene then, Roy. You might have helped me work it out. But all I had at the time were Scoones and Sinclair and Carrie Macleod – and now, Jerome. And although the truth about Conrad had been a private epiphany, I still had no further memory of what had really happened to him, or what his last words to me had been, or of what – if anything – I had seen on the day he disappeared. But maybe Jerome could help me, I thought. His suggestion made sense. If the wall of my hidden past was beginning to give way, then anything – a scent, a word – might trigger another inrush of memories.

'Becks? Are you nearly ready?' That was Dominic, from downstairs.

I looked at my untouched breakfast tray. The thought of eating anything made me feel suddenly nauseous.

'Just a minute!' I called cheerily, and set about looking for how to dispose of my birthday breakfast. Thankfully, the bedroom had its own adjacent bathroom. I poured the orange juice down the sink, followed by the coffee. The drain gave a little hiccup, but seemed to accept the offering. The French toast was more of a problem; eventually, I tore it into small pieces, and flushed them down the toilet. It took three flushes to get rid of them all, as well as half a bottle of bleach, but finally, the evidence was gone.

'Becks? Are you OK?'

'Of course.' I opened the bedroom door. 'I just wanted to look my best for when I meet your family.'

He grinned. 'I know. They can be a bit much,' he said. 'But they're all going to love you. They just need the chance to see you in a – *relaxed* environment.'

A relaxed environment. I suddenly felt like laughing. I'd met Dom's parents once for a meal at a local restaurant, as well as two of his sisters and their respective husbands, but it had *not* been a relaxed environment, and I had spent most of the time in a state of acute anxiety. Dom's family was a close one, but their way of expressing affection seemed to consist mostly of teasing, shouting, squabbling and violent recriminations for a series of childhood incidents.

It was so different to what I had known that I had kept almost silent throughout the meal, provoking the comment from Dominic's Ma: 'Not much of a talker, is she, Dom?'

It was not a promising start; and missing Victoria's birthday had not helped repair the damage. I feared that Dominic's family had found me very dull, or worse, thought that I considered myself too good for them. Of course Dom had denied this, but I didn't believe him.

'I told them you were shy,' he'd said. 'And – I hope you don't mind – but I also told Ma about your therapy, and that business with your brother. No one's going to bring it up, I swear,' he went on quickly. 'I just wanted everyone to know you've been through a lot, and it isn't your fault, and how sweet and wonderful you can be when you let your defences down.'

Of course, he never realized how little he had ever seen of what was behind my defences. I'd lied to him from the very start; our time together was woven through with bright threads of betrayal. But Dominic was a simple man, and assumed that everyone was equally so.

He saw the empty breakfast tray on the dressing table, and smiled. 'Was it good?'

'Delicious,' I said.

He kissed me. I could smell his cologne, and the memory of the joint he'd smoked the previous night before going to bed. And I *wanted* to please him: I wanted to be the trusting girl he thought I was; sweet-toothed, eating my French toast, excited at the prospect of my very own birthday party.

'I can't wait till you open your presents,' he said. 'Emily made you a special card. Word of warning; Ma *always* knits these terrible jumpers for birthdays. I tried to persuade her not to this time, but she's asked me three times what colours you like, so I'm guessing no luck. Estelle will probably bake something. Victoria likes gadgets, so expect something weird, an electric carving knife or a battery-powered back massager, or something. And Myra – you haven't met her yet. She's your age. She's dying to meet you.' He paused. 'Sorry, I'm just so excited. You're finally meeting all the gang.'

The gang, I thought. It conjured up images of childhood, and school, and of Conrad and his three friends. I had never been in a gang. I had never understood those books in which groups of wholesome children went off on exciting adventures. My childhood had been very different; an airless, glassy cabinet in which I had been on display for years, staring at the world outside in silent, sullen disbelief; flawlessly lifelike, and yet refusing stubbornly to perform, like a clever automaton lacking the key to make it work.

Automatically, I said: 'I'm really looking forward to it.'

'Of course you are. Emily, too. I told her to wear something nice.'

Once more I smiled. A woman's smile, I've found, has many advantages. It makes us look unthreatening, approving, happy and sincere. Men prefer women who smile. I've even had men stop me in the street and tell me I should smile more. My body has never really been mine: I simply adorn and take care of it for the passing attention of men. Or at least that was true twenty years ago: now, my body is mine again, like a plaything wrested from a child by an older sibling, to be returned at some later date; broken; no longer of interest. At six years old, my daughter was learning that lesson early. *Wear something nice.*

'And *here* she is!'

She was wearing a pink dress that Dominic had bought her. It was supposed to be a dressing-up outfit from some kind of Disney movie, slightly frayed at the hem, and a little tight in the shoulders. On her feet were her Pooh wellingtons, and on her head, a knitted hat.

I smiled. Perhaps the lesson had not been learnt as thoroughly as I'd thought.

'Aren't you warm with that hat on?' I said.

Emily shook her head silently, looking so guilty I immediately knew that there was something wrong.

'Let me see,' I said gently.

Silently, Emily shook her head.

Dom gave her a warm smile. 'Come on, Milly,' he said. 'What's wrong? You look just like a princess. Princesses don't wear old woolly hats on their lovely shiny hair.'

Emily looked stricken, and I saw tears begin to gather in her eyes. Dom held out his arms to her. 'What is it, darling?'

She pulled off the hat. Underneath, her hair was cut raggedly short; so short in places that I could see the baby pink of her scalp.

'Sweetheart, your *hair*!' I could see that Dom was genuinely distressed. 'Why did you cut it? What did you use? You could have really hurt yourself!'

Emily began to sob. 'I had to,' she said. 'He lives in the drains. He can reach up and pull you in.'

A sudden *muted* sensation, like the feeling you get in your ears when a train goes into a tunnel. The current reality seemed to dim, eclipsed by another memory: myself in my parents' bathroom, books pinning down the toilet seat; red curls falling to the floor. My parents' voices, coming from a place deep underwater:

Why does she do these things, Dad? What on earth is wrong with her?

Don't worry, love. It's only hair.

I said, in a voice that sounded very small and distant: 'Who told you that, Emily?'

Then came her voice, even further away; very small but somehow *charged*, like lightning in a bottle, and doubled, like the echo of a child's voice in a tunnel:

It was Conrad. Conrad told – Conrad. Conrad told me.

2

St Oswald's ~~Grammar School for Boys~~ *Academy*
Michaelmas Term, September 21st, 2006

I awoke this morning with a pounding headache and a sudden, violent longing for my favourite St Oswald's mug. Now that we are an Academy, this piece of St Oswald's ephemera – like those old Prep Diaries – has become something of a rarity. I started to get up, but as soon as I did, the world tilted and I half fell, bumping my knee against the floor. Pain flared, alarmingly keen. Surprising – I should know better. But how little we expect Time's inevitable changes. I suppose we all feel immune to them somehow, as if age would pass us by. Even now I find that I can look into the mirror and see, instead of a man of sixty-six, a schoolboy with an impish face and an astonishing shock of grey hair. My mother, in her dementia years, must have experienced something similar. I often used to find her sitting by the window, looking blankly at the glass.

'That old woman's there again,' she would say. 'Always trying to get in.'

It took me some time to understand she was speaking of her reflection. I wonder what image of herself *she* saw in the mirror.

When I reached the kitchen, I found that the mug was missing. Going over recent events, I remembered I'd left it in my desk. Damn it. There's something about a favourite mug that makes even herbal tea taste more palatable. After an unsatisfactory dose of La Buckfast's hawthorn-liquorice concoction, served in one of my mother's undersized cups, I finally picked up the phone and dialled Kitty Teague's direct number.

'German Department.' The voice on the line was definitely *not* that of Miss Teague.

'Straitley!'

'Why, Dr Devine. Occupying the French again?' A long-running rivalry over office space has existed between us for many years. In fact, a couple of years ago he even managed to temporarily annexe the Latin office, although the victory was short-lived. Even Johnny Harrington failed to repurpose my office, and when my time comes, I shall haunt it, with strange, damp smells, and eerie sounds, and pointed quotes from Cicero.

Dr Devine made the kind of sniffing sound he makes when confronted with a boy who misuses the Perfect Subjunctive. 'You sound peaky, Straitley,' he said. 'Perhaps you should be lying down.'

'*Qui se ultro morti offerant . . .*' I said, aware that I had forgotten the rest of the quotation. Damn this illness; it makes my head feel as soft as a rotten apple. I made my voice especially crisp. 'Well, while you're on the line, perhaps you could ask the Sixth-Form girl, Emma Wicks, to bring me a few things I left in my desk? My copy of Catullus's *Condolences*; my green file of Upper Sixth course work, and –' I left a cunning pause, to ensure that he would not guess the true reason behind my call. 'Oh, while you're at it, my St Oswald's mug. It should be in the second drawer.'

Dr Devine made that sound again. 'Anything else, Straitley? Liquorice Allsorts, or maybe a personal massage from the Head?'

'Not for the moment, thank you,' I said. 'And since she *is* the Head, perhaps you could refrain from the crude allusions?'

There was a small and sniffy pause. 'Well,' said Devine, 'I knew you were ill, but this is concerning. Since when were you and the Head so close?'

I ignored the gibe. 'Just tell the Wicks girl not to forget. I'll probably be back next week. I need to prepare for my lessons.'

I sat rather heavily in my kitchen chair. In spite of the herbal remedy's supposed relaxing benefits, I could feel my heart beating distressingly fast, and with that little fluttering – like the wings of a tiny moth – that never seems to go away. It must have been because I'd skipped breakfast, but my head felt soft and swimmy.

I heard Devine's tinny voice down the line. 'Straitley? Are you still there?'

I tried to reply, but once more I fell – this time, more heavily – onto the floor. And that is where she found me, twenty minutes later; conscious, but unable to rise, and still in my old striped pyjamas and my fuzzy dressing gown.

Of course, old Sourgrape had called her. I tried to persuade her that my fall had been merely the result of over-exertion, but she overrode my protests and called the ambulance straight-away. She rode with me to the hospital and as I looked up from the stretcher on which they had insisted I lie, I saw the sun on her auburn hair, and smelt her perfume – like hyacinth – and I thought of Merlin, the master, trapped and beguiled in the hawthorn tree by Nimuë, the enchantress.

It was a rather peculiar thought. And yet it persisted strangely. The old magician, trapped by his complacency and his weakness for a pretty face. Surely I wasn't like that, I thought – and yet, she *has* beguiled me. Beguiled me with her story; her words. Made me forget my allegiances. It seems somehow appropriate that the tea she insists I drink contains the tree that trapped Merlin.

I closed my eyes.

'That's right,' she said. 'You rest now, Mr Straitley.'

'What happened?' I said, in a voice that seemed to come from very far away, like an untethered birthday balloon, floating off in the distance.

'Don't fret. I'll tell you later,' she said.

And as I drifted away into sleep, I felt a sense of vague surprise that my dreams were not of St Oswald's, and the boy buried by the Gunderson Building, but of the birthday party at the Shanker's Arms, and the red-haired young woman in the green dress, and I thought once again of Nimuë, before sinking into oblivion.

3

King Henry's Grammar School for Boys, July 9th, 1989

Why yes. The hawthorn tea took its time, but it finally worked its magic. Hawthorn and liquorice are both stimulants, not to be taken by those suffering from any kind of heart arrhythmia, as Straitley would have noticed if he'd bothered to read the back of the box. But yes, the print *is* very small. And no, I had no real intention of actually *causing his death*, although I'll admit that would not have been a wholly undesirable outcome. But I *did* need him out of the way for a while, at least until the next stage, and there's only so much misdirection you can achieve by telling a story.

Sincerely, I wish him no harm. But I like him better in hospital. At home, he has too many visitors. Sooner or later, he would have learnt that the Gunderson Building is once more under construction. It helps that the son of our local planning officer has just been made Captain of the swimming team, with a view to entering him in next year's County Team Championships – that is, if our pool is ready in time. As a result, the long-delayed planning application has gone through at last, thanks to the reworked drainage plan, and by the end of the week, I hope we shall see the groundwork completed, and the carbon-ceramic lining finally put into place. After that, I am certain that Gunderson Senior – who happens to be the head of a firm that specializes in swimming pools – will ensure that the building work follows as speedily as possible. By the time Straitley returns to work – if indeed he ever does – the site will be unrecognizable, and the evidence – such as it is – will be buried underneath the most lavish monument to a teenage boy's mediocrity since the tomb of Tutankhamen.

Yes, I have done more than tell stories over the past couple of weeks. In fact, I like to tell myself that I have moved decisively. Straitley has no way of proving what he *thinks* he saw out there; nor have the boys who included him in their little discovery. By the time this is over, all of that will be nothing more than the dream of an autumn night. Straitley will not speak of it now, because it may implicate a friend: and they follow his lead, because they are schoolboys, trained to obey.

I'll admit, I'm looking forward to that. Telling my story to Straitley has been surprisingly exhausting, as well as cathartic. The sooner I get to the end, I suppose, the sooner we can all move on.

They tried to fix my hair, of course. Just as we tried to fix Emily's. I still remember the way my dad tried to make a game of it, talked about Anne of Green Gables, and said it made me look like a pixie. I listened with wry amusement as Dom said the same things to Emily. *Now you look like a pixie, babe. It makes your eyes more beautiful.* In fact, my daughter was rather plain. Pudgy, with her father's eyes. It didn't mean I loved her any less, but now that her hair was clipped so short, I could see the roll of fat that nestled at the base of her skull like one of my mother's draught-excluders under the edge of the living room door. Her soft brown curls had given her a kind of childish prettiness: now they were gone, you could see the plainness that had always been there.

'Don't worry, Emily, it'll grow back.' I wasn't sure whether my words were meant to comfort her or Dominic. His dark eyes were filled with tears: he always was suggestible. I felt a little sting of contempt. 'After all, it's only hair.'

'But why did you do it?' My mother's voice across the years is still just as sharp as ever.

'Conrad made me do it,' I said. 'He told me it was dangerous.'

That was the first and only time I ever saw my father really lose his temper with Conrad. There's something about a girl child's hair – like a girl child's virginity – that seems uniquely precious. And mine was rather beautiful, as well as never having been cut, which might have explained his anger. Either way, Conrad was grounded for three weeks after the incident. No going out with his friends; no pocket-money; no TV. He pretended to accept the punishment, and I was still too young to see the promise of mischief in his eyes. But as Jerome would tell me, some eighteen years in the future, *Conrad had a way of hiding a grudge and taking it out on you later.*

He waited until the three weeks were up before he showed his hand again. It was nearing the end of June, and the summer holidays stretched out just around the corner, green and white and endless. One Saturday, he offered to babysit while my parents went out to the garden centre; and then, as soon as they were gone, Milky and Fatty and Mod came round, promising to *show me something cool.*

It was all part of the plan, of course. But I never saw it coming. Conrad was so *nice* that day; sharing his sweets, even carrying me on his back when I got too tired. We walked through the woods near King Henry's, via the abandoned railway line that once had led to the colliery. I liked that route. It was soft and green, and bordered with elder trees in bloom. The only part of it I didn't like was the cutting that led to the old railway tunnel. Malbry tunnel was just over one thousand yards long, and had been disused for many years. The tunnel entrance was fenced off, and the far end had been filled in. Sometimes, Conrad and his friends would go right to the tunnel mouth and shout into the darkness to make echoes, but even this game frightened me, and we never tried to get in.

We followed the disused rail bed up to the mouth of the tunnel, then climbed up over the top of the cutting and followed the grassy ridge above, where you could see the top of one of the old ventilation shafts, which looked like a little round castle standing alone on the footpath. It was famous in its way. Locals call it the Pepper Pot, and in those days rail enthusiasts often came to take photographs.

But this time, Conrad and his friends did not climb up to the ridge where the Pepper Pot stood guard. Instead, they made for the tunnel, which stood like the half-open tooth-less mouth of an old man sleeping. Conrad was carrying me on his back, and he stepped up his pace as we approached, even though he could see that I was struggling to get down.

'We're going in,' he told me in a deceptively cheerful voice. 'I'm going to show you something cool.'

I was very young, but I knew at once he was lying. *Something cool*, in Conrad's book, was always code for something else. And Conrad, in spite of his outward charm, was spitefully, doggedly vengeful. Even in the case of a child almost ten years his junior, he knew how to hold onto a grudge, and now I knew the reason.

The loss of my hair, and the reason behind it, was still a source of tension between Conrad and my father. My mother had let the incident pass — he'd always been her favourite — but every time my father saw my poor little head with its cropped curls, his anger at Conrad resurfaced. Strange, how I'd forgotten that. I'd always believed that my father was as devoted to Conrad as my mother had always been. But now, in the wake of new memories, I began to remember the anger that had hung in the air between them all that summer; anger ready to erupt at the slightest provocation.

It was not simply the loss of my hair. It seemed to be in *everything*. My father and my brother prowled around each other like wild dogs ready for a fight. And Conrad knew how best to annoy people without seeming to try. The drawl he always adopted when speaking to our father. Those records he played again and again, at full volume, in his room: especially that one by The Doors he'd had on special order for weeks: the one with the tinkling, but somehow sinister, little tune.

Conrad started to hum it now as we approached the tunnel mouth. 'Riders On The Storm', it was called, and even now I can't bring myself to hear it on the radio.

'I want to get down,' I said. 'I don't want to go into the tunnel.'

Conrad didn't say anything. He just kept humming that little tune. The tunnel mouth gaped like an open drain, and all I could do was watch as the boys ran and hooted and hollered along into the mouth of the monster.

Milky got to the barrier first. He was a small and wiry boy, very good at climbing. His blazer was different to Conrad's; with a blue, instead of a maroon, trim, and his glasses were taped at one corner. It occurred to me suddenly, just then, as I was unravelling the long twisted ribbon of the past, that

Milky must be a St Oswald's boy. That would make sense: I never saw him walking to school with Conrad. Mod did, but I never saw him wear a blazer either. Instead, he always wore that battered green parka over his school uniform. For a long time I'd assumed that this was the reason behind his nickname, but the day of the party, I was to learn the truth behind that. As for Fatty, he always walked just behind the rest of them; watching his step on the broken tracks; cautious of the brambles.

'Come on, *Fattyman*, keep up,' said Conrad in a mocking voice, and I remember thinking once or twice that Fatty wasn't even fat; it was just Conrad's way of making him feel small, as he did with everyone.

But now I was too busy processing the memory that had returned as I pulled my hair from the bathroom drain. Like the hair, it was ugly, and yet it was compelling. I could no more have stopped it then than leave that plug of hair in place – even though it disgusted me and filled me with childlike horror.

Conrad told me to do it, I'd said – but that was the last time I'd told anyone. After that, whatever he did – locking me in the bathroom, threatening me with the monster – remained our secret forever. Something inside me was silenced that day, something that found its soulmate on the day Conrad disappeared; something that only now had returned to show its face in the sunshine.

There were daisies on the path leading to the tunnel mouth. This I remembered perfectly. And there, beyond the daisies, was the brick-built entrance to the railway tunnel. It was too dark to see inside, but with Conrad lifting me up, I could look across into the darkness. Not that I wanted to do that now – but Conrad held me up anyway, and started to carry me towards it.

'I don't want to go in there,' I said.

'You want to see something cool, don't you?' My brother's voice was grim. 'This is where Mr Smallface lives. I'm taking you to see him.'

I started to struggle more violently, but Conrad was inescapable. He carried me to the barrier, where the others were waiting. Looking at it, closer, I could see that it wasn't much of a barrier. One side of the wooden fence had been pulled away from the brickwork, and it was easy to get inside. Conrad put me down on the ground and pushed me through the gap in the fence. The others followed after me. I could hear the sound of their feet echoing against the walls.

I started to cry.

'You do that,' he whispered. 'It'll only bring him here faster.'

I pressed both hands to my mouth at once. Milky took a flashlight from his pocket, and shone the beam upward onto his face, so that his features were suddenly those of a grinning, bespectacled troll.

'Dr Terror's House of Horrors presents – The *Milkman!*' he said in a booming voice.

Fatty said: 'Milky, you pillock,' and laughed.

I flinched and looked longingly back towards the mouth of the tunnel. The warmth of the bright summer day already seemed a world away to me; the air inside was damp and cold. There was a whitish residue streaked across the soot-blackened walls: in the beam of the flashlight it looked like melted ice cream. From further into the darkness came the sound of dripping water.

'We're not going right inside?' I said.

'I'll stay here and watch her,' said Mod.

'No need for that,' said Conrad. 'She'll be fine. Won't you, Becks?' Holding me firmly by the arm, he led me into the tunnel. At first, it wasn't quite dark; I could see the reflected glow of daylight against the sooty walls. Every now and again there was an arch in the side of the tunnel; this was where rail workers had to stand if a train went through while they were working. As we advanced, the air grew cold; the tunnel mouth receded, and the falling water from the roof grew to a steady downpour. The narrow beam of Milky's flashlight cast a pallid circle against the bricks and turned the falling water into twisting ropes of silver.

'It's raining,' I said, in a small voice. The shadows snatched my voice away into a librarian whisper.

Conrad laughed. 'It is, yes. But that's not the cool part, Becks. Keep going. It's isn't far.'

To me, it seemed a very long way. My feet were growing tired, but I didn't dare tell Conrad. The smell of the tunnel was dust, and mould, and coal, and rot, and cobwebs. The sound of the boys' footsteps echoed and clattered against the walls. None of them seemed at all afraid, although I was sick with terror. They chatted as we went along. Milky kept lifting the torch to his face, and Mod had his parka hood up, his face lost in the darkness.

'It's like you're the Invisible Man,' said Fatty in a dramatic voice. '*I meddled in things man must leave alone.*'

Mod said, 'Try being me for a week, see how invisible I am.'

All of them laughed, their voices enervating the shadows. I followed numbly into the dark, starting to shiver now with cold.

'You certainly stood out to Miss Macleod.' That was Fatty's voice again, a voice I found oddly greasy somehow, coloured by innuendo that I was too young to understand. 'I mean, you got the lead in the play. Next up, *Junior Showtime.*'

Conrad's voice, unexpectedly harsh: 'Fuck her, and fuck her play.'

Fatty: 'You wish.'

'Don't we all?'

And then, in the beam of the flashlight, I saw something ahead of us. It looked as if the tunnel was blocked, but as we came closer, I could see the thing that reared up ahead of us. It looked like a crazy, haphazard pile of ill-assorted jumble, randomly assembled and reaching all the way to the roof. Refuse sacks, old mattresses, clothes, cutlery, long-decayed fruit; an ancient plastic rocking horse like the one I had at home, but faded and filthy, encrusted with that eerie, whitish residue that seemed to be on everything. The enormous pile of debris twisted and towered above us, and moving forward, I could see that it reached far beyond the roof. There was a kind of chimney up there, a long dark funnel, half choked with junk, culminating in a tiny slotted pupil of daylight, as if we were in a giant drain, filled with the giant's debris. And there was a kind of grating up there – a rusty arrangement of metal bars that looked like the grid of a plughole.

Of course, it was the Pepper Pot. Over the years, people had dumped their rubbish into the air vent. Over the years, it had built up to form this half-digested sphincter of junk. I know that now. It all makes sense. But I still remember the horror of it. The cold; the dark; the chimney with its terrible burden of unloved, unwanted things –

'This is where he lives,' said Conrad quietly into my ear. 'Down here, in the sink hole. This is where he brings the children.'

I started to cry. I wanted to scream, but all I could do was whimper. Conrad lifted me up then, towards the distant mouth of the air vent. I even remember how it smelt; dank and wet and mealy. But that wasn't the worst thing. The worst thing was the *voice* that seemed to come from everywhere, a voice that whispered from out of the dark:

Beckssss. Beckssss . . .

I tried to force myself to scream. I remember thinking that if I could scream, maybe the monster would go away. But all that came out was a whistling sound like air coming out of a party balloon. The world tilted around me, and started to fade alarmingly.

I remember Mod, saying nervously: 'Come on, man. She's just a kid.'

Fatty's voice: 'It's only a joke. Fucking lighten up, man.'

'He's coming,' said Conrad. 'Goodbye, Becks.'

And then he dropped me to the ground and started back down the tunnel.

For a moment I was unable to move, hypnotized by the distant hole. The grid work of bars so far away looked like the grid of a plughole. And I saw – I swear I *saw* – him, coming down for me through the dark; his pale and ghastly features, his beard, like grasping tentacles, his long and somehow root-like hands, and then there was nothing but darkness, suffocating, cold and soft, and everything just slipped away like water down a drainpipe –

I awoke to find myself lying outside on the grass, looking up into the crisp blue sky. I could feel the mossy ground against the newly shorn skin of my scalp, and I could hear tiny insects moving between the grass stems. My trousers were wet around the crotch – *I had an accident, Mummy*. I heard Conrad's voice, and Mod's, from across an acre of sky.

'What if there's something really wrong with her?' That was Mod, who had always been the gentlest of the foursome.

'Don't be a twat. She's fine,' Conrad's voice was as sharp as a paper-cut. 'She's always doing shit like that.'

'But what if she tells your parents?'

'She won't.'

'But what if she *does*?'

'She won't. She'll keep her mouth shut.' He turned and gave me a terrible smile. 'She loves me. Isn't that right, Becks?'

I told no more stories after that. No one – except for Emily, to whom I confided everything – knew the truth about Conrad. The teasing, the scary stories, the threats – I only ever told Emily, and only when we were completely alone. As far as our parents were concerned, I had the ideal big brother. To me, he was a monster that had to be placated – one who could summon terror out of the drains. And so I did what I could to survive. I even came to blame myself. You'd call that Stockholm Syndrome now, but I was so young, and so terrified. And if at night, under the covers, when I said my prayers, I prayed for Conrad to disappear, for Mr Smallface to take *him*, not me, I made sure to use my smallest voice, the one that only God could hear.

4

July 9th, 1989

It took us some time to comfort Emily, and to get her ready to go out. Dominic did most of that, and I let him, because I've never been all that good at expressing sympathy. I suppose it's because no one showed me much of it when I was young; I was just expected to go about my day-to-day business, while my parents built a wall of grief between themselves and the rest of the world.

I wanted to ask Emily more about *who* had told her to cut her hair, but Dom refused to allow it, saying she was already upset enough without going into more details. He now seemed to think that *Conrad* must be the name of a boy at school, and was already making plans to speak to Emily's teacher.

'But today, it's all about *you*, Becks,' he said. 'We're going to throw you a party!'

Thus it was that we found ourselves at the Shanker's Arms at one o'clock, and were ushered into the upstairs room that Dom used for his Labour Party meetings. I'd only ever seen it once myself, and for only a short time. I remembered a dark, bare room, with a few posters and pictures on the walls. Now it was lit up with fairy lights, and pillar candles in tall glass jars. A cloud of balloons occupied one corner of the long room: two laden tables bisected one end. A DJ with his equipment occupied the far side, and there was a small area apparently reserved for dancing, bracketed with coloured lights and topped with a giant mirror-ball. And all around were Dominic's guests, filling half of the big room – eighty people, maybe more. I recognized a few members of staff from Sunnybank Park; people I'd known when I taught there, but not quite well enough to want to stay in touch with. And of course, there was Dominic's family. I recognized Estelle and Victoria, with their respective husbands. The younger one, with the long braids, carrying a baby, I suspected was Myra. His parents, Blossom and Cecil, were there too, along with a very old lady I later found out to be Granny Oh, Dominic's grandmother. There were also at least two dozen aunts, uncles, cousins, and a generous sprinkling of children of all ages. Most were Afro-Caribbean, but there were some from Cecil's side, too, most of them older people. It was a little overwhelming to see them all there, especially when Dominic entered the room, calling: *Here she is!* – and everyone turned to look at me, some of them whooping and calling my name. Then an expectant silence fell, which was worse in a way than the calling. I realized that I was supposed to do something – to smile, to wave, or maybe to hug someone.

Then the young woman with the braids reached out to me with a radiant smile, and I managed to smile back. 'I'm so pleased to meet you at last!' she said, in a voice that was oddly like Dominic's. 'I'm –'

'Myra,' I managed to say, and smiled. 'It's great to see you.'

Myra was rather smaller than I was, with large and very expressive dark eyes. The baby in her arms looked about three months old, and was wrapped in a quilted blanket. 'Mum's been dying for us to meet,' she said. 'Do you want to hold Tootie?' And at that, she thrust the baby into my arms. There was a flash as a camera went off. Dom laughed. I must have looked startled.

'Give her a minute, Bobs,' he said to an elderly white man with a camera. 'Becks, this is Uncle Bobs, my dad's brother. You've already met Myra. This is my Auntie Fedora, and her daughter, Katie. And here's Granny Oh. She's ninety-four. And look, over here, it's Victoria. Come and say hello to the gang!'

The gang. Oh, Dominic, I thought.

I managed to keep smiling as I worked my way through the family group. Dominic kept telling me names, but I forgot them almost immediately. Blossom's genes seemed to be strongest among the family, though Dominic's sister Victoria had lighter skin than her siblings. She dressed differently, too, and ironed her hair. She looked me up and down, and gave me a slightly mocking smile. I supposed she was thinking about how I'd missed her birthday party.

'Rebecca,' she said. 'I hope you are well.'

I tried to smile. 'Yes, thank you,' I said. In fact, I was feeling a little sick. The baby in my arms was surprisingly heavy, and had started to wriggle alarmingly. I looked for Myra, but she had moved away. Uncle Bobs snapped another rapid series of photographs of me holding the baby.

'You'll have one of your own soon,' he said, revealing brown-stained teeth. 'You'll soon get over that trouble of yours when you've got a little 'un of your own.'

I seem to remember the party through a kind of distorting lens. I tell myself now that there can't have been as much noise as I remember, or as many shifting lights. I tell myself that I must have behaved acceptably: certainly Dominic failed to see just how much I was struggling. There was a mountain of presents, I know. Soap and talc sets; baskets of fruit; a knitted pullover from Blossom, which she insisted I try on. Over my dress it looked absurd, reaching almost to my knees. I'd never seen so many presents before, so many gaily wrapped parcels.

'I'll help you open them,' Emily said, and I let her, almost sick with relief. My daughter had always loved parties. She loved the crowd of aunties making a fuss of her. She loved the party food: sandwiches and sausage rolls and piles of chicken wings, and holding court above them, the cake – a giant pile of pink-and-yellow flowers atop a double disc of sponge, layered in coloured icing. The flowers were made of icing, too; the thought of putting one into my mouth was like biting on tinfoil.

'What a lovely little girl,' said Blossom, over Emily's head. 'You must have been *very* young.'

I nodded. 'Yes, I was.'

'You don't enjoy it at that age. Everything comes as a surprise. Next time, you'll be able to *really* enjoy being a mother.'

By then I'd managed to pass Tootie back to Myra. She immediately passed the baby to Dom. *You might as well get some practice.* It seemed as if the entire room was filled with expectations; they charged the air like cigar-smoke. I found myself talking to a white woman in her fifties, who I think was a niece of Cecil's.

'You're such a *pretty* girl,' she kept saying. 'What I call a proper English rose.'

In the light of the mostly brown faces in the room, I found this comment rather distasteful. I excused myself, and, leaving Emily with the niece, went in search of the bathroom. The ladies at the Shanker's Arms was an old-fashioned bathroom, tiled in brown, with a row of high windows in marbled glass, and three cubicles, one of which was labelled: OUT OF ORDER.

I stood for a minute in front of the mirror, listening to the muffled sound of voices from the party room. I thought I looked pale and not very well; I found a lipstick in my bag and applied it.

Behind me, something thumped on the cubicle door. A prickle of electricity ran over my skin like spiders.

I turned sharply, to see Myra coming out of the cubicle, smoothing down her long print dress. She looked amused at my surprise.

'I'm sorry, did I make you jump?'

'I'm just a little nervous today.'

She put her hand on my arm and smiled. 'I know. I guess we can be a bit much. But Dom *so* wanted a party for you. He said you'd never had one before.'

I nodded.

'Because of your brother?'

I nodded again.

'It must have been *awful* for you,' she said, as I knew she would. It's what everyone says. It isn't their fault: they mean well, and the adjectives have all been used. I knew she was trying to be kind, and yet her warmth felt distant, like a homely fireside seen through a window from a dark street. 'And having to go back there to teach – I can't imagine how you must feel.'

I shrugged. 'It was a long time ago,' I said. 'And Dominic's been helping a lot.' I said that because I thought it was what she wanted to hear. Empathic people express concern because *they* want to feel better. Being around someone in pain makes *them* feel uncomfortable.

'Oh, I *know*.' She smiled again. 'Dom's a big brother to the world. And he understands what it must be like. He hated that place too, you know. He never fitted in.'

I was confused. 'King Henry's?'

248

'Didn't he tell you? How typical. He was a pupil there for a year. But it didn't work out. Too snobbish. Too white. He went back to Sunnybank Park instead. That's where we all went. We had a great time.' She took my hand and squeezed it. 'But I'm talking too much. Come back with me. It's nearly time to cut the cake.'

Feeling slightly dazed, I followed Myra back into the crowded party room. I felt even more disconnected and claustrophobic than before. *Dominic? At King Henry's?* Why on earth hadn't he told me? If he was a pupil there, then surely he would have known Conrad?

The DJ had turned up the music, and some of the guests had cleared a space and were dancing at the far end of the room. Dom was by the table, pouring champagne into plastic cups.

'*Here she is!*' he called. '*Over here!*' He said something to the DJ, and the music stopped mid-phrase. Dom caught hold of the microphone. Tapped it twice; there came a warning drone of feedback. 'I want you all to listen,' he said. 'You all know why you're here today.' The room fell silent, except for the sounds of shuffling feet, a few catcalls, and some excited murmuring.

'Dom's going to make a speech,' Myra said, squeezing my hand again. All Dom's family seemed to be very tactile people. I myself am not; I felt my cool, limp hand in hers and wondered what to do with it. It seemed rude to pull it away, and so I simply left it there, like a baby bird in shock, until finally she let me go. Dominic was speaking.

'When I first met Rebecca,' he said, 'she'd never had a party. She'd never drunk a glass of champagne, or danced like no one was watching. And so I brought her home to you, because I knew you'd love her.' He paused, and looked at me, and smiled. 'Maybe not *quite* as much as I do,' he said. 'But give her time. She'll grow on you.'

I became aware I was moving: Myra was guiding me gently forward towards the microphone and the cake. It occurred to me that she must have been briefed to make sure I co-operated. Maybe because she was closest to my age, and I was expected to like her best.

Dominic went on: 'Since then, Rebecca and Emily have become a part of my life. We've shared so much together. It hasn't been long, but I already know that I can't live without you. And that's why I want to ask you now –' He smiled and held out his hand to me – 'Rebecca, will you marry me? Will you become *Mrs Buckfast*?'

5

King Henry's Grammar School for Boys, July 9th, 1989

I often wonder what I might have told him if we'd been alone. In the same way, I sometimes wonder what Cinderella, or Galatea, or King Cophetua's Beggar Maid *really* felt about the men who saved them. Did they fall tearfully into their arms? Or did they acknowledge a debt to be paid? When you've been as we were, Roy, living from day to day on a diet of dried noodles at ten pence a pack and discounted veg from the market; when you've balanced the cost of buying your child a new coat from the charity shop against the fifty pence you need to feed the gas meter, can you turn down an offer of regular meals, a soft bed and the chance of a comfortable future? Consent is a privilege for our kind. And Dominic, being a good man, had no idea what it meant to me to smile, and take his hand, and pose as Uncle Bobs took pictures of us with Myra, and the sisters, and Blossom, and Cecil, and Auntie Fee, and Tootie, and Norma, and Granny Oh, *and all the gang*, as Dominic kept saying.

I suppose I played my part acceptably. I'm good at that: and yet, throughout it all — the celebrations, the cake (which Estelle had made herself), the toasts, the many hugs, the long, slow dance with Dominic, the kiss we shared with Uncle Bobs's camera and what felt like a thousand people – I felt like a dried-out, hollow gourd, rattling the same few seeds over and over and over again.

Dom had been at King Henry's.

Why had he never told me?

Could he have known Conrad?

Might they even have been *friends*?

I managed to survive, somehow, without allowing my mask to slip. If you look at the photographs, you'll see me having a marvellous time. I was photogenic then; there's hardly an unflattering shot of me. Here I am with Dominic, laughing wildly in his arms; with Myra and her sisters, almost helpless with laughter. Here I am with Tootie, gentle and Madonna-like; and here, with a glass of champagne in my hand, wearing Blossom's sweater and looking like a fourteen-year-old dressing up in her grandmother's clothes. Here I am with Granny Oh, with her face like a fistful of wrinkles. And once again with Dominic; a bride, alight with happiness.

Uncle Bobs made an album of all his photographs of that day. I have it still, somewhere, although I seldom bring it out. After Dominic died and I moved out of April Street, the gang seemed to release me on its own. It was almost as if Dominic had been the only working part in that supportive mechanism: without him, the family withdrew back into their circle of grief. It was my fault, of course; I'd failed to live up to their expectations. I supposed they thought I was being cold. But whatever I felt at Dominic's death remained my own, unexpressed and unexplored. I like to think you'd understand, Roy. Maybe you'd even sympathize.

'*To the future Mrs Buckfast!*' The toast came loudly and often. Reckless on champagne, I dared to suggest that I might keep

my name. The look on his face, Roy. The look on his face
– until Victoria started to laugh, and punched my arm, and
said: 'You dope. Can't you see she's joking?'

And so I played along with that too, just as I had with
the party. It wasn't that I was especially sentimental about
my name. Changing it might even help. I wouldn't be *Asda
Price* anymore – although Buckfast had its own challenges.
And Conrad would be one step further away. But it was my
name. My identity. Without it, what would I be left with?

We finally got home that night at about ten o'clock. It
might have been even later, but Emily had school the next
day, which gave me a legitimate excuse. We came home
with armfuls of presents, many of them still wrapped, and
while Dominic put Emily to bed, I showered, and made some
camomile tea. I drank it by the fireside, in my old pyjamas,
and I was just beginning to unwind when Dominic came
back downstairs, triumphant and filled with energy. He'd
drunk rather a lot of champagne, but he was still mostly
high on atmosphere.

'What a terrific party!' he said. 'I *said* you'd have a great time.'
He looked in the drawer under the TV cabinet, where he kept
his bag of weed. 'You want one? I'm going to have one.'

I smiled and shook my head.

Dom began to roll a joint, still talking in that rapid, half-
laughing way that I found a little disquieting. 'Everybody
loved you, Becks. Mum, my sisters, everyone. It was so good
to see you together. I told them if they gave you a chance,
you'd show them what you're really like. And they *loved* you.
It was so great to see. Even Victoria said you were sweet,
and she's a difficult girl to please. And Mum said you were
a natural when you were holding the baby –'

'I've held a baby before, Dom,' I reminded him gently.

253

'Yes, but that was different,' he said, lighting the joint and taking a drag. I wondered in what way he thought Emily could be different, but I'd seen him like this before, and I knew he wasn't really listening. 'And now we're going to be married –' He stopped and sniffed at the teapot on the table beside me. 'What's that?'

'Camomile tea,' I said.

He laughed. 'Oh, you're so *cute*, Becks. Flannel pyjamas and camomile tea. It's like we're an old married couple already!' He laughed again – that night it seemed that *everything* I did was cute. I knew he was drunk and a little high, but, after what Myra had said to me, his laughter made me want to scream. I sipped my tea and closed my eyes, trying to find myself again. Meanwhile, Dominic rattled on: he was ten years older than I was, but sometimes, especially when he was high, he could sound just like a teenage girl. I realized how uncertain he'd been about the success of his party; about my acceptance into his gang; even of his proposal. It should have been endearing, I thought – and yet the fact that he hadn't told me about being a pupil at King Henry's overshadowed everything; an unexpected chunk of ice at the heart of a birthday cake.

'Myra said you'd had a chat,' Dominic was saying to me. 'What did you girls talk about?'

'Not much, really. Girl stuff.'

'Myra's great. I knew you'd get on. What did she say about me?'

I nodded. Now was the time, I thought; and yet I couldn't find a way to begin. 'She talked about Sunnybank Park,' I said at last. 'She said how happy you were there.'

Dominic looked surprised. 'She did? Well, it's a terrific environment,' he said. 'Inclusive, diverse – great Art Department, obviously.' He grinned. 'You'll be relieved to get back there, after you finish King Henry's.'

'Is that how *you* felt, coming back?'

He looked bewildered. 'What do you mean? I'd never teach at that place.'

'I mean when you were a pupil,' I said.

I saw him stiffen. 'Who said that?'

'Myra did,' I told him. 'She said you'd tried it for a year, then decided you hated it. How come you never told me?'

He took another drag of his joint, burning it down to the fingers. '*Fuck!*' He dropped the stub and crushed it against the tiled hearth. The sunny, elated mood was gone; now he looked withdrawn and paranoid. Too much dope sometimes did that to him, although he was rarely immoderate. 'I *wasn't* there for a year,' he said. 'I only lasted a couple of terms. Myra doesn't remember that because she was only a little kid.'

'What happened?' I said.

He shrugged. 'Not much. My mother got this idea that I was gifted – too bright for Sunnybank Park. She put me up for the entrance exam. Third-year entrance. English and Maths. I was supposed to know Latin, too. I didn't know a fucking word. But I came top of the year in Maths, and fourth overall in English, and so I got in on a Junior Scholarship, provided I caught up on two years of Latin as soon as fucking possible.' He started to roll another joint. I wondered how many he'd smoked that day. 'It wasn't the best year of my life. That's why I never mentioned it.'

'But if you were in Conrad's year –'

'I didn't know him,' said Dominic. 'You think that if I'd known him, I wouldn't have told you straightaway? Conrad wasn't in my House, or any of my classes. And besides, by the time he disappeared, I was back at Sunnybank, where I belonged.'

'What was it like?'

'What do you think? People made fun of everything. My accent. My shoes. My schoolbag. I got put in the bottom sets, even in fucking English and Maths. The only other two black lads there were the sons of a Nigerian diplomat. Then there was me. The scholarship boy, in his second-hand uniform. The thought that I might actually be *smart* didn't even occur to them. Fucking Henriettas.' His eyes narrowed – against the smoke, or maybe against the memory. 'Way to fuck up the vibe, Becks. Thanks for nothing.'

'I'm sorry,' I said. 'I needed to know.'

'Well, now you know. Now you know how it feels for me to watch you go into that place every day. To hear you talk about *your boys*.' He gave the word an unpleasant inflection, and I found myself retreating even further into myself. I felt myself starting to apologize again, and stopped myself just in time. But Dominic had always had the power to make me feel like a child, at fault without quite knowing why. I realized at that moment that Conrad had made me feel the same way.

I finished my tea and stood up.

'Where are you going?'

'I'm tired,' I said.

'You haven't opened your presents,' said Dom, with another of those abrupt shifts of mood. 'You can't go to bed without opening your birthday presents, Becks.'

He must have seen my expression, because he stood up and gave me a hug. 'I'm sorry,' he said. 'I was being a dick. Come back and open your presents.'

Dominic was like that, Roy. His bad moods never lasted. They shifted like clouds over the sun on a summer's day. Mine are very different: my nerves were a-jangle with alarm, and I knew that I wouldn't be able to sleep for hours after the little episode. Somewhere in the walls, I heard the sound of a water pipe gargling: I supposed that Emily must have got up to get a drink of water. And yet, in spite of that, I felt a shiver, of something moving in its sleep; something that shouldn't be disturbed.

'Come on, Becks,' said Dominic. 'Don't let it spoil your special day.'

And of course, I stayed, like a good little girl, summoning a smile, although my heart was wrapped in razor wire. I don't remember the presents, although I do remember the wrappings: handmade paper from Victoria; dancing mice from Estelle; rainbows and stars from Myra. And from Dominic, a tiny box, wrapped with a silver ribbon – an ornate ring of reddish gold, topped with a tiny diamond shaped like a baleful, narrowed eye.

'It belonged to my great-grandmother,' he said. 'Do you like it?'

What choice did I have? Once more, my consent was assumed. In fact, I found it old-fashioned and over-ornate; the diamond, like so many old gems, looked dull and strangely unfinished. 'It's beautiful,' I said.

'Put it on.'

My fingers were slender, but not as slim as those of the long-dead ancestor. As a consequence the ring was a little tight, but I managed to push it over my knuckle.

Dominic kissed me. 'Perfect,' he said. He started to collect the wrapping paper that had fallen to the floor. 'Oh, wait,' he said. 'We forgot one.' And from the pile of wrappers he drew out a small parcel, rather clumsily wrapped, in paper with an old-fashioned design of kittens against a pink ground.

I felt a small, cold hand tighten around my windpipe. I knew that wrapping. I'd seen it many times from afar, along with the little envelope, now slightly yellow with age, which had stood on the top of the wardrobe in my parents' room for so long.

'Emily?' said Dominic quizzically, reading the handwritten label.

'An old friend,' I said, still holding the card.

'Was she at the party?'

I shook my head. 'Someone else must have left it.'

'Well, go on, open it,' said Dom. 'Come on, Becks. Let me help you.' And before I could protest, he had torn off the wrapping paper. Inside, was a pink hardback book, with the words *My Album* embossed in gold. The card that came with it – kittens and string – was signed in the same painstaking childish hand as the gift tag:

To BecCa,
LovE FrOm Emily

I opened the album at the first page. The paper was thick, almost like card, with printed frames intended for photographs and souvenirs. Some were labelled with captions in the same cursive gold as the cover. *My Holidays*; *My Pet*; *My School*; *Best Friends*. Under the last caption, there was a photograph of myself at five, and a clumsy drawing of two little girls, one with red hair, one blonde.

'You were so cute,' said Dominic, looking over my shoulder. 'Just look at those curls!'

Quickly, I closed the album. How had it come to be there? Someone must have delivered it in secret to the party. But who? My parents? I couldn't imagine either of them coming as far as the Shanker's Arms. My mother seldom left the house, and my father only ever did to go as far as the corner shop. And yet, without any doubt, the present was the one that my childhood friend had given me when I was five, and which had been kept for eighteen years on top of my parents' wardrobe, awaiting my brother's return. What did it mean? And why today?

Once more I thought of the letter 'from Conrad' my father had shown me. Impossible that it could be genuine, and yet my parents had seemed so sure that my brother would call on his birthday. I considered phoning my parents to find out if anyone *had* come by, but it was getting late by then, and they would have certainly gone to bed. And so I put the book aside, and tried to think of the future. But the past is a stronger current by far, and though I played my part with Dom, I slept very little that night, and dreamt of being in the old railway tunnel, with my finger trapped under one of the rails, and of Conrad, grown to giant size, coming at me out of the dark like a speeding express train.

I awoke to find that my finger was hurting. It must have swollen overnight: and now Dominic's engagement ring, which had been only a little too tight the previous night, was impossible to remove. I tried using soap, to no avail; and Dominic found me almost in tears half an hour later, with my hand in a bucket of ice in the hope of reducing the swelling. Ignoring my protests, he drove me straight to Casualty, where a cheery nurse clipped off the ring with a special instrument. Dominic hid his dismay, repeating that it wasn't my fault, and that I shouldn't feel responsible.

'We can easily have it repaired,' he kept saying, as if to convince himself. 'But if you'd damaged your finger, I would never have forgiven myself.'

'That's a good man you've got there,' said the cheery nurse, as she ushered me out of the cubicle. 'You hang onto him, dearie. He's *definitely* a keeper.'

6

St Oswald's ~~Grammar School for Boys~~ Academy
Michaelmas Term, September 24th, 2006

How quickly, how slowly time passes here. Minutes are so
slow, and yet the days themselves seem to slide away like slices
of melting ice cream. My doctor has changed my medication
again, and wants to keep me here for at least another week
until he discovers what caused my collapse. I know today is
Sunday, because there are so many visitors here. Families, some
of them bringing balloons. Solemn-faced children with an eye
to the sunny world outside.

My ward is a small one of six beds, each with a modest
curtain. If the nurse draws the curtain, it gives me a little
privacy. On the other hand, it also makes me a magnet for
the curious.

Who's in there? Voices whispering. *Is he going to die?*

At least I am by the window, which Sister leaves ajar
throughout the day. A warm breeze comes from outside, where
the leaves continue to turn and fall, oblivious, in the mellow
air. A small commotion outside the room; young voices and
Sister's Irish one, raised together in argument:

You can't come in here. Off you go.

But we want to see him!

Visits are only for family.

He doesn't have a family! If we could come in for a minute. I promise we'd be quiet –

His daughter visits every day. Now be off with the lot of you. I have my work to get on with.

The Head will visit this evening, when the families have gone. An afternoon can be sacrificed, but Sunday nights are sacrosanct. And yet her devotion to duty – to *me* – has never faltered. Does she not have a family? I know she has a daughter. Is there no one else at all? That woman, still young, still attractive – she must surely have *someone*. And yet she never mentions it. I wonder how her husband died. I wonder, too, that she married him at all – everything she tells me suggests that they were not in any way suited.

But Rebecca Buckfast is nothing if not pragmatic. She has somehow managed to reach the top of the patriarchal pole, leaving behind the baffled men she encountered on the way. Dominic Buckfast, Johnny Harrington, Philip Sinclair, Eric Scoones. What does she expect of *me*? How am I serving her purpose? I am not vain enough to believe that she visits me for my own sake. And yet, I am clearly vain enough to believe that she values my company.

There came a tap at the window. A furtive little tap, and a hiss, barely audible over the buzz of the ward, with its many visitors.

'Sir!'

I looked up and saw a familiar face looking over the window sill. Behind him, I could just make out several other figures, crouching in that furtive way teenagers seem to think confers invisibility. My Brodie Boys – including Ben Wild – seemed to have turned up *en masse*. I felt a sudden, sentimental moistening of the eyelids, and assumed the crispest tone I could in my attempt at self-control.

'Mr Allen-Jones,' I said. 'At least, that's who I assume this is, lurking beneath the window ledge.'

Allen-Jones popped his head up again. Speaking through the narrow gap between the window ledge and the sash, he said: 'Sir. The nurse wouldn't let us in.'

'Rules, those pesky things,' I said. '*Auctoritas non veritas facit legem.*'

I straightened my ancient dressing gown and moved a little closer to the window. 'To what do I owe this pleasure?' I said, keeping my voice carefully lowered. 'You seem to have brought half the Upper School with you.'

A pair of eyes peered over the sill, topped by a wedge of ginger hair. It was Sutcliff, also seemingly convinced that he was being thoroughly inconspicuous. 'We wanted to see how you were,' he said. 'No one tells us anything. Ben tried to talk to Ms Buckfast, but she just told him there was no news.'

Him. Those pesky pronouns again. And yet, Ben finds them important. *He's telling us who he is, Sir. When people tell us who they are* −

Ben chimed in. 'We tried to ask about − *you know what.* The Head says it's all been dealt with.'

'But there's been nothing at all in the papers,' said McNair. 'And now they're starting building again. And no one's telling us anything.'

'Building?'

'By the Gunderson Building. There's a whole load of machinery there, and they've brought some new materials in.'

'Really?' That was news to me. I wondered why the Head hadn't mentioned it. I was about to say something else, when Allen-Jones ducked down again − presumably Sister was doing the rounds.

There came a whisper from under the ledge: 'Got to go. Sorry, Sir.' The whisper was briefly followed by an extended hand through the gap beneath the window sash, clutching something in plastic.

'Oh, and we brought you a present, Sir.' He passed it to me through the gap. I heard the sudden clatter of rapidly departing footsteps, and looked at the object in my hand.

It was a packet of Liquorice Allsorts.

7

September 24th, 2006

I found Straitley sitting up in bed, eating Liquorice Allsorts. He
looks rather better than he did yesterday, although there was
a measuring look in his eye that made me a little wary. Who
gave him those sweets? The nurse tells me that he has had no
visitors. And yet, I cannot rid myself of the feeling that my
audience of one is not quite so captive – or as passive – as he
was a week ago.

'Any word from the authorities yet?' he asked, even before
I took my seat.

I shook my head. 'These things take time. For all we know,
there may be other factors we've overlooked.'

He took a yellow coconut sweet and handed me the bag. 'A
friend of mine used to say that you could judge a person's character from the kind of selection he made. Are you a straightforward liquorice stick? A sandwich? A jelly spog? Monochrome?
Vibrantly coloured? Tough or tender-hearted?'

I smiled. 'I don't think I'd feel comfortable, revealing myself
so openly.'

His eyes gleamed. 'Very wise,' he said. 'And yet you've
already told me so much, albeit rather selectively. Why do

you come here, Headmaster? It can't be for my company. Surely, you have someone at home – a friend, a companion. Your daughter, perhaps?'

I shook my head. 'Like you, Roy, I value my space. And I do enjoy your company. You remind me of how far St Oswald's has come, and of what I have inherited.'

Straitley pulled a comical face. 'I'm not at all certain that was a compliment. And although Augustus may have found Rome a city of bricks and left it a city of marble, I happen to be rather fond of our old bricks, and see no real reason to rebuild anything.'

'Fighting talk.' I smiled again. 'But then, Roy, you never did have much of a problem speaking truth to power.'

He smiled. 'Are you sure you won't have an Allsort?'

I toyed with the thought of a coconut roll, pink and sweet on the outside, concealing a black and bitter heart. 'No, thanks. I thought perhaps you might want me to finish my story.'

He nodded. 'But there are so many loose ends. Do you think there's time?'

'Life never ties up *all* the loose ends. But perhaps we could talk about Eric Scoones. I imagine you must miss him.'

He took another Allsort, this time a pink-and-brown sandwich. 'Over sixty years or so I'd more or less got used to him,' he said. 'I can see why he might not have come across as entirely likeable to you.'

Oh, Straitley. If only you knew. I'd always planned to tell you this part; though maybe a little later. In fact, and, in spite of what I may have led you to believe – my story is nowhere near its end. I may not tell you all of it. In fact, I probably shouldn't. But somehow, telling my story this way – and for the very first time, Roy – I hope you see that as a mark of respect. Not even my therapist knows the truth.

You can't just confess to a murder. Even a therapist is obliged to act on such information. But *you*, Roy – with the right kind of groundwork, I've always thought we could be on the same side. We both want what's best for St Oswald's; even though we may not always see eye to eye. Scoones was never like that. Scoones cared for no one but himself and his small, predictable ambitions.

But you struck a nerve, Roy, when you mentioned Emily. I wonder if you meant to. And yes, I *do* value my space, but that isn't the whole story. I doubt I'll ever tell you that, but I hear from her once or twice a year, usually when she needs money. I sometimes wonder what I did wrong; whether I accidentally revealed too much of myself to my daughter. And sometimes, I still wonder what might have turned out differently if I had been capable of being the wife of Dominic Buckfast. Girls read the story of Bluebeard as a cautionary tale. *Don't ask questions, little girl, or you may awaken the monster.* But in my experience, severed heads are the least likely thing for a woman to find in her husband's secret chamber. Far from revealing the monster within, those chambers will often contain nothing but a pitiful collection of weaknesses and deceptions. That was Dom; so insecure that he couldn't even tolerate the thought of my keeping my maiden name. And yet I still worked to placate him; to keep his mystery intact. I have no excuse; I was very young. And, of course, I needed the money.

8

July 10th, 1989

The incident with the engagement ring meant that I was late to work. I arrived halfway through the lunch break, to the disapproval of Scoones, who was marking books by the open window, who now greeted my arrival with ill-concealed scorn.

I tried to explain what had happened, but Scoones was his usual brusque self. 'Some of us have better things to do than chat,' he said, and went back to his marking.

'Don't pay any attention to him,' said Carrie, who was smoking in spite of the hand-lettered sign affixed directly above her chair. 'What happened? Are you all right?'

My finger had been bandaged after the engagement ring incident, but it looked worse than it really was. I told her what had happened.

'Engaged? Congratulations!' she said.

'Dominic's a good man.'

Carrie raised an eyebrow. 'That sounds rather less than joyous. You're not up the duff, are you, sweetheart?'

I laughed. 'Nothing like that. I think I just need time to adjust.' And I explained about the party, and Dom's surprise proposal, and all the family's unsubtle hints about our having a baby of our own. I found myself laughing at my account of the previous night's events, even though it hadn't been funny at the time. That was Carrie's influence; it was hard to feel depressed in the face of her cynical humour.

'I'm really very ungrateful,' I said. 'I get a party of my own, a big romantic proposal, an antique ring, and what happens? My body rejects it all in my sleep.' I waved my bandaged finger. 'Perhaps this is my subconscious saying that it's all going to end in tears.' I meant it lightly, but somehow I thought my voice sounded a little flat. 'I'm having second thoughts,' I said. Until then I hadn't known I was.

She raised an eyebrow. 'Does he know?'

I shook my head. 'It's my fault. If only I'd had time to *think* –'

Carrie gave me a stern look. 'But that's how they do it,' she told me. 'These men. Their romance. They make of it a performing art. They don't give you the chance to respond the way you would in private. That very public proposal, in front of all his family and friends. Oh, and let me guess how many times his sisters called it *romantic*.'

I had to laugh. 'A few,' I said.

'Romance is always their excuse,' said Carrie, sitting beside me. 'We hear it from the cradle. Controlling, violent, abusive men are so often portrayed as romantic. Look at Heathcliff. Or Rochester. And we're supposed to fall for that shit. And we do. Over and over again, we do.' She smiled. 'Tell me, sweetheart, do you think that if he'd asked you face-to-face, just you and him, to marry him, with no performance and no one else there, that you would still have accepted?'

I shrugged. 'I don't know.'

'Why's that?'

'Because I don't really know him,' I said. 'All this time, I thought I did. I thought he was so straightforward. No mystery about him at all. And now I find out he was a pupil here, and he kept it from me all along. Why would he do that? Why would he pretend he didn't know this place, or the people I was working with?'

'What was his name again?'

'Dominic. His name is Dominic Buckfast.'

For a moment her expression changed. She frowned and stared at me for so long that I found myself beginning to doubt whether she remembered him. He'd been there for less than a year, after all. It could be their paths had never crossed. But if he'd been as unusual as he'd led me to believe, then Carrie might remember.

At last she nodded. 'He was only there a year. He left at the end of the summer term, the year Conrad Price disappeared.'

'He was there the whole year? He didn't leave early?'

She gave me an odd look. 'Yes, he was there the whole year, right up to the end of term. He was a good kid. Sensitive. I assumed the business with Conrad must have been too upsetting for him.'

'Conrad and Dominic were friends?' My mouth was filled with needles.

'Yes, they were inseparable. Always up to something. He used to wear a green parka. He was always getting into trouble for that.' She smiled. 'Conrad had a name for him. A nickname. What did he call him?' Briefly Carrie closed her eyes, lost in concentration. 'Conrad had nicknames for everyone. *What* was it?'

'Mod,' I said quietly.

Carrie opened her eyes. 'That's right. Does *he* know you're Conrad's sister?'

I nodded. 'How long have *you* known?'

She shrugged. 'I always suspected. Besides –' She dropped her cigarette into her half-finished cup of tea. 'Sweetheart, hasn't anyone told you, you look *exactly* like him?'

9

July 10th, 1989

We moved to the theatre after that, and I told her the rest of the story. Dominic, Conrad, my parents. Scoones. The blond boy with the Prefect's badge. Even Mr Smallface, and the voice under the Pepper Pot. She listened in silence, occasionally nodding, or frowning in sympathy. When I told her about Mr Smallface, she put her arm around me.

'You poor angel,' she said at last. 'You had a hell of a time of it.'

I had to smile. 'You could say that.'

'But after that, why didn't you get away as far as you could? London Calling, and all that jazz? Why stay here in Malbry? And why, of all places, come to teach *here*?'

It was a reasonable question, and there was no simple answer. Just a tangled ball of twine around a handful of razor blades. I *could* have said it was because my parents needed me; or because I had my roots here. But I have *never* felt rooted. My parents did *not* need me. There was no one I would have missed if I'd simply moved away. I am like the air plant, *Tillandsia* – or that other epiphyte, the orchid – able to take its energy from whatever surrounds it. A tree branch; a creeper; the air itself. Force me to bloom; I will not. Put me in the earth, I die.

I shrugged. 'I really don't know,' I said. 'Maybe I thought I could put him to rest.'

She gave a comical half-smile. 'By finding out how he died? How very Nancy Drew of you.'

I winced. 'It sounds so stupid when you say it aloud.'

She took my hand. 'You're not stupid,' she said. 'But you need to stop living in shadow. The shadow of your brother's death; the shadow of your parents' grief. And maybe ask yourself why you were drawn to Dominic in the first place? Could it have been because, in some way, you already knew who he was?'

It was a startling, sobering thought. 'I don't *think* so,' I said. 'I mean, I was five years old. All I remember was that he was the one who stood up for me, that time by the railway. I don't really remember his face. Just that parka he used to wear. That's all I remember about him.'

Carrie stood up. 'Come with me. This might help you remember.'

I followed as she led me into the corridor outside the theatre. The day was fine, the boys were outside and the corridor was deserted. Only Chris, the caretaker, was there, apparently working on something inside a ceiling panel. He recognized me and lifted a hand. I smiled back at him.

'You ever catch that boy?' he said.

I shook my head.

'Little bastards.'

The corridor outside the theatre was lined with dozens of School photographs. Like St Oswald's, King Henry's had one taken every three years by the same local firm of photographers; Jacob Barrowman & Son. They'd taken my brother's portrait just the week before he disappeared, and their picture of him had appeared in all the local papers. I knew it well:

my parents had bought a copy in the largest possible format, and had kept it over the mantelpiece throughout the past eighteen years. But they hadn't bought a copy of the Full School Photograph: these were quite expensive and, besides, Conrad's face would not have been much more than a blur among the rest. Perhaps they would have bought a copy when he reached the Sixth Form, but Conrad never made it that far.

The taking of the School Photograph – as I'm sure you know, Roy – has always been a laborious affair, which is why it was held only every three years, during Summer Term. It began with the construction of a kind of three-tier platform on the grass in front of the Main Entrance, on which the boys were made to stand (or sit, depending on their height) according to their year and form. First-years sat cross-legged on the grass at ground level. Second-years sat on chairs on the first level; third-years stood behind them. On the next level, fourth- and fifth-years did the same. Then, on the last tier, the Sixth-Formers stood, some in their colours blazers, the rest dark-suited and dapper, with the teaching staff at the heart of it all, all in their academic robes.

'Look for the photo for '71,' said Carrie, scanning the walls. 'I know we had one taken then; it's always a whole palaver.'

It was indeed: you'll know that, Roy. It takes a long time for the boys to be seated; yet more time to settle them down. The photographer uses a tripod and cape with his long-lens camera. He makes several test runs – the process is an expensive one, and he does not want to waste a shot. Then the boys are warned to remain stock-still for a minute or more, as the camera moves from one side of the group to the other for the panoramic shot. Or at least it was true in those days: now, the photos are digital, and the process far less laborious.

The pupils are the same, though; excited by the break in routine; looking for an opportunity to disrupt or misbehave. I remember my mother at breakfast on the day of Conrad's photograph, fussing over his uniform; making sure his Prefect's badge was pinned on straight to his lapel. Eight days later, he was gone: just in time for his portrait to be handed over to the police. Everyone knows that portrait now: and yet, the whole School Photograph had never been published. I wondered why. I found the photo for July 1971 halfway down the corridor. Black-and-white, in those days, of course: the rows of faces poignantly fresh. Conrad was right at the end of his row, looking bright and neatly pressed; I touched his small face with the tip of my index finger. Next to him, Dominic 'Mod' Buckfast was grinning into the camera.

Now, I could see the boy I had known. The resemblance was undeniable. But memory is a landscape that changes perspectives as we grow; and Mod had been a *big* boy to me; almost an adult. Here he was only fourteen; and although he did stand taller than his friends, he looked almost touchingly young.

'Here they are, at the end of the row,' said Carrie from the opposite end of the frame.

'No, I already found them,' I said.

She took a rapid step forward and checked the face at my fingertip. For a moment she stood there frowning, then she turned once more to me. 'The little bastards,' Carrie said. 'How did they get away with it?'

'Get away with what?' I said.

Wordlessly, Carrie beckoned me towards the far end of the photograph. I looked; I touched the shining glass. And there, at the opposite end of the row, I saw Dominic again, and next to him, smiling angelically, the blurry face of my brother.

In every school there is always an anecdotal tradition, during the School Photograph, of pupils attempting to race around the back of the group and reposition themselves before the end of the shot, thereby (in theory, at least) appearing in the photograph twice. Boys at King Henry's were always roundly forbidden to attempt such a thing, but there's always one willing to take the chance, even at the risk of ruining the expensive shot. Conrad had taken his place just in time; there was a suggestion of movement around his hair and the side of his face, as if the camera had caught him in an unexpected sneeze. But there he was, with Mod by his side, both of them grinning brashly. And now that I looked more closely, I recognized Milky beside them –

'But Milky wasn't a King Henry's boy,' I said. 'I thought he went to St Oswald's.'

Seeing him next to my brother like that, I noticed how similar they looked. Both blond, with glasses; though Milky's were cheap National Health frames, whereas Conrad's were gold-rimmed; expensive. Milky's hair was longer, too; falling lankly over his eyes; and at that moment something surfaced in my memory; a scent of something acrid and sharp, like burning tinfoil paper –

Carrie looked more closely at his face, and said: 'My God, I think you're right. Conrad must have helped him sneak in; swiped a school blazer from Lost Property. It's just the kind of practical joke that he would have found hilarious.' She shrugged. 'In normal circumstances, I expect the Head would have pursued it, except that Conrad disappeared so soon after that, and it would have been pretty tasteless to portray him as the troublemaker he was.'

'But he was always so popular,' I said. 'He was even a Prefect –'

Carrie laughed. 'No, he wasn't. He swiped that badge from the props room. Told people I'd made him a Prefect because he was helping with the play. And as for his popularity – let's just say that he was a comedian, never happier than when he was sounding off at someone else's expense. Oh, he could be very charming when he wanted to. But there's a reason his friends were all misfits and outsiders. He didn't get on with the popular crowd. He liked his people – vulnerable.'

My brother wasn't a Prefect. The thought was somehow voluptuous. 'Did he often do things like that? Lie, misbehave in class?'

She looked at me and pulled a face. 'Oh, sweetheart. Your brother was a little shit, spoilt rotten by his parents. Lazy in class, nothing special in sports, and yet he seemed somehow to think that he was destined for greatness.'

I stared at her. 'Wow. I had no idea. My parents always let me believe that he was a model student.'

Carrie laughed. 'Of course they did. No parent ever wants to believe their child is mediocre, or a bully, or dishonest. And when a child dies – or disappears – all we ever hear about is how popular and brilliant they were. No one ever comes out and says: *the only thing that marked him out is how happy we all were to see him go.*'

I took some time to think about that. The thought that my brother had not been the popular, successful boy that my parents remembered was already feeding my hungry heart. Carrie hadn't liked him, nor had most of the other boys. A sudden, fierce curiosity took hold of me: I wanted to know. I wanted to know every detail.

'What did he do?'

Carrie shrugged. 'It depended. Conrad knew how to wind people up. And he knew how to spot weakness. In some classes he was well behaved, in others, he was disruptive. He and I got on at first. He wanted to be in the School play. All the third-years wanted that. It meant a lot of leeway with homework during rehearsals. That year we were doing *Othello*. First time in the Little Theatre. Dominic got the lead role. Conrad didn't like that.'

I tried to picture Dom on stage, before an audience of white faces.

Carrie saw my expression. 'I know. The only black boy in the year, and I had to single him out in that way. But it was 1971. In those days, it was a radical choice. And if I hadn't chosen him, we would have had Conrad in blackface.'

I thought of Conrad's voice then. *Fuck her, and fuck her play.*
You wish.
Don't we all?

'What happened?'

Carrie looked surprised. 'I got him to help with the lights instead. Conrad was too full of himself to settle for a minor role and, anyway, I wanted to give Dominic a chance to shine. He was a New Boy that year, which made it hard to make new friends. Perhaps that's why he became so close to a boy like Conrad. And, of course, there were other problems.'

I thought back to the way Dom had spoken of the School. Yes, it must have been hard for him to be in such a minority. To be a working-class black kid in a place of such visibly white privilege – no wonder he'd hated being there. For the first time since the party, I wondered if I could let it go; just draw a line under Conrad and move on with Dom into the future –

But Dominic had lied to me. He'd pretended he hadn't known Conrad. He'd told me he'd been at King Henry's for two terms, rather than the whole year. He'd let me tell him my story without once correcting my belief that *I* had been the broken one. Did he know something about Conrad's death? Did he *prefer* me broken? And if he did, could that be because *he knew what had really happened to me?*

I don't suppose you think of me as a damaged individual. That's because I have worked very hard to be whole. I have never believed in the mantra 'what does not kill me makes me stronger', but I do believe that what does *not* kill me gives me the chance to fight back. And I have been fighting back, Roy, every single day of my life; fighting back against the past, against cancer, Conrad, Dominic, Harrington, King Henry's, and lately, St Oswald's. I have fought back against all of you, and no one will rob me of my victory. On Monday, the work began again on the Gunderson swimming pool; by the time you return, whatever you may think you have seen will be buried under a hundred tonnes of shielded, reinforced concrete.

You'd be surprised at what workmen will overlook to keep working on site. In this case, it was easy to disperse the remains and rebury the pieces where no one would look. Sometimes, burial is best. Why would you want to dig up the past? Especially when the mystery is so much better than the truth. After all, who would benefit, now that all concerned are dead? And how much would St Oswald's lose to have the story told in full?

I left you when the Sister announced the end of Visiting Hour. I'd been there almost all afternoon, and you were looking tired by then. Tomorrow, I'll be back to deliver another slice of my story, and you will await it hungrily, just as you have done throughout. Dear Straitley. I'm so fond of you. And I know you very well. I imagine, for instance, that Allen-Jones and the others managed to see you today. Those Liquorice Allsorts gave them away. I know their propensity – and yours

– for far-fetched schemes, including the one that ultimately brought down my predecessor. But clandestine recordings will not help you now. You became a part of this the moment I began my tale. The more you listen, the more the fate of St Oswald's – its reputation, its staff, its pupils – lies in your hands. And yet, there is no danger. This is all just sleight of hand. The audience, watching breathlessly as the stage magician cuts up the girl, never for a moment believes that she will not step out of this unscathed. Why then, this remaining suspense? Why do they keep watching at all?

St Oswald's ~~Grammar School for Boys~~ Academy
Michaelmas term, September 24th, 2006

Well, yes. With hindsight I see that I should never have given her that fatal first chance. The sparkling lure was filled with hooks, and I was dragged along in her wake. Now it's too late to turn back; too late to call the authorities. I can imagine only too well how they would receive the news that I and a small group of pupils had discovered a body by the earthworks at the Gunderson Building; and how, for three weeks, I had failed to report it.

I can imagine it clearly; the officer standing by my bed first thing Monday morning – a young man, maybe a new recruit, maybe even an ex-pupil – sent to humour a sick old man. I can see him writing down the details in his notebook, wishing he was elsewhere; asking a dutiful question or two. *And would you say these boys were habitual pranksters, Mr Straitley? So this 'body' that you saw looked just like a bundle of rags? And you're saying the Head is in on it? So – where do you think this 'body' is now? And just how ill have you really been?*

As for La Buckfast's story, none of it is verifiable. Even the fact that she told me at all seems improbable, at best. And she has *not* told me everything – yet. The role of my old friend Eric Scoones remains as yet a mystery. Is that how she managed to pull me in, to hypnotize me as she did? Is that how she will finish her tale, by revealing him as a murderer?

I have to hand it to her, though. I know how ruthless she can be, and still she managed to draw me in. Could all this have been a ploy to make me leave St Oswald's? Does she still see me as a threat? I rather thought she liked me, but that has never stopped her before. I don't believe Rebecca Price was ever the type to let nostalgia get in her way. If she is telling me the truth, it must be for a reason. And if she is not – well, the right kind of lie can reveal almost as much as the truth. And lying here in my hospital bed, I realize that it is the *truth* that matters to me most now. The truth will either kill or cure, for my heart is with St Oswald's, and if one of ours is responsible for the death of Conrad Price, then my heart will have no choice but to hand in its notice. We have our own laws at St Oswald's, regardless of the Law outside. Till then, however, the story goes on. *Quod incepimus conficiemus*: What we have begun, we shall finish.

I I

September 26th, 2006

I arrived at seven o'clock last night to find him dressed and waiting. 'My doctor has finally given me leave to discharge myself,' he said. 'I have booked a cab for eight o'clock, which gives us time for tea and a chat.' He saw my cautious expression and smiled. 'You haven't finished your story. As you can imagine, I'm keen to hear the next instalment.'

I sat next to him on one of the blue hospital chairs. He had already ordered tea – in a couple of hospital mugs – in anticipation of my visit. Not a word about the police, or the work on the Gunderson Building. I no longer have to lead him on; now he follows willingly. Nor did I need a thousand and one nights; I had him practically at hello. But Straitley is no fool, and he still needs to be kept on a short leash, at least until the building work is nearer its completion. My gently redacted version of things will lead him to a blank wall. What will he do when he gets there? Will he simply turn around? Or will he choose to turn and fight?

I remember that final week of term through a veil of unreality. Weeks, and not days, seemed to have passed since my talk with

Jerome; since my birthday; since the letter from *Conrad*. Time had a treacle consistency; moving at the unbearable pace of an encroaching nightmare. I slept badly; dreaming of the green door and the sink hole. More than once I heard Dominic, speaking urgently on the phone, only to hang up almost as soon as I entered the room. Once I overheard him say: 'I don't care what it takes.' When I asked him, he claimed that it was something to do with the wedding, but I no longer believed him. Everything around me was coloured by the knowledge that Dominic was Mod: that he had not only lied to me, but that he had made me doubt myself. Even now, I found myself unable to confront him; as if by staying very still, I could avert catastrophe. So much now depended on him; our future; our security. Emily adored him, and had already thrown herself headlong into plans for the wedding. If I provoked a quarrel – or even worse, a split – I knew she would never forgive me. He had done his work too well – the bicycle, the attention, the holidays by the sea – charming her from under my nose while I obsessed over Conrad. And so, against all my instincts, I did not confront him, and I consigned my suspicions and fears to the twilight of the sink hole.

At work, I tried to hold onto the decaying routine of the final week of term: quizzes, extra-curricular groups, some half-hearted attempts by colleagues (mostly Scoones and Sinclair) to keep to the Departmental lesson plans, while the younger ones (Higgs and Lenormand) allowed silent reading and, occasionally, chess. Surprisingly, I found my relief in the routine of King Henry's; in cups of tea in the Common Room and cigarettes with Carrie. The boys were cheerily noisy, but there was no misbehaviour. I came home late every night that week, not because I had work to do, but to give myself longer in that world where – ironically – things were so much simpler.

Although I waited impatiently for my meeting with Jerome, in many ways, this pleased me. It gave me time to plan ahead; time to think things over. So many unanswered questions had emerged from the past few days, questions which, until now, I had not dared face. Who had sent me the birthday gift from my childhood friend, Emily? Who was the person my daughter called Conrad – the one who had frightened her into cutting her own hair, and had told her about Mr Smallface? Who was the person who had written the letter to my parents, purporting to be my brother? And why would anyone do those things? What possible reason could they have?

Whoever it was knew details of my story that had never been told in any of the articles published around Conrad's death. Not even Catherine Potts, author of *CONRAD: The Lost Boy of Malbry*, had known about the hair-cutting incident, or about Emily's birthday gift. Whoever was behind these things was someone who had *known* me. Someone who had access to my parents and my memories. The drama of that summer term – the boy with the Prefect's badge, the air of hostility in the Department, Conrad's memorial window – all this had created a kind of paralysis in me. I had no longer felt able to trust the evidence of my senses. Now at last I realized that I had been spinning out of control – seeing hallucinations, hearing voices from the drain – so that I'd doubted everything, even my own judgement.

But now, I had found my centre again. Whatever the questionable origins of the blood in the sink, or the boy with the Prefect's badge, that figure in the theatre was *real*. Everyone had seen him. Someone *real* had written that letter to my parents. Someone *real* had frightened Emily into cutting her hair. There was a human origin to all this, which I had allowed to go unchallenged for much too long. A little too late, I realized I should have started with Emily. In spite of his apparent concern, Dominic had dissuaded me from asking about her imaginary friend, but in the light of new information, I started to question his motives. I did not doubt his affection for her, and his shock at her shorn hair had been real. But had he talked to her about me? I knew he'd become very close to her. Could he have told her that story? And if not Dominic, then who had told her about Mr Smallface? It was too late to ask her now. Dominic had claimed her. I wasn't surprised. How could I compete? All I could do was bide my time, and hope for the chance to investigate.

I found the opportunity on the last afternoon of term. King Henry's broke up early that day, which gave me the whole of the afternoon before Dom and Emily came home. I got back at twelve to an empty house; and without even pausing to change my clothes, I headed to Emily's bedroom.

I've never had any compunction in searching my daughter's bedroom. She had always known the rules: if she needed something to be private, she had to be better at hiding it than I would be at finding it out. Emily at six years old was not at all better at hiding. I found her pictures under her bed, in the same dark-green folder that Dominic had shown me. This time there were more of them: all of them horribly familiar. I'd drawn my own version, after all, in the months after Conrad disappeared; clumsy, ominous figures in muddy shades of grey and brown, some of them showing the monster coming out of a cavern or drain, all of them topped with that somehow terrifyingly small, dark head.

But that wasn't what I was looking for. I'd seen my daughter's drawings before. I was looking for something else – a clue that would help me understand how a long-dead monster had somehow managed to claim my child. I never doubted that there was *something* she was hiding from me. Even before we moved into the house on April Street, Emily had always been a quiet, secretive little girl. She didn't have many friends. The girls whom Dominic had invited to sleep over had very quickly drifted away. Only one name kept resurfacing. A friend whose name was *Conrad*.

I'd already made enquiries at school. There was no Conrad in her year. I searched in her wardrobe; her bedside drawers, her toy box, in the hope of finding a clue. Everything was in its place, neat and tidy and harmless. And then I tried her bookcase, where all her picture books were filed in order of colour, size and shape, and found, in between *Sleeping Beauty* and *Cars and Trucks and Things That Go*, a slim, black hardback notebook, labelled: *King Henry's Grammar School Prep Diary.*

I opened it, already knowing the name that I would find. On the flyleaf I read, in an exuberant hand:

Conrad Price; Michaelmas Term, 1971

My brother's school diary. How strange, I thought. All Conrad's possessions had been carefully kept by my parents. How could it have found its way into my daughter's things like this? A diary for a school term that my brother had never known, neatly labelled in readiness for a year he would not see.

I turned the page. There was his timetable, carefully inked, and the list of his Masters for that year.

Form Master: Dr Sinclair
English: Miss Macleod
Maths: Dr Jones
Physics: Mr Fry
Art: Mr Moody
Chemistry: Dr Hillman

Each name was flanked with a crude, but lively caricature of the member of staff concerned. I was unsurprised to see that my brother had been a lover of doodles in margins, of nicknames. Thus, Miss Macleod appeared as her scantily clad alter ego, *Carrie On Camping*. Dr Sinclair was *Shagger Sinclair*. Dr Jones was *Mr Redface*, and Mr Fry was *Mr Smallfry*, which made me pause for a moment, though neither of the caricatures looked anything like the monster of my childhood. Once again, I turned the page. There was his form list; twenty-two names, in my brother's graceless hand. To me at five, barely able to write my name, Conrad's handwriting had seemed impossibly sophisticated: now I could see it for what it was; the shapeless scrawl of a teenage boy who was in every way unremarkable. In a way it was touching: almost disappointing. As if I had pulled aside a mask to reveal something small and pitiful. I scanned the class list and saw Dominic's name. So Dominic *had* intended to stay – at least at the time the list was drawn up. I turned the page. It was headed: *Michaelmas Term: Week 1*.

I suppose I'd expected it to be blank: a symbol of the boy-shaped hole at the heart of my family. Instead, I read two written lines. One, carefully printed now, but in the same kind of shapeless writing as the class list and the teacher notes, read:

Hello, I'm Conrad. Who are you?

And the other, in an uncertain hand, said:

Hello, Conrad. I'm Emily.

PART 6

Mnemosyne
(River of Memory)

I

King Henry's Grammar School for Boys, July 15th, 1989

I read through the rest of the diary at speed, hardly daring to breathe. The entries told their own story: one of a small girl with a vivid imagination and her secret, ghostly friend. And what child could fail to be drawn in? From the entries I guessed that the exchange had begun some weeks ago, at around the time I started at King Henry's.

My daughter was not quite seven years old. Her reading was fair, but not yet up to following adult, joined-up handwriting. Her mysterious friend had obliged by printing all his entries, carefully detaching the words so that a child could read them.

Let's be friends.

And her reply, in a heartbreaking scrawl:

Yes plEAse.

The rest of the entries told their tale. Brief at first, then gaining in sinister detail as they went on. I found the first mention of Mr Smallface four pages in, after a few innocuous entries, brief, but laden with meaning.

What do your mummy and daddy do?

Mummy and Dom They are teechers

Do you like your school?

yes I like drwring and games

What about your new house?

It nice but my mummy prommist she get me a kitn and she did Not

I had to smile at that. Emily had always dreamt of having a pet. Only children often do, just as I had when I was her age. Of course, by then I *was* an only child, except for the absence of Conrad, which seemed a presence in itself, like a cold and baleful dog that followed me wherever I went. Before the house on April Street, a pet would have been impossible. We were living in rented rooms, buying clothes from Oxfam. A tin of cat food cost the same as two packets of instant noodles. And then there would have been vet's bills; flea spray; vaccination fees.

Emily had understood. I'd bought her a stuffed cat toy from one of the charity shops, and she had been satisfied for a while. The stuffed cat was called Marmalade, and sometimes I'd heard her talking to him when she thought I was asleep. Soon after we moved in with Dominic, Emily had started to mention maybe adopting a kitten, but with the new job and my other concerns, the subject had never been followed up, although more recently, Dominic had hinted that, after the wedding, it might be possible. Now, of course, when Emily whispered to herself at night, it was no longer to a harmless old stuffed cat, but to something far more dangerous. Something that could whisper back, in the secret language of childhood.

It's a nice house, the entry went on, **but watch out for Mr Smallface.**

whos that?

He lives in the pipes. Down the toilet. You can hear him knocking at night.

And now it began; the story Conrad had told me, retold in

his diary in almost exactly the same words. At first Emily had seemed to think it was a joke, but soon the entries suggested that she was feeling anxious. Over the weeks, the details had emerged – the sound of the plumbing, the sinks, the drains – and then the stolen children. Emily's replies became gradually more anxious, 'Conrad's' entries gradually more detailed. Now came the instructions:

Mr Smallface wants you to draw him.

Mr Smallface says don't tell your mum.

Mr Smallface wants to pull you down the plughole. He wants to pull you in by your hair.

I felt a sudden burst of rage and slammed the diary shut. Who could be behind this? Only Dominic and I had access to Emily's room. Only Dominic knew enough about my history to use it in this way. And he *had* lied to me. But why? Why would he frighten Emily? And if not Dominic, then *who*?

I realized I was shaking. Although it was summery outside, my fingers had grown stiff with cold. I looked at my watch. Three-thirty. Dominic would be home soon. Emily liked to walk back from school – it was only half a mile from the house, and in those days children walked to school; no one felt it was dangerous. But today, *everything* felt dangerous. I felt as if a layer of the world had been stripped away like paper. In this new world, anything – yes, *anything* – could happen. Dominic could be a liar. My daughter could be taken from me. Now I imagined her, walking home, in her red-and-grey uniform, making sure not to step on the cracks – and someone else walking behind her.

I put the diary back in the bookcase, exactly as I had found it. I needed to think about what it meant before I tried to talk to her. My feet were aching – I kicked off my shoes and walked barefoot to the kitchen. There, I made tea, Dominic's way, with milk and lots of sugar, and sat by the window drinking it, feeling the warmth return to my hands. I was almost ready to face whatever came next when the phone rang.

It was my father. 'Becky, love?'

My father never phoned. Neither of my parents had, not once since I'd moved in with Dominic. And there was an unfamiliar note in his voice; something I couldn't identify.

'What's wrong? Are you all right? Is it Mum?'

I heard him laugh, and I realized that the note I'd heard was excitement. 'Oh no, we're fine. I couldn't wait. I wanted to tell you straightaway. Becky, come over as soon as you can. Something amazing has happened.'

I felt my heart sink. 'Oh no, Dad. Another letter?'

He laughed again. 'Oh no, love. He's been. Conrad's *been*. We've seen him, *talked* to him, both of us. It's him. Your mother's over the moon, and – we just wanted you to know.'

I felt my hands go numb again. The fleeting warmth of the tea had gone. *Oh, God. Not this. Not now*, I thought. I'd seen all this before, you see. The hope was worse than the heartbreak. I wanted to slam down the phone, to cry, to hide under the bedclothes. But I was their only remaining child; this was my responsibility. There could be no hiding away; not anymore. Not from this. And so I kept my voice very calm as I said:

'Hang on, Dad. I'm coming.'

2

King Henry's Grammar School for Boys, July 15th, 1989

Of course he was gone by the time I got to the house on Jackson Street. In fact, whoever had been had left long before my arrival. But both my parents were adamant; it had been Conrad. No room for doubt.

'A father always knows,' said Dad, as if this sorry scenario hadn't already happened a dozen times before. 'It was Conrad. No doubt about it. He was even wearing that badge of his, his Prefect's badge that he was so proud of.'

My mother looked up in agreement, her face made pink and youthful by tears. I'd grown up thinking she was old, but today she looked almost my age. 'He's grown so tall,' she said, 'but his *face*! His face is just like a schoolboy's. He told us it would be easier if he just saw us at first, because there's so much to tell you, so much to take in. He didn't want to be overwhelmed. He wanted you to be ready. But I *know* he'll want you here next time. He misses you so much, Becky.'

I'd found them both in the garden – the first time I'd seen them outside in years. My mother was sitting on the step, with one eye to her cooking in the kitchen. My father was in his shirt sleeves, kneeling by a flower bed. The garden had scarcely been touched in years, but there were roses by the wall, and self-seeded forget-me-nots. Now my father was earnestly trying to pull up nettles from the bed, a tea-cloth wrapped around his hand for want of gardening gloves. Best of all, the radio was not tuned to a numbers station, but to a local station playing Frank Sinatra.

'Oh, love,' he said, 'I'm so glad you came. Will you stay for tea? Your mother's made chilli con carne.'

I didn't want to stay for tea. I wanted to cry with frustration, to tell them how utterly wrong they were. But their happiness was so touching, so new, and both of them looked so different to the grey-faced ghosts of my childhood that I just didn't know how to begin. If I voiced my suspicions now, they simply wouldn't believe me. And I knew better than to question their faith in this 'Conrad' – at least not before I had all the information I needed.

I smiled. 'That sounds delicious. Didn't – er, *Conrad* want to stay for dinner?'

My father gave me a humorous look. 'He said you wouldn't believe it at first. He knows how stubborn you can be. He said you needed to take your time.' He gave me a rough and cheery hug. 'You'll come round, love. I know you will. You were so little when he left. It makes sense you'd feel it differently.'

I decided to humour him awhile. 'I think I'm afraid to believe it,' I said. 'We've been disappointed so many times.'

'I know you have, love.' He smiled again. 'He said you'd probably feel that way. Little steps at first, he said. Like your birthday present. He thought you might like to see it again, after all this time.'

'What?' I thought of the little pink album that had sat on top of the wardrobe for years. 'He brought that to my party? He was there?'

'Of course he was. He wanted us to keep quiet about him until he had time to talk to you. He would have said hello then, but he didn't want to spoil your night. When you meet again, he wants it to be in a nice, quiet place, where you can have a proper chat. He told us you might be angry at first, that you might not even want to see him. He says if so, he understands. He's ready to give you all the time you need.'

'I see. How thoughtful.' My mouth was dry.

'Come inside. I'll make some tea and tell you all about it.'

I followed him into the kitchen, where my mother was stirring a simmering pot. I wasn't hungry at all – Dom and I usually had dinner much later than this – but chilli con carne had always been one of my childhood favourites, and the fact that my parents had thought of me made the invitation hard to refuse.

I sat at the kitchen table, upon which stood a vase of peonies, three plates and some accompaniments to the meal my mother was preparing. I was a little surprised to see fresh chillies and coriander there – my mother had always been an unadventurous cook, and her chilli came from a packet – but this smelt fresh and really good. I said so, and my mother looked pleased. 'You should have brought your little girl,' she said. 'She must be growing fast.'

'She is,' I said, thinking of Conrad's diary.

'Conrad says she looks just like you at the same age.'

I stiffened a little. 'He's seen her?'

'We showed him the photographs,' she said. 'And of course, he's seen her walking home from school.'

I felt a sudden prickle of rage. How long had this man been watching us? And could *he* have been responsible for the entries in Conrad's diary? The thought of some stranger in the house, looking through my daughter's things, filled me with a swooning rage. And of course, if that were so, then Dominic must be complicit. He knew so much about us, I thought. And Dom and Conrad had been friends. Could this imposter and Dominic be somehow working together? And if so, what was the motive?

I said, rather more sharply than I'd intended: 'If this is really Conrad, then where has he been for eighteen years?'

My father put his hand on my arm. 'All in good time, love. It's complicated.'

'Well, did he run away, Dad, or was he taken? Did he tell you *that*, at least?'

'He told us, love. Not the details. But it's not up to us to tell you. Your brother wants to tell you himself, once things have settled down a bit.'

'That's convenient,' I said. 'Well, at least tell me where he lives. What job hc docs. Why he decided to come back now, after all this time.'

My mother was looking anxious by then. I could see her glancing back at me from her place over the stove. Her face was pinched, her colour high, no longer with excitement.

'Don't be like that, Becky,' she said. 'Not now we're a family again.'

I could feel a hot ball of tension forming under my breastbone. It was a very familiar shape, a very familiar feeling. One tug, I knew, and the ball would unravel into a hot red snarl of rage, and I would not be able to hold onto my patience, or my anger.

My father saw it and intervened, saying to my mother; 'Give her time to get used to it, love. She's been through a lot.' It was the first time either of them had acknowledged such a thing. I felt both disarmed, and oddly touched, but that feeling, I knew, was dangerous. This man who claimed to be

Conrad was certainly not my brother. I had to find out who he was, what he wanted, especially as, by his own admission, he'd been stalking both me and my daughter.

I took a deep and calming breath. 'I'm sorry. You're right,' I said. 'It's a lot to take in all at once. And there have been so many men saying they were Conrad. Why is this one different?'

My parents exchanged glances. 'He *looks* like Conrad,' my mother said. 'He's tall, well built, well spoken. And he knows everything Conrad would know. He remembers everything. He even remembered I liked peonies.' She indicated the vase on the table.

'Anyone can buy flowers,' I said. 'As for the rest, it's easy to read up on the case in all those articles and books.'

She shook her head. 'It's different this time. He knows things we didn't tell anyone. Details about his school, his friends. Becky, he even remembers about that imaginary friend you had.'

'Mr Smallface? Mum, *everyone* knows that story.'

She waved a wooden spoon at me. 'No, not him. That little girl. The one you called Emily Jackson.'

3

July 15th, 1989

'But Emily was real,' I said. 'I know. I went to school with her. Mum, I even went to her house. She had a disabled sister –'

My mother shook her head and smiled. 'You were always such an imaginative little thing. You had such funny ideas in your head. That monster who lived in the drains was one. Anything that went wrong was his fault. That Emily, she was another. You even named her after our address.'

'Emily was real,' I said. 'I remember her perfectly.'

But did I *really*, I asked myself? Those memories now seemed too clear, too luminous among the rest of the murk of my childhood. Was it a coincidence that the Jacksons shared the name of our street? And hadn't the family moved away soon after Conrad disappeared?

'Of course she was real,' I insisted. 'What about my birthday present, that pink album Conrad brought? There was a picture of me inside, and one of Emily's drawings.'

My father gave me a sympathetic look. '*You* did that drawing, Becky, love. You stuck in the picture. And you were the one who signed the card. Conrad knew. He was concerned. He wanted you to make real friends.'

I felt my chest tighten. 'That isn't true. Emily was a real friend. I remember her mother, too, and her sister Teresa, who had cerebral palsy.'

I told myself there was no reason to question what I remembered. My parents were the ones who had the memory issues, I told myself. *They* were the ones who had lived in a dream, and who were still dreaming. I had come through the tunnel at last. I was happy, and grounded, and whole –

'Oh, Becky,' said my father. 'Teresa was *your* sister. She died before you were even born, when Conrad was a little boy. *She* had cerebral palsy, and she died when she was three months old. That was *her* album, the pink one. We kept it in a drawer for years. We never got to fill it in. You must have found it and wrapped it up.'

I shook my head. 'I remember Teresa. I remember what she was like.'

My father's voice was gentle, but firm. 'You must have heard us talking, Becks. You'd always wanted a sister. You must have picked it up, somehow, and made it part of your make-believe.'

Once more I shook my head. This wasn't right. I knew there had been another child, who had died in infancy. But that child wasn't Teresa. I was sure I'd never been told her name. And yet it all seemed familiar, like a picture I'd been shown long ago. *She died before you were even born. You'd always wanted a sister.* Show a child a photograph of something that happened before they were born; tell the same story often enough, and they can come to believe they were there, that they themselves were a part of it.

Cerebral palsy. Would I really have known that term when I was five years old? I thought back to my memories of Emily and the Jacksons. Her sweet and caring relationship

299

with her older sibling; her jolly, loving parents. All of them gilded in my mind, polished to a dangerous sheen. I thought of how many times I had wished that I could live with the Jacksons – that Emily could be my sister, that maybe *I* could be Emily. *Could* I have invented them? Were they just a fantasy of my perfect family, projected onto my real life like an image onto a blank wall? I thought of the gaps in my memory, the sink holes that littered my childhood. Could all that really have been the result of an overactive imagination?

I thought of my sister, Teresa; the damaged child I'd never known. I've spent enough time in therapy to understand projection. And now it seemed all too possible that Emily Jackson had been just that – a projection – representing everything that was missing in my life. Was it really plausible that I had no pictures of Emily? No photograph from school, no snapshot taken at her house? And where exactly *was* her house? I must have been there many times. But although I seemed to remember her parents and her sister, I had no recollection of ever having walked there. Instead, there were dreamlike images of both of us together; in a room very like my own bedroom, surrounded by familiar toys –

My head was aching ferociously. Suddenly, I wanted to be home, with Dominic and Emily. I made my feeble excuses and fled, in spite of my parents' protests. But April Street wasn't home. April Street was a mirage; a promise of something built on lies, as comforting and imaginary as my friendship with Emily Jackson. Could I accept a relationship with a man who not only had lied to me but who might have been in collusion with the man who had duped my parents? On the other hand, Emily Jackson proved that I was *not* reliable; that I could recreate my world as a fantasy to serve my needs. What if I was wrong about Dom? What if I was wrong about everything?

These were the thoughts that filled my mind as I drove back to April Street. Everything we had, we owed to Dominic's generosity. Emily had her own room for the first time in her life. We had money to spend on clothes, on toys, on treats, on holidays. Even my car – bought second-hand from his Uncle Bobs – had been a gift from Dominic. Why was I willing to risk all that for the sake of a few lost memories?

I turned down April Street, then onto the drive. The driver's window was open and I could smell the blossom from the hedge. Dominic's car was already there, parked against the grass verge, and at the side of the house I could see the kitchen window was open. From inside, I could hear Cyndi Lauper, hiccuping 'I Drove All Night', and I could smell something cooking; something light and aromatic.

It was all so normal, so comforting. If only it could stay that way –

It can. It can, if you want it to, said a tiny voice in my mind. It sounded so clear and so lucid that I could almost believe it had come from outside. And it was right, I realized. Nothing really had to change. All I had to do was to put those suspicions from my mind. After all, nothing was proven. I could let the matter die. Rather than challenge Dominic, I could claim what he was offering me. An easy life. A comfortable home. The means to bring up my daughter, not as a struggling single mother, but as part of a family. I know that sounds a little cold. But I have never believed in romance. Silence was the practical choice, for my own sake, and Emily's. A successful marriage needs compromise. What couple doesn't keep secrets? All I needed was to let go, and never go back to King Henry's.

You saw something. You know what it means.

Perhaps. But what did it matter now? I didn't need those memories. Conrad was dead, and I would not let him jeopardize my future.

And so I took a deep breath, checked my face in the mirror. I looked a little pale, I thought. I pinched my cheeks for colour. Then I stepped out of the car and, smiling, went inside the house.

4

St Oswald's ~~Grammar School for Boys~~ *Academy*
Michaelmas term, September 26th, 2006

And who would really blame her? I'm certainly in no position
to judge other people's choices. As she says, we all have to
compromise. The past three weeks have shown me just how
much I am willing to compromise for the sake of St Oswald's,
that barnacle-ridden, rotten old hulk, which somehow keeps
on sailing.

She has not yet finished her story. I wonder if she ever
will. Her tale is like the rivers of Hell, leading in every direction at once; brimming over with human tears. I want to
hear the end of it; and yet I cannot lie in bed and have it
drip-fed to me through a tube. Like the young Becky Price
with her Dominic, I have traded the uncomfortable truth for
a fleeting moment of calm. This cannot continue. I cannot
remain Merlin, trapped by Nimuë. This is why, before she
arrived here, I booked a taxi to take me home, in the hope
that this would break the spell she seemingly has over me.
My cab arrived at the hospital a little after eight o'clock. My
doctor was stern, but magnanimous: 'If you insist, Mr Straitley,
then yes, I will discharge you. But on no account must you

return to work for at least two weeks; or I will not answer for the consequences.'

The doctor is yet another St Oswald's boy. There's no escaping them in Malbry. They are like homing pigeons; they go off to university, filled with hope and ambition, and before you know it, they're back here, looking slightly furtive, but still lording it over the rest. This one, Dr Massey, was never actually one of *my* boys – a fact that gives me some relief, given that I can never look at my GP without remembering him as an undersized little grinning boy with the unfortunate habit of slipping his shoes off under his desk and kicking them about as he worked on his grammar.

This one, at least, stirs no memories, except of a name on an Honours Board, and a distant, boyish face in the crowd. It also means that he has no fear of voicing his professional concern: in his opinion, I am risking a relapse of my as-yet-unexplained condition. But I am a grown man, he says, with a look on his face that suggests he thinks quite the reverse, and I am free to leave if I must. In a wheelchair, forsooth, although I am quite capable of leaving the premises by my own motive power, as I pointed out when we reached the door and with it, thankfully, the limits of the man's authority.

He shot a glance at La Buckfast, who I think he believes is a relative. 'Will you be taking Mr Straitley home? If so, perhaps you could try to make sure that he gets some rest. He needs no further excitement.'

The taxi was parked pleasingly close to the hospital entrance. 'I am perfectly capable of taking myself home,' I said, making for the idling cab with as brisk a stride as I could manage. 'Ms Buckfast has other demands on her time than supervising recalcitrant staff.'

La Buckfast smiled. 'Of course,' she said. 'But I'd rather stay with you. Just in case you had the idea of dropping by somewhere else on the way. The Gunderson Building, for instance.'

I started. 'What?'

She waited until I had settled myself on the back seat of the cab before sitting beside me. 'Admit it, Roy. It had crossed your mind.'

So shoot me. Maybe it had. I said; 'What of it? It's only half a mile from my house.'

'Half a mile, on foot, through a park, at half past eight in the evening. I don't think so, Roy. Not today. There's nothing to see there, anyway.'

I leant forward to speak to the driver. 'St Oswald's, main entrance, please. I'll be about ten minutes.'

La Buckfast shrugged. 'As you wish.' She handed the driver a note. 'Just don't drive away while we're out there.'

It was dark when we arrived. I'd forgotten how fast the nights draw in during the first half of the Michaelmas term. The main gates were closed, but the Porter's Gate, which served the Porter's Lodge, was not. There is a prefab by the gate, from which our Porter, Jimmy Watt, supervises any comings and goings. A bank of security lights came on as we passed (the new St Oswald's is protective of its investments), and Jimmy's head appeared from a window.

'Who's there?' he called. 'Oh, Mr Straitley. Everything all right?'

'Yes, thank you, Jimmy,' I said. 'Just having a look at the building works. Nothing to worry about.'

'OK, boss.' Jimmy's head withdrew, and La Buckfast and I headed the few hundred yards to the fenced-off part of the playing fields, which once had been a seasonal lake, and now seemed set to be the largest and showiest monument to a boy since the School was founded.

The question was, *which* boy? Rupert Gunderson or Conrad Price?

The site was surrounded by fences, mobile cabins and machinery. Here too there were security lights, placed on a bank of scaffolding. They came on as we approached, lighting up the building. Because it *is* a building now; larger than I'd imagined it, and shaped like the prow of a kind of ship, all curves and sharp angles. The glass (there will be a great deal of glass) is not yet in place, but the shell of the building, the skeleton and much of the concrete floor are in place, and in the harsh security lights, I can see the pool itself; an empty blue plastic rectangle surrounded by brushed concrete.

'The changing rooms and facilities are at the back of the building. Boys on the left, girls on the right, just under this big archway. And right here, under the glass wall, there'll be a seating area, with potted palms, vending machines, more bathrooms and a kitchenette.'

I gave her a look. 'And the body?' I said.

She smiled. 'There are sixty tons of concrete in that floor. I think this time we can safely assume he isn't going to resurface.'

'But why?' I still didn't understand why she, of all people, would hide the truth. 'He was your brother. You spent so long trying to find out what happened to him. Why would you want to bury the truth, when finally you could be free?'

Once more, she smiled. 'Oh Roy. You know why. St Oswald's is my legacy. My gift to the girls of the future. Do you think I'd give that up for the chance to give *him* more attention?'

I stared at her. Her eyes were clear; her face illuminated by more than the lights.

'You have to understand,' she said. 'I've lived with his story all my life. I've never had an identity. To my parents, I was the child they *had*, not the one they wanted. To Dominic, I was the memory of a debt he had to pay. In all those books and articles, I was the key to unlocking a door that led to Conrad's murderer. No one ever asked themselves if I deserved a door of my own. And now I have my door, Roy —'

'*Audere, agere, auferre*,' I murmured, almost reverently.

'What?'

'Oh, you just reminded me of somebody else for a moment,' I said.

She nodded as if she understood. 'I hope you can see my perspective,' she said. 'From where I was standing, there wasn't a choice. St Oswald's has suffered so many blows over the past few years. One more might have ended us. And I know we don't always see eye to eye on matters of School policy' — she gave me a satirical look — 'but both of us want the School to survive. Both of us know our priorities. And both of us are capable of making a personal sacrifice. For the sake of the School, Roy. For the sake of St Oswald's.'

The taxi was still waiting by the time we got back to the gates, although we had been gone for over twice as long as I'd promised. It was just beginning to rain; the kind of soft rain that sometimes sets in at the tail of a long, dry summer, and it smelt of damp earth, and fallen leaves, and the alchemy of petrichor. It is a deceptive kind of rain, which settles softly into the air like pollen, barely seeming to touch the ground. And yet it is relentless, finding its way into every crack and fissure; every broken seal. Nothing can withstand it long; not stone, or oak, or slate, or glass. And little by little, it fills the lakes, and ponds, and wells, and reservoirs.

I looked over at La Buckfast, as she handed the driver another note. In the light of the street lamp, her hair was torched into hectic brightness. There were tiny droplets of rain caught in the fur collar of her coat. She turned towards me and smiled. 'Well?'

'I want the rest of the story,' I said. 'I've followed you this far, after all.'

'Very well, Mr Straitley,' she said.

We set off home in silence.

5

The house was cold when we arrived. I turned on the fire in the living room and made a pot of Darjeeling tea. The herbal tea has served its purpose; and it might be a long night. I found some packets of UHT milk hidden in the pantry, along with some sachets of sugar. I loaded Straitley's mug with both, and settled into an armchair.

Memory is an organic machine, made of many connections. Take one away, and the machine will try to bypass the missing reality, making its own connections, reaching out towards the light. Emily Jackson was one of these; a series of hopeful images, made to conceal a missing part; the gap at the heart of my childhood. It finally came clear to me, as I entered the house on April Street, that not only was I missing the memory of Conrad's disappearance, but that of *everything else* I thought had happened to me over the years. None of it could be trusted now; none of it had substance. Soap bubbles in the sun; bright and shiny as baubles of glass, but vanishing at a single touch.

Plato believed that Memory was like a piece of sealing wax, upon which a man could imprint the facts irrevocably into its surface. But Plato also believed that the written word was the enemy of memory, robbing the goddess Mnemosyne of her ancient tribute:

They will cease to exercise memory because they rely on that which is written, calling things to remembrance no longer from within themselves, but by means of external marks.

No, Mr Straitley; you're not the only one with a Classical education. At Mulberry House we learnt all about the mother of the Muses. Some of the ancients venerated her as a Muse herself – perhaps the greatest of all of them; for what good are poetry, theatre, dance, history or song without the means to remember them?

Perhaps Plato was right, I thought as I greeted my fiancé with a kiss, just as if nothing odd or upsetting had happened that day. Perhaps I had allowed other people's words to rob me of my memories. The newspapers, the studies, the books had overwritten my memory, so that I had drunk from the wrong stream – Lethe, and not Mnemosyne.

You saw something. You know what it means. All you need is the key –

'How was your last day of term?' said Dom.

'Fine. A bit of a shambles,' I said. 'Can't say I'm sorry to be home.'

He gave me his warm and brilliant smile. 'Can't say I'm sorry to see you,' he said. 'Oh, and here –' He reached in his pocket and held something out in the palm of his hand. 'It's your ring. I had it fixed. It should fit you properly now.'

It was indeed the engagement ring that I'd had removed a few days before. It had been expertly mended, with nothing but the smallest ripple to show where the gold had been cut. And yes, it fitted perfectly, gleaming like a narrowed eye.

I smiled. 'You're an angel.'

'Not really. You might even say I've got skin in the game.'

You see how it was for me, Straitley. The ring; the warmth of his smile; the flowers he'd bought on the way home – not peonies, but wallflowers, sweet and rich and golden-brown; the cup of tea he handed me; the scent of something good from the stove. It was as if I'd been given a choice – I could have all this, I thought, or the key to a door that led nowhere at best, or at worst, to a chamber of horrors.

So, Roy. I chose all this. I chose to become Mrs Buckfast. I told myself I could be *one of the gang*; give Emily a father. All I had to do was say nothing; but instead enjoy what was offered me, forget the past, and never go back to King Henry's. And just then, for that evening, with the summer holiday stretching out like a beach of sun-warmed sand, and the scene at my parents' house fresh in my mind, I really thought I could do that. Write to King Henry's, telling them that I'd decided to go elsewhere; cancel my meeting with Jerome; let my parents deal with their imposter as they chose. I went to bed feeling strangely relieved, and awoke in a burst of clarity at two o'clock in the morning to the sobbing of the water pipes, and knew there was no choice to be made.

I had remembered the shape of the thing that had troubled me at my parents' house. The thing that I was meant to know, but which had been lost.

The green door.

Where had it been?

You heard something, Becky. You know what it means.

And now, perhaps, I thought I did. Behind the sobbing of the pipes, I heard my father's voice again, saying: *It was Conrad. No doubt about it. He was even wearing that badge of his, his Prefect's badge that he was so proud of.*

And it tasted of bitten tinfoil, and burning, and sour suds, and chocolate, and however much I tried to turn over and go back to sleep, those words kept coming back to me, and with them, a realization. My memories were a locked door to a garden left abandoned for years. Over those years, the garden had changed; the beds overrun by brambles and weeds; the shrubs grown into oppressive trees. It had become a frightening place, filled with reflections and shadows, and I had come to believe that I would be happier leaving it locked for good.

But I had the key to open the door. Only I could use it. I'd *always* had the key to the door, in spite of my mind's reluctance to look at its shape, to try it for size, to turn it over and over, to feel its connection with my past. And now that I knew the shape of the key, there could be no walking away.

I had been sleeping for eighteen years. Now, at last, I was awake.

6

King Henry's Grammar School for Boys, July 15th, 1989

I went to my rendezvous with Jerome without giving rise to suspicion. That meant pretending to Emily that I didn't know her secret; pretending to Dom that I didn't know his. But we learn our lessons young. A woman knows how to smile when she doesn't feel like smiling. She knows how to rein back her anger so as not to be thought too shrill or overly confrontational. She knows when looking pretty counts more than looking competent. You ask yourself where my coldness began: it began when I was a child. *Little girls should be seen and not heard* is a maxim that grows into womanhood. Women are valued mostly when they are pretty and attentive. I was both, and I found that men – Johnny, Dom, even you, Roy – too often assumed that this was because I had nothing important to say.

Paul the Apostle wrote: *I suffer not a woman to teach, nor to usurp authority over the man, but to be in silence.* Not what you'd call an endorsement for the Headmistress of a grammar school. But I have found that speaking one's mind is far less rewarding than listening. That's why in the course of my career I've become an excellent listener. Men have told me their secrets without a second thought; revealing themselves, piece by piece, believing that somehow I didn't count. I am not complaining. I have made a good career out of being seen, and rarely heard. I have opened the narrow door and, quietly, made St Oswald's my own. If I could say anything to my younger self, the one who still longed for inclusion, it would be this: *Stop hoping for the crumbs from the cake. One day, you'll be running the bakery.*

I arrived at King Henry's that Saturday just a little early. It was already a hot day, the hottest day of the summer so far, and I was wearing sandals and shorts, my hair tied up in a ponytail. I carried an oversized canvas bag, containing, among other things, the little red satchel I'd found in the theatre. I didn't yet know why I wanted it, but the satchel had been with me that day in 1971, and if I was to unlock my memories, I knew I needed it with me.

Arriving at the entrance, I found a side door standing open, and went in, to find the caretaker, Chris, now dressed in jeans and a T-shirt, his hair tied back from his angular face, his glasses hooked over the neck of his shirt. A toolbox lay open on the parquet floor.

He looked surprised as I came in. 'Can I help you, Miss?' he said.

'I came in to tie up a few loose ends. Is that all right? I won't get in the way.'

He shrugged. 'Fine by me, Miss. Dr Sinclair's in the Departmental Office with Mr Scoones, if you need him.' He grinned at my expression. 'I take it you *won't* be joining them?'

I smiled at that. 'How did you guess? I thought the school would be empty.'

'Oh it is, mostly. Sometimes members of staff come in to tidy up, or to work on next year's curriculum. Mr Scoones says the school is at its best when there are no boys on the premises.' He gave a comic intonation to the words that summed up Scoones's manner perfectly.

I had to laugh. 'I see you've met.'

'Several times,' he said, and grinned. 'In fact, he got me expelled from school.'

'He did? You went to King Henry's?' I said, trying not to show surprise. King Henry's boys do not, as a rule, end up as ancillary staff. They go to Oxford, or Cambridge, and return with laurels and doctorates.

'Actually, I was a St Oswald's boy,' said Chris, with a little grin. 'But I had friends at King Henry's. We used to meet at the chess club, then bunk off and get up to all sorts of things. Scoonesy caught us out one day and reported me to the Head. I was on a scholarship, so out I went.'

'I'm sorry,' I said, trying to imagine my parents' shame if the same thing had happened to Conrad.

'I was an idiot. Most boys are. My brother's kid's a pupil there now. Let's hope he does better than I did.'

That scent of burning tinfoil was back, twice as strongly as before, and with it, a kind of memory, uncertain, but persistent. I tried to imagine what Chris would have looked like as a boy, eighteen years ago. Blond hair, a little too long. A pair of National Health glasses.

'Milky. They called you Milky,' I said.

He gave an involuntary laugh. 'That's right! I looked like the Milky Bar Kid. God, how I hated those glasses. But they were free on the NHS, and there was no way my mum was going to turn down something free.' He squinted at me. 'How do you know?'

'Because you knew my brother,' I said. 'Because you were friends with Conrad Price.'

Chris – *Milky* – grew very still. 'Oh, shit. That was *you*? Oh, shit.' His dismay seemed genuine. 'How much do you remember?' he said.

'I remember enough,' I said.

Milky rubbed the bridge of his nose. It was an oddly childish gesture, and it made him look younger, more vulnerable. 'It must have been tough for you,' he said. 'I mean, you were just a little kid.'

I nodded. 'Tough enough.'

He sighed. 'Not knowing must be the worst. Wondering if he'll ever come back. I once had a cat that disappeared. Not knowing if he'd ever come back was worse than if I'd seen him run over.' He rubbed the bridge of his nose again, and I felt a tiny sting of something that might have been anger. 'Do you remember me?' he said. I thought he looked uncomfortable.

Once more I nodded, thinking of the railway tunnel, the sink hole. The way he'd used his flashlight to make his face that of the monster. And was he also the one who had whispered my name in the shadows? I thought he was.

'I remember being under the Pepper Pot,' I said. 'I remember that very well.'

He looked back at me, almost pleadingly. 'I shouldn't have gone along with it,' he said. 'I told you I was an idiot. I had a kid brother of my own, and I was used to pranking him. And Conrad' – he rubbed his nose – 'Conrad's pranks were something else. I mean, they were legendary.'

'Like crashing the School Photograph?'

Milky looked rueful. 'Among other things. That was how Scoonesy caught us. Caught *me*. Someone ratted me out. Scoonesy was my form teacher, and somehow he got word of it. Conrad got away with it, of course. But that was schoolboy stuff. Nothing bad. Not like that time on the railway.' That oddly childish gesture made him look fourteen again. 'That was a bad thing we did that day. I never meant to upset you. I'm sorry.'

I was surprised. It's not often that a woman receives an apology from a man, especially not in such circumstances. I am far more used to being told: *You need to learn to take a joke*, or; *Why must you be so sensitive?* Little girls are taught the lesson almost from the cradle. *Boys will be boys. It's a man's world. It's because he likes you.* Working at King Henry's, and later at St Oswald's, I had always had to be tough on myself, and gentle on men. Men are so very fragile, Roy; so unused to being challenged. I felt a sudden surge of an emotion I barely recognized, as well as a tiny prickle of doubt. Was he *really* talking about that day under the Pepper Pot? Or could he have meant his apology to refer to something else?

'Thank you,' I told him, and I was alarmed to find that there were tears in my eyes. '*Thank you.*'

According to legend, Mnemosyne is the counterpart of Lethe, the domain of a goddess older than Zeus, and the secret sixth river of Hades. Initiates were given the chance to drink from its waters and escape Lethe's oblivion. I always imagine them salt, Roy; those waters. Salt, like memory. And as my tears began to flow, I felt the waters of Memory pressing against the locked door of Time, bringing with them the flotsam of years, suddenly and sharply released.

I began to sob, not from sadness, but from something deeper and more true; a visceral reaction to the words of the man before me. I sobbed, and the tears came burning like napalm; tears of salt, and grief, and fire, and, once more, of *remembering*.

7

King Henry's Grammar School for Boys, July 15th, 1989

Some memories come fully fledged; some in a flutter of dark wings. This one came in the colour green, and a scent of something burning.

There's something behind the green door. Something big.

Of course, to five-year-old Becky Price, *big* was a matter of perspective. And yet I seemed to remember myself clutching my little red satchel, and something huge in the shadows; and then a hollow crashing sound, like the door of an empty crypt slamming in the darkness.

The green door. Mr Smallface. The taste of bitten tinfoil. The taste of tears, a feeling like sunburn on my streaming face. That *door.* Where had I seen it before? None of the doors at King Henry's were green. In most cases, the doors at King Henry's were made of dark and natural wood, with some of the cheaper ones – for instance, the ones in the toilets – painted black.

But the door of my memory was *green,* the exact same green as the colour of a tin of Golden Syrup, and edged in that sickly, unnatural light, like something out of a nightmare. *Out of the eater came forth meat. And out of the strong came forth –.*

'Miss?' The voice was filled with concern. 'Miss, are you all right?'

I took a breath and opened my eyes. Milky was standing close to me, looking uncertain and troubled. Men rarely, if ever, know what to do when a woman shows any sign of distress. In films, the answer always seems to be some kind of an assault – a violent kiss, or a slap in the face, or maybe a flung glass of water. Of course, most films are made by men. A woman would know better.

'I'm fine,' I said, forcing a smile. 'It's just – *remembering*, you know?'

'OK.' He was still looking cautious. 'If you're sure –'

'Perfectly sure. You've got to love those hormones.' My smile was more convincing now, and I saw him relax a little. I could almost hear his thoughts. *Hormones. Thank God. Just hormones. Nothing to do with me.*

You men. You're so predictable. You're so easy to divert – with tears, or sex, or hormones. You fight your way to the mystery of intimacy like a storybook knight, hacking his way through the undergrowth of our mysterious feelings. *If only you could be like us*, you tell us with your hopeful eyes. *If only you weren't so emotional, so vulnerable, so unexpected.*

I wiped my face with the tail of my shirt. 'I have to go. If Mr Jerome comes looking for me, I'll be on the Lower Corridor, somewhere by the Little Theatre and the Middle School cloakroom.'

'OK. I'll keep an eye out,' he said. 'Mr, er – Jerome, you said?'

'That's right. Do you know him?'

He shook his head. I thought he seemed eager to get back to work, now that the crisis of my tears had been safely averted.

'Well, point him in my direction,' I said, 'if he comes in this way.' I turned. 'Oh, and by the way,' I said, 'do you happen to know if there's a green door anywhere in the school? Do you remember a door like that?'

'Not that I can think of, Miss,' he said, sounding almost sullen now. 'Maybe there was something once, years ago, before my time.' He bent down to take something out of his toolbox, a gesture both of dismissal, and so I couldn't see his eyes. 'Anyway, better get back to work. I'll never be finished otherwise.'

8

King Henry's Grammar School for Boys, July 15th, 1989

I left him kneeling by the box and made my way to the Middle
School cloakroom. The cloakroom was where I had always
waited for Conrad after school. Surely if there *was* a green
door, that's where I must have seen it. But so far there had
been little chance for me to investigate the cloakroom without
the distraction of pupils or staff, and besides, my first encounter
with Scoones had made me somewhat reluctant to try.

I turned the corner, past the theatre and the wall of old
School Photographs, trying to notice everything as if for the
first time. The polished floor; the double doors; the smell of
floor wax and old wood. The sound my school shoes made
as I walked; the echo of my footsteps. The day Conrad had
disappeared, I'd been wearing new shoes. Patent-leather Mary
Janes; red and fascinatingly shiny. I'd spent the whole day
looking down to admire them as I walked. I tried to imagine
them now in the place of my summer sneakers: the sound of
their soles against the wood; their candy-apple shine.

It was working. I could tell. Like a trail of breadcrumbs
through a wood, I followed the memory of those red shoes
towards the empty cloakrooms.

I'd walked down the road from Chapel Lane when I saw Conrad wasn't at the school gate. I'd reached King Henry's fifteen minutes later; the cloakroom was already half empty. Conrad wasn't there, even though he was meant to walk me home; he had a play to prepare for, and I was looking forward to my very first birthday party. I remember sitting on the bench in front of Conrad's locker and watching the last of the stragglers leave. No one hung around that day. None of Conrad's friends were there. Silence settled onto the school like a layer of dust. I waited. And waited.

Had Conrad left? Had he forgotten to pick me up in his excitement over the play? Just *when* did my brother disappear? Those questions had been asked before, many times, over eighteen years. But now that I was here again, the oddness of it struck me once more. Where had my brother been that day? And who else had been there with him?

The Middle School cloakroom was in a basement room, just around from the Middle School entrance. A worn stone flight of steps led down to the place where, eighteen years before, I had waited for Conrad to return. One of the cleaners found me. It had been six o'clock by then. I had been hiding right inside one of the empty lockers, knees drawn up to my chin. The cleaner – a lady called Pat – had given me a bar of Fry's Five Centres, which I had accepted in silence, big-eyed and unsmiling. Five segments of flavoured fondant, coated in dark chocolate – her little treat, for after work. I left the coffee segment.

That scene stands very clear in my mind. I can even still taste the chocolate. I bit against a piece of tinfoil, and the taste of it was like a burst of static from a radio station against my teeth. I could almost feel it now, and yet it felt *too* real, somehow; as real as a story told so many times that you start to believe it happened.

So many of my memories are simply remembered photographs, or newspaper stories, or things I've heard from other people. Who can I trust? My memory is riddled with inconsistencies. Mr Smallface; Emily Jackson; the memory of the cloakroom, with the late sunlight shining through the window, and the taste of chocolate in my mouth – all those things *seem* like memories now. But as soon as I reach for them, they fall away like paper dolls. Nothing is certain; nothing feels safe. I am a child in a fairy tale, surrounded by walking statues.

Such were the thoughts going through my mind as I went down the steps to the cloakroom, smelling the very familiar scent of football boots, disinfectant, dust, Lynx deodorant and the peculiarly ripe and biscuity reek of teenage boys the world over. Boys have a very particular smell; it must be the testosterone. Even now, after the end of term, when every part of the school is cleaned and disinfected, that familiar smell lingered on; it seemed to have been ingrained into the very stones and plaster.

A school is a kind of time capsule, Roy. For all their new theatres and swimming pools and toilet facilities for girls, schools are stubbornly resistant to change. This was certainly true of King Henry's Middle School cloakroom. After eighteen years, it looked the same. The chapel-high ceiling; the mottled walls; the smooth and age-worn flagstones. The banks of gun-grey lockers, scarred and scratched and battered. A double rail of coat pegs running down the length of the room, above a line of benches and cubby-holes for muddy boots. Damp had worked its way through the walls, making the paint rise like pastry. I touched one of the risen spots with my fingertip; it was soft and flaked away, revealing a whitish, powdery stuff that looked like lemon sherbet.

I looked down at my shoes and recalled doing the very same thing eighteen years ago, and feeling a sense of silent dread, that even the walls, which seemed so sound, were nothing but pressed powder. I'd put my finger into my mouth to see what the wall-sherbet tasted like: it had been sour and cottony; the brackish spoor of a monster. Once again, I touched the wall and put my fingers to my mouth; the familiar taste came rushing back, sending me further down the path after those scattered breadcrumbs.

There was a stuttering strip of lights fixed above the cellar steps, but most of the light in the cloakroom came from a long, narrow, ground-level window, high up near the ceiling, which ran the length of the locker room, and let in a pale and watery light. The window was made of solid glass bricks, and you could look up and see the feet of boys running past in the yard high above, and hear their echoing voices, like sounds heard from an aquarium.

Of course, now the school was deserted. No voices rang from the courtyard. Slowly, I walked the length of the room, following the benches. The coat pegs were bare, except for a single blazer, no doubt forgotten by some boy in a hurry to get home. The lockers had all been left open – any boy leaving property inside his locker after term was likely to incur a fine – and a door swung open as I passed, revealing a metal interior, like an old-fashioned oven. Scraps of ancient sticky tape remained on the inside of the door where, year after year, generations of boys had stuck their timetables, pictures of bands (and maybe a centrefold or two, tucked away at the very back). Conrad's locker had been full of pictures cut from magazines; *Sounds* and *Melody Maker*. *The green door. Mr Smallface. The sound of a crypt door slamming.*

The only entrance was via the Lower Corridor steps. There was no inner door. Nor was there any space for one: there were lockers against every wall. The lockers were in blocks of six, the lower ones larger than the top, and were numbered by means of small metal plates fixed into the door. Conrad's locker was 73. I used to sit on the bench opposite, looking at the metal plate, and hiding under the row of coats that hung on the pegs above me.

I went to find my usual place, under locker 73. Conrad's locker was on the top row, and I remembered sitting on the bench, looking up at the metal door. There had been a sticker there, a round one with some writing. Now there was no sticker; not even a mark to show where it had been. The door was shut.

I sat on the bench. It felt surprisingly low to me now: my knees were practically touching my chin. I remembered how I used to climb up there and swing my legs. I don't know why the fact of having *grown* always comes as such a surprise. I closed my eyes and tried to imagine myself at five years old, swinging my feet up and down and looking at my shiny shoes.

The green door. That's where he went.

The memory was close now; so close I could almost taste it. A green door. A garish light. A scent of paint, and wood, and smoke. Dark clouds in the rainbow sky. A groaning sound from the water pipes. A big, dark shape descending. My little red satchel. A slamming sound. And a voice, saying: *Now be a good girl and wait here. Forget you ever saw us.*

Whose voice was that? A boy's voice. My memory would not release it. But I did remember his *shoes* – black, with broken laces. Summer-term shoes; dusty and worn from a whole year of football games in the yard, climbing trees and kicking stones. Shoes that had not seen polish since the start of the Michaelmas term; stretched out of shape, scuffed grey at the toes. But Conrad's shoes, like mine, had been new. My mother would never have let him wear those cheap and scruffy shoes for school.

I felt a pang of excitement. A clue. An unexpected gift from the past. Could those shoes have been Milky's, I thought, or Fatty's, or even Dominic's? The thought made me shiver. Conrad's friends had always claimed that they had gone home after school that day; but their parents had still been at work. They could have lied. One of them had. And the thought that Dominic might have been there was suddenly, strangely, believable. *Why* had Dominic chosen me? Why was he so protective of me? Could it be that somehow he felt the need for a kind of atonement?

I heard a sound from above my head, like light footsteps running past in the yard. I opened my eyes and looked. Nothing there. Nothing but the silent boom of a deserted building. Suddenly the smell of old sweat and football boots and damp plaster was sickening. There was no green door; there never had been.

What am I doing here, really?

I stood up. Locker 73 was now at the level of my eyes. I touched the metal surface, and realized the door was locked. Some boy must have forgotten to take out his things at the end of term. Or maybe, like my brother, he simply hadn't had the chance —

Once more, there came that sound from above; a sudden quick rattle, like boys' shoes on stone. A pupil, I thought; curious to see the School after term's end. Except that I didn't think that at all — I knew *exactly* who it was. I looked up at the strip of glass bricks and saw the blurry outline of someone standing close to the wall; a pair of shoes; grey trousers; a King Henry's boy in uniform.

And then, as I watched, the boy knelt down to look through the clear wall into the locker room. He pressed his face to the glass bricks, and I saw his blurry image there, grotesquely distorted where his face had pressed against the marbled glass —

It was the boy with the Prefect's badge.

9

This time, there was no paralysis. This time, I reacted instinctively. I was wearing sneakers and jeans, rather than my usual heels, and I stood up and ran up the cellar steps towards the Middle Corridor. He must have seen my movement, because he was already running when I burst through the side exit door and out into the open air. He had almost reached the grass verge that stood by the near-empty car park, and was heading across to the main gate, his shirt tails flapping in the breeze.

'You! You, boy! *Stop there!*'

He ignored me, disappearing between the trees that lined the long main entrance. I decided to cut through the car park that lay to the side of the building. There was a side entrance in the wall that ran around the school grounds; maybe I could catch up with him as he joined the main road. I sprinted through the car park; jumped over a small raised flower bed; reached the line of cherry trees at the back of the theatre – and ran straight into a familiar figure, who looked at me, and said:

'What happened? Are you OK?'

It was Jerome, looking natty in his striped boating blazer over a pair of pressed jeans, and wearing that Prefect's badge in his lapel.

I nodded, slowly becoming aware that I was hot and out of breath, and that my hair had escaped from its bun to fall haphazardly over my face.

'I'm sorry I'm a bit late,' he said. 'Are you sure you're OK? You look a bit —'

I glanced over his shoulder towards the School's main entrance. The boy was no longer visible; I'd missed my opportunity.

'There was a boy. I lost him,' I said. 'You must have seen him. He was right there.'

'I'm sorry. I didn't see anyone.'

'He was there,' I insisted. 'Blond, wearing King Henry's uniform.'

He looked at me. 'Like your brother?'

'Yes.'

He gave me a sympathetic look, but I knew he thought it was crazy. He put a hand on my arm, and said, 'Let's go back inside, Becky. Let's get you a cup of tea.' I followed him into the building. He seemed very much at ease there. He led me without hesitation to the staff room, at the far end of the corridor.

Milky was no longer there as we passed through the entrance hall, though I saw the theatre door standing open. Had it been Milky's voice I heard? Had it been *his* worn-out shoes?

In the staff room, Jerome made tea. Without asking me, he added sugar. 'I'm sorry I was late,' he said. 'I can see you've had a shock.'

I drank the tea slowly. *Had I?* I thought. The excess adrenaline still roaring through my veins made my hand shake a little.

'I wasn't afraid,' I said at last. 'I only wanted to see his face.'

He smiled at me. 'Just finish your tea. Tell me what you remember.'

So I told him about the dirty shoes, and the green door, and that sound of a hollow vault, slamming. 'Someone knows what happened that day. Someone warned me to keep away. After what I remembered today, I think it might have been Milky.' And I told him what Milky had said to me, and how he had tried to apologize – for that day under the Pepper Pot, but maybe also for something else. 'I could see he was uncomfortable. He wanted to tell me something. If I could talk to him again, I'm sure I could find out what it was.'

'Maybe,' Jerome said. 'But first, I think maybe we should –'

He did not finish his sentence. Instead, the staff room door was flung open and Philip Sinclair and Eric Scoones came rushing in together. Scoones was the colour of Parma ham; Sinclair, pale as plaster. Scoones stopped short on seeing me, a fixed expression on his face. Sinclair made straight for the telephone and dialled a three-digit number.

'Ambulance. King Henry's School. Theatre entrance,' Sinclair said. Then, he allowed himself to collapse in a chair by the phone and said; 'Hurry, please. I think there's been a rather dreadful accident.'

You probably read about it at the time, although you may not remember it. It was one of those regrettable accidents that sometimes happen in old buildings: a combination of bad luck, hybrid wiring, live cables and human error. Christopher Milk, the school caretaker, was generally agreed to be at fault, as well as being the only casualty. Between themselves, King Henry's staff agreed that it could have been worse. It could have been a pupil.

I don't remember much about the rest of that day, apart from the smell of burning. I do know that the ambulance arrived almost immediately after the call, and that Jerome prevented me from going into the theatre. I know that Scoones kept glaring at me, as if I were the one responsible, and that Sinclair ushered us out of the building as soon as I seemed recovered. I understood that this was the end of my plan to recover my memories. Henceforth, the School would be out of bounds to everyone except the police.

But even so, I already knew more than I had expected to find. Milky *had* been in school that day. His stammering little apology; his eagerness to see me gone; all pointed to something far greater than mere social awkwardness. He had tried to tell me so. And that's why, however much it might have *seemed* like an accident, I already knew without a doubt that Christopher Milk had been murdered.

IO

July 20th, 1989

After that, there was no further chance of exploring the School at leisure. The police searched the Little Theatre for clues, and brought in an electronics engineer to confirm the cause of the accident: but that was only because the School's insurance needed the details.

Death by misadventure, they said. The victim – not a trained engineer – had omitted to check whether a cable was live before inserting a metal screwdriver into a wall socket. Well, Roy, Health and Safety wasn't the same in those days as it is now. The staff of King Henry's, though shocked by the news, were not especially surprised. After all, Christopher Milk had never been very reliable.

Of course, I couldn't tell Dominic that I'd been there when it happened. I had to wait for him to find out about the accident from the *Malbry Examiner*. By then, nearly a week had passed (the *Examiner* came out on Thursdays), and I had been ill for most of that time with what Dom thought was end-of-term flu.

'It happens all the time,' he said over breakfast that morning. 'You run on fumes till the end of term, and then, as soon as the kids break up – *poof*! You're flat on your back for a fortnight.' He smiled and handed me a mug. 'This'll get you back on your feet. It's my mother's recipe. Lemon, hot water, cinnamon, clove – and a healing dose of rum. You'll feel better in no time.'

I took the mug and watched him butter a slice of toast. Emily was eating cereal, sorting out brown shapes from golden ones. The discarded wholegrain cereal hoops looked like a rising pile of dead bees.

'Wow. I used to know that guy.' Dominic had finally seen page two of the *Malbry Examiner*. Milky hadn't made the front page. I watched as Dom read the article, pretending to drink my flu remedy. There was a lot of rum in the mug. The hot fumes made my eyes water.

'What happened?' I said.

Dominic shrugged. 'Accident at King Henry's. The care-taker. Did you know him?'

'I've seen him around a couple of times, that's all. Poor man. You said you knew him?'

'We were at school together,' he said. 'We weren't exactly friends, but yes, I do remember him. We used to call him Milky, because we thought he looked like the Milky Bar Kid.'

He seemed so very casual, I thought. There was nothing in his manner to suggest that he and Christopher Milk had known what had happened to Conrad. Nor was there anything to suggest that he and Milky had stayed in touch, or that he could have known anything about the incident. And yet, I felt uncomfortable. Dominic had already lied to me once about King Henry's. The thought that he was lying now would not completely leave me alone.

'You knew him at King Henry's?' I said.

He gave me a sharp look. 'Of course not. He went to Sunny-bank Park. What makes you think he went to King Henry's?'

I shook my head. Of course, the newspaper gave no such information. It merely said that Christopher Milk, an unmarried man of thirty-four, had died while making routine repairs in the Little Theatre at King Henry's. A photo showed the victim at some kind of family gathering; a much larger photo beside it showed the day of the opening of the Little Theatre: with Margaret Thatcher standing beside a much younger Carolyn Macleod.

'Let me look at that,' I said.

Dom passed me the paper. From the half-page of a local newspaper devoted to his life, Christopher Milk smiled out at me between an older version of him – a brother, I guessed – and a boy who looked about twelve. The newsprint was grainy, and the boy was younger than I'd seen him last; and yet I recognized him at once. It was the boy in uniform I'd seen the day that Milky died, looking down through the marbled glass into the Middle School cloakroom.

PART 7

Asphodel
(Land of the Dead)

I

St Oswald's ~~Grammar School for Boys~~ Academy
Michaelmas term, September 28th, 2006

I have not looked outside for two days. The rain has been incessant. Without her visits, I don't think I would have bothered to leave my bed. My Scheherazade – or is she Nimuë? – has exercised a kind of paralysis over me, so that I feel like an animal in the headlights of an oncoming train, helpless to move or to look away as the monster prepares to run me down.

I tell myself that all this ended a very, very long time ago. All the protagonists are dead – except for La Buckfast, of course – all this was played out two decades ago. This story is like a collision of stars, reaching the Earth a million years after the drama is over; now nothing more than old light, and yet I feel it with all the pain of a recent wound. Once more I find myself playing the sleuth. Scoones was at King Henry's that day. Could he have been somehow responsible for the death of the caretaker? I don't see why, and yet I find myself repeatedly playing out scenarios.

Mr Milk, a word, please?

That's Eric's voice to perfection. Rather gruff, but with the kind of politeness that caretakers do not often receive from staff.

337

It has come to my attention that one of the sockets is broken backstage in the Little Theatre. I'll show you where it is. No, I have not entered it in the Repairs Book. It shouldn't take more than a few minutes to replace. Shall we?

School caretakers are usually men-of-all-work; seldom trained in anything. I can see him now in my mind's eye, squinting impatiently at the broken socket through his little round glasses. *Bloody Eric Scoones*, he thinks. *Still, it won't take long. Better get it out of the way.*

He checks the circuit board backstage; turns off the circuit breaker. He makes his way back to the socket, removes the plate and looks inside. Milk is not an electrician. He does not have a test meter. He takes a screwdriver from his belt and inserts it into the socket to loosen the terminal. His other hand rests gently on the metal box to which the socket was installed. All it would take at that moment would be for someone at the circuit box to just reset the breaker –

It seems horribly plausible. The investigative team would simply have assumed that Milk had flipped the wrong switch, unaware that the terminal was live. The rest was easy. All the murderer would have to do next would be to 'discover' the accident, and allow the drama to unfold. And then there's the fact that Eric had never been clear about why he left King Henry's that year, except for his gruff assertion that *the place was going to the dogs.* Could he have been involved, somehow? Had Chris Milk known something about the disappearance of Conrad Price?

Whenever there's a crime of this type, you always read the same witness accounts. *He was such a nice, quiet man. We never suspected anything.* And, of course, no criminal wants to be caught. No criminal who has gone so long without being caught *looks* like a criminal. And yet, in spite of everything, I cannot believe that Eric Scoones was capable of murder. Eric, who always came second in French. Eric, who always shared his sweets with me at Break times, whose shirt was always untucked at the back, who called me *Straits* for fifty-five years. Eric, whose ambition had soured into sullenness and resentment; Eric, who secretly liked to translate French poetry into English; Eric, who dreamt of travelling, and who had died less than three miles away from the house where he'd been born.

I know. That's maudlin. I apologize. It isn't like me to be maudlin. I miss St Oswald's, that's what it is. My Brodie Boys; my classroom; my daily clashes with Devine. And Eric. I still miss Eric – not for what he *was*, perhaps, but for what he represented to me. The other night, on the playing fields, I felt like a warhorse hearing the call: even the monstrosity of the Gunderson Building felt like coming home, somehow. I wonder how I shall feel when I walk past that building in daylight, knowing there is a body buried under the concrete. I sometimes worry that I will feel relief, or worse, nothing at all. I used to think the truth was more important than anything. Now, after so long alone with my thoughts, I realize that St Oswald's has always taken precedence over the truth, over human beings, even over virtue. St Oswald's, my constant; my Northern Star throughout the years of my Century; St Oswald's, the broken old pirate ship to which I have given the best of myself.

Amare et sapere vix deo conceditur. Even a St Oswald's Master finds it hard to be wise and to love at the same time. I think that perhaps I have not always been wise. But I *have* always been loyal. Boys and Masters – even Heads – will pass, but the stones and spirit endures. La Buckfast's story is safe with me, however it ends; not for her sake, or Eric's, but for the sake of St Oswald's.

The girl who brings my groceries came at one o'clock today. What was her name again? Emma something. I forget. A pretty girl, with the prettiness that comes with youth and privilege and genes, and inexperience of anything but her small and moneyed existence. That she is now a St Oswald's girl still makes the hairs on my neck stand up. But St Oswald's has moved on. Under La Buckfast's captaincy, the old ship has been refurbished and the new recruits are a different class. Well, of course they would be: gone are the days when a boy from a humble background could aspire to a full scholarship. Nowadays, the pupils are all from the kind of families that can afford to spend six thousand a term (plus uniform, trips, and supplies) on a Classical education based, not on grammar and literature, but on the kind of soft approach introduced by Call-Me-Jo, in which pupils read poetry in translation and watch gladiator movies as a means to understanding the culture that shaped our empire.

I despair. I really do. At least I have my Brodie Boys, but they are the last of the old crew. After them, I suppose it will be the fields of asphodel – which is to say, retirement – or plastic desks, and IT labs, and pretty girls called Emma.

I said as much to La Buckfast as she called at her usual time after school.

'You're still looking under the weather, Roy,' she said, as she made a pot of tea. No herbal tea, thank all the gods, but Tetley's decaf teabags, with a decadent splash of semi-skimmed milk.

'Yes, but you bring the sunshine,' I replied gallantly, and, sitting in my kitchen chair, I drank my tea and prepared myself for one more of my thousand and one nights.

2

July 29th, 1989

I remember that summer as I remember some of the days of my childhood. Nothing seemed real, although it was: everything real was imaginary. My mind was like a box of abandoned jigsaw pieces; luminous fragments that caught the eye, but never connected to anything. My flu – if that's what it was – improved, and by the end of July I was back to something like normality.

Except it *wasn't* normal – my life had become a series of well-lit scenes from a stage play. I watched from the wings as Dominic and Emily continued to plan the wedding; occasionally walking onto the stage to smile, and approve, and look happy. Outwardly I looked fine. Dominic took pictures. Here I am in the garden, in a yellow sundress and shades; here I am with Emily, playing a game with the sprinkler. I look so convincing: happy, fresh-faced; the picture of youth and beauty. But underneath, there's a sink hole, not of memory, but of doubt: an opening rift in the ground that stares out like the eye of a monster.

Dominic had arranged the date of the wedding for August 28th. It would give us the chance to celebrate, and maybe even enjoy a little honeymoon before the start of the new term. Dom made all the arrangements, and I followed like a sleepy child going through a bedtime routine that requires nothing but obedience.

'So, just a little ceremony. Nothing big or grand,' said Dom. 'Just the gang at the registrar, then off to the pub for the party. We'll ask Estelle to make the cake. And Ma's just *dying* to make your dress.'

'Oh.' I hadn't thought about that. 'I thought I might just get a normal dress. Something I can wear again.'

'What, no dress?' said Dominic. 'Oh no, you can't do that. Ma's been talking of nothing but, ever since our engagement. She's really good at sewing and stuff. She'll know just what will suit you.'

And so it was decided. I would wear magnolia, and Emily would be my flower-girl, and the sisters would be bridesmaids, in peach, just like Victoria's wedding. Dominic's mother invited us to lunch, with the fitting afterwards.

'She'll probably need to go up a size by the time she's eaten all that,' said Dominic, seeing the table laden with food.

'She needs a little flesh on her bones,' said Blossom, piling chicken and scampi and rice onto my already loaded plate.

Blossom had a sewing room, which had once been a bedroom. Now it was neatly stacked with rolls of fabric, boxes of lace, balls of multicoloured wool. Two sewing machines stood side by side on a work table: a dressmaker's dummy stood by the door.

'Oh, and some of Dominic's old things,' she said. 'I've packed them into boxes for you to take away with you.'

She indicated three cardboard boxes, stacked up by the door. 'I've been thinking I should have a clear-out,' she said, 'but I thought you might like to go through them first. Get to know Dominic when he was a boy. You can tell I'm sentimental, can't you, my dear?' She indicated a wall that was covered in framed family photographs.

I made a sound that I hoped she would take for approval.

'And, of course, I made all these,' she said, indicating a portrait. 'Here's my Victoria's dress, over here. And here's Myra's, and Estelle's.' She smiled at me, and put her hand on my bare shoulder. 'I made the bride clothes for *all* my girls,' she said. 'It's just plain wicked how much they cost if you go to a wedding shop. And besides, if you're starting a family, you'll need to save money, not spend it.'

That made me feel uncomfortable. This was not the first time Blossom had assumed I was starting a family. What had Dominic said to her? Had he led her to believe that I was giving up teaching?

But Blossom had already moved on. 'Just take your jeans and top off, dear. Let me take your measurements, and then we'll look at fabrics.'

She had already bought the fabric for my wedding dress: it was a lovely raw silk, as close to white as possible. She draped it around me carefully, clucking and nodding to herself. 'I thought something simple and classic for you. Bare arms. Maybe three-quarter-length.'

I let her turn and drape me. I felt like a moth in a cocoon. From time to time I smiled at her and said all the things she expected of me, but I felt nothing at all; no joy, not even curiosity. I kept thinking of Christopher Milk, and the way he had apologized for an incident eighteen years old. I wished I'd had the courage then to pursue the conversation.

'What about your parents?' said Blossom. 'They must be so excited.'

I smiled and nodded convincingly. In fact, I had not heard from them since my visit two weeks before; the day they told me Emily had been an imaginary friend. It made me feel guilty to think of it, and yet the prospect of going back there – of maybe even meeting the man who claimed to be my brother – was too much to face. Perhaps I believed that telling them about my engagement would make it real; or perhaps I was trying to keep them away from a situation I already knew would be painful.

'I'm so looking forward to meeting them,' said Blossom. 'They must be so proud.'

I smiled again. *Smile. Turn. Stand up straight. Look pretty.* I wondered whether Milky would be buried or cremated. I wondered which option his family had chosen. Cremation, most probably. Burials are expensive. I thought of the boy in the photograph, and whether I had imagined the resemblance to the boy I'd seen at school. And then I realized something so obvious that I'd missed it, and took a breath so sudden that Blossom, who was pinning folds of silk around me, assumed she'd stuck me with the pin.

'Do you have a copy of this week's *Examiner*?' I said.

'By the TV. In the newspaper rack.'

Ignoring Blossom's protests, I ran out into the living room, still trailing yards of oyster silk. I found the newspaper, turned to the Obituaries page. There he was, Christopher Milk, in a little black-bordered box. I felt my heartbeat quicken. The scent of burning filled my head. Blossom called, from the sewing room: 'Hey! Don't you know it's bad luck for the groom to see the wedding dress?'

I dropped the paper back into the rack, and said something about wanting to check the layout of the marriage notices, and went back into the sewing room, where Emily was impatiently looking at spools of lace, and ribbons, and buttons, and sequins, and veils. I felt a sudden pang for my plain and earnest daughter, so young, and already so desperate to conform to expectations. 'Look at me, I'm a bride!' she said, draping a scrap of veil around her head.

Blossom gave an indulgent smile. 'Give it a few more years,' she said. 'You'll find your handsome prince, you'll see.'

Emily did a pirouette in front of the full-length mirror. 'I don't want a handsome prince. I'm going to marry Dom,' she said.

'Your Ma might have something to say about that.' Blossom smiled indulgently. 'Although you're right; my son's a catch.'

But I was barely listening. I already had what I wanted. I resumed my position at Blossom's side, heart beating a little faster. Throughout the fitting I silently went over and over the place and date of Christopher Milk's funeral, while my prospective mother-in-law pinned silk and gauze around me, and my daughter capered and danced like a moth with a flame: Pog Hill Crematorium: 15th August: 11 a.m.

3

August 12th, 1989

By then, of course, I was long overdue for a visit to my parents'.
I'd been putting it off for a while, partly because I'd been ill
with the flu, partly because of the wedding plans, but mostly
because of Conrad.

My daughter's imaginary friend had been quiet since
the end of term. From time to time I heard her talking
to herself in her room, but otherwise there had been no
more writing in the journal, or mention of Mr Smallface.
Instead, she played with her school friends, or rode her bicycle
down the lane, or listened to the radio (she had recently
discovered New Kids On The Block, and was alarmingly
smitten), or helped Dom in the kitchen. Dom had always
loved cooking, and planned to spend the holidays teaching
Emily to make some of his own childhood favourites. And
so they cooked pholourie, with split-pea batter and peppers;
and coconut bake; and Trini pelau, and curried chickpeas
and flatbread. That hot, dry, endless summer was filled with
the sounds and scents of Dominic's cooking, and with the
hits on the radio; and afterwards I could never eat any of
those things again without hearing New Kids On The Block,

and smelling cut grass, and tamarind, and the tinfoil scent of scorched chillies.

That was the scent of Blossom's house, too: the healthy scent of a family home with lots of comings and goings. I think that was what gave me the idea of dropping by at Jackson Street after the fitting, and walking home; leaving Dominic to drive back with Emily and the boxes. It was a good idea, Dom said: it would give him and Emily time to start on making dinner. At that I gave a comic groan, and said: 'Oh, *no*! Not *more* food!' which made Emily laugh, and Blossom smile, and Cecil said: 'Get used to it, love, you're a Buckfast now,' and for a moment it was almost as if we were a real family, with a history, and a future of shared and silly jokes.

By contrast, the smell of my parents' house was a tunnel back into the past. Lavender polish, stale smoke and the kind of smell that comes from rooms filled with old and unused things; my brother's clothes, hanging there; his books, untouched and forever unread; his records unplayed; his music magazines, foxed with age. When I arrived, feeling dull dread, my mother was in her housecoat; my father was doing the dishes, the kitchen window was closed in spite of the steam and the summer sunshine. Neither showed any surprise at seeing me, although it had been a month since my last visit. Nor was there any sign of the energy they'd shown that day: they seemed to have fallen back into the usual aimless pattern of things. Worse still, the radio was on again: against a veil of static, an inhuman female voice intoned a string of numbers.

I accepted a cup of milky tea and a slightly stale Bourbon biscuit, then asked if they'd had any visitors. I refused to say Conrad's name, or play to their delusion, but I needed to know if the man claiming to be my brother had been to the house again, and if so, what they'd given him.

'Oh, Conrad had to go away,' my father said, with a sideways glance at my mother. 'He travels a lot in his work, Becks, and he couldn't wait forever.'

'Wait for what?'

'Well *you*, of course,' my father said. 'He wanted you to be ready. He said he wanted to give you as long as you needed. But he couldn't stay all summer. He had to get back to his other life. He said he'd stay in touch, and come back when you were ready to see him.'

'How much did you give him?' I said.

My father's face fell. 'Oh, Becky,' he said. 'This is *Conrad*. I know how you must feel, but I promise you, this isn't like the other times.'

'If you've given him money, Dad, it's *exactly* like those other times.' I was trying not to cry, but I could feel my eyes burning. I could feel my anger, too, rising like something out of the ground. My parents had some money put by, mostly Conrad's savings account, into which they had placed a sum they had raised to fund the search for my brother. The search had petered out, of course; but some forty thousand pounds had remained, gaining a little interest, though the terms were not especially favourable. Of course, my parents had refused to use any of the cash for themselves. A holiday would have done them good, as I'd told them many times, or a move to a more modern house, but they'd treated the idea with the same horror they had shown when I'd suggested changing Conrad's room.

'Don't be like that, Becky love. It's his money. It always was.' My father wouldn't quite meet my eyes. I feared the worst, and I was right.

'You didn't give him all of it. Dad, please, say you didn't.'

My father shrugged. 'You don't understand.'

'How often have you seen him since?'

My mother was starting to look agitated. Her hands in the lap of her housedress were like a knot of angleworms.

My father gave me a warning look. 'Don't. You'll upset your mother, love. He said he'd be away for a while. But that doesn't mean he won't be back. He said he had business to deal with.'

Of course he did. They always do, these imposters. This one was convincing; but it didn't take much to convince them. A smiling face, a few anecdotes that anyone could have picked up. My brother's disappearance has provided excellent business for true-crime writers, publishers and journalists. Conspiracy theories abound. The volume of material published over the years has made it possible for anyone with a little imagination to create a plausible story. And, of course, my parents had paid him in cash, taking the money straight from the bank and providing no paper trail.

'Well, he'd have had to pay tax otherwise,' explained my father, who held a long-standing grudge against the tax man. 'Why should he pay tax on his own savings?'

There was nothing I could say. I felt anger, sadness, disgust – but it all felt so distant, so meaningless. My brother just kept on taking, even when he was someone else. And no, it wasn't the money; it was the fact that I'd been there all the time, caring for them – *loving* them – and still, at the mention of Conrad, they were willing to follow the piper. I knew right then that I couldn't tell them about the wedding. It was already too much – the gang, the dress, the party – without my having to deal with them. I would make sure there was nothing in print; no notice in the paper. I didn't suppose it would matter. They wouldn't have noticed anyway. As for the imposter, I had no desire to discuss him, or hear about him any further. I knew what he'd done. That was enough. Anything more was irrelevant.

Besides, I already knew who he was. All I needed now was proof.

I took the long walk back to April Street, through the woods round the back of St Oswald's, and then on to the disused railway line, the Pepper Pot, and the two miles of cinder path that led me to King Henry's. It had been a long, long time since I'd walked that childhood path, and once more, the ghosts of my brother and his friends walked along beside me. The route must have grown less popular, I thought. The path seemed narrower than before, the hedges taller and thicker; and drifts of rosebay willowherb, its flowers long since gone to seed, had gathered in the cutting like snow. *Fields of asphodel,* I thought, *lining the path to the Lands of the Dead.*

I'd always thought that asphodel was a kind of lily. In fact, Roy, as I imagine you know, it is one of the Lands of the Dead, named after the pale and dismal weeds that grew in its endless wastelands. The path along the railway bed was surely one of these, I thought; abandoned to willowherb gone to seed, and stands of swaying nettle.

Certainly, it was abandoned now. Since the mouth of the railway tunnel had been blocked in the Seventies, fewer rail enthusiasts had come to photograph the site. Bindweed covered the Pepper Pot, which made it look even more like a fairy-tale castle, in which a princess might be asleep, waiting for her prince to arrive.

Stupid. There's no sleeping princess. Anything inside there is dead.

But the building didn't *look* dead. There was more of the willowherb growing all around it, sending up clouds of gossamer into the sleepy summer air. And as I stopped to listen, I thought I could still hear that sound through the ventilation shaft, and I wondered what might be sleeping there, down in the darkness, awaiting its time. I thought of the Trapper-Lad, ten years old, and the men of the Smarthwaite Colliery, who had gone underground in 1912, and never come up to the surface again. Conrad used to tell me how people heard their voices, pleading and calling from under the Malbry streets for nearly a week until, one by one, they finally fell silent. I thought of my brother, long dead, and yet still so present in our lives; and about Mr Smallface, who had returned to haunt my six-year-old daughter.

There's nothing. There are no ghosts, I thought.

The Pepper Pot stood, seeming to smile in the mote-ridden sunlight.

'There are no ghosts,' I said aloud. 'Conrad's dead. He won't come back.'

There came a sudden thudding sound from deep inside the Pepper Pot.

Rats, I thought. *There must be rats*. I remembered the terrible, trailing plug of refuse and abandoned things, reaching all the way from the mouth of the vent to the railway tunnel. There must be thousands of them there; trapped, unable to climb out –

But now came the sound of a rustling in the long grass by the vent. Then, a sudden, sharp movement; a thud too loud to be caused by a rat. I felt my chest tighten; my breathing catch. Slowly, I started to back away.

There came another sharp movement, releasing a plume of gossamer seeds. Then something started towards me, fast; sending the plumes of willowherb into rapid, frenzied activity. The kaleidoscope air was suddenly filled with seeds like the flakes in a snow globe. And with it came a memory; a dazzle of light from the ceiling; the sound of something heavy in motion on the bare boards. *There are no ghosts*, I told myself, and yet, I did not believe it. After all, what else would I find on the road to Asphodel?

Once again I started to move backward along the cinder path. But the creature – whatever it was – was fast; and in my rising panic I tripped and fell into a patch of nettles. I gave a cry and closed my eyes as the creature rushed towards me –

Then came the sound of barking. I opened my eyes and saw a brown Jack Russell on the path, barking and wagging his stumpy tail. A surge of relief went through me. *A dog. It was only a dog.*

I started to get up and saw the nettle stings rising fast on my bare arms. Then I saw a man on the path, wearing a brown tweed jacket and carrying a dog lead.

'Are you all right?' said a voice, which came to me through a cloud of floating seeds. 'The dog's just excited. He doesn't bite.'

I scrambled quickly to my feet and brushed the cinders from my palms. The man's voice was familiar, but in that moment I couldn't think why. He came a little closer, and I saw his face in the sunlight. It was a very familiar face, wearing an unfamiliar look of concern. I hadn't recognized him before, because I was so used to seeing him in a suit and academic gown; but now it was unmistakable.

It was Scoones.

4

St Oswald's ~~Grammar School for Boys~~ *Academy*
Michaelmas term, September 29th, 2006

Of course, I remember: old Scoones had a dog. In fact, it belonged to his mother, but as she grew older and less able to cope, it was always Eric who walked it. I remember that he always used to refer to it only as 'The Dog', though his mother called it Biscuit. Maybe old Scoones felt it was beneath his dignity to go around shouting 'Biscuit!' whenever the dog got off the leash. Of course, the dog died years ago, but her account of him walking it along the disused railway line (probably via St Oswald's fields, and the scrubland that lies beyond it) was oddly, surprisingly touching. I found I could *see* Eric as she spoke; wearing his old tweed jacket; maybe carrying a stick; his usual rigidity softened by sunlight and solitude. And he *did* have a softer side, although we rarely saw it then; a glimpse of the boy he used to be released by the scents of summer.

I wished she had seen that softer side. Maybe she would have understood. I can imagine them both that day on top of the old railway tunnel, with the dog barking wildly, and those willowherb seeds, whirling and spinning and clouding the air like the snows of yesteryear. I know them well, those long-gone snows. I feel their wintriness in my bones. It makes me feel melancholy and old, and in need of another Gauloise. No, she has not found them all. I have a small supply of them in a biscuit tin under the coffee table. I allow myself just one a day, and I smoke it outside, so as not to alert La Buckfast to my transgression. But I do miss Eric, for all his faults – yes, even his felonies. I miss our little talks over tea and biscuits in the Common Room; I miss his absurd formality when he was offended. I miss his idiotic mug with the photo of Princess Diana. I miss his ridiculous pretence of not taking sugar in his tea. I miss the querulous sound of his voice through the glass of his teaching room door – *Now boys! That's enough, boys!* I miss the way he called me *Straits*.

This Sunday will be October the first. Soon it will be the time of golden leaves and Bonfire Night, and clear and frosty mornings. I've always loved this time of year; its accent of smoke and fallen fruit; its graveyard scent of petrichor. Don't tell La Buckfast, but I went for a walk outside today. Only to the park and back; but it felt like freedom. There is an old horse-chestnut tree that I remember from childhood: its leaves are frazzled from summer's drought, and it has shed branches over the years, but it still stands, monumental; the grandest tree in Malbry Park.

A few horse-chestnuts had fallen, and I put them in my pockets. I don't know why I do this. And yet I never can resist their plump and glossy thoroughbred shine. Today was oddly blustery; sunny, with a little rain. The air smelt faintly of the sea, although we're seventy miles from the coast; and the light had a golden quality, like a window on to the past. I ventured a little way into the park, and saw a group of schoolboys there, in St Oswald's uniforms. They're not supposed to leave the grounds at lunchtime, but some always do, if only for the horse-chestnut trees. I watched them from afar, and thought I recognized their voices: but boys never change. Scoonesy and Straits are still out there, playing truant, with conkers.

On Monday I will go back to school. I have played truant for too long. On Monday, whether she finishes her story or not, I will confront my long-delayed responsibilities. *Perfer et obdura*, Straits. It may mean difficult choices – but since when did I ever turn away from those when it came to St Oswald's? One more conker, for old times' sake. Into my jacket pocket it goes. Who is the boy buried in the concrete of the Gunderson Pool? Tomorrow, Scoones, I will find out the truth. By Monday, whether she plans it or not – I *must* know the answer.

5

August 12th, 1989

'Mr Scoones?' I almost didn't recognize him without his suit and Master's gown. He too, seemed uncertain; as if being outside King Henry's had robbed him of a protective layer. He looked at me, then glared at the dog, which was barking playfully.

'Biscuit! *Biscuit!* Here, boy!'

The dog ignored him and lapped at my hands, tail wagging furiously. Scoones looked aggrieved. 'It isn't my dog. It's my mother's. *Biscuit!* Come *here*, Sir!'

I couldn't help laughing. I imagined him sounding just the same in front of an unruly class. I stroked the dog, which rolled over. 'It's all right,' I told Scoones. 'He's just being friendly.'

He glanced over his shoulder, and made a kind of dry sound in his throat. I wondered if it was just my presence that was making him uneasy, or something else. Scoones made a lunge at the dog, and caught it by the collar. He fixed on the lead, and pulled the dog, still protesting, to his side. He stood up, once more looking more assured.

'Well, Miss Price. I'll be on my way.' And he turned back from where he had previously come, the dog seeming reluctant, as if he had expected a different route.

A few minutes further down the path I passed a trio of boys, aged ten or eleven; their unselfconscious scruffiness marking them as Sunnybankers. It occurred to me as I walked home that a man with a borrowed dog is a magnet for boys; the perfect excuse to stop and chat, maybe even to make friends —

I wondered why Scoones had been so quick to change direction on seeing me.

I thought of the graffiti I'd seen on the desks at King Henry's.

Mr Scoones is the Eggman.

Mr Scoones is a nonce.

I was still lost in thought when I reached the house on April Street. Dominic and Emily were in the kitchen, listening to New Kids On The Block. Emily was giggling; Dom was dancing and singing along, using a wooden spoon as a microphone. They were making so much noise that they did not notice me arrive.

Three cardboard boxes stood by the door, labelled in Blossom's careful hand: *Dominic — School Things.* I looked inside the first one. It contained a stack of old exercise books; some plastic toys; some art pads. Inside these, a young Dominic had drawn exuberant battle scenes; superheroes; dinosaurs. The exercise books were all cheap, buff-coloured jotters from Sunnybank Park. There was nothing from King Henry's.

I opened the second box. Here were more art pads, showing how much Dominic had improved through the years: instead of the superheroes, I saw portraits in pencil and pastel chalks. Many were of fantasy girls; their features vaguely familiar. Some were nudes. I leafed through these, feeling slightly uncomfortable. And here at last were King Henry's books; English, Maths and History. I noticed that his writing was much neater in the English book than in the rest. And right at the bottom of the box I found a smaller box – maybe a shoebox; containing some black-and-white photographs, a Bic lighter, a couple of tiny bottles of Spiritual Sky patchouli oil, and a programme for *Othello*. I looked inside. His name caught my eye. *Dominic Buckfast: Othello*. And on the opposite page was the colour photo of the cast, holding masks and in lavish Venetian dress, on a set that consisted of nothing more than some curtains, a bed and an open trapdoor, through which a green light seemed to shine through a shimmer of dry ice –

It felt like an electric shock. *The light! Not the door itself, but the light!* And the memory came with an acrid scent, and the sound of something striking the stage; something heavy that thudded and slid, and someone telling me to run –

'Hey, Becks!'

It was Dominic, his shirt sleeves rolled to the elbows. His hands were all white with flour; he was still holding the wooden spoon. Emily was behind him, wearing a giant apron that enveloped her like a cocoon.

'What are you doing?' Dom's voice was bright, but I could hear the edge in his words.

I had no choice but to brazen it out. 'Checking out Blossom's boxes,' I said. 'Looking for the evidence of your vile youthful depravity.'

He laughed. It sounded convincing. 'Oh, there was plenty of *that*,' he said. 'You should see some of the comics I drew. But for the moment, close your eyes. We have something to show you!'

I closed my eyes, and Dominic led me into the kitchen. He and Emily had made a batch of coconut dumplings with mango jam. 'Just like Granny Oh used to make,' he said. 'I hope you're hungry!' And between the dumplings, and Emily's pride, and the game he made of the washing-up; and the movie we watched as a reward (*Labyrinth*, Emily's favourite); it took me some time to notice that the boxes he'd brought from Blossom's house had disappeared from beside the door: and when I asked him where they were the next day, he looked at me with a sheepish grin and said: 'I put them out with the bins. I'm sorry. I know you were curious,' he said, seeing my expression. 'But I just couldn't face you seeing all those comic books I drew. So many teenage fantasies. So many boobs. Forgive me?'

Of course, I couldn't make a fuss. Not in front of Emily. And so I laughed and teased him about his teenage hormones, and tried not to think of what more I might have remembered if only I'd had a proper look at that old theatre programme.

The green door had been a *trapdoor*. Only the *light* shining out had been green. Had Conrad been pulled through the trapdoor by someone wearing the void-face mask that Carrie had called the *moretta*?

'You're not upset with me, are you, Becks?' he said. 'You know it was all just rubbish, right? The sort of things only mothers keep.' He took my hand and kissed it. 'I want our life together to be a completely fresh start for both of us. You want that too, don't you?'

'Of course.'

He smiled and kissed me again. 'Besides, if you want the *real* dirt, my Ma's got three dozen albums filled with *the* most embarrassing baby pictures ever, and trust me, if you give her the slightest bit of encouragement, she'll talk you through *every single one of them* –'

I smiled at him. 'I can't wait. I bet you were adorable.'

'I still am,' said Dominic, and without that glimpse of the green door, I almost could have agreed with him.

6

August 12th, 1989

What do you do when you suspect your fiancé of betrayal? Of betrayal, or something worse? In my case, the answer was *nothing at all*. I simply went on as I had before. I know that must be hard to believe. But I had fallen prey to a kind of strange, consuming lethargy. I moved on through the summer days like a stone through fathoms of water, passing through layers of darkness; watching the light recede until there was no light left at all.

Meanwhile, everything else went on; the plans for the wedding; the cake; the dress; the bookings. Emily's excitement at all this seemed enough to satisfy Dominic, who was happy and energized; making arrangements; cracking jokes; filled with ideas for our future. He knew nothing of my dreams, or my doubts or suspicions; or even the fact that my parents had given their savings to a stranger. And there were times when he was sweet, and there were times when it was good; and I felt as if it could almost be real – or at least, as real as Emily Jackson.

'I hear there's a job coming up at Sunnybank in the autumn,' he announced one day over breakfast. 'They haven't even advertised it yet. You can get in before they do. Helen from

RE's pregnant: she'll be taking six months off from October.'
He saw my puzzled expression and smiled. 'I know it's not
your subject, Becks, but face it, *anyone* can teach RE, plus
you've got a great record at Sunnybank, and it would put
you in a good position when it came to something more
permanent. *And* it would get you out of King Fucking Henry's
Grammar School. No, listen –' he said as I tried to reply.
'You've been so much better since you left. No nightmares,
no sleepwalking, no zoning out. And Emily's been better too.
No Mr Smallface. No Conrad.'

Well, yes. I'm good at faking things. I smiled, and said:
'Perhaps you're right.'

He looked relieved. 'OK,' he said. 'I'll make a call to the
Head of RE. Stan Collier – remember him? Good man. Party
member.'

I smiled again. 'Thanks, Dominic.'

'Happy to help. He'll listen to me. We'll be Mr and Mrs
Buckfast by then. And he likes you, Becks. He does. I mean,
who *wouldn't* like you?'

I thought about that for a moment. Did Dominic like me?
Or did he like the *idea* of me, the cheery, tasteful packaging?
I laughed. 'You wouldn't say that if you'd seen the way Eric
Scoones looks at me.'

He gave a shrug. 'You're well shut of him. You're better
off taking cover at a proper school like Sunnybank than trying
for a permanent post at a place like King Henry's.'

'Perhaps you're right.' I said again.

'Good girl,' said Dominic.

That's all men want, Roy, most of the time. For women to
smile and tell them they're right. It's such an easy way to keep
them thinking that they're in control: meanwhile, you take

what you can – what you want – without them even noticing. It worked with Johnny Harrington; it worked with Dominic Buckfast. It may even still work with you, Roy, in spite of your little rebellion. Yes, I know you're planning to go back to St Oswald's on Monday. You called Dr Strange this morning, to warn him to cancel your cover. Not everyone would have thought of that; but you were always so correct. And we'll still have the weekend. Two nights to finish my story. Eric Scoones has been my trail of breadcrumbs throughout this tale. After this, they will be gone. What then, Roy? I like to think you will do as I did, for the sake of the status quo. After all, what good would it do, so long after the end of it all? And how would you justify an act that would mean the end of St Oswald's?

But I am rushing ahead again. By Monday, you may feel differently. For now, bear with me a while longer. We have a funeral to attend.

7

August 15th, 1989

Pog Hill Crematorium lies a few miles outside Malbry. A modern building of no great interest, comprising a waiting room, a chapel and a memorial garden. This was where I waited for Milky's service to begin, sitting on a wooden bench dedicated to *Gloria Green (Gone But Not Forgotten)*.

The hearse arrived at 10.14, closely followed by a black Ford Sierra, from which emerged a woman in her seventies, whom I took to be Milky's mother; a man in his thirties with a strong resemblance to Milky, whom I assumed must be his brother; his wife; and a boy I recognized, even out of uniform. It was the boy from the photograph: the boy from the theatre. Conrad.

I watched the whole thing from my bench. The hearse. The procession. The guests – no more than twenty; all of them in rather more expensive clothes than I would have guessed from a caretaker's family. Once they were all assembled in the little chapel, I listened from the waiting room. The ceremony was simple. A little speech from the celebrant: *Christopher was a man who loved life*. A reading by his brother. A hymn. A slightly distorted recording of ELO's 'Mr Blue Sky'. And then they all trooped out again, heading for the Ring o' Bells, the well-placed pub across the road which catches most of the funeral trade.

There was a beer garden at the back. I guessed the boy would sit there; the day was warm, if cloudy, and he wasn't old enough for the bar. I watched as the bar staff brought food: the same kind of food that the Shanker's Arms had served at my birthday party. Sausage rolls; sandwiches; coleslaw; tea; cakes with fluorescent icing. I waited until the food was served, and the adults were in conversation, then I came to sit at a table just behind the boy. He was sitting alone, his plate piled high.

I said: 'I'm sorry about your uncle.'

The boy turned at the sound of my voice, and I saw his expression of guilt and alarm. 'I didn't know him well,' I went on. 'But maybe you can tell me more.'

The boy looked cautiously around, as if for a means of escape. I could see him measuring the distance between us; trying to assess what I might do if he just stood up and ran for the doorway.

I said: 'I wouldn't, if I were you. Not here, in front of these people. Imagine what your parents would say if they knew what you'd been up to.' I tried a gambit. 'Or even your school. I imagine that kind of behaviour doesn't impress at St Oswald's.'

The boy seemed to consider this. Now I could see him properly, he didn't really look like Conrad at all. His face was clever and narrow, and like Milky, he wore glasses, although his looked more expensive than Milky's National Health frames. His pale hair was nicely cut, and his tie was watered silk. Borrowed from his father, no doubt. I'd been right about the school. This was no Sunnybanker.

The look of alarm had vanished by now. The boy looked calm and in control. 'What do you want?' he said at last.

'Maybe we could start with your name.'

'Darren Milk,' said the boy.

'Pleased to meet you, Darren,' I said. 'Now tell me who put you up to that prank on me at King Henry's, and why.'

He seemed to hesitate. Behind the small-lensed glasses, his eyes were cool and wary.

'I won't tell anyone,' I said. 'I just want to know the truth.'

Once more he seemed to hesitate. Then, he nodded. 'Fine. OK.'

It was an old school friend of his uncle's, he said. This man had paid Darren twenty pounds to wear an old King Henry's uniform and play a joke on a colleague who would be in school after the end of term.

'But why?'

He shrugged. 'I didn't ask. I thought it was just a wind-up. And besides –' He gave me a cynical look. 'Twenty quid is twenty quid.'

I agreed that twenty quid was not a sum to be sneezed at. 'So, who *was* your uncle's old school friend? I'm assuming you know his name.'

'You won't tell him I told you?'

'Not a word.'

'His name is Fentiman,' said the boy. 'But sometimes, he called him Fatty.'

9

August 15th, 1989

'*Fentiman?* Are you sure?' For a moment I was bewildered. I'd been so sure that I already knew the culprit that the name took me by surprise. Fentiman?

Fattyman.

Yes, I thought. It might be that. How slow I'd been to make the connection. But that was because I'd been *so sure* –

'What's his first name?'

'Jerry,' said Milk.

'Jerry, as in Jerome?' I said. I'd assumed from our first meeting that, like so many of my male colleagues, Jerome went by his surname.

Darren nodded. 'Yeah. I guess.'

'Thank you. I see.'

Some revelations are dazzling: some come upon you like a stroke. Some come in a gradual series of nudges in the darkness. I realized what they were now. His presence in the theatre. His eagerness to be my friend. My father telling me that day: *He was even wearing that badge of his, his Prefect's badge that he was so proud of.*

And the fact that he was Fattyman, the fourth member of my brother's gang, chimed so neatly with the rest. Fentiman was

Conrad. As Conrad's friend, he knew details that would make his story believable. As *my* friend, he had access to knowledge that he could use to his advantage. I thought back to what I had told him that day in the Thirsty Scholar. The numbers stations. My brother's shrine. My parents' joy at receiving a letter from their long-lost son. Now I saw that all this had given Fentiman the information he'd needed to make his imposture believable, while keeping me distracted with theories and phantoms.

And Milky? He must have been part of the plan. His awkwardness around me; his attempt at an apology. That day outside the theatre, he'd lied, allowing me to believe that a King Henry's boy had been the masked apparition. The truth was shockingly clear to me now. The masked man must have been Jerome. He would have known about the trapdoor, the moretta mask and the disguise, as well as having plenty of time to re-enter the theatre in darkness and to hide in the disabled toilet while I was in the trap room. Only Milky would have seen him coming into the theatre. Therefore Milky must have known. I left the funeral party discreetly, through the garden gate at the back. My mind was making connections so fast that I could hardly keep up with them. Everything I'd learnt so far – the scene in the Little Theatre, Jerome's deception, Milky's lie – spoke of a planned attempt to undermine my confidence – even, perhaps, my sanity. To drive me away from King Henry's and into a new life with Dominic. Dom, who had been so quick to dispose of the box from King Henry's. Dom, of the furtive phone calls. Dom, whose disapproval of my taking the job at King Henry's had led to such bitter arguments. Dom, whose role in *Othello* had been lit by green light from a trapdoor.

It was no longer possible for me to try to write these things off as coincidence. If Fentiman was guilty, then Dominic must be complicit. But why? Fentiman's motive was easy: he had walked away with forty thousand pounds of my parents' savings. And Milky? I remembered Darren Milk saying: *Twenty quid is twenty quid.* Easy to bribe the caretaker to ignore a practical joke. But Dominic, the union man? Whatever his role in this affair, I couldn't believe it was for money. He loved me. He loved Emily. He wanted to protect us. Everything he'd done had been to distance me from my memories; from what had happened to Conrad. And I could see only one reason for that: because he was somehow culpable. The green door of my memory was a trapdoor lit with a green light. Dominic had been there, with Conrad in charge of the lighting. Did *Othello* hold the key to Conrad's disappearance? And if so, why would Dominic want to keep me from finding out? A sudden memory of Dom, saying: *It was all just rubbish. The sort of things only mothers keep.* And suddenly, I knew where I needed to go; where I might find some of the answers.

I hadn't been to Jackson Street since the day of the wedding dress fitting. To be frank, I was dreading it. My parents had given their savings to the man they thought was my brother, and it was only a matter of time before the truth descended upon them. In the past, this process had taken something between three and twelve weeks, depending on the sums involved. My father always responded with rage; my mother with a further descent into deeper dementia. When I arrived at Jackson Street, the signs were already visible; the living room curtains were tightly drawn, and the small patch of grass at the front of the house was overgrown with ragwort. I knocked and went in without waiting. The house smelt of my childhood; of old magazines and the scent of desperation. My father was in the kitchen; my mother was nowhere to be seen.

'She's having one of her headaches,' he told me, when I asked him. 'I told her to have a lie-down. I was going to do the dishes.'

A glance at the kitchen sink confirmed that the dishes hadn't been done since my last visit. This too was part of a pattern: first came the cleaning, then the neglect. My mother had already taken to her bed; possibly for weeks or months. My father was slower to wind down, but the kitchen radio was once more tuned to one of his numbers stations. I could hear the sound of a female voice, underscored with harsh static, repeating over and over again: *Nine. Zero. Two. Nine. Zero. Nine. Zero. Two. Nine. Zero.* Perhaps he had a notebook in which he wrote the numbers. Perhaps he was simply waiting to hear a number that he recognized – the date of Conrad's birth, perhaps, *Seven. Nine. One. Nine. Seven. One –* that might bring some kind of closure.

'Don't,' said Dad as I reached to turn the radio off. 'I like it.'

'I don't,' I said, more sharply than I'd intended.

He shrugged like an adolescent. 'It'll be proved one day. You'll see. There are people researching them.'

I did not ask who *they* were. Aliens, Secret Servicemen, gangs of high-profile Satanists – my father always turned to his conspiracy theories when things went bad. And all I wanted today was the chance to go through Conrad's school things. I knew my parents had kept them all. He had been involved in the play. And if he'd had a programme –

'Listen Dad, would you make us some tea? I just need to look for something.'

I need not have bothered with an excuse. My father barely reacted as I left the kitchen for Conrad's room. There were a number of cartons there, stored since his disappearance: the police had had them for a while, after which they had gone to Catherine Potts, author of *The Lost Boy of Malbry*, who had returned them in due course to their place at the back of his wardrobe.

I found the programme, helpfully stored in a folder labelled: *Theatre*. There it was, along with a notebook labelled: *Othello – Lighting Notes*. I took the whole thing, not wanting to be in the house a moment longer, and drove to the end of April Street before parking the car to investigate the contents of the folder.

I flicked through the handwritten notebook. It was filled with scene references, cues and instructions, some in my brother's shapeless handwriting, some in a cursive, adult script: *Colour spot: green. Denotes jealousy. Fade to Desdemona. Smoke machine!* I closed it and moved to the programme. For a moment I studied the cast photograph: at its centre, Dominic, in Venetian dress, standing beside Desdemona. *Fresh out of Girton, and stagy as hell.* Of course; who else would have played the role? And Dominic looked – well. I've seen that look. That look of adoration. Of course, it isn't unusual for a young pupil to have a crush on an attractive teacher, but Dominic in 1971 looked a lot more mature than his friends. He might have been a sixth-former, or even a first-year University student. And Carrie – who in the photograph, *did* look a lot like Diana Rigg – had been caught in a moment's aside, her head turned as if imparting a confidence, a tiny, tender smile on her lips.

Green.

Green denotes jealousy.

Green denotes jealousy.

I remembered Conrad saying: *Fuck her, and fuck her play.*

You wish.

Don't we all?

And then, I saw on the opposite page, in the small photo labelled *Tech Crew*, the thing I had been looking for. It was a tiny photograph, but I could see both boys clearly. Underneath, were both their names. *C. Price: Spot Operator.* My brother was in his safety harness, grinning at the camera. And next to him was a stocky boy I'd only ever known by his nickname. But there he was: *J. Fentiman* – known to my brother as *Fatty*, although he was barely overweight, and to me, more recently, just as *Jerome*.

10

St Oswald's ~~Grammar School for Boys~~ *Academy*
October 1st, 2006

Jerome Fentiman. Of course. I *knew* I remembered that name
from somewhere: but at my age, names don't come easily. I can
always remember the names of my boys; but I find that in the
longer term, these names often slip out of usage, to be replaced
by more current ones. The same goes for colleagues; and
Fentiman, of course, was not a colleague for long. I remember
his appointment: in those days we still had an empire, and
Classics was still the beating heart of our core curriculum.

We interviewed Fentiman in early July – the old Old
Head, the Head of Department and I. We'd had to advertise
the job late, and he was the best of the applicants. Perhaps a
little lightweight, but there was no sign that he might be the
kind of man who abandons his class for such a small thing as
a practical joke – a spider under a desk lid, forsooth. But his
CV read Balliol, Oxford, *and* he had been a King Henry's
boy – at least until 1972. Our decision was unanimous. The
rest of the applicants were too young, and one at least was
female. Did Becky Price apply for the job? Too long ago
to remember. All I recall is that Fentiman wore his College

372

blazer to the interview, and was both persuasive and person-
able, and seemed to fit the criteria, and thus the Old old Head
approved of him.

Of course, all this must have happened while the man was
befriending Becky Price. And six weeks after Fentiman's disastrous loss of nerve, Eric Scoones had returned to St Oswald's to
fill the space the new man had left. At the time it had seemed
providential. But now, I can't help but wonder if the urge to
leave in the wake of a schoolboy's death was the same that
had led my old friend to flee St Oswald's in the first place.
La Buckfast continues to take her time. Her tale unfolds like
an onion; leaf by leaf, layer by layer, soon to reveal the thing
at its heart that must make an old man weep. I force myself
not to interrupt, not to demand more than my due. To tell
you the truth, I begin to fear the conclusion of her story. I
fear it almost as much as I fear that she will never finish at all.

But now I see the end in sight, as her tale and mine
move together. Darren Milk. Eric Scoones. Jerome Fentiman.
Rebecca and Dominic Buckfast. The Prefect's badge from the
Gunderson site is still in my jacket pocket. Repeated handling
has worn the broken fastening almost smooth. If only that
could happen to the broken pieces of our lives; lost friendships;
summers past. If only gentle handling could soften our rough
edges. But as her story reaches its end, I sense there will be
no softening. Only the cruel conclusion of something that died
thirty years ago; a grinding of machineries run ragged by the
passing of time. And then, when it is over, I will have to make
a decision. To bury them forever, or to dig up the skeletons
of the past. Either choice will cost me dear. But I can see no
alternative. Seneca said it best, I think: *Veritas numquam perit.*
Heads may rise and heads may fall; but the truth stands eternal.

PART 8

Tartarus
(Land of Eternal Darkness)

I

August 19th, 1989

I think you know what it feels like, Roy: to learn that a loved one is not as they seemed. That sense of disconnection: that creeping unreality. I felt like a tiny creature among a herd of stampeding cows; unable to run for safety; unable to face what was coming. Jerome's betrayal; Dom's deceit; Carrie, as Desdemona.

There she was again, I saw, as I flicked through the lighting notebook. This time, it was a drawing: half a page torn from a ring-bound pad and slipped between the pages. The style was juvenile, perhaps, but I recognized Dom's work. Looking through the book, I found more, all of the same subject. Carrie in profile; Carrie full-face; Carrie topless, in orange chalk, hair loose over a pillow. There's something about a drawing, I think, that reveals more than a photograph. A photograph reveals the photographer. A drawing reveals the relationship between an artist and model. And suddenly it occurred to me then that Dominic had never drawn *me*. It's easy for adults to forget the violent passions of childhood. Too many adults assume that children, with their short attention spans and changing moods, experience the world in a lesser way, and with less intensity. In fact, the opposite is true. The things we feel as children are extraordinary. Violent passions; terrible grief; rage that burns like paper and evaporates like gunsmoke. Dom's drawings of Carrie were like that. Flamboyant and shy at the same time; both tender and possessive.

I remembered Carrie saying to me: *Conrad knew how to wind people up. He knew how to spot weakness.* And now I knew that my brother had found Dominic's weakness – his secret – and hers, too. I thought of those two little bottles of scent in the shoebox of theatre stuff. *Incense, patchouli, and long, loose hair.* Those drawings, hidden in Conrad's things. And Dom, who was gifted and sensitive, and looked much older than fourteen – I felt like a child in a mirror maze, every surface a broken mask. There were no answers to be found; simply distorted images, with only the promise of broken glass at the end of it. I'd been so quick to assume that Dominic had betrayed me. That he had lied to me in order to better keep me under control. But this suggested that he too, had been a victim of abuse –

No one ever questions the term when the abuser is a man, and the victim a teenage girl. But when the gender roles are reversed, there's all too often a tendency to overlook the damage, or to dismiss it altogether. And Carrie was desirable, charming, intelligent – *different.* Too easy to portray her teenage victim as lucky, rather than damaged. *That hippie Drama teacher,* he'd said. Thinking back to those bottles of patchouli oil, so often used in the Seventies to conceal the pungent scent of weed, I wondered if Carrie had been the one to introduce him to marijuana. Certainly, none of his family seemed to share his habit. Carrie might even have seen it as a kind of education.

I felt a rush of confusion and guilt. I'd been so sure that Dominic was lying to me about Conrad. But what if he had lied to me to hide his connection with Carrie? It would explain his reaction when I'd suggested inviting her. It might even explain why he left King Henry's. Was *this* Dominic's secret? And was his controlling behaviour the result of his experience? Still dazed from this new knowledge I went home to April Street, hiding the programme and notebook under the bed with the satchel and Conrad's old school diary. I said nothing to Dominic. The thought that he'd been a victim – and not, as I'd thought, an abuser – had overturned my perspective. I'd assumed his motives were aligned with those of Jerome Fentiman, but now I could see another set of reasons for his behaviour. It made me feel guilty; deceitful. Looking at Dom with Emily, I shivered to see how close I'd come to throwing away our future. I'd always found it easier to trust a woman than a man. Perhaps that's why I had been so quick to believe Carrie, rather than Dominic. Now I could see how kind he'd been, how understanding of my needs. My mistrust of him had come from my belief that I did not deserve to be loved; that I was not *capable* of love. Now I promised myself that I would try. *Fake it till you make it.*

And so, over the next few days, I wrapped my new life around me like spun silk around a moth's cocoon. Events unrolled like coloured yarn: the wedding preparations; the suffocating parade of gifts. These things all passed around me like the revolutions of a kaleidoscope, in dizzying patterns of colour and sound.

I tried to embrace my good fortune. I've always been good at showing others what they want to see. But in the intervals between, I saw the darkness of my descent, and watched the marionette of myself dancing on the surface. And the worst of it was that no one guessed: not Emily, not Dominic. I went through the movements, just as I had done throughout most of my childhood; and if there were dreams, they stayed beneath that dark, unbroken surface. Until one morning, just over a week before the wedding, I awoke from an uneasy dream in the living room at April Street barefoot, in my pyjamas, and with Conrad's diary on my knee and a ball-point pen in my hand.

For a moment I was confused. It had been weeks since my last sleepwalking episode. Dawn was breaking; the room was lit with a greenish, undersea light. The clock on the wall said just after five, and the house was completely silent. Dominic and Emily were both sound sleepers, and I knew that neither of them would stir until at least nine o'clock. I pulled on a sweatshirt of Dominic's, which he had left on the sofa, and looked at the open diary. There was a new entry.

You can't hide from him, I read.

The writing was the same as before. Juvenile, rather shapeless, in the same blue ball-point as the pen that had been in my hand when I awoke. I must have held it very tight; there was still an indentation on my middle finger, and a smudge of ink on the tip. I turned the page. A new entry.

He'll take everyone you care about. Then he'll come for you.

Blurrily, I shook my head. That couldn't be my writing. I went to check the front door. It was locked. The back door, too. Upstairs, Emily and Dom slept. I remembered what my mother had said: *You had such funny ideas in your head. That monster who lived in the drains was one. Anything that went wrong was his fault.*

I went into the kitchen and made myself a cup of tea. I drank it slowly, watching the sky turn from green to shocking pink. *Had* I written those entries myself? At last, the mystery made sense. No one had crept into the house to write in Conrad's diary. No one else had been here at all. These were the things that came out of the dark; the voices from the sink hole. But why would I frighten Emily? I'd tried so hard to protect her. I'd never even spoken to her about Conrad, or Mr Smallface. From the day she was born, I'd tried to give her a childhood as bright and untroubled as mine had been dark. Why then would I spoil it for her, just as we'd reached a safe haven?

I'd started to make more tea when the phone gave a sudden, alarming bray. I ran to pick up the receiver; I caught it on the third ring. No one expects a phone call at six o'clock in the morning; at least, no one expects good news. And I knew, Roy. I already knew with the certainty of a broken bone. I hadn't seen them for over a week, hadn't called, hadn't even thought of them. Except that in the darkness, I'd known, even as I descended. I'd seen it in my father's face; I'd heard it in the litany of the numbers station. And even as I picked up the phone, I heard the distant sound of static, and the numbers: *Seven. Nine. Seven. Three. One. Seven. Nine. Seven. Three. One –*

'Dad? Is that you?' My voice was sharp.

Once more, the static. The numbers.

'Dad?'

A distant sound, like that of a drain. '*Beckssssss –*'

'Daddy? Is that you?'

The static was thick as alluvial mud. The numbers floated out of it like dead fish onto a greasy lake. I suddenly felt very cold; the hairs on my arms stood up like spines. I tried to make out my father's voice through the numbers and the static, but all I could really make out down the line was a kind of sludgy dragging sound, like something buried deep underground in a tunnel full of whispers.

'Dad are you all right? Is it Mum?'

'*Beckssss.*'

'Stay there. I'm coming.'

I slammed down the phone and ran for the car without even stopping to put on my shoes. But even as I drove to the house, clenching my fists on the steering wheel, and cursing at every traffic sign, I knew I was already too late. I could taste it in the air, just like the scent of burning.

2

Surely, every child must dream of the death of their parents. In stories, that's where it all begins. The adventure; the journey; the handsome prince; and it ends with a fairy-tale wedding. I certainly dreamt of all that often enough as I was growing up; it had always seemed to me inevitable that the sudden – and preferably painless – removal of the two haunted figures on Jackson Street would herald the beginning of my personal adventure.

In this case, it worked rather differently. The story, the fairy-tale wedding, were all by necessity put on hold to make way for a different story. You may remember the details, Roy; it made the national papers, in spite of Dom's efforts to suppress it. *Tragic Accident Claims Lives of Parents of 'Lost Boy of Malbry'* was hardly the catchiest of headlines, but the story ran alongside *that* photograph of Conrad, and was thankfully low on detail.

The coroner decided on a verdict of misadventure. The gas fire in my parents' bedroom had been out of order for years; it leaked, and they never used it. That night, they had turned it on, and closed the door, and gone to sleep hand-in-hand on the coverlet, dressed in the outfits they wore to church, a photo of Conrad between them. I'd found them the next morning; still warm, but then, of course, the gas fire had been on all night, and it was mid-August. Why did I not tell the police about the fake Conrad's imposture? There certainly was no doubt in my mind that this was the cause of their suicide. Not so much the money, perhaps, but the false hope and the foolishness of having been taken in yet again. But I had no real evidence to link Jerome to those letters, and he had been very careful not to mention money. Nor would he have been careless enough to transfer the cash to his bank account. It would have been my word against his, and he was very plausible, while I was a young woman with a history of mental instability. No one would have believed me. Not even my parents had believed me over him.

I don't remember their faces. I don't think I even looked at them. Instead, I opened the windows, turned off the gas and removed Conrad's photograph from the bed. I put it back on the mantelpiece, along with the others like it. The bedside phone was off the hook, and I replaced the receiver. I also turned off the radio, still tuned to the numbers station. Then I stood in the kitchen, where all the dishes had been washed and put away in the cupboard, and a new cloth placed on the table, in case the neighbours came to look. I found the letters from 'Conrad' by the clock on the living room mantel-piece. There were about half a dozen in all, handwritten in that cursive hand on smooth, expensive paper. I also found Conrad's bank book, empty now of savings. I put them all into my pocket. I didn't want them to be found. Then I made a cup of tea with just the right amount of milk, and drank it very slowly before I phoned for the police, feeling the dark-ness grow and grow, and listening to the sound of the pipes.

My parents' house had always had the noisiest of plumbing. Even before Mr Smallface, I'd found it terrifying. Now, alone at last in the house, I heard the gurgling and hissing of the water pipes, which had always sounded like something alive moving inside the brickwork, and I thought of something in a black mask, coming down a chimney.

Suddenly there came the sound of something moving in the sink. A tiny, queasy scratching sound, like that of a long, long fingernail. *That's where he lives*, said Conrad's voice from far away. *In the sink hole. He'll take everyone you care about. And then he'll come for you.*

'There's nothing there. It's only the pipes.' My voice was unexpectedly loud.

Silence.

Then came the scratching sound again, like a finger from out of the plughole. I put down my empty cup of tea and walked over to the kitchen sink. There was a mouse there, trying to climb the slippery sides of the basin. It was trapped: I could see its eyes like droplets of black treacle. Its mouth was open: it made no sound, but I could see it was suffering. I picked it up gently in my hand, and took it to the front door, and let it go on the newly cut lawn, and hoped it wouldn't die of shock. Mice do that sometimes. They die of shock even when the danger's past. I meant to check on it later, when the police had come and gone, but I never did. I hope it lived. But there's no way of knowing.

I remember the rest of that awful day in pallid snaps, like Polaroids. The two police officers – one woman, one man. The ambulance, idling at the kerb. The open windows letting in the scent of grass and gardens. *No, officer, I didn't touch anything. Just the gas and the windows.* The woman officer made me some tea – too milky, and with sugar. *No officer, there wasn't a note.*

I always called on them regularly. The gas fire leaked. They both knew that. My dad was going to have it fixed. Yes, I am the only child. No, I'm not married. Not yet. I drank my tea obediently, from a thousand fathoms down. My words floated up from my drowned face like fragments of confetti.

Eventually, Dominic arrived. They must have called him from the car. He'd left Emily with Blossom, and driven straight over from the house. I noticed that the car was still full of bags of shopping.

'Oh sweetheart. You don't even have any shoes.' He folded his arms around me. *Down. Down into darkness.* 'Sit down, my love. I'll make you some tea.' More tea, too milky, too sweet. I looked down at my grubby feet.

And then, from afar, I heard Dom say to the male officer: 'Oh, God. We're getting married on the twenty-eighth. What am I going to tell everyone?'

3

August 27th, 1989

So there it was. My story. My happy-ever-after. My fairy-tale wedding, my handsome prince, all scattered to the winds like pieces of torn-up paper. Dominic and his sisters did most of the clearing of the house; my parents' things, and Conrad's room that they had kept intact for so long. I like to think he searched for them – the lighting book, the programme, the drawings of Carrie Macleod, glimpsed through the lens of infatuation – but maybe he simply bundled up all the papers and books he could find and dumped them with the rubbish.

In any case, he kept me away while he made all the arrangements. There are a lot of arrangements to be made when someone dies; organizing the funeral; closing bank accounts; stopping mail. There was no family to inform; no investments to handle. Dominic was rather surprised at how little savings there were, and spent some time searching the house, hoping perhaps for a hidden cache. But I had taken the bank book, and Conrad's account was empty. No one – at least, as far as I knew – was aware of the forty thousand pounds that had been removed only a few weeks before. No one except Jerome Fentiman and, of course, myself.

'Are you sure there's nothing you want from the house? A souvenir? A photograph?'

I shook my head. I'd already told him I wanted nothing from Jackson Street. Everything that could be sold had already been taken by the clearance firm. Not that there was very much: some decent, but old-fashioned furniture; some clothing for the charity shop. A handful of true-crime fans had called, wanting mementoes of Conrad: Dominic had sent them away, and made sure the more desirable items of memorabilia were burnt. And rather than sell the house on the open market, we had opted to sell it at auction. There would be less money, of course, but at least it would be over sooner.

I'd assumed that because of the funeral, the wedding would have to be postponed, but Emily's anguish at the thought persuaded me to change my mind. Besides, there was Dominic's gang to think of. In the days that followed my parents' death, no morning or afternoon went by without some member of the family dropping in with *something* – a cake, a casserole, a voucher for the beauty shop, a book of uplifting essays, a cassette tape of religious music. Blossom was especially persistent, sometimes calling twice a day. Her sympathy was genuine, but I found it almost unbearable. Her rosy view of my parents, reunited with Conrad and looking down approvingly from their place in Heaven; her collection of cheering aphorisms; worst of all, her assumption that my parents wanted only the best for me, which, according to Blossom, was for the wedding to go ahead as planned.

'It's what they would have wanted,' she said. 'For you and Milly to get on with your lives. And besides –' Besides, as I already knew, the wedding was booked and paid for. 'Not that we'd begrudge you *that*, if you felt you couldn't go through with it. But I think it would be good for you both to draw the line and move on.'

Draw the line. I heard the phrase so many times over the course of that week. As if my grief were an irksome task – a pile of ironing, perhaps – to be completed before the celebrations could start.

'It's not as if you were close,' said Dom. 'And Milly barely knew them. Perhaps she ought to stay at home on the day. We don't want to upset her.'

And so we held the funeral at Malbry crematorium, at nine o'clock the day before the day set aside for our wedding. It was short notice, but Dominic had a friend there who was able to find us a ten-minute slot. It rained that day, as it rained all week, and would continue to rain until well after the end of the month. I wore my navy trouser suit. Dominic chose the music. I had no idea what my parents had liked. I sat through the service without a tear.

4

August 28th, 1989

I remember my wedding in slips of time, between great swoops of shadow. The scent of the church, like Jackson Street; all damp and lavender polish. White umbrellas in the rain. The cornflowers in my bridal bouquet, between the sprays of pale-pink rose. Blossom in a yellow dress, with Cecil in a matching waistcoat and a jaunty fedora. Emily, big with importance, with her little basket of sweets, a flower crown on her cropped hair. I do not remember the ceremony, but I do remember that as we arrived, the rain stopped just for a moment, to allow a faint gleam of sunshine.

Blossom was dismayed to find that there was no one to give me away. In fact, I had no guests at all; no friends from work; no family. In different circumstances, I might have invited Carrie, but the memory of those drawings, slipped between the pages of Conrad's lighting notebook, had made me profoundly uneasy. I need not explain to you why, Roy. A child's infatuation is all too easy to abuse. Carrie should have known that. Carrie should have walked away.

'Does *anyone* have to give me away?'

'But, sweetie, it's traditional.'

I've always hated those traditions. The passing over of the bride from one man to the other. The changing of her birth name from that of one patriarch to the next. It seems so condescending, as if women can't be trusted, even to hold onto a name.

In the end, it was Cecil who gave me away, as well as playing the role of best man. 'I don't think I want to give her away,' he said. 'I think I'll just keep her.'

Dominic grinned. He was in his element; making jokes with his parents; teasing his sisters, complimenting Blossom on my dress.

'She's a cracker,' Cecil said.

A cracker. Something beautifully wrapped, later to be pulled apart between two competing factions. That seemed to sum up my feelings quite well, and I gave an involuntary cry of laughter.

Then came the photographs outside the church, and the thin rain falling. Then a reception at the Shanker's Arms, rather more subdued than last time. There were no more than twenty guests, all of them from Dominic's gang, plus the wedding photographer, who had followed us from the church. I remember music. A cake with fondant roses. A speech, in which Cecil toasted the bride. *Welcome to Team Buckfast!* Then Dominic, speaking of how we met in the staff room at Sunnybank Park, and how one look had been enough – I was starting to feel dizzy. Far too much had happened over the course of a couple of weeks. I felt disconnected, lost; surrounded by too many colours and sounds. I suddenly wanted to be alone, somewhere dark and quiet; somewhere I could close my eyes and let reality slip away. Instead, I had to smile, to laugh: I could hear myself from a long way away, sounding forced and mechanical. I closed my eyes; from across the room I could hear Emily, sounding shrill and overexcited. *'Team Buckfast! Team Buckfast!'*

I opened my eyes and realized that Dominic was still talking. 'When I first met Becks,' he said, 'she had never had a birthday party. Never been on holiday. Never drunk a glass of champagne. And Milly had never ridden a bike, or had a friend to stay over. But now we're going to make up for all that. Now that she's a Buckfast.' Dominic looked at Emily. 'Milly, how's that sound to you? How would you like to be Emily Buckfast?'

'*Yay!*'

He smiled. 'I think that's settled, then.' He poured me another glass of champagne and sat down by my side. 'OK?'

'OK what?' I said.

'I want to adopt Milly. Give her the family she never had. And besides, now you're Mrs Buckfast, it would look odd if she was Emily Price.'

It made perfect sense as he said it, and yet I felt a pang of unease. This was another version of that very public proposal, aimed this time at Emily, and just as difficult to refuse. Did I *want* to refuse it? Emily seemed delighted. So why did it trouble me so much? Was it just that Dominic hadn't consulted me? Or was it simply the casual way he'd assumed possession of my daughter?

You may smile, Roy, but names are powerful. Forenames, surnames, nicknames. Each has its own unique energy. Masters use the surname as a disciplinary tool. Pupils use nicknames like rhyming slang, as a means of defying authority; or in the case of my brother, as a means of wielding it. From the beginning, Dominic had called my daughter *Milly*, even though she had always been Emily to everyone else. And he'd always called me *Becks*, the nickname Conrad had for me.

Becks. *Becksssss*. Like gas from a pipe.

'Becks? Are you OK?'

I smiled. Men always comment when we do not smile, as if our default expression should be one of delight at their presence. 'Of course. I just thought we'd discuss it first.'

'I wanted it to be a surprise.' I could see his expression beginning to change, like clouds across a summer sky. 'And look at Milly, how happy she is.'

I looked across at my daughter, now dancing with Cecil, to applause from Blossom and Victoria. My quiet, solitary child had somehow become an extrovert. Perhaps a change of name can bring about a change of nature, I thought, once more with that feeling of *shadow*, as if my reality were a flickering reel of unmoving pictures, with darkness around. I said: 'We were happy before, Dom. We didn't need you to save us.'

He lowered his voice. 'For fuck's sake. You're not going to do this today, are you?' The clouds were overhead now, the brief slice of sunlight extinguished. 'You do this every time, Becks. I try to do something to help, and you just go the other way.'

'I'm sorry. I'm used to my own way.' I hated the childish sound of the words; my instinct to placate him.

'And look how far *that* got you,' he said, still speaking in that lowered voice. 'Hearing voices from the drains. Passing it on to Milly. Obsessing about King Henry's instead of caring for your daughter. Between you and your parents, it's a miracle she's turned out as normal as she has.'

My anger was back, and I realized that it had never gone away. I had simply banked it down, like a fire under ash. Now it was back; that conviction that *damage* was what attracted him — damage like his own, perhaps, but it made him none the less dangerous. His grandiose gestures, designed to impress; the force of his personality; his genuine warmth; his possessiveness; his overwhelming family. These things had taken me in at the start, and as my doubts about him had begun to emerge, I'd blamed myself for my coldness. Now I saw that Dominic's generosity was driven by an insatiable hunger for both approval and gratitude: the unconditional gratitude of a dependent child. That was one of the reasons he'd grown so close to Emily. That was why I could never be the woman he really wanted. And right there, at my wedding, I began to see how it would end; the inevitability of our descent; and how he would fight to keep Emily with every weapon at his command.

I remembered what Carrie had said when we were discussing Conrad: *Oh, he could be very charming when he wanted to. But there's a reason his friends were all misfits and outsiders . . . He liked his people – vulnerable.*

How could I not have seen it before?

How much do you love me, Becks?

I reined in my anger and smiled again. 'I know. You're right. I'm sorry.' And I was – not for being the person I am, but for what would have to happen. And I drifted along in the slipstream of those strange late-summer days like a piece of ash on the wind, consumed by that growing darkness.

5

St Oswald's ~~Grammar School for Boys~~ *Academy*
October 2nd, 2006, 7.30 a.m.

I arrived at the old place just before seven-thirty this morning.
It was still dark, and the street lights were on, which made me
realize just how long it has been since I left my desk. A Master
of St Oswald's never leaves his post; and yet I have been away so
long. Even my classroom smells different now; less tobacco, less
dust, less chalk, and more of a kind of floral scent, as if they have
changed the cleaners again. I suppose it might be the scent of girls.

I notice that someone has tidied my desk. Nothing is missing,
except for a number of used handkerchiefs, some empty ink
cartridges and a single Liquorice Allsort (blue), which I kept
for nostalgia's sake. Additionally, I notice that all my books
and papers and pens have been neatly compartmentalized. I
detect the hand of Dr Devine, whose love of this kind of
minutiae hides an equally trivial mind.

I sat at my desk and smoked a Gauloise to try and dispel
the floral scent, then opened the window to dispel the smoke.
I was just crushing the last of my cigarette into the inkwell
when the door opened behind me. It was the man himself, no
doubt alerted by the smell of tobacco. He did not comment

openly, but the nose – which in his case has always been the most reactive part of the man – twitched eloquently.

'Ah, Straitley,' he said.

I nodded. 'Devine.'

Thus have our conversations eased over the past twelve months or so. A year ago, such easy banter would not have been imaginable.

'You're back, then,' he said.

'*Libens. Volens. Potens*,' I said, indicating my readiness.

The nose twitched again. 'I thought you were away till half-term.'

'What? So that you can annexe my office again?'

He sniffed. 'You still don't look well, Straitley. Too little exercise, too many of *those*.' He indicated the crumpled packet of Gauloises sticking out of my trouser pocket. I should have been wearing my gown, I thought. A gown hides a multitude of sins. I looked for it in its habitual place on the peg at the back of the door, and saw with alarm that it had gone.

'Where's my gown?' I said. 'It isn't where I left it.'

Devine shrugged, as if to absolve himself of responsibility. 'Maybe Miss Malone tidied it away,' he said. 'She's been in charge of your form for a while.'

'The *Foghorn*?' Words failed me. 'They put The Foghorn in charge of my form?'

'Miss Malone has managed quite well, given the circumstances,' he said. 'And after all, how much effort does it take to control a Second Form?'

I found my gown in the stock cupboard. It was hanging on a coat hanger that certainly hadn't been there before. It looked and smelt suspiciously clean, and I finally traced the floral scent to a can of fabric freshener, also a new addition to my collection of papers and books.

I shrugged on the gown with displeasure. Masters are terri-
torial, but I draw the line at scent-marking. 'Good thing I got
back when I did,' I said. 'Another three weeks and they'd have
remodelled the whole place.' I glanced out of the window,
where my once-familiar view of the chapel, with a vista of
fields in the distance, now encompassed the angry tip of the
Gunderson Building. 'That eyesore,' I said.

He followed my gaze. 'I think it's rather handsome.
Modern.'

I gave a snort. 'You would.'

Devine gave me a satirical look. '*Non progredi est regredi.*
Isn't that how the saying goes?' he said.

'*Not to go forward is to go backward.* I'm impressed at the
Latin, if not at the sentiment. Many things survive quite well
without *ever* going forward.'

He smiled. 'I suppose you'd have us stay in the Middle Ages.'
But there was no sting in his words today, simply a kind of
affectionate tolerance that I found most unusual. Could Dr
Devine have mellowed? It was a slightly alarming thought. Dr
Devine's disapproval has always been one of the pillars of my
career. The thought that he might actually *like* me now, after
all these years, is more than a little disturbing. I lit a defiant
Gauloise, which, to my relief, caused him to shudder, then,
when he had retreated back to the safety and hygiene of the
German Departmental Office, I went out onto the balcony
– long since declared out of bounds to boys for Health and
Safety reasons – and smoked it, counting the gargoyles on the
roof and watching the sun rise softly out of the autumn mist.

St Oswald's is the only place I've taught where there are
actually gargoyles. Most of them are on the roof, but a few
of them are on the staff – an old joke, but one I still make
regularly, to break the ice with parents. I am not entirely

unaware that I look rather like a gargoyle myself, which is presumably why some of the boys refer to me as Quasimodo. This, plus my home in the Bell Tower, and the fact that my features, never Classical, now resemble a birthday cake that has been left out in the rain. None of this troubles me at all. The likes of Devine may embrace such things as exercise and aftershave: I prefer to inhabit a body built for comfort, not speed. And yet, as I stand on the balcony, feeling the October mist and smelling the October leaves from down there in the Middle School Quad, I feel that something is out of place. No, not *out of place*, exactly – but surely the gargoyle closest to the edge of my balcony seems more modern than the rest; unmarred by smoke, as yet untouched by the lichen blooms of time.

I move a little closer, avoiding the broken parapet that caused Devine, in his days as Health and Safety Officer, to designate my balcony unsafe to pupils.

Yes, as I thought: the sculpture has been added recently. And it is baked clay, not stone, like the creatures that adorn the Natural History Museum: modelled into a creature wearing something like an academic robe, with a not-unfamiliar face and, at the base, an inscription. Leaning dangerously out into space, I managed to decipher the text:

Caesar adsum jam forte
Brutus aderat

For a moment I was baffled. A portrait of myself in clay, flanked by one of the oldest and silliest of all my Latin jokes, carefully sculpted, oven-baked, and mortared in place on top of a ledge alongside the previous residents. Who could have done such a thing, and how?

Then I remembered Allen-Jones and the others, talking about a prank that would put to shame the classic pranks of earlier generations, and I began to laugh so hard that the invisible finger finally intervened with one of its admonishing prods, presumably to slow me down before I fell off the balcony. And that was how she found me, sitting at my old school desk, still grinning to myself as the current 2S filed in for Registration.

'Mr Straitley!'

'Headmaster.'

She gave a rather tight-lipped smile. 'We weren't expecting you today.'

'And yet, behold me, Headmaster,' I said, indicating my person.

'Well, you *do* have cover today,' said La Buckfast, still smiling. 'I know you contacted Dr Strange, but I thought it best to keep them on.'

'Well, I'm sure they can be redeployed,' I said. 'I've been looking forward to this. Back in the saddle, after – how long? Three weeks? That's more time away from my desk than the whole of the rest of my career.'

She shrugged. 'Very well, Mr Straitley. I hope you won't exhaust yourself. And maybe we can finish our chat after school, at four?'

'I'll be here, Headmaster,' I said.

She raised an eyebrow. 'Here?'

I said: 'Here, on my own quarterdeck.'

I saw her consider this carefully. On previous occasions, she had always had the advantage. I had been ill; in hospital; in her office; on her terms. For us to meet in Room 59 gave me back my authority. I took a deep breath of the air of the place; that scent of wood and chalk dust. In my absence, the old desks have not been removed; nor has my ancient blackboard, and the fleeting scent of Miss Malone's air freshener has already been displaced by that of my Gauloises and the outdoors. I grinned to myself once again at the thought of that addition to my balcony: a gargoyle of my very own, modelled to my features. The spiteful finger under my ribs poked, and then moved on again.

Finally, she gave a shrug. 'I'll bring the coffee, Roy,' she said.

6

October 2nd, 2006, 9.45 a.m.

The stubborn old fool. He still looked unwell, and yet he insisted on staying. And there's only so much a Head can do in the face of such determination. And so I shifted his cover to another Department, and waited until the time of our final meeting. Because it *will* be the last one, I know. Here, I will finish my story.

Why have I taken so long, do you ask? Because I wanted your silence? That was what I thought at the time, but now I see that I needed to tell my story as much as you needed to hear it. I have not told you everything. I'm sure you must already know that, Roy. Some things cannot be spoken aloud, or even entirely remembered. That's why I never told Dominic, or asked him about Carrie. Nor did I ever feel the need to seek her out and confront her. It was a different time, Roy. The power dynamic was different. That doesn't excuse her in the least, but I know what it's like to take power. I know what it's like for Masters and boys to look at you in *that* way. I imagine she was flattered at first. To have his adoration. Dominic was talented. I can see from the cast photographs – stills from the show, in black-and-white – how expressive his face was, how certain, how spontaneous his gestures. Adding to that his undoubted artistic talent, I can see how Carrie might have made him her special project. Was that what Conrad envied? It must have been hard for my brother to see the new boy earn so much attention. Conrad himself, in spite of our parents' adoration, was never more than average: in sport, in chess, in everything. Did Milky beat him at chess that day in the Smarthwaite Library? I think perhaps he did. Is that why he talked him into crashing the School Photograph? Could he even have been the one who reported Milky to Mr Scoones? I think perhaps it was. My brother was good at hiding a grudge until it was time to take revenge. What kind of revenge had he planned to exact on Dominic, for his special relationship with Miss Macleod?

Fuck her, and fuck her play.

You wish.

Don't we all?

Had Fentiman been in on it? I was inclined to believe he had. Would Milky have been involved? Maybe not, especially after he'd been expelled from St Oswald's. But *Fentiman* – I remembered him as a follower, not a leader. A quiet boy, who spoke up mostly to reinforce what my brother had said. The older Fentiman was the same; quick to know what he was expected to say; changing from ally, to confidant, to old school tie, to one of the boys, to Prodigal Son, and all with an effortless ease that suggested *he*, and not Conrad, should have been in the theatre. What role did he play, then? *Tech Crew*. That could have meant almost anything. Conrad had the lead role; the one with the safety harness, there to ensure that he did not fall from his place on the lighting tower. Fatty had the supporting role, as always. The stalwart. The convenient stooge. Had Fatty known of Conrad's plan? Had he even planned it himself? I could imagine it all too well. What would it be? Something public, no doubt. Something designed to humiliate. And something to hurt Carrie, too, for choosing Dom over Conrad. I remembered Carrie telling me that she'd once been engaged to Philip Sinclair. Could Conrad have been behind the split? It wouldn't have taken much. A word, a hint – or one of those pictures of Dominic's –

Of course, I could have asked Dominic. He would have told me, eventually. But that would have meant confiding in him, telling him about Fentiman. By keeping silent, I could at least pretend that things were normal. I could at least pretend to be the woman he believed I was. And I *enjoyed* being that woman. I liked her vulnerability, her innocence. I liked the way she brought out Dominic's protective side. I liked her willingness to accept the things over which she had no control. And maybe I already knew, Roy, that if I were to hear from him that he was complicit, that he was *there*, I would have no further choice.

I would have to kill him.

7

St Oswald's ~~Grammar School for Boys~~ Academy
October 2nd, 2006, 12.30

An old warhorse never forgets the sound of battle. In spite of
my three weeks' absence, it was almost surprising how quickly
I fell back into the routine. Thirty seconds of awkwardness
– I'll never get used to seeing girls in the class – and then
we were fine. A Second Form first, and then an Upper Fifth,
then Break, which I spent in my room with a cup of tea and
a biscuit, kindly brought in by Kitty Teague. A fine young
woman, Miss Teague, and a worthy Head of Department. I
said as much to her, and she smiled.

'I'm very glad you're back, Roy,' she said. 'It isn't the same
without you.'

I took a bite from a Custard Cream. 'I'm not the same
without St Oswald's,' I said. 'The barnacles on the old ship
only survive when in motion. Take us onto land, and we die.
Stop us moving for too long, we die.'

Kitty looked at me anxiously. 'You're feeling better, aren't
you?' she said. 'You don't want to overdo things.'

I smiled. 'My life has until now been a positive orgy of
excess. I believe it suits me.'

After that I taught a Mulberry form the difference between Latin and Classics: a somewhat fraught experience for the girls, who had expected the normal routine of gladiator movies and colouring-in, but I think that, by the end of it, we had reached an agreement. Then it was Lunch Break, during which I managed a quick cup of tea and a furtive cheese-and-ham sandwich before sneaking out for a Gauloise on my tiny balcony.

I flipped my cigarette butt into the autumn air, and turned to see a welcome quintet at the door: my Brodie Boys, with Allen-Jones looking especially *louche*, and watching me through the classroom door as if I were a rare specimen in a tank. I suppose perhaps to them, I am: a quasi-legendary creature, like the Kraken, emerging from the depths only to die, gasping, on the surface. I suppose that must be why they chose to depict me as a gargoyle.

'*Quod agis, Magister?*' piped up Allen-Jones.

I stepped inside the classroom once more, assuming a ferocious expression. 'Come on in, you reprobates. I imagine you haven't assembled here simply to watch me.'

Ben Wild gave me a cautious look. 'You saw it, Sir?'

'That excrescence? That foul caricature of me on the body of the dear old Bell Tower?'

'It was a prank, Sir,' said Allen-Jones.

'A *prank*?' I repeated.

'Yes, Sir.'

Seeing their faces so full of dismay, I couldn't keep up the pretence any longer. I erupted with laughter, and had to sit back on my chair for a while as the invisible finger played its cakewalk on my ribs. My Brodie Boys relaxed visibly, spreading out to occupy the front-row desks, each hastening to tell his part of the tale. Meanwhile, I drank a cup of tea, and waited for the details.

'It was Ben's idea,' said Sutcliff. 'We made the model out of clay. Ben managed to talk the technician into letting us use the Sixth-Form kiln.'

'Did she?' I said, without thinking.

'He, Sir,' said Allen-Jones.

I looked at Ben and nodded. Boys will be boys, I told myself. And sometimes, children teach us more than we could ever believe.

'But how did you manage to get it up here? Please tell me you *didn't* steal a crane.'

Ben smiled. 'Not quite, Sir. We got Jimmy to use the cherry-picker. The one he uses for changing the bulbs on the outdoor security lights.'

'I see.' I put down my empty cup. 'Well, gentlemen, my work here is done. Under my command, you have learnt all of Life's essential skills. Subversion, persuasion, bribery, deceit, *and* all the Latin you need to know. If you don't end up ruling the world, then I will be extremely surprised.'

The five of them grinned at each other. 'I thought you'd like it,' said Allen-Jones. 'Now you'll be here forever.'

8

The next two periods were free, and I was able to sit for a
while and enjoy the relative peace of the day. Outside, the
sky was overcast; soft curtains of mist had fallen. I opened the
window, and watched the sky darken gently. By four it would
be almost night. I remembered one of Eric's French poems, I
don't remember the author now:

> She comes with the night from as far as the night
> Wind-footed, wolf-shod –

It describes her rather well, I thought. The victim-turned-predator,
subtle as smoke, armed today with nothing but words. I admire
her more than I can say; she has achieved the impossible. Girls
in the School; a new regime; a masterly defeat of one who
thought he was up to every game. But her account is not over.
I still do not know the truth. Sitting here in Room 59, with
the scent of old wood and chalk dust and mice, I wonder why I
want it so much. And yet I do: without it, all this is nothing but
dust and kindling. I dig into the pockets of my tweed jacket,
hoping for an Allsort. There are none, but in the lining, I find

a couple of conkers. A little wizened now, but just seasoned enough for a game.

I smile. This will be our final night; the final chapter of our tale. I'm glad I was able to spend it here, among the things that mean most to me. I'm glad I was able to spend it with you. I'm glad of the chance to hear the end of your tale, back here, where it all began. We have come a long way together. We have shared more over these few weeks than most people do in a lifetime. And yet we must come together again for one last time, before we are done. Once more, as the night falls and the mist swirls around the old stones. Once more, for my conscience's sake, and for the sake of our honour.

She comes from the night from as far as the night –

Once more, for St Oswald's.

9

September 4th, 1989

Meanwhile, I had not forgotten Conrad's old friend, Jerome Fentiman. I already knew, via Darren Milk, that, failing the job at King Henry's, he had accepted a post at St Oswald's. Interesting choice, don't you think? It's almost as if he'd chosen a place where he could pursue his alternative career as a confidence trickster and extortionist. There was no lack of potential there. Eric Scoones, David Spikely, Johnny Harrington, Harry Clarke – St Oswald's had at least as many skeletons as King Henry's, and men like Fentiman always seem to find the right person to serve their needs. You might have thought it a risky move, except that his latest victims were dead, and their daughter had nothing but theories to link him to the imposture. Besides, people like Fentiman have always hidden in plain sight. An Oxford man, an Old Boy, a friend of Daniel Higgs, he came with his passport already stamped. He had no need of the narrow door. St Oswald's gates were open wide in welcome to receive him.

It took just a little arranging. St Oswald's starts its term a week earlier than the state schools in Malbry, so Dom and Emily were home. But in the wake of my parents' deaths, I

409

had taken to going walking along the disused railway line: I sometimes stayed out for hours, and Dominic was used to that. Thus I was able to make my plans under the cover of my grief, while waiting for Fentiman to emerge. Darren Milk had been easy to bribe. A note slipped into the teacher's desk on the first day of the new term was enough to deliver Fentiman to a rendezvous spot.

> Dear Conrad,
> I'm waiting at the side gate.
> Your little sister,
> Becky

The spider was Darren's own idea – a harmless prank, but in the end it proved to be invaluable.

The Porter's Gate at St Oswald's is usually a busy place. It's where the school buses drop off the boys and pick them up at the end of the day. It's where the Porter had his lodge – now a simple prefab – and where parents of the rugby team come to watch their offspring play. But during lesson times, the place is usually deserted. There's always the risk of encountering a wandering Master or boy out of class, or maybe the Porter doing his rounds, but it was far less of a risk than meeting him after school, or in the morning. Of course, I had no idea then of how the encounter with Fentiman would end; but you can probably guess, Roy.

It was raining a little when I arrived at St Oswald's. It had been raining for almost a week, and the rugby pitch was water-logged. The puddle at the near end of the field had grown into a moderate lake, which had already almost reached the path, and the two wooden benches by the gate. A half-hearted attempt had been made to stem the progress of the water: a low barrier of sandbags and stones ran along the side of the path, although it did little to stop the flood. I arrived just before the second period, which was when Darren Milk had his Latin class, and waited by the shallow end of the pool, in which a number of crisp packets, a satsuma and what looked like the side of a gate post already floated mournfully. I had made no special attempt to look unobtrusive. Only a knitted hat over my hair, and a waterproof jacket against the rain. Anyone could have seen me, except that no one was around; there are no sports on the first day of term, and anyway, it was raining.

Fentiman arrived some twenty minutes into the lesson. He must have had time to greet the class, set them to work and open his desk, where my note was already waiting. I doubt if he saw the spider; though later its presence served as excellent justification for Fentiman's sudden departure. Certainly, no one went looking for him beyond the initial half-hearted attempt: the man was clearly not up to the task of teaching at St Oswald's.

Not that I'd planned to kill him right then; it takes a special mindset to admit to that kind of thing. I simply didn't see myself as being capable of murder. Of course, I know now how absurd that is; we are all of us capable. Even you, Roy. Even me. Even your old friend Eric Scoones, whose green car *was* at King Henry's that day. He had driven young Christopher Milk in to see the Headmaster in order to apologize for his role in the crashing of the School Photograph. The old Old Head would certainly have asked to see my brother that day, too; except that my brother was nowhere to be found when the prints were delivered.

Fentiman was wearing his Oxford blazer underneath a drab-coloured mac against the rain. His Prefect's badge was in the lapel, and I wondered whether that was what had persuaded my parents to trust him. Absurd, of course: they would have trusted any passer-by who happened to mention my brother's name. But that Prefect's badge had registered. It had put them at their ease. No matter that it was a cheap thing, mass-produced by the same local firm that makes those school Prep Diaries. The fact that he was wearing it now filled me with a low rage, but I managed a smile in greeting.

'Nice of you to meet me.'

'How could I resist?' he said.

Fentiman was outwardly calm, but I could see his agitation. My note had got his attention, at least. But behind it, there was another look; one of quiet complacency. *I'm wearing the badge and the blazer*, it said. *I fit. Do you? Do you really think that if you walk into St Oswald's now, their ranks won't close to protect me?* He didn't say it aloud, but I knew. He had walked in through the wide front door. Mine was the narrow entrance, and if I wanted entry at all, I would have to fight my way in.

'I know who you are,' I told him. 'I know what you did.'

'Oh, really?' he said. 'In which case, I'm surprised you haven't been to the police.'

'I might. I have your letters. I know my parents gave you money.'

He looked at me with sympathy. 'I'm sorry about your parents, Rebecca. But you must have known how unhappy they were. And as for the letters, I think you'll find that anyone could have written them. Even a handwriting expert might have difficulty with copperplate.'

'Maybe you're right. But I don't suppose St Oswald's would relish the scandal.'

I thought I saw his eyes narrow at that. 'If this is about the money —'

'It's not.'

'Then what do you *want*, Rebecca?'

I took a breath. The air was sour with rain and stagnant water. A seagull landed briefly on the top of the side gate, then flew, *crawk*-ing, into the white sky. 'I want to know what happened,' I said. 'I want to know about Conrad. I want to know why he disappeared. I want an end to all of it.'

'What, still?' He looked at me with what seemed like genuine concern. The man was a consummate actor. 'Trust me, you're better not knowing,' he said. 'You've got a good man in Dominic, and Emily seems like a nice kid. You're free of the past. Enjoy what you have. Don't go digging up corpses.'

I felt that flash of rage again. 'I'm not a child,' I told him. 'I don't need your advice, or your protection.'

He raised his eyebrows. 'That's not what I've heard. In fact, everything you've told me so far suggests you'd do better to just walk away.'

'I think it's a little late for that.' I tried to keep my voice even. 'You were the one who brought up the past. You even involved my daughter in your filthy little deception.'

'I've never been near your daughter,' he said, and I thought his surprise looked genuine. 'I've never even been to your house. Why would I bother, when Dominic was already right there?'

'Dominic was in on this?' My mouth was suddenly very dry.

'Are you sure you want to know?'

I nodded.

'Of course he was in on it.' His voice was almost regretful. 'He wanted you out of King Henry's,' he said. 'He thought it was a bad idea for you to be back where it happened. He told us to do whatever it took to make certain that you didn't stay.'

'*Us*? You mean you and Milky?'

He shrugged. 'Milky was already working there. That made it easy to get a foot in. Besides, I already knew the place. It didn't take much to know what to do. Forgive me for saying so, but it's not like you were a great fit to start off with.'

'What about my parents?' I said. 'The letters from Conrad?'

He shook his head. 'Dominic didn't know about that. I told you, this was all about you. I saw my chance, and I took it, that's all. Dom didn't ask any questions. But if you *did* get any ideas about making trouble for me here, I promise you I could make a *lot* more trouble for him over at Sunnybank Park than you could here at St Oswald's.'

I thought about that for a moment. Yes, Jerome was probably right. Places like St Oswald's are designed to look after their people. Any investigation of a complaint against a member of staff would be conducted internally – if indeed it was conducted at all. In Fentiman's case, it was doubtful: after all, I wasn't even a parent.

I reached into my pocket and pulled out a pack of cigarettes. I'd started smoking again after the death of my parents, though not in front of Dominic. I lit one with fingers that were starting to turn numb and red with cold, and drew the smoke into my lungs with a kind of gasping relief.

'I'm not going to make a complaint,' I said. 'I just want to know what happened.'

Fentiman looked at me. 'You mean you really don't know?' His hair was plastered to his forehead now, and his coat had darkened with the rain. His initial look of unease had veered to something almost avuncular. 'Trust me, Rebecca. There's nothing you need to remember about that day. No one you need to prove anything to. It's over. Forgotten. You have to move on –'

'Don't patronize me, you bastard.' My voice was low and

furred with smoke. 'Tell me what happened that day.'

For a moment he didn't say anything. Instead, he looked at me with a smile of barely concealed complacency. It was the smile of every man who looked up my skirt on a staircase. The smile of every Master who mistook me for a Secretary. The smile of every man who thought he could be my protector.

How much do you love me, Becks?

How much do you love me?

'Haven't you worked it out?' he said. 'Haven't you guessed, after all this time? I can't believe that for all these years you've managed to keep the truth hidden away, even from yourself.'

'I don't know what you mean,' I said. And yet, wasn't there something familiar in the rhythm of his words; something that brought back my parents' house, and the sound of the numbers station? *That monster who lived in the drains was one. Anything that went wrong was his fault. That Emily, she was another. Emily Jackson, you called her.*

'What do you mean?' I said again. 'Tell me. *Who killed Conrad?*'

10

September 12th, 1989

It's funny how we see ourselves. Until we commit a murder, we do not think of ourselves as murderers. Even afterwards, we try to frame the act as something else. A crime of passion. Self-defence. An accident. An act of God. A momentary lapse of reason.

Certainly, I did not think of myself as any kind of murderer. He turned away, and I picked up the thing that looked like a broken gate post. A piece of wood maybe three feet long, with a couple of twisted nails at one end, and something that might have been part of a hinge. It had been in the water some time; the wood was like a soaked sponge. I lifted it like a hockey stick and hit him in the back of the head – he must have seen me coming, because he started to turn, and instead of striking him in the nape of the neck, I caught him in the jaw instead, and he spun sideways and fell face down into the shallow water.

They say you can drown in a puddle. I can attest to the truth of this. He hardly even struggled. I think the blow must have unhinged his jaw, because he barely made a sound. I stood with my foot on the back of his neck for about ten minutes, wondering what I would do if someone – a boy, a Master – happened to pass at that moment. I had no plan. My head was filled with images, all released by a single action, like Proust dipping his madeleine. Even then, I was aware of the absurdity of the comparison. But dipping Fentiman in the pool had a similar effect: the past began to unravel like pulling hair out of a drain, and everything began to clear. And I remembered the green door, and the sound of something falling through, and the face of the monster, and I could taste, and I could see, and I could hear, and I could *feel*, not just the story that I'd told and woven around myself like a cocoon, but the memory inside, like biting the stone at the heart of a fruit.

For a time, I was overwhelmed. Anybody walking past would have seen me standing there by the Porter's Gate with a look of intent concentration and a dead man at my feet. Then, as my world began to shift and reassess its axis, I dragged him by the trouser leg until the water covered him, and piled some sandbags over him to hide him from immediate sight. I had no idea what to do next. His murder had been an impulse. I could already feel myself mentally reframing his death; recasting myself as a witness, traumatized by what I'd seen. I went home and waited for the police: two days passed, and then a week. The unseasonal rain had long since stopped. It was only a matter of time before someone noticed the body in that absurdly shallow water.

I did not return to King Henry's. Instead, I applied for the job at Sunnybank Park, never expecting to last that long. Every day the papers came, and I searched them for news of Fentiman. Nothing came. And then at last I did what no murderer should ever do: I went back to the scene of the crime. And I understood what had happened then, and why no one had reported a body. Three lorryloads of topsoil and grit had been spread over the sunken area of the playing fields by the Porter's Gate – part of a regular attempt to deal with mining subsidence. Tons of packing, rubble and earth had been tipped onto the waterlogged field, after which a machine had rolled it flat, and the area had been fenced off to protect the new-seeded grass. Looking at the tiny shoots already pricking the surface, I guessed that this had all happened within forty-eight hours of Fentiman's death.

It's hard to believe how they managed to miss the body of a grown man in barely a foot of water. But we see mostly what we *expect* to see – sandbags, a discarded overcoat. At best, a pile of debris shaped amusingly like a body. St Oswald's, like King Henry's, has always been so complacent, unquestioning of its certainties. These men, who think they run the world. A woman would have noticed.

But no one went looking for Fentiman. No one reported him missing. Thanks to Darren Milk and his tarantula, the staff of St Oswald's – you included, Roy – assumed that he had simply lost his nerve. He had no close family; his house was leased, and his landlord reclaimed the property when the bills stopped being paid. Six months down the line, there was a small and half-hearted investigation on behalf of an elderly couple who claimed that Fentiman had embezzled them out of their savings – the amount was small compared to the sum that my parents had given him, but it was enough to explain the man's sudden departure. The story appeared in the *Yorkshire Post* and the *Malbry Examiner*, but it was never headline news. I had escaped detection. I was – once more – a murderer.

I I

October 2nd, 2006, 4.18 p.m.

Memory is a river that leads to all the lands of the Underworld. Some tributaries run to Lethe and the blessing of oblivion. Others lead to Tartarus and the torments of remorse. I have never felt remorse. In some ways, that might have been better. Instead, I simply spun a cocoon, adding layers of detail until the truth was perfectly hidden. And I had *believed* the story; just as I'd believed in Emily Jackson, and Mr Smallface. But now the truth had been revealed. The dam had been broken. The river ran.

On the afternoon of July 9th, 1971, it was raining. I remember the droplets of water on my shiny new red-patent shoes. I went into the cloakroom to wait for Conrad to arrive. I sat in front of his locker, then, after fifteen minutes or so, I looked into the corridor to check if my brother was nearby.

A Master and a boy were passing in the corridor. I recognized Milky, and understood that he was somehow in trouble. I imagine, Roy, that the Master was Eric Scoones, who had been Milky's Form Master that year, and took his responsibilities seriously. I didn't know Scoones, of course, but I

419

remember his loud voice and the black gown he wore, so like the portrait in the Smarthwaite Library. I waited behind the locker room door until they were safely out of the way. I remember the sound of the Master's shoes, heavy on the wooden floor. Then, when it was silent again, I came out to investigate.

An empty school sounds different, you know. You'd expect it to be silent when all the boys are busy in class, but there's always a kind of hum in the air, like a drowsy beehive. Absence has a sound of its own, and the school sounded *empty* that day; empty as a beehive where all the bees are dead. There were no after-school clubs or sports so close to the end of term. Most of the staff had gone straight home. The cleaners were due to arrive at five. The last performance of *Othello* was supposed to start at eight, which gave everyone concerned the chance to go home, have a meal and come back in time to prepare for the show.

Holding my little red satchel, I stepped out into the corridor. My new shoes made a pattering sound on the polished floorboards. I knew where the Little Theatre was. I'd been there before, and I remembered the design of interlaced masks – Tragedy and Comedy – over the door. I didn't like masks. They frightened me. I pushed the door open and went inside.

It was dark inside the theatre. The house lights were off, and a vivid green light shone around the empty stage. The scene was an interior; stone walls like a castle tower, with pointed windows that somehow reminded me of the Pepper Pot. The green light came from an open trapdoor, and broke into a pattern of leaves that dappled the curtains and scenery. From far away, I heard the sound of voices; distant laughter.

'Conrad?'

The sound of voices stopped. I came a little closer. There were steps leading up to the side of the stage. I paused for a moment, then climbed up. From the green-lit trapdoor, there came a kind of dragging sound.

'Conrad?' My small voice sounded very big on the hollow-sounding stage.

The dragging sound came closer. It seemed to come from under my feet, as if something had awakened there. At the same time, there was a hissing sound from a box in the wings, and smoke began to pour onto the stage; thick, white smoke that smelt chalky somehow, chalk and rubber and sawdust. The green light caught the smoke like powder paint dispersing in a bowl of water; that bright and somehow poisonous green spilt over the toes of my party shoes. And it was *cold*: I could already see the condensation on the little red satchel that I clutched so tightly to my chest.

I called for Conrad again, this time in a choking whisper. The dragging sound was closer now, and I thought I could hear a voice; a soft and very *familiar* voice that whispered: *Becks. Beckssssss.* It came from the open trapdoor, where the smoke had made a kind of lime-green puddle; and then, from out of the green smoke, came a head, with a grotesquely *small* blank face upon its giant shoulders –

There are two kinds of people, Roy. Those who freeze under pressure, and those who go on the attack. I reacted instinctively. I swung my little red satchel by its strap towards the trapdoor. There was a kind of metal strut holding the trapdoor open. The satchel hit the metal strut, which fell away, whipping the strap from my hand. The monstrous figure disappeared, the heavy trapdoor slammed shut with a sound that seemed to fill the whole world. From under the stage, there came the sound of something heavy falling. Then silence; then a voice raised in wordless, warbling dismay.

I'd lost my little red satchel. It had fallen through the trapdoor. My distress at losing it wholly eclipsed the rest of the scene. Children are like that, Roy: they have their own priorities. They see the world from their own, very small, peculiar perspective. Adults live in a kind of blur, far above their heads. Their thoughts and actions are strangely intense; determined by childish rituals that adults do not understand. Thus, the death of my brother went almost unnoticed in the face of a larger tragedy; the loss of my little red satchel into the lair of the monster.

My adult self can see it now. Through hindsight's flawless rear window, everything falls in its place. The boy in the *moretta* mask and the black robe around his shoulders; the other boy, at the foot of the steps, waiting in the trap room. The child slamming shut the green-lit trapdoor as she so often closed the toilet seat, to mute the sinister sound of the flush and to guard against the monster. The trapdoor was heavy; it smashed the boy's skull. Conrad was dead within seconds.

'It's shocking, how fast it all happened,' Fentiman had said by the pool. 'For a minute I couldn't believe Conrad wasn't faking it. Alive one second, dead the next. I guess I lost it for a while.'

I smiled at that, not unaware of the irony of my position. And he was perfectly right, of course: it always comes as a surprise just how easy it is to take a life. Films and TV shows make it look so difficult, so dramatic. But like the best Classical drama, Conrad's death happened off-stage. All I knew was that I'd fought back; slammed the door in the face of my tormentor.

With the help of Fentiman, I put together a sequence of events. Conrad and Fatty had been in the trap room, planning their trick on Miss Macleod. It wasn't a complicated plan. A simple sachet of itching powder in the front panel of Desdemona's dress; just the kind of trick I knew Conrad would have found hilarious. Dominic had gone to meet Milky as he came out of the Head's office. Scoones was still in there with the Head; his ponderous accents penetrating even through the study door. Both boys had heard Fatty's cry of dismay, and followed the sound to the trap room. They had seen the red satchel on the ground beside my brother's body and, all together, had gone in search of me.

They found me in the cloakroom. I only really remember their shoes; Milky's shiny black school shoes; Fatty's brogues; Dominic's scuffed and dusty toes as they gathered around me. Fatty was trying to explain what he'd seen – the satchel, the trapdoor, Conrad. His voice, sharpened by alarm, distressed the air of the cloakroom. Remember, I was five years old. Those fourteen-year-old boys were like adults to me. Their voices clapped and bounced like flung basketballs against the hard, high ceiling. I found an open locker and crept inside, safe in the enclosed space.

It was Dominic who took charge. Dominic, who spoke to me in his calm and quiet voice, through the gap in the locker door, while the others went back to the trap room and argued over what to do.

It's OK, Becks. You stay in there. You stay in there, where it's safe. Where's Conrad?

Conrad's gone. Mr Smallface took him away. You remember that, don't you?

In the dark, I nodded.

Don't tell anyone we were here. Otherwise he might come back.

Once more, I nodded, and pushed myself further into the locker space.

Now be a good girl and wait, he said.

And like a good girl, I waited.

According to Fentiman, it had been Dominic, in the end, who took the lead in Conrad's stead and suggested a course of action. 'We can't tell anyone about this.'

'What do you mean?' Fentiman said. 'We have to tell *someone*.'

'No, we don't,' Dominic said. 'If you want to tell someone, you go ahead. But you were alone when it happened. You'll just have to explain it all. Including what you were doing there together in the first place.'

'It was an accident,' Fatty said. 'He was messing about with the trapdoor, trying to frighten his sister.'

'You think his parents will buy that? They'll be looking for someone to blame. You think they'll believe *any* story where Conrad wasn't the hero? Look at what happened to Milky.'

Fatty looked at Milky, who shrugged. 'Anything to pin the blame on someone who wasn't from here.'

'They'll say we were fighting or something,' said Dom. 'They'll say we shouldn't have been here alone. They'll say we had it in for him, and we *did* – he was always winding people up. They'll call the police. They'll have to. And then we'll have a record. We'll be on their radar *forever* –'

I guessed that Dom's experience of the police was different to that of his friends. In any case, he was convincing: and the others were already nervous enough to go along with his idea.

'So what? We make him disappear?'

'First, we clean the trap room floor. There's bleach in the cleaners' cupboard. Then, we find somewhere to hide him. Somewhere no one's going to look.'

★

'There were suitcases in the trap room,' Fentiman had told me. 'We found one with wheels that would fit him, then we took it to the Pepper Pot.'

It must have taken them over an hour to drag the case across King Henry's playing fields, into the woods at the back of the School, then finally along the path that led to the railway tunnel. They had been lucky not to be seen; but by then the grounds were deserted, and besides, it had been raining heavily that day, which meant no dog-walkers on the path, or railway buffs taking photographs. They had climbed up the side of the Pepper Pot, hauling the suitcase behind them on a piece of theatre rope. Then they had tipped the suitcase into the mouth of the Pepper Pot, along with the bags of refuse and broken toys and unwanted things.

Then they had all gone their separate ways – Milky back to his own part of town, Fatty and Dominic home for tea before coming back for *Othello*. Of course, by the time that happened, the cleaners had already found me, and Conrad's failure to bring me home was already ringing alarm bells.

After that – well. I already know how unreal it seemed to them. Life went on as normal, except that Conrad was no longer a part of it. They avoided each other at school. At home, they watched *Dr Who* on TV, and *Hawaii Five-O*, and *Z-Cars*. They listened to the radio, with 'Get It On' at Number 1. They brushed their teeth in the mornings. They ate fish and chips on Saturdays and looked forward to the end of term. *Those* things were real. *Those* things were *them*, not the suitcase in the Pepper Pot. And as the search for Conrad cooled, and the hot summer holidays began, the three of them went their separate ways – Milky to the seaside at Scarborough for a fortnight with his mum, Dominic to Trinidad to visit his mother's relatives, and Fatty to Cornwall with his folks, where he paddled in rock pools and ate ice cream and secretly revelled in the fact that no one would ever call him by that ugly nickname, ever again.

You see, Roy, I do understand. As my life became ever more distanced from what it had been, theirs became ever more normal. They had put the events of July 9th into a suitcase, and thrown it away. And in my way, I did the same. I tried to fit my memories into the story of my life. And when they asked: *Where did Conrad go?* I told them the truth, as I'd seen it. I told them about Mr Smallface. I told them about the green door. And the more I retold that story, the more authentic it seemed to me, until the *rest* of the memory – the trapdoor, the sound of him falling, the shoes of the other boys shuffling around, and their voices raised in argument – had vanished into the slipstream of what the press called the *Conrad Price Affair*.

And remember, a five-year-old sees the world from a different perspective. They asked me about *faces* when most of what I saw was feet. They expected me to concentrate when all I wanted to do was play. Mr Scoones was called in to give evidence; and so were Miss Macleod, and Mr Sinclair. I remember the man with the small head and the habit of pulling at his hair, but I didn't know what they wanted of me when they asked me if I'd seen him. And memory likes to normalize what it sees as irregular. It papers over the cracks in the world. It cocoons us from trauma. In the case of Conrad's friends, it must have been easier to let go. To draw a line under Conrad, and to forget they were ever involved. Oh, maybe it scarred them, a little. Dominic Buckfast left the School, and ended up at Sunnybank Park, where his considerable talent for art was eventually channelled into teaching. Christopher Milk left school at sixteen and ended up four years later as a caretaker at King Henry's. And Jerome Fentiman, after a brief stint at Oxford, became a confidence trickster, taking advantage of old folk and robbing them of their savings.

Well, of course, they're all dead now. Dead, and mostly forgotten, Roy — like those episodes of somnambulism that accompanied my brief stint at King Henry's. Sufferers from the condition have been known to do extraordinary things when in the grip of an episode. Cooking a meal, for instance. Or writing in a journal. Anything to direct the sleeper away from the spring of Mnemosyne — that spring that reveals past and present — and into the arms of Lethe.

As for Dominic Buckfast, he died at a birthday party, only six months into his marriage, of a bad reaction to Ecstasy. His family resolutely denied that he had ever been a user, although his penchant for marijuana was known, and dated from his early adolescence. No one admitted to having provided Dominic with the drug. No one at school knew his dealer. The police showed a deplorable lack of interest in these significant details, which, had he been white, I believe might have raised a number of suspicions. But then, our police have never been good at looking beyond the stereotype. If they had, who knows what else they might have uncovered?

He never did adopt Emily, though by then the process was under way. He left us the house, and his savings, which, added to the small inheritance I already had from my parents, guaranteed our security. My daughter changed her name to his as soon as she reached the age of eighteen, but by then she'd almost forgotten him, except for the stories I told her; the legends that eclipsed the truth — and, of course, the photographs.

★

I look at my watch and see that it is after six o'clock. The coffee has gone cold, and you, too, are already cooling. I didn't see it happen, Roy. I think it must have been very quick. A massive heart attack, brought on by the strain of returning to work too soon. No, of course I had nothing to do with it. I told you, Roy. I'm fond of you. You look very calm: eyes closed as if enjoying a quiet post-prandial snooze. I am glad you lived long enough to know your friend Scoones was innocent, at least of this particular crime, and that your beloved St Oswald's is safe once more from the vultures of scandal.

Besides, I'm well aware that, to you, retirement would have been a curse. How would you ever have managed it? The past few weeks have proved to us both that the sedentary life was not for you. Instead, a quick and painless death, here in your very own Bell Tower, wearing your old tweed jacket, seems the kindest option. And thanks to your Brodie Boys, you'll always be here – yes, I know about the gargoyle, Roy. Of course I know. How could I not? A Head's business is to know everything.

I think I will discover you on my way out of the building. Maybe I saw a light still on at the top of the Bell Tower. I am shocked and saddened, of course. I may even shed a tear. But first, a quick look through your pockets for anything a little too interesting. A diary. A letter, perhaps. Maybe even the Prefect's badge that kicked off this whole affair.

But no. Your pockets are empty, except for a handful of conkers. That seems rather appropriate. Some people cannot pass a horse-chestnut tree without stopping to fill their pockets.

Goodbye, old friend. And be assured that St Oswald's is in good hands. The girls your colleagues so despised will thrive here, and grow into women; strong, ambitious and principled.

The narrow door is open wide: no longer will they stand aside to make the way easier for men.

Goodbye, old friend. I'll miss our talks. But I know you'd understand that this is really for the best. *Audere, agere, auferre.* To dare, to strive, to conquer. A motto, dating back to a time when women were little else but chattels. But you and I need something else; something that acknowledges the struggle we have had so far: your death, my life.

Mors tua, vita mea.

Epilogue
Elysium
(Islands of the Blessed)

St Oswald's Grammar School
1 October 2006

Dear Allen-Jones, Sutcliff, Tayler, McNair and Wild,

There comes a time when even the most tireless warhorse must be put out to pasture. I have no idea when my time will come, but the events of the past few weeks have put things into perspective. I have survived a Century of teaching at St Oswald's; a worthy achievement for one who began his career as a budding reprobate.

Now, to the next generation of reprobates, I leave this account of the past few weeks, including conversations I have had with the new New Head. You will, I am sure, find them of interest, although I leave it up to you to determine what action – if any – to take. So far, my account is unfinished. I hope to complete it very soon. But sitting here in my form room, the room I have occupied for thirty-odd years, I feel a kind of urgency. There is a small stone ledge beneath the gargoyle you made for me. I shall keep my diary there, where I know you will find it, wrapped in a waterproof covering, in case the Reaper comes for me without warning. There too I leave the Prefect's badge. I lacked the courage to put it to use. Maybe you will feel differently. Or maybe you will decide to give it – like the rest of this tale – a quiet and final burial.

433

I hope you know that teaching you has been the highlight of my career: my Brodie Boys, whose chaotic good cheer has never failed to brighten my days. I hope you will continue with your Latin studies; at the very least it will annoy Dr Strange, and besides, a good knowledge of Classics has always been an advantage in Life. Lastly, Mr Allen-Jones, if, as I presume, you are attempting to emulate Mr Bugs Bunny, it should be: 'Quid agis, Magister?' As I am sure you must recall, the adjective interrogative pronoun 'quod' would imply 'what', or 'which', rather than the more usual; 'What's up?' I point this out at the risk of appearing pedantic, of course, but as I'm sure Mr Wild would say, it never pays to overlook the pronouns.

Affectionately yours,
Roy Straitley

Acknowledgements

Just as a School is more than its Head, it takes more than one person to make a book. I owe special thanks to my agent Jon Wood; my editors Harriet Bourton, Lucy Frederick and Anouchka Harris; copy editor Marian Reid; jacket designer Tomás Almeida and illustrator Micaela Alcaino, marketing manager Jennifer Hope and marketing assistant Tanjiah Islam, publicist Alex Layt, and the rest of the great staff at Orion. I see from social media that my Brodie Boys are no longer boys, but rather excellent human beings, which continues to make me happy. I also feel the passage of time, which is both a little melancholy, and very much as it should be. Several Old Centurions and Tweed Jackets have fallen over the past couple of years; I know they won't be forgotten, but I still owe them my heartfelt thanks, and maybe a little glass of something raised in front of St Oswald's Honours Boards. I also owe thanks to everyone who helped keep me sane over the past two years; to Kevin Harris, Christopher Fowler, Bonnie Helen Hawkins, Nicola Solomon, Philip Pullman, the Board members and the wonderful, hard-working staff of the SOA and the ALCS. Thank you to all the bookshops and festivals who have organized readings during this long, strange time, and to the many readers who embraced online and virtual events. Thank you to the dedicated workers of the NHS, who have been such a source of strength and support to me, and to so many others. And of course, as always, to my bluebirds of Twitter, whose daily interactions have been my staff room, my water cooler and, sometimes, my lifeline. Writing is a lonely business during a time of lockdown, and you have your place on the Honours Boards, too. Thank you for following Roy Straitley, his boys, his colleagues and the perennial tragicomedy of St Oswald's for so long. And always dare to stand, to strive; to question and to conquer . . .

Credits

Orion Fiction would like to thank everyone at Orion who worked on the publication of *A Narrow Door* in the UK.

Editorial
Harriet Bourton
Lucy Frederick

Copy editor
Marian Reid

Proofreader
Jenny Page

Contracts
Anne Goddard
Jake Alderson

Design
Tomás Almeida
Rabab Adams
Joanna Ridley
Nick May

Editorial Management
Charlie Panayiotou
Jane Hughes
Alice Davis

Production
Ruth Sharvell

Publicity
Alex Layt

Marketing
Katie Moss
Jennifer Hope
Tanjiah Islam

Finance
Jasdip Nandra
Afeera Ahmed

Elizabeth Beaumont
Sue Baker

Audio
Paul Stark
Amber Bates

Sales
Jen Wilson
Esther Waters
Victoria Laws

Rachael Hum
Ellie Kyrke-Smith
Frances Doyle
Georgina Cutler

Operations
Jo Jacobs
Sharon Willis
Lisa Pryde
Lucy Brem

Help us make the next generation of readers

We – both author and publisher – hope you enjoyed this book. We believe that you can become a reader at any time in your life, but we'd love your help to give the next generation a head start.

Did you know that 9 per cent of children don't have a book of their own in their home, rising to 13 per cent in disadvantaged families*? We'd like to try to change that by asking you to consider the role you could play in helping to build readers of the future.

We'd love you to think of sharing, borrowing, reading, buying or talking about a book with a child in your life and spreading the love of reading. We want to make sure the next generation continue to have access to books, wherever they come from.

And if you would like to consider donating to charities that help fund literacy projects, find out more at **www.literacytrust.org.uk** and **www.booktrust.org.uk**.

THANK YOU

*As reported by the National Literacy Trust